Stirring the Hornet's Nest

by Lind

CW00500018

Prologue

Although there was a bitter chill to the night, clammy beads of sweat dripped from her forehead making her hair sticky. She pushed a strand to one side, feeling its coarse candy floss-like texture rough against her cheek. The streets were silent; there wasn't a soul in sight. She was fully aware that a person wearing a threadbare Barbour jacket, Wellington boots and pushing an overladen wheelbarrow must cut a suspicious figure at this ungodly hour. She hoped for the thousandth time over the past few weeks, that nobody was watching.

The wheelbarrow was heavy and the wheels jerked against the uneven surface of the road. Its contents, wrapped in black plastic, jutted awkwardly and moved at odd, jarring angles. As if by strange instinct, the insides of these polythene parcels, were trying to make use of their last chance to break free from their confines, having guessed their final resting place was close by.

Above, the milky question mark of a crescent moon hung in the sky, contesting her actions. It was much too late for that. She needed to push on and get the job done. Not too far ahead, the trees would give her the welcome cover she needed and she must stay focused on that. Almost certain that she heard a rustling in the bushes; she cast another wary look over her shoulder. Thankfully, there was no trace of anyone.

With great difficulty, she manoeuvred the wheelbarrow from the footpath onto the narrow path into the woods. There was still much work to be done. The screech of a nearby barn owl startled her and her load wobbled precariously. She steadied it, straining her muscles, until eventually she reached the spot. To her right, next to a clump of trees, she could see the spade poking out from the ground as if a marker on the path of some nature trail. Ditching the wheelbarrow next to it, she peered down into the hole like an Alice in Nightmare land. Was it deep enough? For weeks she had been digging at this space, piling up mounds of soil on either side of the pit. She had chosen what she hoped, was a secluded spot. But was it? Had anyone come across her handiwork? With any luck, if her efforts had been seen, they would be thought to be the work of children making a woodland den.

Taking a deep breath, she began pouring the contents of the wheelbarrow into the hole. She did not dare to picture what the insides now looked like. Mostly, the parcels of plastic sunk with ease into the hole, like the lumpy mixture of a fruit cake, moving from bowl to baking tin. But certain ingredients stuck like stubborn, glazed cherries, refusing to budge, and needed the help of a hefty kick. Beneath the rubber soles of her boots, she imagined she could feel knives of splintered bones digging into her feet.

Once all the packages were in position, she looked at her watch and began to quickly shovel back the soil, filling the hole. By now her arms were aching terribly, but goodness only knew how much worse they would be hurting tomorrow. But that was of little consequence. She needed to keep going. She must keep concentrating on the task in hand. Even now, an early or very late dog walker might happen upon this route. And if questioned about what she was doing, she could hardly claim to be planting trees.

This night had been planned for some time. She had calculated, that the event of the new moon would be best, so as not to shed too much light on her. After all, this unforeseen complication no business whatsoever in the present and should have remained buried in the past where it belonged. Nobody could have foreseen these recent, unwanted developments and the road construction coming into play. Checking once more for unwanted company, she did a slow, circular turn, before throwing in a final sombre, spadeful of earth. There was, for certain, no need for procrastination here, she just had to roll back those big rocks into place and her work would be done.

As she left the woods, she thought she heard a movement behind. Then, as she crossed over the field back to the estate, she was convinced she could feel eyes boring into her. Drawing nearer to her house, the closed curtains behind neighbours' windows seemed to be moving and twitching. No, that was impossible; everyone would be asleep at this hour. This was just her imagination playing cruel tricks. Her house came into sight and she ran the last part of the way pushing her lighter load.

First, the wheelbarrow went back in the shed. Then the wellies were placed in the utility room, aligned tidily next to her husband's along with the collection of mops and brushes. The clean, running water in the basin quickly turned murky, as she washed her hands. She desperately wanted a shower but it was just too risky, as he might hear. At last, with clothes shoved in the washing machine and her nightie retrieved from a hook, she crept up the stairs. When she listened to the familiar sound of snoring, she felt some comfort and slid her icicle limbs between the sheets.

Chapter 1

Julia

'Have you seen this?' Neil waved a piece of paper about.

'Well, obviously not.' Julia looked up from her phone. As it was Saturday, it was lovely to be able to chill out and take a little time to enjoy the autumn sunlight streaming into the kitchen. She was still dressed in her favourite kingfisher-blue, silk pyjamas, and was enjoying drinking her first cup of coffee of the day. Although she had just risen from her bed, her chestnut bob of hair was immaculate, as even at weekends Julia's first port of call was with her hair straighteners.

A well-earned lazy morning, after the hard week's work was really just what the doctor ordered. So, Julia cast her husband her practised, frosty glance, as she wanted to stay put in this precious weekend moment. She was not really anticipating, that this letter would bring any unwelcome drama, especially as it seemed to be the source of Neil's annoyingly playful mood.

'Well, from looking at the expression on your face,' said Julia. 'I'd take it to be good news,' She returned her attention to her phone.

Neil gave a smile, one of his little secretive ones that he reserved solely for teasing his wife.

Then, pretending to scan once more, the mysterious contents of his letter he spied on his wife from under his eyelids. Feigning indifference, Julia wondered if some distant relative had left him some money and her mind shot forward to possible holiday destinations – ancient ruins, balmy beaches, and quaint little villages somewhere in Tuscany, just aching to be explored. She tried not to let her husband see this, as she wanted to read her Facebook updates and not play his silly little games. Eventually, as her curiosity got the better of her, she succumbed.

'Well?' She asked. 'Who is it from? A solicitor? Just tell me …'

Neil's brown eyes were twinkling. 'It's the council actually …'

'A little early for next year's Council Tax bill isn't it? I mean it's only November and it doesn't usually come till the New Year.' Julia rolled her eyes in exasperation and wondered whatever letter from them could generate such childish giddiness. This was just another example of her husband's immaturity.

'No, listen.' Neil's face switched to one of more seriousness. 'They're thinking of building a new bypass. You know, with all that congestion going into town … I mean it's mental in the morning especially, isn't it? Recently, I've been late for work loads of times. It must have made your getting to school touch and go too.'

'Yes, I suppose so. It is annoying. But Neil … it's Saturday morning, do we really have to talk about this?' Julia was baffled as to how traffic problems and new roads could be any cause for her husband getting himself all in a tizzy but that was Neil for you.

'And guess *where* the road they are planning to build is being projected to pass through? You'll never believe it.' Neil began babbling, as he often did when all fired up, and Julia felt a sick lump in the pit of her stomach. Instantly, she guessed what was coming next.

'Well, would you believe it?' He continued. 'They want to –'

'They want to build it through our back garden don't they?' Julia interrupted. But Neil, caught up in his own thoughts was oblivious to the strange look that had suddenly passed across his wife's face, as if someone had just marched over her grave. He also failed to notice the peculiar monotone voice she was using.

'Julia, look, the plans are here.' He moved over to the seat next to her and was bouncing up and down like a jack-in-the -box, waving the letter in front of her face. 'It's only the bottom quarter of the garden. We wouldn't miss it but think … I wonder how much money they'll give us? We could pay off the mortgage. We could give up work. We could travel …'

Of course, it would be that particular part, she thought, next to the rose bed. She was feeling increasingly more queasy as each moment passed.

'Be quiet Neil.' She stood up and glared at him. 'This is all just a proposal. It might come to nothing …'

'What's wrong with you woman? Might come to nothing? Well, it sounds pretty definite to me?' Neil's eyes were whirling like the dollar symbols on a fruit machine.

'Neil, you know what these plans are like … most of the time … well, they just realise it's not financially viable and that's the last you hear of them.' This is what she hoped anyway, as she tried to stop her hands shaking.

'Anyone would think you didn't want it to happen? Are you crazy?' Sometimes Neil just couldn't fathom his wife's train of thought, 'This finally could be just what we have been waiting for … '

'No … it's not that.' Julia snapped. She couldn't meet her husband's eyes, but she knew that she needed to pretend as if this development was of little consequence, when in fact it was the very fabric of her worst nightmare. 'It's just. It's silly getting our hopes up and if this comes to nothing …'

'Comes to nothing? Look, here are the plans and the route. It cuts right through the bottom of our garden. We don't need all that garden. Especially, not that old-fashioned flower bed.'

'It's a rose bed, Neil.' Julia's eyes had a wild look and she tried to blink away tears.

'Whatever. The point is do we really need it? Just think what compensation the Council will pay.'

'But it might not happen.' Julia's voice quivered as she turned away from him to look through the French windows down into the garden.

'Sometimes, I really just don't understand you.' Neil slammed the dining room door in exasperation and went upstairs to sulk in his study. He intended to check out some further details about the road scheme on his lap top. Left alone downstairs, Julia attempted to disguise her sobbing by turning on the radio and chewing frantically on her fingernails.

Neil

Neil flounced upstairs to his office, where he had spent a great deal of time lately, allegedly working from home. Next to his computer screen, like a ready to be lit bonfire, was strewn an ominous collection of unpaid bills, final demands and unopened letters. Julia rarely came up here in Neil's domain to work, as she preferred to do her marking, planning and other such schoolwork downstairs in the kitchen, where she was now. But nevertheless, further stress and confrontation from that department, was the last thing he felt like dealing with today. Angrily, he shoved the troublesome papers into a drawer.

For the first time in ages, he had felt a glimmer of hope about the future and she as usual, had seen fit to rain on his parade. So typical of Julia these days, but just recently things had just gone from bad to even worse. What they really needed, she thought, was a break away to

some exotic location. Well unfortunately Julia, Shangri-La was certainly not on the cards in the immediate future. How, in the current state of play, they could possibly cope being in each other's company 24/7, no matter how exclusive the location, he really couldn't imagine. But this, wasn't even a consideration because currently, unbeknown to her, every penny they owned was accounted for and more …

Neil worked as an Estate Agent or had done so until fairly recently. For years, Oak Elm Ash Residential Sales and Lettings had leeched the very blood from his veins. All those hours he had spent, charming the clients, racking up the sales, bringing in the money for Charles Lavender and his inept son Max. And how had they rewarded him? Unbelievable. All those years' service he had given to them and what appreciation did he now get? Now that Max had completed his Mickey Mouse Degree, in artistically arranging envelopes and paperclips, from the University of Never Neverland, Neil's services had conveniently become surplus to requirements.

For the past few days, Neil imagined that Julia would have thought it odd, that he had begun spending so much time working from home. This had never happened before. Neil's "office" was really just his excuse for a "Man Cave", with a top of the range plasma telly , fine collection of rare, vinyl records, first-edition, mint condition comics and splendid hoard of single malt whiskies. After dinner most nights, Neil liked to retire to his lair, while Julia marked books and watched rubbish soap operas downstairs.

Here, he could sit and bask in his comfy leather swivel chair to shoot the breeze or whatever he chose to do. After a hard day's work, it was a reward he had earned. He could have a few drinks, surf the net, watch the latest films, play his records and have the odd cigar. This was the only room that Julia permitted him to smoke in. She couldn't stand the smell and a further reason she kept well away from his office. Any activity pursued by Neil on his latest state of the art laptop, was for mostly recreational purposes.

All his financial dabbling was purely for his own amusement and in no way connected with his job.

Neil's talent was for selling properties, not sitting behind a laptop screen. But he had assured Julia, it was just Charles Lavender's way of being more efficient with his business.

By sending his son out on more of the everyday, lacklustre property viewings, it would enable him to concentrate on the more important jobs. As yet she hadn't questioned him about the precise nature of these, but the word 'marketing' he had ready to hand as a plausible answer. Anyway, so far she hadn't asked. Yet, after her odd behaviour tonight, something was definitely boiling in the cauldron and he needed to be on guard, should she decide to do some snooping. Thankfully, she didn't know the password for his computer, as the recent history of his browser was certainly inconsistent with hours spent in gainful employment. Neil pushed to the back of his mind those insalubrious sites he had been viewing, for therein lay the real source of his problems.

Here it was: The Gateshead Planning Department Website. He found the section on the new road and the familiar Cheshire cat grin spread once more across his face.

"Plans confirmed for a new road to be built from Sunderland to Newcastle.

Heavy congestion in both the morning and evening rush hours has made plans for the building of a new road to be put into action sooner rather than later, as there was no sign of the problem diminishing in the foreseeable future. Councillor Bill Nelson has confirmed that many people were finding it impossible to reach their place of employment on time and this was having a devastating effect on the local economy. A tipping point had been reached. It was essential to get this new road up and running as soon as possible."

Furthermore, the money for this new venture will be financed from the tolls to be imposed upon vehicles entering the city centre so this will place no real burden on Council finances. Soon, the final details will be revealed but those people whose land lies on the proposed path would have a handsome, financial reimbursement. In fact, those dwellings most likely to be affected have already been informed.'

Well, that seemed pretty definite to him. After all, they had actually had a letter that day. Once more, Neil felt angry about Julia's crushing negativity, as he'd had such great visions of the Golden Goose finally coming to lay her bountiful egg. Maybe, for once everything would be fine. Perhaps, he ought to come clean with Julia regarding what had happened with his job and the rest ... but no, not just yet, especially not with her pessimistic mood today. His wife's glass half empty attitude was contagious, he decided. This clearly wasn't the time for him to lay his cards on the table and make a clean breast of it. More than likely, the new road would take some time he sighed glumly, as he headed once more for the situations vacant page.

Julia

Meanwhile, Julia was sitting staring through the French windows at the rose bed, down at the bottom of the garden. Now, there were no flowers to be seen anywhere just those malicious bushes with their evil thorns. Any colour they could generate at this time of year would be from pricking unsuspecting fingers and thumbs till they dripped with blood. She shuddered for only she knew what lay beneath, and now, after all these years, the secrets that those red petals had longed to scream each summer would soon be revealed – unless, she could think of an alternative solution.

Neil – for goodness sake – honestly, her husband was unbelievable. Did he really think she was so stupid? Apparently so. But it was his problem and he needed to find the solution. Even if some money was given to them as a result of this new road … well surely it would be far too late by then. She suspected that they were already behind on mortgage payments and such like, but that had always been Neil's responsibility. They had no children and as a result had always had plenty of money, to spend as freely as they pleased. Julia bought the food and Neil sorted the bills. That had been the way it had always been. The arrangement had suited her fine, as she had never really had to bother thinking about money. And Neil, as a silver-tongued estate agent with his handsome bonuses, had always ensured they had more than enough.

However recently, she had noticed a change in his behaviour. He had been turning down the heating even though the weather was now getting chilly, changing the conversation when she had mentioned the next holiday, and making disparaging comments about wasted food. This was totally out of keeping with his usual spendthrift ways. Definitely, something was afoot and it wasn't fair on her because she still had her stressful teaching job to contend with, as

well as doing the cooking, cleaning and washing. Why on earth would Charles Lavender be asking him to work from home? It just didn't make sense. Neil, with his fast-talking sales patter needed to be out sweet- talking his clients, not wallowing upstairs in their house. It all pointed to one possible conclusion, Neil must have lost his job. Charles Lavender had sacked him. There was no other plausible alternative. But why would that happen?

Charles Lavender and he were as thick as thieves, in both in business and friendship. They went back years and had even been at school together. Ever since she had known Neil, their property business had successfully weathered the various financial doldrums of the last couple of decades and always seemed to manage to keep afloat. In fact, it had largely prospered, even during those periods of bleak recession. Various other estate agency businesses had come and gone, but the combination of Charles' excellent business sense and Neil's superb sales skills, had proven a winning combination.

Although, officially OakElmAsh Residential was Charles's company, as he had financed it from the spoils of his parent's inheritance, they had always seemed to her to be much more of an equal partnership. The success was due as much to the charm and endeavours of Neil, as it was to Charles, who, it had to be admitted, presented himself as a surly and unprepossessing individual. It was only when he was in Neil's company and fortified by stiff drink, that a slightly more jovial and likeable person emerged.

How his wife Pamela, a nervy, anxious woman with an unhealthy appetite for the latest gossip, had endured his company for so long was beyond her. Pamela must be perpetually on edge, trying to satisfy the demands of her dour, critical husband, while he must be constantly irritated by her meek, fussy ways. Anyway, the old adage that opposites attract had proved to be true and they each deserved the other. This at least spared them inflicting themselves on other unfortunate spouses. However, the greatest misfortune of all was the mixture of their gene pools to produce that son of theirs, Max. If in a bizarre, scientific experiment, the genes of the cheerless Charles and the prissy Pamela had been blended together in a cement mixer, their inept, idle and tongue-tied result of a son could have been accurately predicted.

Admittedly, Julia had known that the time would come when Charles would want to include

his son in the business, but surely he couldn't just expect awkward Max to step into her husband's shoes just like that. Max of all people. Charles must be losing his faculties. Neil, she would be the first to admit had many faults but as far as successfully selling properties was concerned he knew he had the golden touch.

Chapter 2

Pamela

The Lavenders lived in a large, detached, red-brick house, in a street of similarly smart homes. All the windows were freshly painted on a regular basis, with fresh white gloss and gardens immaculately maintained (many employing gardeners), with finely mowed lawns and neat herbaceous borders. At Christmas, there would be the annual unspoken competition for the most elaborate and expensive outdoor decorations. Prancing reindeers, guffawing Santas and throngs of cherubims, with wings like the Angel of the North would hold a nightly dance off from the rooftops. In Newcastle, the department store Fenwick's set the standard with their seasonal window display and Valley View Drive strove to emulate this. Now, in November it was time for preparations ~~being made~~. to begin.

On this Saturday morning, Pamela Lavender, a fussily dressed woman when even at leisure, was wearing a pink floral dress, with a ruffle of red lace like a turkey snood at the neck, and smart coral-coloured, court shoes. Her blond pageboy cut, pristine as ever, was fixed to her head like a helmet, and her reading glasses were perched on the end of her nose. At that moment, her efforts were concentrated on a tricky three thousand piece jigsaw puzzle of the ruined water wheel in Jesmond Dene. As the picture was mostly sky, stone, water and leaves, it was challenging and Pamela had already been kept occupied by it ~~already~~, for at least three days. So far little progress, apart from the border, had been made. She had a special board for her puzzles which sat perfectly on their walnut coffee table. After clearing her throat, she took a sip from her very strong coffee (the third that morning) and triumphantly placed a greenish outside edge piece of some grass between two others of a similar colour. a piece of grass

Charles Lavender was sitting in an armchair opposite his wife reading the Telegraph. He was a thickset man in his early fifties, who when younger had played rugby, but now his muscle had turned to flab. His head still sported a thick thatch of steel-grey hair and his small, watchful eyes sat upon florid cheeks like over-ripe plums. Similarly to his wife, he didn't embrace the casual look and on weekends favoured comfy slacks and smart pullovers in pastel shades. Today, he wore a custard-coloured sweater, which pulled unattractively over his ample stomach, as he reclined in the chair, and biscuit-coloured pants with an oatmeal fleck.

While most people favoured having two sofas in their sitting rooms, the Lavenders opted for the traditional settee and two armchairs in theirs. They were upholstered in a neutral beige with a matching array of scatter cushions that Charles was in the custom of throwing on the floor. The room had a replica Victorian fireplace featuring William Morris tiles, a massive television, and an Axminster carpet in autumnal shades of russet, scarlet and gold. Pamela and Charles always sat in their preferred seats, husband to the right of the fireplace and Pamela to the left, while Max favoured the sofa.

'Have you any plans for this afternoon? Anything we need to do?' Charles did not look up from his newspaper and hardly sounded thrilled by the prospect of whatever tedious activity his wife might suggest.

'I was thinking …'There was a long pause before Pamela finished her sentence, as she was trying to gauge whether her husband would find this an agreeable suggestion. 'We might visit that garden centre. You know the one near the airport. You know … we are well into November aren't we? And most people will have already decided what ...' Pamela's voice was becoming increasingly squeaky and shrill before she was interrupted.

'Yes, very well. If that's what you wish. It might be very crowded though.' Charles didn't sound very enthusiastic, as at the moment, ghastly Christmas decorations were the last thing on his mind.

'Well I think it's time we did don't you. In a couple of weeks it'll start, you know. And if next door have anything like those reindeers again. Do you remember last year Charles? Our

Santa … well it let the whole street down didn't it? We need to get planning and quickly. I mean, last year … I felt too embarrassed to go out. I'm sure the neighbours … well Charles. I would just die if we had another Christmas like last year.' Pamela reached for a cardigan which she placed around he shoulders, as if the recollection of last year's humiliation was creating a nasty draught.

‘Very well.’ Charles folded up his newspaper and walked over to the window. ‘Oh look, here comes Max’s MG round the corner. It must be time for lunch. What are we having today?’

‘It’s only just gone eleven Charles.’ She looked at the large antique grandfather clock which

had only just chimed a few moments ago. ‘I don’t know, I’ve had other things on my mind. Do you know Charles … don’t say anything to Max, but I think he’s a bit worried.’

‘Worried? What’s he got to be worried about?’ Charles snorted.

‘Well he’s never really had a job before … I mean I don’t know the first thing about it of course but… selling houses. Wouldn’t it be better if Neil was there … to teach him. I mean. I don’t understand why Neil isn’t ….’

‘No, you don’t understand it. That’s exactly right, you don’t understand it. Now just leave it. Go and make lunch.’ As usual, his wife’s gibbering was beginning to grate.

Pamela was used to her husband barking orders at her, so she nodded and placed the box lid on top of the puzzle. Charles hadn’t told her what had happened between Neil and himself. Pamela was dying to know what had occurred. It must have been something truly terrible but she didn’t like to ask him, as altercations with him were best avoided. She knew her husband had a short fuse; Charles could rouse himself into a tsunami of a fury over the slightest of provocation, and even more so, it seemed of late. Nevertheless, his bewildering decision to sack Neil impacted on Max, who must be feeling very worried at the moment. And he didn’t even know that his supposed would be mentor, wouldn’t be there tomorrow. Furthermore and more importantly, what was she going to say when she bumped into her friends? After all, relating all this about Neil to others would be something to be relished, as it really would be news hot off the press.

‘But Charles … What am I going to say if I see Julia when I’m out shopping or anybody else who knows Neil for that matter? They will want to know…’

‘Leave it Pamela. You don’t understand. It’s none of your business and it has nothing whatsoever to do with bloody anyone else. Now, don’t let Max hear you talking about this.’ Charles sat down once more, pretended to read his newspaper and listened for the sound of the key in the door.

Unusually for Max, he had got up early and taken himself off to Newcastle for a mooch around the town. Usually, he preferred to stay in bed in the morning, for as long as possible. Often, he chose not to surface until after noon, much to the concern of his mother. This morning, he had just felt the compelling urge to get away from the house. It felt like the walls were closing in on him. It seemed as if his parents were increasingly invading his personal space, like the green mould on his favourite type of cheese (Max was very partial to cheese and his favourite was Caerphilly). Who was annoying him the most, his mother with her constant fussing and blethering or his father with his misjudged attempts at bonhomie? It was just too difficult to decide.

For some reason, it had always been a foregone conclusion that one day, in the dim and distant future; he would enter into the family business. That day had unfortunately arrived, rather sooner than he had expected. The sudden urgency in itself though was peculiar, as Max's degree had been completed nearly six months ago. Since then, he had been permitted to drift aimlessly in no particular direction without mention of any employment. Then a couple of days ago, completely out of the blue, his father had sprung this unexpected position that had emerged for him in the family business. It was all highly peculiar and most unwanted from his point of view.

Somehow to his surprise, Max had managed to achieve a Third in media Studies from a little known college, in Framwellgate Moor, just outside Durham. This in itself was amazing, as he had little interest in either the subject nor had he applied himself greatly to the course. Media Studies as a subject had been selected by him, as it sounded much more interesting than the business course his father had suggested. Also, the college had been impressed by his attendance at the Royal Grammar School and had been prepared to overlook the unfortunate matter of his disastrous examination results.

Anyway, since graduating, he had been allowed to waft about the house like a mildly contented ghost, playing on his laptop and hanging out in a few coffee bar and pubs with his like-minded friend Nigel. Why the sudden panic should somehow occur, that he should have to start working in two days' time he really couldn't fathom. What on earth did his father expect him to do? Property was bound to be even more boring than Media Studies and he didn't have the foggiest notion how to go about selling someone a house. Wasn't that super-smooth Neil's job? Max doubted that he was going to take too kindly to having to take someone like him under his wing.

Most would consider that Max had enjoyed a privileged upbringing. From an early age he'd had all the latest toys and gadgets lavished upon him. The swish, red MG he currently swanned about in, had merely been the customary, generous gift from his parents, that he would have expected for his twenty-first birthday. Certainly the fees at the Royal Grammar School in Jesmond hadn't come cheap, but Charles Lavender had wanted nothing but the best for his only son. Max had hated it there, for academically he wasn't bright. To make matters worse his dyslexia had only been diagnosed quite recently and it seemed more than likely that much better provision would have been made for him in a state school. Furthermore, he had absolutely no interest in any sports whatsoever. So, he had hung around the periphery of the social gatherings of the Sixth Form, like a fish out of water, in pretty much the same way he had skulked around the edge of the playground in his earlier preparatory school days.

However, he was quite fond of computer games, particularly violent ones. This was one of the interests he shared with Nigel, his solitary friend. In fact, he had spent his time in Newcastle that morning, browsing in the Apple store. Here he had made half a dozen purchases. With these he intended to fill the rest of the day, from the seclusion of his messy bedroom and having as little contact from his parents as possible. Hopefully, they would be going out this afternoon, as they usually did on a Saturday, to some really boring garden centre or equally mundane place.

'Is that you dear?'

Max hadn't even taken his key out of the door before she started.'Well it's hardly the bogey man is it?' He should have stayed out longer, and then they might have already gone out.

'What would you like for lunch? Your father and I were just going to have a tuna sandwich. Would you like one?' Pamela was in the kitchen, listening to Graham Norton interviewing Olivia Coleman on the radio.

'No. Not hungry. I already had a burger in town.' Max disappeared upstairs to his room.
'Did you have a nice time shopping? Did you buy anything of interest?'
Pamela's questions remained unanswered and there was no way he was showing his mother what he had bought.
'Pamela,' Charles shouted from the front room. 'I think I'd rather have a burger than a tuna sandwich for my lunch.'

Chapter 3

Zoe

After making herself a much needed cup of tea, Zoe plonked herself down on the last available chair in the staffroom. Unfortunately, it was the one which was directly facing Hazel Swan, the head teacher, and Zoe looked unhappily at the clock. Around the walls were stuck all the rotas of who was to be doing what and where. It put her in mind of attempts at pinning the tail on the donkey. There were many pieces of paper and lots of jobs to be done. It would be an hour at least before the meeting would be over and she could sort out what was needed to be done for tomorrow.

She hated Mondays, what with it being her yard duty and everyone always seeming subdued; the weekend was over and the week stretched ahead like an overly-complicated, obstacle course. Behind where Hazel was perched, there was a large calendar, which had all the completed days ticked off, putting one in mind of an on-going prison sentence and she could see that five long weeks were to be suffered until the Christmas break. And this term was always so mad busy.

Hazel Swan, shuffled some papers about on the coffee table in front of her and cleared her throat. She always made a point of being particularly smartly dressed on Monday, as if she had spent all day on Sunday preparing the outfit specially. Later on in the week, the combinations became a little more haphazard. Today, she wore a charcoal pin-striped suit with a jade-coloured blouse which Zoe thought suited her copper-coloured choice of hair colour.

Zoe flattened down her own wild, orange tresses that also had some chemical assistance and straightened the skirt of her short ruby-red pinafore dress. Everyone fixed their eyes on Ms Swan, wondering what further workload would be inflicted on them this evening. Julia was sitting in the corner, out of the way (she must have got here early to get that prime seat thought Zoe). She tried to make eye contact with her friend but Julia was staring into space, totally oblivious of her attempts to attract her attention.

'Now as you are all well aware, we could be due an inspection at any time and it is essential that we are all prepared.' Hazel addressed her staff as if she were behind a pulpit. There were groans and mutters from under breaths, as she had been banging on about this old chestnut for the past two years. Also, as Hazel was well into her sixties and due to retire at the end of the summer term; it probably wouldn't even affect her.
'Anyway,' her brow wrinkled in annoyance, but she chose to ignore any signs of insubordination from the ranks. Once, and not very long ago, this wouldn't have been the case. 'As I have been telling you for some time, the goalposts once more have shifted. No longer are they going to be focusing on the work in children's books but they are going to be actually asking the children about what they have learned. You can definitely guess which ones they will ask too.' She shook her head in exasperation and looked pointedly from face to face. 'Has anyone got any bright ideas what we can do about this?' Zoe quickly cast her eyes down to the green carpet and there was a long silence.
'Well luckily,' Hazel continued. 'I have been talking with Linda and Karen and they have some ideas about making sheets to stick in the children's books with questions about each topic they have been learning. Personally, I think this is an excellent idea 'Linda and Karen smiled smugly at each other as they passed around some examples of their handiwork. 'Humph', Zoe thought, this looked extremely time-consuming. Once more, she tried to catch her friend's attention, expecting her to be twisting her face at the sound of this laborious task.

Zoe, was the curriculum leader for Geography and Julia had the delights of Religious Education. All teachers had one subject or other, some more than one as it was a small school. However, Julia was sitting there as if she were in a trance. Something was definitely wrong with her and she wondered that she hadn't spotted it before, but Mondays were such busy days.

When she had wished her a 'good morning', earlier Julia had only grunted back. Noticing that unusually Julia had turned in late, Zoe thought that probably she had been stuck in the dreadful traffic that seemed to be getting worse every morning. She was no doubt feeling flustered. So, she had thought nothing of it and let her be. Later in the morning though, when she was on the way to the yard, she walked past Julia's classroom and heard her shouting. Julia never shouted and her class were lovely, not like the monsters Zoe had in hers. But Julia had been almost screaming, as if she had lost her temper *big time* and was in real danger of was losing control. There was obviously much more to this and it was probably something in connection with *that* Neil.

'So Zoe,' Hazel slammed a ruler on the coffee table. 'Do you see how this. Will fit into your Geography curriculum?'

'Sorry' Zoe pulled herself up in her chair like a sleep-deprived soldier, summoned to attention. 'Could you repeat that again please?' A look of thunder passed across Hazel's face. Too well, Zoe knew of the wrath of Hazel.

'Well I am sorry, that you don't find this very interesting Zoe.' Zoe glanced around the room and she could see Karen and some of the others, covering their mouths with their hands, stifling the sniggers. 'Nevertheless, I was wondering about your opinion on how these sheets might work for your subject.'

'Oh yes,' She looked at the example sheet in front of her on Anglo-Saxons. 'When Year 3 is studying the… Water Cycle erm … I guess if vocabulary words like … precipitation and condensation were already in their books it would be really useful.' Zoe gave a triumphant smile, as she congratulated herself on her magnificent transformation from rabbit caught in the headlight to magician's bunny performing clever tricks.

Max

With relief, Max closed his bedroom door, opened the top button of his shirt and took off his tie. Thank goodness that awful day was over. 'Could that really have gone any worse?' he asked his reflection in the mirror and ran his fingers through his newly-shorn hair. Then he looked into his own sad, grey-green eyes, pale, forlorn face and nondescript brown hair, that had been ordered to be trimmed into tidiness by his mother a few days earlier. In fact he hardly recognised himself and didn't like what he saw. Not one little bit. Max the Estate Agent – who was kidding who?

After an uncomfortable breakfast, with Pamela fussing round the table like some deranged mother hen, the journey to the office in his father's Jag had been tense. Despite Charles's assurances about how well he would get on with the other members of the team and of how fortunate he was to have this opportunity, Max either ignored any questions from his father or answered them with a belligerent grunt. Eventually, Charles gave up and they travelled the last part of the journey into Newcastle in silence.

When they arrived at the estate agent's office, which was located quite close to the football ground on St James Street, Charles parked his car in his personal space outside the building. Taking a deep breath, he surveyed his empire 'OakElmAsh – Residential Sales and Lettings' in big, golden letters on the top of the office front and announced with pride,

'Now son, one day this will be all yours. Not for a good while though … hopefully'. Charles guffawed; laughing at what he considered was an hilarious joke. 'Until then however … there are a few tricks of the trade that you need to learn. But learn them you will son, and this will be the making of you.' Charles attempted to put an arm affectionately around his son but Max sidestepped to avoid it and hopped uncomfortably, from foot to foot.

There was only one other private parking space in the small car park, he noticed. That was for Neil, his dad's second in command, which was empty as he obviously hadn't arrived at work yet. Max wondered when Neil would come to the office, as he assumed he would be working closely with him.

Walking into the reception, a place he had been on numerous occasions before, for the first time he noticed how disturbingly bright everything was. He blinked and wished he had brought his sunglasses. It was as if the whole room had been hurriedly whitewashed in an attempt to cover any growths, blemishes or stains. On the wall, were examples of the most attractive properties available, accompanied by the usual hyperbole of why the purchase of this particular residence was an opportunity not to be missed. 'With this house all your dreams will come true' sat alongside, 'Why wait for heaven when this house can bring it to you'. Max felt sick.

'Max, let me introduce you to Tracy.' He had met Tracy before and she beamed at him with her ultra-white teeth, platinum-blonde hair and dazzling, white blouse. Whether she was best

suited to a toothpaste or washing powder commercial, he couldn't quite decide. But the smile didn't quite extend to her icy- blue eyes that remained cold and unwelcoming. He knew from earlier visits that original thoughts on both sides were confirmed – mutual hatred.

'Now, Tracy is going to be showing you the ropes today. 'Unfortunate turn of phrase, thought Max. Did his father wish him to hang himself, in a spot this female Grim Reaper suggested? 'She has the list of potential buyers you will be meeting.' He would be meeting clients today? Max's nausea grew by the second and he imagined his face to have reached an appropriately blanched shade of green to match the room. 'As you haven't brought your own car with you there is a company van you can use and don't worry, there's an up-to- date SAT Nav inside.' Charles threw a bunch of keys at his son.

'But Dad, won't I be going out with Neil? I thought I would be working alongside him today. Where is he?' Clearly alarmed, Max cleared his throat wishing his voice sounded a little less whiney. While Tracy raised her eyebrows, and gave her boss a, "*How are you going to explain this one*?" face. Charles ignored both the question and look.

'Come on Son, I'll bet you can't wait to meet all your colleagues. I know they're dying to meet you.' He said unconvincingly, pushing open a door and gesturedfor his nauseas son to follow.

Then his father led him through a number of rooms where he was introduced to his various employees, who were all beavering away on computers. Most of them smiled and feigned some slight interest in him, as they didn't want to get on the wrong side of Charles. Everyone knew Charles was ruthless, didn't suffer fools, and if at first you couldn't cut the mustard with the first knife, then you didn't get a second.

Before his father went to attend his own important e mails, phone calls and business, he delivered his son back into the hands of the ice queen. Tracy made little effort to conceal her contempt.

'Well Max here is the list. Your first appointment is with Mr and Mrs Evans at eleven.

The address is over in Fenham, but in this folder are all the postcodes and necessary bumph. I suggest you read all this before you go to each property. For example, this first one, Tindale Gardens, well it hasn't got much of a garden but it has a nice tidy garage. So you need to point this out to the client. Do you get it?' She challenged him as if knowing his card was well and truly marked for inevitable failure but Max was too mesmerised by her gleaming teeth to pick up on this.

'Well, have you got any questions? She continued.

'I don't think so.' Max had many questions but he felt tongue-tied and didn't know where to begin. He had been well and truly thrown in the deep end and most what she had just told him sounded like murky, underwater noise. 'Mr and Mrs Elf did you say … the first ones?'

'No Evans, Max. You're not going to meet a couple of garden gnomes you know.' She sneered at him and removed an imaginary speck, from the silvery, immaculate polish on her nails. 'Anyway, it's half past 10, so … I suggest you get a move on. After all we don't want to keep these wee folk waiting do we?' Smirking at him unkindly she added, 'And remember "Sales make your Salary". Hasn't your dad told you the company motto yet?'

Max was glad to escape from the serpent-like woman, as he fled from the building in search of the company van which thankfully he found in the backstreet behind the premises. If he could just get through today, then surely Neil would be back tomorrow. It was very strange though, how his father was being so evasive on that matter.

* I felt van was white maybe "the apple on Tracy's desk"

Chapter 4

Neil

Neil was glad when his wife left for work, as he no longer needed to stick to the charade that he was working from home. After making himself a further cup of coffee, he sat downstairs and watched some morning telly. When 'Homes under the Hammer' came on, he flicked to another channel. Once it had been a favourite, but for some reason, it had now lost its appeal. On the whole though, he quite liked it in the house when he was alone and didn't have to pretend anymore. As the sun streamed through the window, he realised he had all day to do exactly as he liked and this was a still an unfamiliar luxury to him. Neil stretched out on the sofa and Mabel, their large silver Maine Coon cat came to sit on his lap, engulf him in fur and make her little, chirruping noises.

Neil had worked his socks off for Charles for over twenty years and the man owed him. He couldn't believe that Charles had been so resolute. It wasn't as if he had actually stolen any money. He had just borrowed it and it would only have been for a short time. Until, he got himself sorted. Also, it wasn't as if it was actually such a great deal. It was only a few thousand. Well perhaps maybe more than a few but for heaven's sake, it wasn't as if OakElmAsh didn't have plenty of cash spare was it? And his bloody motto, "Sales make your salary", well who was responsible for most of those sales? If it hadn't been for him, no way would that company still be up and running. Neil was stroking Mabel with such an increasing speed and pressure that the poor cat jumped off his knee with a yelp.

Charles might be good at organising money but if it weren't for him, well there wouldn't be any around to organise, would there? He had felt proud when he heard others discussing his abilities to sell snow to Eskimos or sand to Arabs, but no, this was just fact, because he was excellent at his job. Pretty soon Charles would be all too absorbed in the business of robbing Peter to pay Paul, to make his books balance. Especially, if he thought he could just replace him with his numpty of a son, Max. It made his blood boil. Maybe he should have one last try at appeasing Charles. Perhaps he could offer to show Max some of his marketing magic tricks and share at least some of his expertise with the lad? Admittedly making a silk purse out if a sow's ear wouldn't be easy but he could give it a go. It wasn't as if it was the first time he had *borrowed* money from the business, it was just the first time that he had been caught. However, if this road should happen to be built then some immediate problems could be solved. And despite Julia's reservations, they didn't really need a garden of the size it was.

Admittedly, there would be a lot more noise from traffic but plenty of people had houses on busy roads. Surely, you would just get used to the noise. Perhaps, there was more to all of this than met the eye. They had been together for over twenty years but Julia had lived here for much longer. In fact, this was the house that Julia had been brought up in. Julia's parents had died tragically in a car crash and as an only child Julia had inherited the house from them.

True, it looked very different from when her parents had lived here, because when they had married, Neil had thought the place old fashioned and had been in favour of them moving elsewhere. Julia had flatly refused, but agreed to some modernisation. Nothing had been done to the place since the 1970s, when Julia had been a child. Central heating, double glazing, loft conversion, garage – the list of essentials just went on. In fact it probably would have been cheaper to buy a new build. Yet, this place had obviously meant a lot to Julia and still did.

Even now, if Neil were to suggest downsizing, her reaction he suspected would be a vehement no. So, after they had taken out the various loans to pay for these home improvements, it had seemed a sensible idea to consolidate these into a small mortgage. At that time both of them had good jobs and it wasn't a problem. So, for them to fall behind on mortgage payments was ridiculous, when you compared theirs to the massive monthly amounts some friends had to find. But *somehow* they had and it was down to him he supposed, but he didn't really want to think about that.

So he put this chagrin from his head and decided to go outside for some air. Although, there was a definite chill about, it was good to fill his lungs with the fresh air. Funnily enough, although the house had changed from all recognition since he moved in, the garden remained largely the same. The same holly bushes in the corners, rose bed at the bottom of the lawn, and dilapidated shed, with its even more ancient tools. Julia always professed to enjoy gardening and that suited him, so he just let her get on with it. But maybe that was it.

This was Julia's link with her parents. She was always particularly meticulous in tending the rose bed. Each year she spent ages deadheading flowers. Of course how stupid of him, he thought. The penny finally dropped. The rose bed had been her mother's pride and joy. When the new road was built, it would destroy her shrine to her parents. Now Neil thought he understood why Julia was behaving strangely. This was why she had behaved so oddly at the mention of the road. Having made some sense of her hostile reaction, he felt greatly calmed so he went inside once more to see what Mabel was doing and if as usual, she was ready for some food.

Julia

Julia couldn't believe it, when she saw there were four-way traffic lights in operation on her way to work that morning. All the cars were gridlocked, as no one could move whether the lights were green, red, yellow or even blue. She was going to be late. But she just couldn't get out of her head thoughts of Neil's lies, roads being built, and rose beds. One day, when she could definitely have done without any extra stress. Monday mornings were bad enough usually, what with the planning that needed to be printed out and handed in, resources to be organised and the classroom being set up. Thank goodness for Emily her classroom assistant, but still she needed this delay like a hole in the head. Upon arriving at the bursting full car park, she found a place to squash her car in, pulled her heavy bag of marked books from the boot and chased into the school.

Vaguely, she remembered a few people wishing her good morning but she had no time for pleasantries or even a cup of tea. She headed for the computer suite. Luckily, everyone else was too busy to speak to her. They were stabbing at the keyboards and after having finished all their printing, they scuttled off back to their classrooms like hardworking, obedient spiders. Thankfully, the printers weren't playing up and as she finally collected her sheets, she saw the clock heading for nine. Damn, the children would be coming in. As she ran down the corridor she caught the headteacher, Miss Swan watching her from her office.

When she arrived at her year 4 classroom, the children were already there. Emily must have brought them in from the yard. The children fussed about the classroom, pushing and shoving each other, and Emily looked frazzled. .

'Miss, Danny's just hurt me,' Imogen squealed loudly.

'Lucy's thrown my coat on the cloakroom floor… and it's all muddy. My mam said I have to keep it clean,' Lacey screamed across the room.

'Shaun just said my mam's fat.' Christopher punched Shaun, who promptly burst into tears..

'Children – be quiet. Please, just sit down. What's all this noise?' Julia could feel herself sweating and her fringe began to frizz. 'This isn't what I expect from my lovely Year 4 class.' The children settled down eventually, some looking subdued, while others presented her with a – '*if you can't be bother to get here on time, then why should I behave* ' face. Then she looked down at her feet and to her mortification she realised that she was wearing odd shoes. As if things could get any worse … but they could.

The children were writing some improvements to the stories that they had written last week and that Julia had spent a sizable portion of the weekend marking. Individual comments like *you could add more detail to your description of the forest* or *include some more dialogue with contractions such as don't*, meant she spent a long time on each book. Pushing worrying thoughts of roses bushes and roads from her head, she attempted to explain calmly what they needed to do. But they just wouldn't stop fussing.

'Miss, my pencil's blunt.'

'I don't understand.'

'What does this say?'

'I can't find my book.'

Several children seemed to be bleating in unison, whining and whingeing on and on and on.

'Will you all just sit down and shut up. Just SHUT UP NOW …' Julia shrieked in a voice so loud and high-pitched that the words seemed to resonate and bounce off the ceiling like arrows. Everyone, including Julia herself was shocked.

All eyes stared at the door expecting Ms Swan or maybe the police to come running in to see if a murder or some such atrocity had occurred. But thankfully the door remained closed. Miraculously, for the moment Julia's histrionics had been undetected but she knew instantly

this wouldn't be the end of the matter. However, as far as the children were concerned, her outburst seemed to have done the trick. Sheepishly, the class seemed now to know what to do and returned to their tasks like little lambs. The children were perturbed because they had never seen the miss lose her temper like this before. Likewise Emily, was now very worried as she had seen a darker side to the usually mild-mannered Julia. Mrs Latimer seemed at least temporarily to have completely lost the plot.

Zoe

At this very point Zoe had walked past the classroom on her way to the yard. Quite literally, she had done a double take, at the unrecognisable, screaming banshee noise coming from Julia's classroom. And the bloodcurdling, 'Shut up …' rang through her ears repeatedly, as she drove alongside the Quayside in her yellow Fiat 500 on her way home. Zoe lived in a small two bedroomed house, in the St Peter's Basin marina development, close to the Ouseburn area of Newcastle. It was always good to cross the river and feel to be nearly home. Although the school was just across the water from where she lived, it felt comfortably far away, as the journey home usually took half an hour due to the traffic.

Zoe had failed to catch her friend after the meeting as Julia had bolted out of the building like a bat out of hell. She would ring her tonight, as something clearly was very wrong and she suspected that husband of hers to be the culprit. Neil was no doubt behind all of this.

On the few occasions that she had met Neil, she wasn't much impressed. Slimy. That was her opinion of him. Despite the fact he must have been well in his fifties, Neil wore the clothes of a much younger man. Those suits with the narrow legged trousers and tight fitting shirts looked ridiculous on the middle-aged man. True, he might not have let himself run to fat, but she was sure that was due more to good fortune rather than any effort on his part. But then with a vain peacock like Neil, one never really knew to what lengths he would go to remain an eternally youthful Peter Pan. or a youthful P Pan

Also, she was sure that strange tawny hair came out of a bottle. While it was expected for women to give Mother Nature a little help in the follicle department, the same didn't apply to men. Zoe shook her own titian tresses, knowing they looked good on her. She always liked to dress in rich, jewel shades like amethyst, topaz and emerald, which she knew complemented her fiery locks. But Neil with his strange orange head glow … well he just looked plain ludicrous.

But it wasn't only that. The way Neil spoke and flirted with women of all ages was ridiculous . The insincere flattery that spewed uncontrollably from his mouth wasn't just laughable, it was plain cringe worthy. Really it was. And while it didn't impress her one little bit, no doubt some others were fooled by his fawning. But then again he was an estate agent. Yet was that really any excuse? How Julia put up with his behaviour she couldn't fathom. If anyone was a candidate for playing away from home and extra-curricular activities then Neil must come top of any list. Once or twice, when she and Julia had been out for drinks, her guard had slipped and Zoe had been on the verge of saying something but she had thankfully managed to bite her tongue. They must be well overdue another night out.

But that was the problem, Zoe had a daughter and although she was almost a teenager, she didn't like to leave her alone in the house. At the age of twelve, Chloe was very young for her age, although lately she had taken to spending a great deal more time in her room listening to loud music and playing on her ipad. Those awkward teenage tantrums and sulks would soon be surging out of the hormonal bag, but not quite yet. Zoe was thankful for this. For the present, Chloe remained a pleasant and biddable girl who still enjoyed the company of her mother. Once Zoe had finished marking her books and Chloe had finished her homework, the two would sit together. Companionably, they would watch the soaps, while Zoe enjoyed a few glasses of wine and Chloe drank her Pepsi. Regrettably, Zoe realised these halcyon days were numbered and needed to be cherished.

Yet, Zoe was only human and she needed time to herself. Part of the reason she had bought the place where she lived in St Peter's Basin, was because round the corner from the house was the marina, with its collection of candy-coloured buildings and boats. Often after a particularly hard day at school, she found nothing more soothing than a walk around the basin to let her imagination run riot. Zoe was fascinated by the flotilla of yachts and vessels that appeared permanently moored there. They rarely seemed to go anyplace but sadly spent their days tethered up in the harbour, like poor neglected pets. This seemed like such a shocking waste, and sometimes Zoe thought she heard wailing and crying noises coming from their timbers. Of course that might have just been the seagulls shrieking but she had always been gifted with a vivid imagination.

Zoe liked to imagine she owned one of the larger yachts, and indulge in thoughts of being a pirate about to set sail on the seven seas. One boat called 'Rebecca' particularly captured her attention. She fantasised that one day she and her daughter could embark on 'Rebecca' for adventures, wearing high, black-leather boots with shiny, gold buckles and tricorn hats worn at the very jauntiest of angles. Along with them they could take Julia's pet, the splendid Mabel, as the ship's Maine-Coone Cat. Often she would walk around the Basin imagining returning from her nautical travels, and regaling folk with her swashbuckling tales of derring-do. Then she quickly dismissed these fanciful thoughts and considered what needed to be done for the next day at school.

Also, 'The Merchant's Tavern' in the Marina, was the sort of place she could go for a drink after a challenging day and pretend herself to be in a Mediterranean location like St Tropez. In fact, the amount of shorts and t shirts worn by other patrons on quite unsuitably chilly days, suggested she was not alone in these notions. There was nothing that Zoe enjoyed better than a few drinks down the pub and a chat with her friends but there was always Chloe to consider. Soon, she would be able to leave her daughter to her own devices, but not quite yet.

Sometimes her mother could be persuaded to come over and stay so Zoe could go out. But increasingly she was becoming very busy with her social activities of ballroom dancing and playing bridge. Since Zoe's father had died and her mother had given up work as a shop assistant in the department store Fenwick's in Newcastle, she had discovered a new lease of life. Also, she seemed to have acquired an assortment of men friends. The word boyfriend seemed entirely inappropriate for these ageing Lotharios in their seventies. Nevertheless, Zoe thought it most unfair that her mother was having much more success in this department than she was herself.

When her husband Gary and she had split up, things hadn't been easy. She had been bitterly hurt and now she was reluctant to trust men again. Apart from anything else it wasn't fair on Chloe. Although it was three years ago now, balancing a full-time teaching job and being a mother was tricky. When she had been replaced with a younger model and her daughter by a newer version, Zoe had understandably felt very bitter. Also, she had struggled to get any maintenance off the bastard. There was something of Neil that reminded her of her arrogant policeman, ex-husband and therein lay the problem. For whatever Neil did, she just couldn't help but dislike him and thoughts of gang-planks entered her mind from somewhere. Something was clearly upsetting Julia and *he* was the most likely cause. She would wait until Chloe was in bed then she would ring her friend.

Earlier that day, after finally completing her jigsaw, Pamela stood and stepped back to admire her efforts. When she had completed a difficult puzzle she always got a feeling of great satisfaction. She loved the sensation of running her fingers across the pieces correctly slotted together. Her feelings of euphoria however were short-lived as her thoughts wandered to OakElmAsh and she wondered how poor Max was coping with his baptism of fire.

It really was most unfair of Charles to land him in it just like that, especially without Neil being there. She had always liked Neil actually and sometimes she wished her husband was a little more like him. Whenever their paths had crossed, he always had something nice to say to her.

'Oh Pamela, don't you look lovely in that green dress. It's gorgeous. Is it new? It really suits you.' She must have had that particular dress at least ten years. Or, 'My Pamela you must have been to the hairdressers today. Don't your locks look shiny? You always look so fetching' Pamela always had her hair exactly the same and it never looked any different from day to day. And sometimes 'What delightful perfume you're wearing.' She always wore the same perfume – Youth Dew by Estee Lauder.

Pamela enjoyed these interactions with Neil and she was almost sure that he carried a secret torch for her. He always made her feel quite giddy and girlish. Charles had never had that effect on her, even when they first got together. Why couldn't Charles be more like Neil? Julia was a very lucky woman. She supposed Julia would be at school at the moment as it was two o'clock. Well, she needed a few things from the shop, so she supposed she had better go now as she certainly didn't want to run the risk of bumping into her and of having to answer any subsequently difficult questions. But just why had her husband sacked Neil? Maybe he was jealous of him because although they were of a similar age, Neil was wearing his years much better.

Aware of her husband's increasing girth, she tried to cook healthy meals for Charles but he was always hankering for fattening foods and after most meals he would sneak into the kitchen to forage for biscuits and cakes. She bet Neil didn't do that.
Charles had always spoken so highly of Neil and especially of his ability to make sales happen.
'That Neil's a bloody magician.' She had often heard her husband say as he rubbed his hands together when he looked at the company accounts. Perhaps Neil had lost his Midas touch? And now, her husband was expecting Max, who was certainly no alchemist, to do his job. Well much as she loved her son to bits, she was well aware of his shortcomings and even she, no matter how hard she tried, could not see him making a very successful salesman.

Max

When Max arrived late at Tindale Gardens, Mr and Mrs Evans had already been there for half an hour at least and they were not impressed at being kept waiting. They were sitting outside the property in a grey Ford Focus, sheltering from the persistent mizzle. As soon as he saw the white OakElmAsh van pull up outside the semi- detached house, Mr Evans leapt out his car. Mrs Evans found manoeuvring herself from the vehicle more problematic, as she was heavily pregnant. Neither of them seemed at all pleased that Max was late.
'Hello you must be Mr and Mrs Evans My name is … ?

'And what time do you call this me lad?' He was looking at his watch, so Max found no need to answer this rhetorical question. Mr Evans spoke with a bluff, Yorkshire accent and Max derived a strange sense of satisfaction from his short stature. Mr Evans couldn't have been more than five foot five and his wife who was even smaller, had the ungainly appearance of a beach ball, in her colourful checked material coat and advanced state of pregnancy.

'Well, come on. Stop gawping at us and get a move on. We have another property to view in twenty minutes.'

'Certainly Sir.' Was this the correct form of address? Max had no idea of Estate Agent's protocol. 'If you come this way.' Max opened a rickety, rusty gate which creaked and came dangerously close to falling off its hinges.

'As you can see um …' Max looked from the hostile pair of small, beady eyes that belonged to Mrs Evans to the more belligerent, protruding ones of her husband. 'The house has a very nice garage.'

The pair of them looked at each other in disbelief. 'Get the door open lad. We don't have long and the bloody garage is neither here nor there, we need to see th' insides.' Shuffling uncomfortably over to the blue door, which was now looking neglected and in need of some serious TLC, Max tentatively put the key into the lock. As the door swung open, Max didn't have good feeling about this place and neither did his clients.

Mr and Mrs Evans followed him uneasily into a dark hallway that smelt of damp or something worse. Max smiled at them apologetically, as if he were an actor who had lost his script.

'This is the front room,' said Max.

The reluctant couple followed him into a room that seemed unchanged since the 1960's. Mrs Evans wrinkled her nose in disdain, looking at the yellowing walls, threadbare rugs and filthy, net curtains that prevented much light from entering the dingy room. Mr Evan's ran a finger across the filthy tiled mantelpiece, where there was a layer of dust as thick as a carpet underlay. Also, the unpleasant smell extended its bouquet here to include nicotine and cat's wee. Max wondered how on earth Neil could have possibly waxed lyrically about such a room but that was obviously what was required of him.

'As you can see there is a nice view of the road from this window and it's an ideal place for… ' He cast his eyes about looking for some inspiration. 'Sitting and watching the telly or … doing a jigsaw. '

Mr and Mrs Evan's were taken aback by this unlikely description of the hovel and the suggestion that they had the time for doing silly puzzles. Meanwhile, Max considered the unlikely picture of his Mother sitting in this room.

'Are you for real?' Mr Evans put a protective arm around his wife. 'Claire, as I'm sure you have noticed, is about to have our child. Do you really think this is the sort of place we would choose to bring up our baby?'

‘If you would like to follow me through to the back … there is, ‘Max reached for inspiration from the company brochure and read aloud, ‘A charming dining room and kitchen leading out to the garden.’

‘I think we’ve seen enough. Come along Claire. Let’s get out of here.’ Mr Evan’s moved towards the door.

‘But Eddie, come on we might as well have look while we’re here.’ She grabbed her husband’s arm.

‘Yes, you might as well … I mean, I know the place maybe needs a little work doing, but you must admit that it’s reflected in the price,’ said Max. Yes, this must be the type of thing Neil would have said, as it must be admitted it was very cheap for a semi-detached house and this wasn’t a bad area. ‘I’d say it’s a bargain actually. Maybe someone has died here and the family just want a quick sale to get rid of the place …’ Big mistake. Max watched the expressions on Claire and Eddie’s faces shifting from aghast, to horror before settling nicely into fury.

‘Come on Claire. Let’s get going. How dare you insult us like this?’ said Mr Evans. Claire was now crying. ‘Come on love, let’s get away from this place.’ Eddie‘s face was scarlet with rage as he shook his finger at Max. ‘And someone’s paying you to do this job? Don’t you worry, Oak, Elm and bloody Ash will definitely be hearing from us. Certainly, I don’t want to waste my time being insulted by a rude, incompetent whippersnapper like you. Honestly, in this day and age, there’s no need to employ clowns like you.’

Chapter 5

Julia

Not wanting to stay at school, but equally not being able to face going home, Julia felt trapped in her cage of a car, as she drove about, killing time. Eventually, she arrived at Saltwell Park which seemed as good a place as anywhere to be. At this time of day and year there were few people around which could only be a bonus. Julia was in no mood for chats with random strangers. The sun was low in the sky, casting eerie shadows off the trees, like witches waving their arms across her path. In the dusk, she could still make out the crenelated parapets and giant, salt and pepper pot chimneys of the glorious Saltwell Towers. Once, it had been the home of Victorian stained-glass manufacturer, William Wales. It now sat like terracotta, wedding cake in the centre of the well-tended ornamental gardens of the park and served as a coffee shop and picturesque venue for those getting married.

In her current frame of mind however it did nothing to impress Julia, as grubby stains from the decaying leaves were spoiling her suede boots and there was a damp, moist drizzle in the air. Normally, she would be bothered about frizzy hair, but today she couldn't care less. It wouldn't be long before the gates would be locked and she would we forced to either leave or spend the night here. All matters considered, she suspected that maybe the latter option would be the better choice.

There was just so much to think about. Julia rubbed her hands through her hair, which now had the texture like the twigs of a badly tended bush. Thoughts she had been trying to push unsuccessfully to the back of her mind all day, buzzed around her head like angry wasps. She felt sick. Also, she had never lost her temper the way she had today. Not in all the years she had been teaching had she felt so completely out of control and the thought scared her. That must never happen again.

Naturally, the children would pick up on her anxieties – that was the nature of the beast, and Julia imagined them as scavengers, eager to sink their teeth into her as roadkill. But she was the adult and the one in control. Teachers should never let children see the chinks in their armour, should they? Goodness knows what Emily had thought and it was a wonder that Hazel Swan hadn't been stirred from her pit to see what was occurring. Thankfully, she hadn't but she had definitely noticed her lateness that morning. If she took some sick leave, it would give her more time to think clearly about what needed to be done. But sometimes, the more you thought, the worse the problem became, like a ladder in a favourite pair of tights; the more you wore them, the longer the run.

Julia pulled her coat tighter round her shoulders and watched the sun setting into the bleak, grey sky. She turned her thoughts to happier times and recalled when she and Neil first met. She remembered how she had felt trapped in a tunnel, but then a light had appeared when he had come into her life. She tried to focus on the blissful period in her life when they had laughed all the time like imbeciles, from the moment they woke until going to sleep. Well, that's what she remembered, for there was always such a lot of drink involved in those early days, and bedtimes were a little blurry to say the least. In retrospect how they managed to get up each morning for work was a mystery in itself. Always, they were either down the pub, out for meals, going to parties or off on holiday. It was as if money were no object. Dinkys (double income no kids yet) is definitely what they were. For they both had well-paid jobs, plenty of surplus cash for fun but the no kids yet turned into ever.

Looking back even further to her previous relationship with Trevor, it had been so appalling , that all she could feel was relief when it ended. The whole chapter in her life had been the most abhorrent time imaginable and she winced at the very thought. At first, his constant criticisms and put downs she had stupidly misconstrued as him wanting the best for her. It had taken her far too long to realise it was not only his lack of altruism that was the problem, but his complete make-up being comprised of a twisted, perverted misogyny.

Although her parents had died tragically when she was still a teenager, she was deemed by the authorities to be of a mature enough age to care of herself. However, she had just felt like an abandoned orphan. In retrospect, she wished that she had been able to go away to study, but that of course had been out of the question. The house was the familiar territory she had craved where she felt safe. She could not have contemplated leaving the place she had grown up in and at that time she had needed any comfort blanket she could lay her hands on. Her

parents had not encouraged her to be independent or wanted her to spread her wings. So, by studying locally she felt she was doing what they would have wished.

However, if she had taken herself off to London or Manchester, then her life would have been very different. But then, she could hardly pin the blame on her parents, for they had hardly expected to die at such a young age. So she had just got on with the unhappy business of being alone. But she had hated it.

Julia reflected that although she had found it easy enough to get boyfriends, their attentions soon drifted elsewhere. So many times, they had finished with her unexpectedly without providing her with any credible explanation. This had left Julia feeling baffled and worthless in equal quantities. Now, she could see they no doubt found her too clingy and demanding. Nobody at nineteen, wanted a millstone round their neck, as the pathetic creature Julia must have seemed to them at that time.

The few girlfriends she had, tried to tell her that she needed to *play it more cool* but their words fell on deaf ears. That was until she met Trevor. Instantly, she knew this one was different. Trevor was older and wasn't a student. He didn't just want to play games. Understandably, she was overwhelmed and flattered by his attentions. It was as if he wanted to spend every moment of every day with her. She loved that he fussed over and cossetted her as if she were the most important thing in his life. Not since her parents had died had she felt so safe. That was until the slavish devotion took a more sinister turn.
'Penny for them?' Julia turned to see that she had company on the bench. 'You look deep in thought. You'll have to be off soon. They'll be locking up for the night.'
'Yes I suppose so.' Julia tried to pin an age on the sorry individual with whom she was sharing a bench. With her coat appearing like a sack, long multi-coloured scarf wound several times round her neck and wellington boots, Julia suspected that she was a homeless person. Her wrinkled skin, straggly grey hair and missing teeth failed to

indicate her age which could have been any number from forty to seventy. But her eyes, like bright buttons, hinted at an intelligence and spirit that refused to be crushed.
She pulled a bottle from her bag and took a long swig before offering it to Julia.
'No thanks.' Julia stood up feeling uncomfortable.' You're all right. I guess I need to be on my way home.'

The woman nodded.'Are all right? You look like you're carrying the problems of the world.' The woman took another drink from her bottle.
'Yes, I'm fine. It's getting cold and I need to be going home.' Julia shivered as she hadn't realised how chilly it had become. 'And what about you?'
'Oh don't you worry about me. I'll get by. I don't suppose you'd spare a couple of quid?'
Julia took her purse from her bag and feeling guilty, as more than likely the woman would be sleeping rough tonight, she gave her a twenty pound note. Upon receiving this, her face lit up and Julia recognised the woman was probably much younger than she was.

Tracy

Tracy was flicking through a glossy magazine and just about to lock up the OakElmAsh office, when the phone began ringing. Oh for goodness sake. She noticed the time on the office clock and really she could do without this now. An angry-faced Charles with a miserable Max had just left. At last, she was the only one left in the building and she was eager to be on her way to the gym. She had a Boxercise class that evening.
'Hello, OakElmAsh Estate Agents. Can I help you?' Tracy was checking that her pristine white trainers were ready for action in her fluffy, exercise bag.
'I want to speak to the owner of this … joke of an Estate Agent. That Mr Lavender … that's his name I believe.'
Oh dear, somebody didn't sound very happy. She wondered who had rattled his cage and pulled the receiver away from her ear, as Mr Evans growled down the phone, getting louder and louder.

'Well I'm sorry, but he isn't here at the moment.' Tracy replied. 'If you wish to speak to him, then you'll have to ring back tomorrow. Can I be of assistance? Or give him a message …' Hopefully, this phone call wouldn't last too long, as she needed to be on her way.

'For starters … you can tell him I wish to launch a complaint about th' idiot who showed me around that Tindale Gardens shambles of a place today.'

A little smile of schadenfreude quivered around Tracy's candy-pink lips, as she realised who he was referring to.

'Oh, I am sorry sir was dissatisfied with *Mr Lavender junior*. 'She said the name pointedly.' What exactly was the problem?' She now affected her most concerned manner.

'Well to be honest, it was mostly his general demeanour and lack of erm … professionalism. Yes, that's the word.' Eddie was now calming down a little, pleased to find a sympathetic ear to which he could vent his spleen.

'In what way can I ask? I shall tell *Mr Lavender senior* tomorrow.' She was keen to labour the relationship between these two, as she was still baffled herself by the ridiculous nepotism deployed in this crazy appointment of Max as lead salesperson.

'To begin with he was at least an half an hour late. I mean, that's not on is it? And my poor wife is expecting a child soon you know … and waiting around isn't good for her condition. '

Tracy remembered now when this client had made the viewing appointment last week. He had been overly pernickety and annoying then, insisting on very particular time slots. However, if Neil had dealt with them, he would have soon had them wrapped round his little finger.

'Oh I'm very sorry to hear that. Anything else?' When she planned on ringing Neil later, this information would cheer him up no end and he would just love to hear all this.

'I don't think it is necessary to go into all the details … he was just generally very rude and … it was as if he was taking the micky … if you know what I mean? '

Tracy was pleased that Max's obvious nervousness had been so wrongly misinterpreted.

‘Well I can only apologise Sir. ‘If she kept pushing, she was sure to get the splendid reward of some more amusing anecdotes that would be good to share. ‘But if you could give me a few more precise details … that would be useful for our company to improve its services.’
‘It was as if he was … well, looking down his nose at us. As if that dump of a house was all we were fit …’ Eddie Evans bit his tongue, realising that this wasn’t a path down which he had intended to tread and expose his own insecurities. ‘Anyway, you can tell Mr Lavender Senior … that I shall ring back tomorrow.’ He now had no intention of ringing back because the useless lump was obviously none other than the boss’s son.
‘Well of course. If you are sure there is no other way I can help you.’ Tracy realised she had milked this conversation as much as possible. ‘Don’t worry I shall report back to Mr Lavender exactly what you told me about our new employee. Personally, I don’t feel he is up to the job. So I suggest you ring back tomorrow and tell my boss yourself.’

Eddie Evans put his phone back in his pocket, not all together sure who had come out of this conversation seeming the greater fool. It was best he put the whole sorry event to bed, and right out of his mind. As Tracy headed off for the gym, she wondered if there were going to be any more messages left on the phone tomorrow from other dissatisfied customers. She hoped so, and was feeling a lot happier than she had in days.

Charles

Charles wondered if it was possible that his son Max was being even more surly and uncommunicative on his way back from work, than he had been on the way there. The lad just needed to get over himself. Honestly, most kids of his age would bite off an arm and a leg to have the opportunities handed to him on a plate. When he was Max’s age, he was just starting the business off and he’d had nothing to speak of. But all those years of hard work and graft had paid off big time. And his son was now going to reap those benefits wasn’t he? Charles really couldn’t understand what his problem was.

‘So son, how did you enjoy your first day as part of the flock?’ Clearly Max just needed a little chivvying along.

‘Well, what do you think Dad? Yes, I showed some people round some houses, but it was awful. I hadn’t known what to say to them. They didn’t like the houses and they didn’t like me.’ Max stared glumly out of the passenger window at the mocking row of houses that came into view, refusing to make any eye contact with his father.

‘Now then son. Don’t be too hard on yourself. It was your first day after all. Who knows? Tomorrow, your clients might be back on the phone asking for a second viewing or even making an offer. You just wait and see. Remember the company slogan – “Sales make your salary”. He winked at his son, who still wasn’t looking at him and took a yellow, pear drop sweet, out of the glove compartment of his Jaguar car. ‘Would you like one of these?’

Max shook his head. ‘It will be better I guess … when Neil comes back.’

Charles ignored this observation, knowing the impossibility of it happening.

Max turned to face his father. ‘Well, where was he today?’

‘Who? Where was who?’ Charles knew full well to whom he was referring.

‘Neil, your golden salesman and friend … the one who was supposed to be showing me what to do.’ Max’s voice sounded like he was being strangled and was becoming peculiarly high pitched.

‘Neil? I guess he was at home.’ Charles kept his eyes on the road ahead.

‘So is he ill?’

Charles wished his son would stop bleating. ‘I’m not sure. Anyway I wonder what your Mother has made us for dinner tonight. I hope it’s shepherd’s pie. She sometimes makes that on a Monday night but then often she makes a casserole. ‘

‘Dad there is something you aren’t telling me. Is Neil seriously ill? Is that why it was so important that I started work today? Has he got some awful disease … like cancer? I can’t understand why he wasn’t there today. Has he been in accident?’ Charles was surprised by these outpouring from his son in the car, as Max hardly ever strung more than two or three words together.

Charles sighed. ‘No it’s nothing like that. Look Max. I know you’re not going to like this. I know even more, you’re not going to understand this. I have had to … how shall I say this? I’ve had to let Neil go.’

'Let him go? What? What do you mean? Do you mean you've sacked him?'
'Well not really sacked … certain matters came to my attention that I just couldn't overlook.'
'But Dad that's crazy. I … I mean he was brilliant at his job. How am I going to bring in a fraction of … *the sales that make your salary*, like he did?'
'Max. Neil's just a jumped-up salesman. People like him are two-a-penny. Look Max, it was your first day today. Just take it easy. Wait and see. Rome wasn't built in a day you know?'

As the car swung into the driveway, Charles was keen to end this conversation.' And don't say anything of this to your mother. We don't need to worry her. Just pretend you've had a great day and that will put her mind at rest and give me a little peace this evening.'

Neil

Neil hoped Julia would be back soon. He had been on his own all day now and he was feeling bored by his own company. Often on a Monday she was a little late because there was a staff meeting but he was sure she was usually back by this time. Perhaps he should make tea, as he had been at home all day, but no, that would arouse suspicions. Neil listened to Mabel's contented snoring sounds, along with the ticking of the clock, as he sat thinking of the details of his and Julia's life.

Over their many years together, Julia and he had shared some great times. He thought of the Julia he had first met, with those haunted eyes and that sadness, that hung from her shoulders like a cloak fashioned from a shroud. Neil was feeling unusually poetic that afternoon. She was the polar opposite from all his previous girlfriends but he was fascinated by her. Much to the amazement of his drinking mates, he had persisted with her. The lads had thought her gloomy and boring but he could see another Julia beneath the tragic façade. With his usual self-assuredness, he had been certain that with his charm, he could release her from her sadness. It was some challenge, but quickly he began to see the results.

Neil and Julia drank cocktails in the swankiest bars, ate fillet steaks in the best restaurants, and splashed out on extravagant weekend mini-breaks to Paris, Barcelona and Rome. Julia surprisingly, embraced this new way of living with great enthusiasm, as for the first time in years she smiled, laughed and fell in love with this fun-loving man and his hedonistic lifestyle. Despite having an appreciation of art and an interest in history, she had never travelled. Neil to his own amazement, enjoyed learning all about mythology and ancient civilisations from her, as they wandered around the Louvre or the Colosseum – she was a school teacher after all.

Also, the fact that Julia had owned this house outright was not without its attractions. This meant he could sell his bachelor pad, with its massive mortgage and they would have lots of disposal income for living the high life. Spending money was a pastime that Neil had always entered into with great gusto and Julia was soon swept up and corrupted by his infectious joie- de-vivre. This lifestyle was also reflected in dramatic home renovations. There was no comparison between the dowdy, out of date house pre-Neil and the smart place they lived in today.

However, for some strange reason she had put her foot down several times about the garden. Neil had thought some decking would be a useful addition for a seating area, when people came over for a barbecue, but Julia wouldn't entertain this. Only a couple of years ago, after having a great time staying in a log cabin, Neil had broached the subject of having a hot tub but Julia would have none of it. Then, Neil had mentioned to her, that some of their friends had a lovely pond with coy carp. He thought that Mabel would love one like this to sit and watch the fish, but again Julia had said no, vehemently.

This was very odd, because the slightest whimsy of Neil's, relating to changes in the home had all been willingly indulged by his wife. In the dining room, was the special table which could be cleverly converted into one for playing pool. There was a once well-stocked but now of course empty, kitsch bar with optics in the front room. Well, it was the purpose of drinks to be enjoyed. And the third bedroom of the house, Julia had allowed it to become Neil's precious man cave. She had even permitted the expensive, high maintenance Mabel into their home, despite the fact she was allergic to cats and didn't particularly like them. However, Mabel was a special Maine Coon cat with her lustrous silver fur and beguiling purr. It had taken very little time for Mabel to win Julia round. Mabel stopped snoring and opened her eyes briefly; as if aware she was being thought about, before drifting back off to sleep.

Neil had never found out all the details of what had happened with Julia and her first husband Trevor, but he hadn't needed to. Sometimes, what had happened in the past was best left there. However, there had definitely been something very wrong there, for him to have affected Julia in the way that he had. Whenever the subject of her past with Trevor arose, Julia was always evasive and didn't want to talk. By contrast when Julia spoke of her childhood, she was happy enough to wax lyrical of these times. She needed little encouragement, to relate tales of happy days out, picnics on the beach and idyllic holidays spent walking in the Lake District with her beloved parents Carol and Michael. She must have been devastated by her parent's untimely death in some awful motor accident.

Neil's mind swam back to Julia's first husband, Trevor the shark, as he liked to think of him. He must have just preyed on the vulnerability of a young girl. Julia had been still in her teens and he suspected that Trevor must have been a lot older. A pliable girl with her own property must have been an extremely attractive proposition to the loser. No doubt marrying Julia, had given him a much better lifestyle than he would have on some meagre shop assistants wage. Although the house wasn't a patch on what it was now, it was no doubt much better than one he could have afforded.

He wondered what had happened to Trevor. Neil bumped into his exes from time to time in supermarkets, restaurants and pubs. Only last week, he had seen Nicola, or had she been called Natalie? He'd met her in Sainsbury's, and they had had a brief chat. Julia was

never fazed in the slightest when Neil regaled her with tales from his colourful past, but Trevor was never mentioned. It was almost as if Julia wanted to pretend he had never existed, yet he must be prowling around somewhere. Perhaps, he had found their breakup so traumatic, that he had moved completely away from the area. Or maybe he hadn't and was stalking the pair of them to this very day. Neil looked through the window and imagined the ghost of Trevor wafting around in the garden. After all, that was just the kind of creepy activity he imagined that Trevor would engage in.

Neil had never seen any photos of Trevor, but he pictured a short, bald, over-weight man with a handlebar moustache. Trevor's he imagined would be the just the kind of person to have such a facial appendage. Of course, Julia was hardly likely to have any of his pictures on display now but perhaps she had some hidden away. Neil now had plenty of time on his hands for a little digging around in the attic. Obviously, not now for he was sure Julia would be back at any moment.

Neil heard his phone ringing. When he saw it was Tracy, he let it go to voice mail.

Chapter 6

Thirty Years Earlier

Trevor

While Trevor ate his evening meal, which on that particular evening had been fish and chips from round the corner, he liked to read The Evening Chronicle; the local paper. Trevor lived in a small bedsit on Coatsworth Road in Gateshead, above a Kosher bakery. It was an area popular with the Orthodox Jewish community and indeed his landlord Solomon Goldstein, with his long ringlets and austere black clothes was an important figure in the local community. However, the rent he charged was reasonable and essential to Trevor given his limited finances. His job as a Pharmacy Assistant didn't pay well. Although the green paint was flaking from the walls like garden waste and there was an unattractive damp patch spreading like an infected abscess on the ceiling, it was convenient for him to walk to the nearby chemist shop where he worked.

Before he screwed up the paper and threw it in the bin, something caught his attention. A middle-aged couple, Carol and Michael Mason, had been involved last week in a fatal car crash. This had happened surprisingly, on a quiet country lane close to Birtley. He recognised those names but from where? It seemed they had been involved in a headlong collision with a stationary vehicle. There had been a terrible inferno and Mr and Mrs Mason had only been identifiable by their dental records. How awful. It seemed a very odd place for such an accident to have occurred and Trevor wondered, disapprovingly if they had been drinking.

Trevor didn't drink and he frankly found drunkenness not only abhorrent but a shocking waste of money. This was along with smoking, gambling, eating in fancy restaurants and paying exorbitant prices for tickets to the theatre or football matches. He didn't much like plays or sport anyway. For an occasional treat however, particularly on a Saturday night, he would allow himself to a visit to the cinema or, like that night, indulge in a take-away meal.

Returning to the newspaper article, he saw that they had left an only daughter of nineteen named Julia. Julia Mason, of course, that's where he recognised the name from. The Mason family had once been his neighbours. Before his own mother had died, Trevor had lived with her in the little terraced house which had been his home since his birth. The two-up, two-down house seemed even smaller than it actually was, being crammed with the bric-a-brac his mother randomly collected over the years. He recalled ladies wearing crinoline dresses waltzing across the window ledges, while toby jugs smirked knowingly from the mantelpiece.

His father, a coal miner had been badly injured in a terrible accident, when a shaft collapsed leaving him paralysed. His devoted mother had nursed her bedridden husband for several years before he at last passed away. His mother only had a small widow's pension, and they had been forced to live frugally, but once he got his job at the chemist's, life for them both was a little easier. At last they could afford to heat the house properly and eat decent meals.

He had happy memories of having teas of liver and bacon with his mother when he came in from work, of them watching Kojak on the television together, and their equal allied curiosity, when the new houses began being built across the street. Mother and son stared through the window transfixed, as first foundations were laid, bricks put in place, drives filled with concrete and then all the fixtures and fittings added until everything was good to go. There had never been such excitement in the street and the drilling, banging and shouting didn't bother them in the slightest; it just added to the interest.

Eventually, the new families moved in and living in the house directly across from them, was Mr and Mrs Mason with their new baby daughter. Mr Mason was a tall man who went to work each day at an accountancy firm wearing a grey suit, a sombre face and carrying a carefully polished briefcase. His wife favoured flared trousers, wedged heeled shoes and brightly coloured floral dresses. Although she didn't appear to go out to work, once she had established herself in the area and acquired a network of friends, she became an avid organiser of Tupperware, Pippa Dee and Avon Cosmetics parties. This was according to his mother, for Trevor was unsure of what these gatherings might be, but was positive they sounded decadent.

However, it was neither Mr nor Mrs Mason that Trevor found of particular interest. From behind the curtains, he watched the daughter Julia, in fascination (his mother had spoken with Mrs Mason and found out their names), as she changed from small toddler, to little girl and then teenager. He had never spoken to her. Not once. No doubt she was completely unaware of his existence but he had never forgotten her even to this very day.

'Trevor, come away from that window. Your tea's ready.' His mother had shouted from the kitchen.

'I was just watching that new family across the road. The ones with the baby.' Trevor was perched on the arm of the badly stained sofa, peering at them from behind the shield of lace curtains.

'It's the Mason family and the baby's called Jane, Jenny or Julia. Something beginning with J.' Trevor remembered the conversation word for word.

'The Mason family.' He repeated as he sat down and smoothed the tablecloth.

'Now Trevor.' His mother put a plate of sausage and mash in front of him. 'Don't keep staring at them out of the window. If they see you … well, they'll think you are odd, won't they?'

'I'm not doing any harm though…' Trevor produced a sulky face.

'Well I know that… but in this day and age you need to be careful.' His mother pointed accusingly at him with her fork.

Once his parents had both died, Trevor had been forced to move out, much to his annoyance, as the property was rented and too expensive for him alone. After a search through the ads in the Chronicle, he came upon Mr Goldstein's and when he discovered its proximity to his place of work, it was an obvious solution. Mr Goldstein appreciated his punctuality with paying rent and hadn't increased the price once in five years. Now he looked around his cramped, miserable flat, and compared it unfavourably with the lovely house the Masons had

lived in. Poor Julia would be there all alone now wouldn't she? Perhaps now it was time for Trevor to make a move and Mr Goldstein to find a new tenant for his hovel.

The Present

Julia

When Julia eventually arrived home, she was surprised to find Neil in the kitchen, chopping onions. Even Mabel was watching him from her large cat basket, with a bemused expression on her face.

'Alright love? How's your day been then?' Neil was trying his best and she noticed he had spilt tomato sauce down the white shirt he was pretending to have worn for work that day.

'Not one of my best I'm afraid. 'Julia took off her coat and hung it on the back of one of the kitchen chairs.'The kids were playing up and I've had a horrible headache all day.'

'Well why don't you sit down? You do look a little peaky. Here's a nice cup of tea for you. And I'm making the food tonight 'Neil proudly, gave her one of what he thought to be his most endearing smiles. 'Spaghetti bolognaise – that alright?' Julia wasn't feeling particularly hungry, but she was glad she didn't have to think about cooking a meal for them both.

'Yes that sounds lovely.' It was very unusual for Neil to attempt to cook and judging from the mess of red sauce and vegetable peelings everywhere, it was obviously going to take some clearing up.

'So have you had a busy time at work today then?' she asked, but Neil didn't meet Julia's eye, as he concentrated on mixing the gloopy concoction in the pan as it splashed merrily onto the top of the cooker.

'Not too bad. Just the usual stuff. Same old.' Neil continued stirring the sauce.

Julia yawned and rubbed her eyes. 'You must have got back early to have started making tea.' Considering that he had probably been sitting on his backside all day, she thought it really was the very least that he could do. However, she hoped she wasn't going to have to clear up all of his debris.

'Well no actually. I'd just come in. In fact you're the one who's late.' Neil put the pasta onto boil.

'Not really, I'm often later on a Monday because of the…'

‘Staff meeting. Yes I remember.’ He looked pleased with himself, as he finished her sentence.
‘So has Charles’s son Max started working at the office yet?’ After the awful day she’d had, she couldn’t resist a little Neil baiting.
‘Erm no …I don’t think so.’ Neil unsurprisingly, seemed rather vague on this matter.
‘Well he mustn’t have done then, must he?’ She watched her husband looking uncomfortable, as she knew he had no way of answering her question.’ I am sure you would have noticed him if he had. I hope you haven’t had that stain down the front of your shirt all day. A messy look like that wouldn’t be a good example to set to the boss’s son now would it?’
‘No, I’ve just done it.’ He pulled a face when he saw the awful state his white shirt was in.
‘You usually take your work clothes off when you get home.’ It was fun to watch Neil squirm. ‘I bet that mark won’t come out of your good shirt.’

Ignoring this remark, Neil served up their tea. It didn’t appear very appetising as the greasy mixture trickled down the side of the green pasta bowl and seeped onto the checked table cloth. Both Neil and Julia played with their spaghetti, winding it around their forks, before allowing it to slurp back into their dishes.
‘I’ve been thinking,’ said Neil. This sounded ominous thought Julia. ‘When this money comes through from the Council.’ Julia could feel the look of panic flitting across her face at the very mention. ‘We could give our jobs up. I mean neither of us are getting any younger and just think of all those places in the world that we haven’t visited. I bet you wouldn’t miss those staff meetings would you when you’re sunning yourself on a tropical island?’
‘There are a lot of people older than us still working Neil.’ Julia was no longer in the mood for banter.’ Anyway however would Charles and OakElmAsh survive without you?’
‘I’m sure they would manage.’ Neil said slowly, wondering if Julia had guessed about his sacking. Sensing that his culinary efforts had neither been appreciated nor enjoyed, Neil went upstairs, leaving Julia to clear up the bombsite.

Once Chloe had taken herself off to her room at around half past nine, Zoe was well into her fourth glass of wine and wondered about the sensibility of ringing her friend. Well, if Julia didn't want to speak with her, then she could just ignore the call couldn't she? She fished out her phone from down the side of the sofa and typed in Julia's number. Just before the phone was about to go to voicemail Julia picked up.

'Zoe is that you? What's wrong is everything ok with you?' Julia sounded a little flustered as she didn't often get calls this late. She had debated for several seconds as to whether to pick up the phone or not and immediately wished that she hadn't.

'Yes I'm fine but I'm worried about you. I tried to catch you after ssschool but…' Zoe was slightly slurring her words. Julia was pleased about this, as she thought it might give her the upper hand when the awkward questions began.

'Oh yes … I had to dash off. I needed to get some … dry cleaning before the place closed. You know what Neil's like with his suits.' Julia could really have been doing without this conversation.

'Is everything ok with you and Neil? Is he with you? Can you talk?' Here we go thought Julia, she assumed either Neil was having a torrid affair or he'd been hitting her. She loved Zoe to bits but sometimes her misandry totally clouded her judgement. For all his faults, Neil was not Gary.

'He's upstairs. Why should anything be wrong?' Julia was sitting in her conservatory, also having wine but she was only on her second glass.

'Well it's just you didn't really seem yourself today … during the staff meeting, you were miles away.' Zoe was sure that if she asked her friend what the meeting was about, she wouldn't have had the foggiest notion.

'Oh I just had a bit of a headache … but it's much better now.' This was true, as she'd had a splitting headache all day.

'You should stay off tomorrow.' Zoe wished she could stay off tomorrow, but at least Tuesdays weren't quite as bad as Mondays.

'No honestly I'm fine now.' She had seen the look in Hazel Swan's eye, when she had clocked her arriving late yesterday and knew she needed to tread carefully. A sickie was simply not on the cards.

'Julia ...' Zoe bit the bullet. 'I heard you screaming at those kids.'

Damn. Julia hoped she hadn't heard. 'Oh I just lost my rag ... they were being really awful and fussy.' She tried to make light of it but she realised Zoe knew her too well and wouldn't be fooled.

'No Julia ... I know there is more to this. It's Neil isn't it?' Zoe was like a dog with a bone.

'Zoe honestly it's nothing to do with him. I just didn't feel very well.' Julia was exhausted and desperately wanted this phone call to end.

'You can tell me you know. The last time we were out ... you were going to tell me something about him, weren't you? Do you remember?' Zoe's unrelenting probing was the final straw.

'Zoe, I know you mean well but I'm just so tired. I need a bath and early night. Look, can we talk tomorrow?'

'Well as long as you are sure ... there isn't anything I can do.'

Julia was at the end of her tether. 'Good night Zoe. See you tomorrow.' Julia put down the phone. Zoe poured herself another glass of wine and thought through the conversation, for any clues as to the source of the problem. It all pointed towards Neil. Julia went upstairs to rn herself a bath and wondered whoever Neil could be whispering to on his phone.

Tracy

Tracy had been trying to contact Neil persistently throughout that evening, but he seemed have his phone switched off. She was looking forward to retelling the events of the day and was piqued that he must be otherwise occupied. No doubt serving some penance with his dreary wife Julia.

Tracy completely failed to grasp what the attraction was there, from Neil's side at least. However, she could clearly see that old fuddy-duddy Julia, must have thought she had bagged quite a catch. Julia with her sensible boots, frumpy woollen jumpers, drawn face and schoolmarm's manner was in no way his equal. Also, in her eyes, it was impossible to believe

the

that she and Julia were of a similar age. If truth be told, Tracy thought that she looked more like Julia's daughter. Tracy preened herself in mirror, admiring her gym-toned body, botoxed skin and the crowning glory of her platinum blonde tresses. Age was just kinder to some more than others, she reckoned.

On the few awkward occasions that their paths had crossed, Tracy had found Julia to be dour, surly and boring. When Tracy had made her customary jokes, Julia hadn't even bothered to raise an inkling of a smile and when she attempted to make conversation with her, the rude cow had shown absolutely no interest whatsoever in celebrity culture. And when she thought Tracy wasn't looking she was almost sure she saw her rolling her eyes at her husband. Tracy had a very low opinion of Julia.

Mind, she had heard that Julia had been left a house and plenty of money by her parents, who she had unfortunately lost at an early age. Rather careless, Tracy thought to lose not just one parent but two. She remembered that quote from somewhere and congratulated herself on her wittiness. Poor Julia, not … rich, lucky Julia. It was the only possible reason that Neil would have had anything to do with the drab creature. And supposedly her first husband, who she must have snared in a similar manner, had peculiarly

disappeared without trace. By all accounts he had been a bit of an oddball, but his mysterious vanishing act, in a puff of smoke, had never been fully explained. How convenient for the witch Julia, enjoying living the life of Riley with husband number two. But just what had happened to his predecessor Tracy wondered, picturing Julia as a black widow spider.

The office just wasn't the same place without Neil and she was pretty sure that Charles would soon see the error of his ways. When Tracy had heard that he had been sacked, well she had been flabbergasted. Once Charles found out what a pig's ear of a job Max was making … well, it was just a matter of time. And to her delight, when she rang Neil at ten o'clock, this time he picked up.

'Hello Trace. How are you?' Neil whispered.

'Oh Neil' She gushed. 'How lovely to hear your voice. Everyone at work is missing you so much.' Neil closed the door to his study

'Really?' She might be, but he doubted very much that was the case for Charles and some of the others.

'Well Neil, I definitely am. And Max … well you wouldn't believe the mess he made of things today.'

Neil wasn't surprised.

'Late for appointments, upsetting clients …' Tracy continued. 'Honestly I've never known a day like it.'

'To be fair Trace, if nobody has shown the lad what to do. It's hardly his fault is it?' After all, he had been thrown in at the deep end.

'Well you would expect that a twenty one year old would be able to tell the time wouldn't you?' she smirked. 'But then I guess most school teachers aren't up to much these days, are they?'

Neil ignored this little jibe at his wife. 'So how did Charles seem? Did he say anything about …?'

'Charles was just the same boring so and so … as usual.' Tracy affected a yawn.' But his son – what a jerk! Do you know I've already had his first client of the day on the blower complaining about his rudeness .You would think with the amount of money that he's had spent on his education, he would have been taught some everyday manners wouldn't you?'

'I guess so.' Neil hoped that Julia couldn't hear him talking.

'And I just wonder when I get into work tomorrow … how many other dissatisfied customers I'll have to deal with.' He imagined Tracy shaking her head, a much practised move to display her albino-like mane of hair to its best advantage. 'Mark my words Neil, by the end of the week Charles will be begging for you to come back.'

‘Hmph, I wouldn’t hold your breath Trace.’ Neil couldn’t be bothered to flirt with Tracy as he usually did and he knew this would be annoying her.

‘Oh come on. So you’ve had some little tiff. So what? That must have happened lots of times.’ Tracy really had no idea about what had happened.

‘It’s a little bit more serious than that.’ To say the least, he thought, but if it hadn’t been for that bloody over-keen accountant, his dubious but well-concealed financial situation would have retained its status quo.

‘What did you do then? Did you call him fat? I bet he wouldn’t like that. But have you noticed the greedy pig never stops shovelling food into his gob.’ Tracy’s voice held a sanctimonious note.

Neil knew Tracy despised gluttony and was always very careful to control her own calorie intake. ’No Tracy it was just a small misunderstanding … about some money.’ There he had said it.

‘Well Neil, he is very fond of his money. But if it wasn’t for you the state of his precious business would be a completely different kettle of fish wouldn’t it? Surely some little financial anomaly will be quickly overlooked. Just you wait and see.’

Little? Neil couldn’t bring himself to divulge the amount of money he was talking about.

‘Look Trace, it’s getting late. If you want to talk … it’s probably better that you ring me during the daytime …’ Neil thought that he could hear his wife running a bath.

‘Yes Neil, I get it. When Julia’s at work. I get the message.’ And he knew Tracy was most definitely miffed, as she cut him off dead.

Chapter 7

Twenty Five Years Ago

Trevor

After reading the newspaper article, Trevor made it his business to find out as much as he could about Julia Mason and her whereabouts. He began by catching the old familiar bus ride to his childhood home and this he enjoyed very much. Once he had known every inch of that route. And while some places had changed, shops opened and closed, mostly things were largely the same.

When he arrived at his old street however, he found it disturbing that his own house now appeared in a much better state of repair than when he had lived there with his mother three years ago. The door was painted a fresh yellow colour and the windows looked sparklingly clean. There were pansies, freesias and petunias hanging from a basket outside and the missing tiles off the roof had been replaced. Compared to his present home this seemed like a palace. This annoyed him further, as he didn't like to think of other people living in his old home and taking better care of the place than his adored mother had done. The new occupants obviously had too much time on their hands.

Nevertheless, this wasn't the reason for his visit and he looked across the road at number eleven, which seemed exactly the same as it had then. The seventies new build still looked appealing in the eighties, with its generous garage at the front and neat garden. This gave him a feeling of warming, like a thickly buttered crumpet, and he pictured fifteen-year-old pony-tail swinging Julia, with her bag crammed full of school books, skipping along the path.

Not wishing to draw too much attention to himself, he stood at the bus stop where he still had a good view of the house and could watch for any comings and goings. Buses came and went; people got on and alighted from them, while Trevor remained there for at least two hours. Nobody paid much attention to him. Trevor was a rather nondescript man of thirty-six, with no distinguishing features. He was shorter than average, of medium build and had dark brown hair. Coupled with an unremarkable taste in clothing, wearing jeans and a navy zip up jacket on that day, he was almost invisible. Trevor thought he had a chameleon-like ability to blend into whichever surroundings he was in. This had always served him well and enabled him to keep out of trouble.

Fundamentally, there was nothing particularly unattractive about Trevor's appearance. The reason he had never had a girlfriend, was purely due to a lack of interest or effort on his part. Several women and girls had attempted to strike up a friendship with him in the Chemist's, but he had remained oblivious and indifferent, so they had soon moved on. Now however, it was different with Julia, as he had a definite purpose for pursuing her and felt anyway, that he had known her for almost all of her life, which he just about had. It was as if she provided a welcome link with happier days when he had lived in this street with his mother, but most importantly she could be the solution to all of his problems.

On this occasion, he'd had no sighting of Julia but this didn't matter as he could always return. At one point he wandered further away from the bus stop, nearer to the house to try and peer through the windows. Then, he remembered his mother's warnings about odd behaviour and thought better of himself. His next day off from the Chemists was Wednesday, so maybe if he could get up here early, he could find out exactly what she did with herself and precisely where she went to.

The Present

Pamela

Pamela was feeling even more worried than usual, as she was expecting her husband and son to be home at any moment and she couldn't possibly imagine how the day could have gone well for either of them. The table was set just how Charles liked, with the carefully polished cutlery and the place mats with the pictures of tropical fish. His favourite shepherd's pie had been cooked to perfection with the cheese bubbling on top.

The vegetables had just been put on to boil and a bottle of his Bordeaux, was breathing on the side. He liked his meal ready for as soon as he arrived, which was usually around six. Glancing out of the window, she wondered what Charles would find fault with tonight. The furniture gleamed with polish and the fresh smell of beeswax filled the air. Every surface was clear and there wasn't an item out of place. Something would be wrong though. It usually was. When Charles couldn't find a fault, he would either invent one or become peevish and she wasn't sure which was worse.

It was more than likely that her husband would have bigger fish to fry this evening. He would be too preoccupied with more important matters to be checking if all the surfaces were dust free. Charles, would be too caught up in Max's performance that day, He was unlikely to be inspecting the kitchen cupboards to see the tins were lined up correctly, with their labels facing outwards, like soldiers on parade. This evening would be all about their son. How could Charles possibly imagine that their dear, but hardly worldly-wise son could possibly metamorphose into a super- confident salesman overnight? It was an unrealistic expectation which was just typical of her husband.

When she and Charles first met she had been a shy young woman who had led a very cosseted and protected life. Her father, now long passed, had been an Anglican Vicar whose Parish Church had been in the small country village of Wylam, not far out of Newcastle. He and his wife and daughter, had lived in one of those charming picture-box cottages with roses round the windows and a plump tabby often curled up on the doorstep. When it became clear that Pamela was not the most academic of girls, they lowered their expectations for their daughter and merely wanted her to be happy. Leaving school as soon as possible, she was encouraged to busy herself with needlepoint and flower arranging in the Church, and they took pleasure in watching her successfully complete jigsaw puzzles. His wife had taught her how to bake delicious cakes and prepare traditional meals. Mother and daughter loved their shopping trips to Newcastle, from which they always returned with an assortment of boxes and bags filled with fancy new outfits to wear.

Although, this would seem an idyllic life to many, it had left Pamela poorly prepared for her future. Not being witty or particularly attractive, she had always found it difficult to relate to other children and preferred to exist in the tight bubble of her family. This suited her parents, for they wished to keep their little Pamela with them for as long as possible, and were quite relieved that she had neither the inclination nor ability to aspire to a further education. When she left school, she had no girlfriends to speak of and virtually no opportunities to meet members of the opposite sex.

When the unlikely happened and Pamela had met the young, ambitious Charles at some church social event (quite why Charles was there was always a mystery), she was bowled over by his confidence and smart suit. On their first date he took her to watch some awful, rugby match, which she hated but didn't let it be known to him. When she introduced him to her parents, all agreed he seemed the most suitable match she was capable of making.

However, soon after the marriage, his bad temper and controlling ways soon emerged. Her prissiness and ignorance as he referred to them, only served to further irritate her husband. On one occasion, a client's wife told Pamela she had a terrible tennis elbow, Pamela had asked her if she played a lot of tennis. How was she supposed to know the two weren't connected?

When they went to social events Pamela chose frilly, floaty dresses to wear, that she thought looked lovely. Just recently, Charles told her she always looked plain silly and nothing like all the other elegant wives of his friends. He said they just laughed and ridiculed her behind her back. It was only because she was so stupid that she didn't realise. But his most hurtful comment was when he had said that her favourite dress would be better served being placed on top of a giant, toilet roll!

While Pamela had everything materially she needed, she lacked the warmth and affection that other women like Julia had. Neil and Julia always seemed to be having fun, laughing and talking about the next holiday they had planned. Pamela could never see anything funny to be laughed at. Certainly not at those boring charity events she was forced to attend, when she would much rather be at home nursing a mug of cocoa and tackling a tricky jigsaw puzzle. Furthermore, Charles had even said that she ought to take a leaf out of Julia's book when it came to dressing suitably for these occasions. Pamela always thought Julia's dresses seemed too understated and frankly rather plain. After all 'a little black, blue or beige dress' could never be any more than it said on the tin.

Pamela knew she wasn't the brightest of women but no one could deny she ran a tight ship of a household. Also, she had been a good mother to Max, who hadn't been the easiest of sons to raise, and had always had his challenges to face. But was that any wonder with his bully of a father? If only Charles were more like affable Neil. However, Charles had sacked Neil for some mysterious reason and as a result she and her boy were both being made to suffer. When she saw her husband's car pull into the drive she checked her hair was neat and applied some more coral-coloured lipstick.

Neil

Julia had long gone to work when Neil crawled out of his bed. After a hot shower he went downstairs to clean and tidy the kitchen. Julia had accused him of leaving a big mess with his cooking, but it obviously hadn't taken her very long to tidy up. Now all surfaces were gleaming, as they usually did. After all that effort he had gone to, and she still hadn't seemed very happy with her food. He had watched her play around with her pasta, but then to be fair, he had done the same with his. Admittedly, when she made spaghetti bolognaise it didn't seem to have that strange burnt taste, but nevertheless, he had tried his best, hadn't he?

He wondered if he would get anymore phone calls off Tracy today, but as she had sounded decidedly miffed with him last night, this was unlikely. He liked Tracy well enough. She was always up for a laugh and he had never been adverse to an innocent bit of flirting. However, he suspected her intentions were rather more serious than those of his own. Neil enjoyed the company of women and always had. But much as Julia infuriated him particularly of late, his interests didn't lie elsewhere. The grass wasn't always greener, and life with Julia for the most part so far had been great.

However recently, Julia's first husband Trevor had been constantly playing on his mind. He was like one of those irritating songs he had heard on the radio, when he used to go to work, and couldn't get it out of his head all day. Julia had hinted that there had been big problems with the marriage and it had only lasted a few short years. He knew there had been a significant age gap between them both, and Julia must have been barely out of her teens when they married. Yet to him, it seemed unlikely, that even at such a tender age she would have allowed herself to have been bullied. His wife was a strong-willed character, even if she sometimes became stressed. But even when young, he couldn't have imagined her putting up with any nonsense whatsoever. As Neil knew from experience she was more than capable of sticking up for herself. Maybe it was the other way round and she had been the one doing the controlling.

He quickly dismissed this thought, as he remembered that enigmatic sadness of the Julia he had first met and fallen in love with. Throughout the high life they had enjoyed, this creature had been put to rest and remained hidden from view. But just recently he had seen glimpses of her once more and he knew that was most likely due to him. But this manifestation of gloom was not originally of his making was it? This misery was of Trevor's creation. What could he have done to her and where was he now? By comparison, his money worries were of little consequence. He needed to find some old photographs of this monster that Julia had chosen to be her husband number one.

Before Neil began his detective work, he felt the pull of the familiar siren luring him upstairs. For Neil's Achilles Heel was always close to hand, and when he was alone it was literally under his fingertips. When he and Julia first met, the casino was just another of their play toys. Money was lost and won, sometimes in alarming amounts, but its significance had been hidden by their overall lavish expenditure on drink, expensive meals and the general good life. Julia had never really shared his enthusiasm for gambling, but at first would just go along with anything he wanted to do. If his passion had been hand gliding or trainspotting, Julia would have been up for it.

hang / seems unusual

However, after a few heavy roulette sessions and Julia realising how much money they had actually squandered, she completely lost interest in this pursuit. And Neil, feigning shock at the thousands lost, bit his lip and thought it unwise to mention the cash they had previously won and frittered. He imagined her aversion to casinos and gambling would wane. He assumed it would quickly re-establish itself into the fabric of their weekend routine – but it didn't. Once Julia got a grip on how much money they had wasted in those dens of inequity, as she called them, she flatly refused to set foot them ever again. She even made him cancel the holiday they had booked to Las Vegas. Neil had protested, reminding her that she had always wanted to see the Grand Canyon, but she just gave him that *look*.

For a while he had started sneaking out late at night, when Julia was ready for bed. On school nights, she liked to be in bed before midnight and this was when he went out for his fix. At first she imagined him to be having an affair and threatened to leave him. So he had no choice but reveal his whereabouts and after many screaming matches, he promised to stop – but he couldn't.

'Neil, come on. It's time for bed.' Julia was tucked up with her Kindle, no doubt hoping it wasn't to be another of *those* nights.

'Not be long dear.' Neil could remember hearing the annoyance in her voice and wished she hadn't heard the door opening.

'You've got to be joking. It's nearly midnight.'

'Erm … I'm just going for a little walk … you know, get some fresh air.' Neil had checked he had his wallet safely in his pocket.

'Stop lying Neil. We both know exactly where you're going.' Neil had caught the familiar sob in her throat and he despised himself for his actions. But what could he do?

'I'll not be long. See you shortly.' His voice held all the lightness and cheer he could muster.

'Neil you promised you wouldn't…'

Neil quietly closed the door. And Julia without doubt, would have burst into tears and not slept a wink until he returned. That was until he discovered *Casino Royale*.

Mabel was watching him reproachfully from under the kitchen table. He opened a fresh can of kitty food for her but knew fine well, this wouldn't placate the source of her disapproval. Turning his back on his judgemental pet, Neil proceeded to make himself a strong coffee before disappearing to his office.

Chapter 8

Twenty-Five Years Ago

Trevor

After several surreptitious visits to Lowfield Avenue at varying times of the day, Trevor was delighted to discover that Julia, looked pretty much the same as she had three years ago. Although she no longer had her hair in a ponytail or sported a school uniform, Trevor liked what he saw. She wore her long dark hair hanging down past her shoulders like a shiny, chestnut curtain, was slim and looked to be slightly smaller than him. This was a fact that pleased Trevor, as he had issues with his own short height and the prospect of a future wife towering over him like a block of flats didn't really appeal. Physically, Julia fitted the bill perfectly as suitable wife material, as he had known all along that she would.

It seemed that she caught the bus into Newcastle each day at around eight a.m. and returned at about roughly five in the evening. Usually she was wearing jeans, trainers and dressed too casually for Trevor's personal taste. He would have preferred to have seen her in a neat, little blouse maybe tucked into a smart skirt. This slovenly dress style led Trevor to the assumption that she must most probably be a student of some type. No office girl or shop assistant would be dressed quite so informally. Not ideal, as a working wife would be more desirable from Trevor's stance, but this matter could be rectified at some point in the future he felt sure.

So one day, when she left the bus and cut through Eldon Square turning right on to Percy Street and into Newcastle University, he followed her. The town was busy with the morning rush of clockwork mice scurrying to their places of work, so it was easy for him to blend into the crowd. Trevor wondered what she was studying, but felt reluctant to pursue her into the actual building. So he hovered about the entrance for a short time like a predatory wasp, before leaving. Universities were unfamiliar territory to him and he felt uncomfortable there. Trevor had been forced to leave school at sixteen in order to get a job and make some money. Many people at that time had failed to realise that your earning potential later on would be increased if you collected the necessary qualifications. This road wasn't for the likes of him. If he had obtained a Pharmaceutical Degree, no doubt he would in possession of his own chemist's by now but at that time his mother had tutted at the very idea. Not wishing to court his mother's disapproval, the matter had never been raised again.

Whenever his schedule allowed and he wasn't working, Trevor would either wait at the bus stop in Eldon Square or get himself over to Lowfield Avenue early, so he could follow her on the bus. Julia, too caught up in her own world, never noticed him. Usually, she was alone but sometimes she was in the company of another female student. The two of them sat on the bus together and giggled. Trevor tried to hear what they were talking about, but was too scared to draw attention to himself, so didn't like to sit too closely to them on the bus. He remained sitting towards the back; a tortoise watching and listening intently from underneath his shell.

Once, when she didn't appear at the bus stop until at least an hour and a half later than usual, Trevor understandably had worried as to her whereabouts. Eventually, two girls appeared rather worse for wear, flushed and laughing loudly. This wasn't the way that his Julia ought to be behaving. Trevor could tell instantly that they had been drinking and this was unbecoming to both of them. The other young woman with the vivid red hair, too short a skirt and holes in her tights, seemed to be in the worse state of inebriation. She was swearing loudly, as she tottered about on silly, strappy high heels like a wobbly giraffe. This particular girl must be the bad influence who had no doubt initiated this unsavoury escapade and when the time came he would put an end to this friendship with great relish.

Another time when Trevor was waiting in Newcastle, he saw Julia approaching the bus stop in the company of a young man. Who was this? To Trevor's horror they were holding hands, looking into each other's eyes and in deep conversation. Then Julia put her arms around the gangly youth's shoulders and the two of them kissed. This behaviour was not what you expected from your future wife. Trevor was gobsmacked for he hadn't seen this one coming. Staggering like a wounded animal, he collapsed onto a nearby seat and watched as Julia waved goodbye to her 'boyfriend' from the bus. A bewildered Trevor sat on the bench in a trance and tried to process this new information.

The Present Day

Zoe

Zoe was sitting in the computer suite at school, printing off the learning objectives to stick in the children's books for that day's lessons. She was wearing an orange and yellow oversized shirt with her black leggings, which was a comfy and favourite outfit of hers. Her class would be learning about the properties of 3D shapes in maths, making bullet points about the characters in Roald Dahl's 'The Twits' in English and after P.E. in the afternoon, they would be delighted to be retelling the parable of The Good Samaritan in R.E. Not.

It would definitely be a challenge, getting some of those silly boys to knuckle down to writing, after they had been all hyped-up from running about the hall. Never mind, at least by then the day would be nearly over she thought, as she looked out of the window to see if there was any sign of her friend Julia arriving yet. In the car park, there was just Ms Swan checking her phone, as she slammed the door shut on her old bashed-up Astra.

Although admittedly, it was quite late when she had rung her on the previous night, she had the distinct impression that Julia didn't really want to speak to her. All the precise details of the conversation were a little blurry, due to the old vino and no doubt the cause of Zoe's splitting headache today. But she had needed to speak to her, as something was clearly very wrong for her to be shouting at her class like that. It just wasn't behaviour you would expect from Julia. And Zoe had known Julia for a very long time.

The two of them had met while they were students doing their Teacher training. They had hit it off immediately. Zoe had introduced Julia to the delights of cider drinking, boys, and the pub. She could remember several occasions when they sat on the bus legless, both just avoiding throwing up. Well mostly, apart from a couple of incidents when the bus driver had literally thrown them off the bus. They had found it hilarious and laughed at first, then quickly sobered up because it was way too far for them to walk home, especially for Julia who lived much further away from Newcastle than she did.

It was only much later that she actually got to visit Julia's swanky home with all the latest gadgets. There was the cocktail bar, the pool table, the state of the art bathroom and kitchen … the list just went on. Zoe's little two up, two down terrace, was a shoebox by comparison, but at least it was all hers. Once she and Gary had split it was all she had been able to afford from her half of the proceeds. But it all belonged to Zoe and Chloe too of course. She didn't have to share with any bloody husband, thank God. No Gary, no Neil, no …. Trevor. Why she had almost forgotten about him. Now Julia really did have the most appalling taste in men. After the first one, you would think that really she ought to know better. Once bitten twice shy and all that. For certain things she missed a bloke but Jeez there were limits to which you could stoop.

Yes for the first two terms at uni Julia and she had been thick as thieves. Then everything changed all because of that freak. Julia looked pretty good for her age now, well rather better than she Zoe did. She was aware of her maybe one or two extra pounds and premature lines on her face from scowling at children. Nevertheless, her brightly coloured hair and flamboyant dress sense she felt more than compensated for this. Zoe appraised her choice of attire for the day favourably. But now as then, Julia never did herself any favours with her drab style of dress. Back in the day though, Julia could have her pick of boyfriends and she did. After Zoe had taught her a trick or two about flirting, she seemed to take to it like a duck to water. Which was all well and good, but with having just recently lost her parents, she was too needy.

Poor Joe, she had been only seeing him for a week or so and Julia kept insisting that they looked at the rings in jewellers shops. Zoe could hear the alarm bells ringing a mile off.

His uncomfortable body language spoke volumes. First, was his obvious reluctance to stand close to her. Then, came his monosyllabic replies to the all the incessant questions she fired at him. They were like desperate bullets, fired in an attempt to avoid any lapses in their conversations. She had watched with some sympathy for him, as whenever Julia had tried to grab Joe's hand he quickly shot it into his pocket to search for an imaginary coin. To a nineteen year old lad, a girl with a commitment obsession was about as attractive as a bad case of halitosis. Julia though, she was just lonely … and then at the very right, or wrong moment, depending on your stance, along came Trevor. Joe had just finished with her and she couldn't understand what she was doing wrong. Zoe couldn't believe it when Julia introduced her to Trevor. It was the creep who had been hanging around the bus stop for weeks gawping at them.

Then everything kind of changed. It was as if she was avoiding Zoe and made up the very lamest of excuses not to go to the pub or even hang out with her. It was as if he had brainwashed her. And, he was always *there* looking down his nose at Zoe. It wasn't as if Trevor, the measly shop assistant was any catch. Back then newly qualified, or probationary teachers didn't get a great salary, but Trevor wouldn't have even earned that piddling amount. Also, he must have been almost old enough to be her father. Julia had been a complete fool to have been blinded by his sickly effusive attentions. And his clothes … well, they were not merely square but positively cube-like. Julia had never been the snappiest of dressers, compared with Zoe of course. She had just started to begin taking Zoe's advice over the colour of lipstick to wear, and best skirt length, when she became contaminated by him. Then all of Zoe's good work had just been thrown out of the window. Within days, he had put his stamp on her and must have been telling her how to dress – abominably, as it turned out. In their matching anoraks and twee woolly hats, the pair of them looked like a couple of twitchers.

Zoe guessed that in Trevor Julia had been looking for some weird kind of father figure, but as far as she could make out, he had been one massive mistake. But once his nasty web had been cast, all influence Zoe had on her friend no longer carried weight. In the summer term she had seen very little of her friend, who seemed to have gone to great lengths to avoid her. Then in the second year, there had been no Julia at all; she had just dropped out off the course. Zoe never heard any more from her. No prize for guessing whose idea this had been.

Anyway this was a long time in the past, but when the new Year 4 teacher started five years ago, Zoe had thought she looked vaguely familiar and with very good reason. Almost immediately, their old friendship rekindled and Zoe quickly was made to understand that Trevor was a no go subject of conversation. Now, of course, it was all about Neil and although she was loathe to admit it, he appeared to be lesser of the two evils. Just. But he was still no good.

Looking once more out of the window she saw Julia getting out of her white mini.

Twenty- Five Years Earlier

Julia

Julia was standing at the bus stop and still in shock from the conversation with Joe on the previous night. How could he just decide that he didn't have time for a girlfriend at the moment, before giving her the old, *it wasn't her but him,* garbage. It just wasn't fair. The same pattern just kept repeating itself, like the tessellating shapes of the tiles on the floor beneath her feet. As Julia's eyes filled with tears, the ground blurred to crazy paving. Only a few weeks earlier, Steve had delivered almost the same verbal missive, as if reading from a script. And before that it had been Chris and then …

'Excuse me my dear but are you all right?' Julia found herself looking into a pair of very kind brown eyes, belonging to an almost middle-aged man, who seemed genuinely concerned as to her well-being.

'Yes, I'll be fine thanks.' What an idiot she must seem blubbering like a baby at, the bus stop of all places. Thank goodness there were only the two of them waiting here, which was unusual given the time of day. She needed to get a grip.

'Well, if you don't mind me saying. Something is clearly upsetting you. And I don't like to see young ladies in distress … especially not such pretty ones.' Julia doubted she could be looking at her best, with her puffy face and red eyes but nevertheless, she managed a weak smile.

'Would you like to tell me what the problem is?' The man gave her a look of encouragement. 'You know what they say don't you.'

'Not really, no.' Julia shook her head.

'Well they say.' He raised an eyebrow, as if about to say something profound. 'That a problem shared, is a problem halved.' Julia had been expecting something more poignant than this, but it was so the sort of thing her dad might have said, and that it in itself was rather comforting.

'Oh, here comes the bus.' Trevor raising his arm assertively to attract the bus driver's attention by semaphore, but it was unnecessary, as the vehicle was already coming to halt. 'Are you getting on this bus into town?' Julia nodded and he stood to one side, to allow her to get onto the bus first.

Once seated on the half empty bus, she took out a book from her bag to read. Almost immediately, she felt a gentle tap on her shoulder. 'Do you mind if I sit here next to you?' As there were plenty of empty seats on the bus, Julia guessed she ought to find it slightly odd that this older man, with his old-fashioned anorak, should want to sit next to her, but what was stranger still, was that she felt slightly flattered.

'So what takes you into Newcastle this morning? Perhaps if something or somebody has made you sad … you deserve to stay at home?'

'I have a lecture at nine.' She lifted the sleeve of her coat to check the time.

'Well… I don't think you'll be making that one. Do you?' It was already ten past nine.

'No, I guess not.' She looked a little sheepish.

'Well in that case. Would you accept my offer of a nice cup of coffee in …' Trevor was racking his brains for a place which he thought might impress her. 'Fenwicks.' He announced as if he were suggesting she should join him on a trip to the moon.

Julia thought about this for a moment. She knew that Zoe's take on this would be a definite no, but she had a couple of hours to kill and after all what harm could it actually do? There was something to be said about the undivided attention of an older man.

Especially, one who was being so thoughtful towards her. She was feeling more grown up and yet more childlike at the same time. She decided she liked this feeling, as if an adventure were about to begin.

'Why not?' She smiled at him as the bus pulled into Eldon Square. Maybe, she had served her apprenticeship with little boys and it was time she graduated to a proper man. One whose name she didn't yet know yet nor neither did he hers, but she had an exciting feeling that these exchanges would be the beginning of something rather special.

Chapter 9

Almost the Present Day (two weeks earlier)

Charles

For some time Charles had been nursing some niggling suspicions about his so called friend Neil. Certain small anomalies in the company accounts just didn't add up. Recently, mysterious withdrawals had become not only more frequent but for larger amounts, significantly larger amounts, and so it was something he could no longer ignore. He hadn't wanted to dispatch with the services of Neil, who he had been friends with for as long as he could remember, and even more importantly he was an excellent property salesman. For some months, Charles had tried to hide the dust under the rug, as he was well aware that much of the success of the company was due to Neil's silver tongue, persuasive skills and ability to close deals fast. He really didn't want to rock the boat, but it was wobbling so much he felt sea sick. Furthermore, he was beginning to wonder, if the man had the actual audacity to blatantly steal wadges of cash from under his very nose.

It wasn't as if Neil actually needed the money. At least from Charles' viewpoint, he couldn't see how he could possibly need it. He was paid a very attractive salary, which combined with his sales bonuses and that of his wife's money from her teaching job must all amount to a tidy sum. How many outgoings could they possibly have? They didn't even have a mortgage because Julia's parent's untimely death had left her owning that house outright. Admittedly, recently the two of them didn't seem to be jetting off on holidays as much as they had once … but surely that would leave them with more cash not less.

This was why for ages, he had just thought he must have been imagining things. That was until he came upon a mysterious expenses account which was syphoning trickles, streams and then gushes of cash, until it could no longer be pushed to one side. The account was entitled Various Expenses which sounded so plausibly vague, that it seemed kosher. It could have covered travel and deal-clinching meals expenses, but he had no recollection of setting up any such account. Actually upon closer inspection, it might have proven a very good idea for a little tax deduction, however this was no one else's call but his own. The finger of suspicion pointed directly at Neil, as no one else had direct access to the accounts. This discovery was the final straw, Charles needed to get his head from out of the sand and investigate immediately.

When Charles had eventually questioned Neil, he had been evasive and claimed no knowledge of any such account. Then, came the certain shifty look that he had noticed of late, appearing in his right hand man's eyes rather too often. That was when Charles knew for certain that Neil could no longer be trusted and action was required before the slippery salesman ran his estate agency into the ground. This hurt him to do so, but business was business. He had his and his family's own interest to consider. So, he brought in the services of Obadiah Goldstein, a young hot shot accountant, whom he was assured would swiftly resolve the matter. Charles knew a can of worms would be opened, but far better that Obadiah's hands were stained with poison than those of his own.

A couple of weeks earlier, Obadiah had arrived at the office of OakElmAsh Residentials to raised eyebrows, to say the least. He had come highly recommended to Charles from the barman at the golf club and although he had met the man before, Charles had not expected the full Kippah, ringlets and tassels of an Orthodox Jew to come flouncing through the showroom. At the golf club, his attire had seemed much less extreme.
'Yes. Can I help you?' asked Tracy, assuming him to be a prospective house purchaser. She recognised him to be a Jew, but had never seen an Orthodox one in such close proximity before. She had heard however that they had plenty of money. 'What type of property is sir looking for?'
'I have come to see Mr Lavender.' He had a strange clipped voice, as if he took no nonsense and wasted no time.
'Could I ask to what business this applies?' Tracy was intrigued by this unusual individual, with his distinctive nose and beady eyes peering at her from behind little round glasses.
'Just tell him that Mr Goldstein has arrived to see him.' Tracy tossed her platinum tresses and widened her eyes, expecting him to elucidate further as to his mysterious purpose.

Her efforts were wasted, as Obadiah was oblivious to her charms and in fact found her artifice rather distasteful.

Tracy rang through to her boss's office and Charles quickly appeared at the door. When he saw Mr Goldstein standing there, he felt uncomfortable. Not because of the young man's unusual appearance, but because of the job he had been employed to undertake.

The Present Day

Neil

Neil just couldn't believe his bad luck. Only two hours ago he was £2,000 up and was feeling that at last the tide had finally turned and things were on the up. But in typical form, Neil hadn't walked away from the virtual table. No, what had stupid reckless Neil done? He had poured himself a congratulatory large whiskey (it was midday after all) and returned once more to play. And now at quarter past two in the afternoon, not only had he drunk half the bottle, but on the top of losing all of his earlier winnings, he had continued to play the table and lose a further £1000. How had everything just gone so badly wrong for him?

Still, he thought, he mustn't carry on drinking. He needed to sober up for when Julia came home. Neil went downstairs to make himself a strong, black coffee. Mabel was looking at him with accusatory eyes as he put the kettle on to boil. She growled and flexed her claws, like ten retractable ball point pens, as he bent to stroke her silky, silver fur.

'Oh Mabel, what have I done? It just isn't fair is it?' Mabel swished her long fluffy tail from side to side angrily, as Neil stroked her. 'Don't worry. I'll sort it out somehow. What do you think? A nice coffee will clear my head, won't it? Then if I go back up there … well I can win the money back and more surely – don't you think?' Neil rubbed her coat more forcefully, hoping for some positive affirmation for his next course of action. But Mabel was making a curious noise somewhere between a snarl and a hiccough, while baring her little pointy teeth at him. Neil thought he sensed her displeasure, but really, she was only a cat.

'Mabel you're just a silly creature. As if you understand any –'

Mabel took a swipe at him with her long talons and scratched a deep cut down his cheek. Neil yelped. 'What the – ?' He ran to the mirror and was horrified to see a red gash and blood trickling down his cheek. He was shocked to see the recalcitrant cat sitting with her back to him in her basket, purring, oblivious to his pain.

After Neil, had washed the wound and applied some antiseptic, he decided not to feed the animal and keep out of her way for a while. Still, that feline fiend had managed to dissuade him away from Casino Royale, for at least that day and her actions had sobered him up more quickly than any coffee. It was a pity that Julia hadn't had a pet such as Mabel when Trevor had been living here, as she would have kept him in order. He imagined a faceless man shouting nastily at Julia. Then, Mabel bounding across the room, sinking teeth and claws into his bleeding limbs like a ferocious tiger. This image he found pleasing and brought Neil's thoughts back to the subject of his predecessor, how their marriage had been and what had become of him.

He knew that Julia kept some old boxes in the attic and that would be the best place to begin his research on mister creepy Trevor. Mabel the monster was best left hungry and sulking in the kitchen. As he pulled down the ladder, he wondered if the malicious creature would attempt to climb up after him. If she tried, then clumps of her fur would more than likely get stuck in the rungs and that would serve her right.

Looking all around the dark space with a flashlight, he could just make out a jumble of boxes everywhere. Then as his eyes grew more accustomed to the darkness, he saw strands of golden tinsel spilling out of one of the nearest boxes. This clearly held last year's Christmas decorations. The second one he opened revealed an ancient blue tent and some camping gear, which he couldn't ever remember using. Camping wasn't really his thing; maybe that's what she and Trevor did for their holidays. What fun they must have had, he thought sarcastically, as he couldn't have imagined anything worse. Sleeping on the hard ground with lots of insects everywhere, he shuddered with distaste at the very thought.

After inspecting the contents of several suitcases, crammed with ladies clothes and shoes, which judging by the dated styles must have been her mother's rather than Julia's, he finally struck gold. There was a large tea chest full of albums which could only contain photographs. As it was so heavy, he dragged it to the ladder opening and started throwing the books onto the landing below. Grumpy though curious Mabel, was sitting near the base of the ladder. She was startled by the loud thuds and bolted downstairs. Then Neil scrambled down the ladder himself, to continue on his Trevor quest.

The first album revealed orange faded photos, arranged like a seventies clothing catalogue. Pictures of a beaming brown eyed toddler leapt from the pages, with her attractive young mother, showing off her long suntanned legs in tiny yellow shorts. This was clearly Julia with her mother Carol, who he had never met, but judging by these photos, he would have very much liked to. As he flicked through the pages, Carol posed for the camera as if model, in a range of halter-necked tops , flared trousers and long boots, using her daughter as a fashion accessory and often kitted out in a matching ensemble. In one photo, the pair of them in matching green mini dresses stood next to a camper van, in front of a familiar blue tent. Carol's smile, with slightly wonky teeth, (cosmetic dentistry hadn't been so popular back in the seventies) actually added to her attraction, giving her a kooky, quirky appeal. He could see from where Julia had got her looks.

Clearly, the photographer of these holiday snaps must have been Julia's father, Michael, as he featured on only a few shots, obviously uncomfortable. Seemingly, he must have been happier behind the camera where he had more flair than his wife. In the pictures of Michael, he often had half his head missing and he had been caught a couple times with an unattractive scowl on his face. Still, he wasn't a bad looking man, with his smart casual Jacquard pullovers, wide–collared shirts and Farah slacks. He had to admit the Masons had made a handsome couple, back in their day, a little like him and Julia, more than forty years later. Nevertheless, they wouldn't look like this now would they? Neil wondered how this now grey-haired, elderly couple would have fared in today's world. This world pre-occupied with the internet and mobile phones, no doubt would seem incomprehensible to them.

Still, it must have been awful for Julia to have lost them at such a young age and so needlessly, in some bizarre car accident. Carol and Michael must have been younger than he and Julia were now. Spooks. How dreadful and unnecessary. How could Michael have crashed the car on a quiet country lane? However this wasn't today's puzzle. Neil had other irons in the fire. He opened the next album – and bingo.

On the first page of the photograph album was a picture of the young Julia, almost the double of her mother but less flamboyantly dressed. In fact she was wearing a very odd, white frock. He remembered the eighties to be time of wide shoulder pads and poufy hairdos but he had no recollection of this strange fashion. She was quite clearly standing outside Gateshead Civic Centre on what must have been her wedding day and next to her was the elusive Trevor.

Twenty- Five Years Earlier

Julia

Julia had woken on the day of her wedding feeling deliriously happy. This was the last time she would be the tragically orphaned Miss Julia Mason. Tonight, she would retire in blissful happiness to bed, with her beloved, husband as the proud Mrs Julia Squires. It had been so strange sleeping alone last night, the first time she had done so almost since she and Trevor had met. They had spent every night together because he loved her so much and he had been adamant he would move in with her after seeing her for only a couple of days. Julia had imagined that he had some very swish bachelor pad, close to the city centre. She was flattered: imagining his urgency to come and live with her at the boring semi-detached house in Lowfield Avenue was proof of his devotion to her.

Julia thought back to that charmed day, almost two months ago now, when he had taken her for a coffee in Fenwick's department store. It was as if their meeting had been decided by fate. If she hadn't missed the earlier bus … well their paths might never have crossed. He must have been telepathic to know that Fenwick's would become her very favourite café bar of all time. She remembered fondly the lime green walls, bamboo furniture and old black and white photos of an earlier Newcastle on display there.

She had sat there enthralled, listening to fascinating tales about the properties of different medicines and his very important job as a chemist. Julia had never known a chemist before and it seemed such a grown up occupation to have. All the boys she knew from college wore jeans, jumpers and trainers but Trevor in his light blue shirt, navy tie and shiny polished shoes, seemed like a real man. Taking the tiniest of sips from her cup, she had just wanted that moment to last for ever. It was like she was in some beautiful dream that she never wanted to be woken from. Then to her utmost delight, he had suggested they went to the cinema the next night. She had no recollection of what the film had been about. It was some science fiction film, the type that she usually hated, but she was enraptured just to be there, sitting next to her sophisticated date.

Since he had moved in with her, their trips out had been far and few between, but that was because he was so wise and sensible. Her very soon-to-be husband had asked why they needed to go out. As long as they were in each other's company, what else did they want? After she had cooked their tea each night, they sat and watched the documentaries he enjoyed about the Second World War and suchlike. She hadn't really been that bothered about those 'silly soap operas and mindless murder mysteries' that the sad Julia had once thought to enjoy. Also, what was the point of paying for fancy restaurants when Julia was such an excellent cook? She hadn't been aware that she was and took this as a compliment. Especially as most of their meals came from the frozen food section in Safeway, but he wasn't to know that.

It was very fortunate, that Trevor wasn't too keen on shopping in supermarkets and he didn't see what they were eating until it arrived on the table in front of him. Also, it wasn't really that much more expensive to buy food for two rather than one. Well, it was a little more, but money was one thing she had never had to worry about. Her parents had left her plenty and once they were married … well, he would take care of that side of things. She wouldn't have to 'worry her pretty little head about it' and she rather liked the idea of that.

Then, when only six weeks ago, he had asked her to marry him, she could no longer contain her elation. He had been so sure of her answer, that he had already booked the ceremony. Trevor was so perfect he just knew what her answer would be. What was the point of a big fancy ceremony when it was just the two of them? Since they had become an item, they were everything to each other so there was no need for anyone else to attend. They could just grab a couple of witnesses off the street. It was as simple as that.

Since a child, Julia had always dreamed of a beautiful wedding gown, like the one her mother had when her parents had married. It had a beautiful bodice studded with mother of pearl sequins and a full billowing skirt. She had always hoped she would have one similar. But then Trevor had made her see the sense of how unnecessary this was. After all, they had no need to get married in a flashy church. Their simple wedding service in the Registry Office would be much more dignified. Trevor had made it clear that a dress similar to her mother's would be inappropriate, a wicked waste of money and even more to the point, she would just look ridiculous. In the end she had found an old white dress of her mother's at the back of a wardrobe. It was a shift style of a dress and only a little too big. Trevor said it was much too short for her to wear and fashions had been different then. Now it was more important to be modestly dressed.

Fortunately, she had been able to sew a piece of material around the bottom, although her sewing ability was on a level with that of her cooking. She thought it looked a little odd and tuttled, but Trevor said it looked perfect and after all he was the one who was marrying her. Also, he suggested that by wearing her Mother's dress, it would seem like her parents were actually there at the wedding too. Wasn't that a marvellous idea? She didn't think it was possible to love him anymore than she did at that moment.

Before leaving to catch the bus, she had a last look at her parent's lovely wedding photograph and caught a glance in the mirror of her grubby white dress with the mismatched material sewn on to the bottom. For a brief moment, she wished that things had just been a little bit different. Then she put such thoughts to the very back of her mind. Tonight, for the first time she would lie in the arms of her husband in the full sense. For although they had shared a bed for several weeks, nothing improper, as Trevor referred to such matters, had occurred, but tonight as man and wife, matters would be very different.

Chapter 10

Two Weeks Earlier Than The Present Day

Charles

Charles knew that the outcome of that day was going to be extremely uncomfortable and the findings of his new auditor, would without any shadow of a doubt confirm his very worst suspicions. When he showed Obadiah Goldstein how to locate the relevant files, he had deliberately not mentioned any problems with the accounts. Obadiah just thought this was a general run- of-the-mill audit for routine tax purposes. However, when Obadiah had revealed the full extent of Neil's duplicity, Charles was so furious he felt he could blow several gaskets.

When Obadiah arrived, Neil thankfully was out of the office, busy with viewings. Charles had instructed Tracy to make sure his diary was full that day, which in itself was odd. She had immediately recognised something was amiss when she realised the Orthodox Jewish man was not a lucrative house hunter. He actually had an appointment in Charles' office and she quickly became very worried. There was no way she would imagine that it was golden boy Neil's future on the line. She was fearful for her own back. Tracy thought she must be in trouble for not pulling her carefully maintained weight and failing to organise sufficient property viewings. Charles received a phone call from an anxious sounding Tracy, to say that a Mr Obadiah Goldstein had arrived to see him.

Obadiah, Charles noted, with his tall, gaunt frame, yellowy pallor and black clothes had the appearance of a Hasidic grim reaper. He nodded enthusiastically as Charles explained the brief to him and directed him to a table in the corner of the room. Clearly, a man not to waste words, he took a lap top and a little red notebook out of his bag. Then he began opening files, scowling at the screen and sighing deeply. When Charles asked if he would like a coffee, he shook his head and continued applying himself diligently to his task. Charles thought he would leave him to it and went to make himself a drink.

In the showroom Tracy made a show of unnecessarily busying herself with papers, as he walked through.

She cleared her throat. 'Is everything all right?' she asked nervously.

'Yes. Mr Goldstein has just come to do the auditing. Nothing for you to worry about.'

Tracy immediately relaxed and gave him one of her practised smiles.

'It's not the usual one? Isn't it Mr Smith who normally does our accounts?'

Mr Smith, who had done the auditing for years, was well into his seventies and although his services were very reasonably priced … no doubt for good reason. If, as he suspected, Neil had been operating his scam for several years, then maybe Mr Smith had let slip, or had been persuaded to let personal expenses slip conveniently through the net.

'Mr Smith has retired I believe.' Charles wondered what dirt was being dredged up by Obadiah.

When he went back into his office, Obadiah wasted no time. 'Mr Lavender …'

'No, Charles, please, I insist.' Charles kind of didn't want to hear this but he needed to.

'It's about this personal expenses account.' Obadiah waved his pencil at the screen as if casting a spell.

'Yes, I must admit I have been a little baffled about that too.' Charles felt sad, knowing that he was about to hear affirmation of what he had suspected.

'Thousands of pounds have been transferred into it and have disappeared.' Once more the accountant brandished his pencil like a magic wand. 'What is it for? Meals, hotels, dry cleaning?' Obadiah was clearly shocked by such extravagance and the look on his face showed quite clearly that he didn't believe this conniving estate agent. 'Well if you haven't spent this money … who has?' Obadiah took a sidelong glance at Charles' florid face and his stomach bulging over his trousers.

'I was rather hoping that you could help me with that.' How dare this Jewish boy be judging him?

'Who else has access to these accounts?'

At last he was getting to the point. 'That is a very good question and one to which I have no answer,' said Charles. 'Well, my next in command is a Mr Neil …'

Obadiah's eyes once more became glued to the screen and his hands were shaking with the full realisation of what he was discovering.

'Could that be N. Latimer? 'Obadiah's lips stretched into a demonic grin. 'There seems to be copious withdrawals and transferrals made to his name.'

Charles couldn't have imagined this man could become so excited that the kippah skullcap actually fell from his head.

'Yes, it's as I suspected. I just needed verification.' Charles shook his head. He thought he ought to feel pleased that this man no longer suspected him of such profligate waste, but he just felt bereft.

'He's siphoned off thousands … and that's just in the last few months. What will you do?' Obadiah placed his cap back on his head attempting to maintain some decorum.

'I don't know. I'll have to have a think …' Charles sat down on his chair and took a sip from his now stone-cold coffee.

'You should ring the police. This is fraud.' He stressed the last word with an almost manic fervour.

'Yes I know but … if I give you access to the accounts for the last five years can you find out exactly how much money Neil's personal expenses account has dissipated?'

Obadiah Goldstein nodded and thought he had never had such a thrilling day.

The Present

Julia

After the events of the previous day, Julia wasn't looking forward to the Tuesday at school one little bit. However, she just intended to keep her head down and stay out of everybody's way. She suspected that Zoe probably couldn't remember much of the previous night's telephone conversation and would no doubt be feeling embarrassed, which suited Julia just fine.

As she had arrived in plenty of time this morning, she made a point of addressing Ms Swan with a forced, cheery greeting, as she passed by her office. Ms Swan was opening some mail and she jumped. She was irritated that Julia had startled her. Then, Julia made her way to her classroom where she was pleased to find everything looking in order and just as it usually did. By the time Emily arrived, the children's books were all organised on the tables, the worksheets and learning objectives in place and Julia was giving the appearance of sitting serenely at her desk with a mug of tea.

'Good morning Julia. How are you today?' The concern in Emily's voice was apparent.

'I'm fine Emily. I'm sorry about yesterday. I wasn't feeling very well. You know, the time of the month.' Emily was a good ten years younger than her and was surprised that middle-aged Julia was still bothered by such things.

'Just as long as you are … ' began Emily.

'Well this morning.' Julia was keen to change the subject. 'In English the children are going to write some character descriptions of either Robin Hood or the Sherriff of Nottingham. So, if you could just work with your usual group. If you get them to write it on their whiteboards first and check what they have written for sense before it goes in their books. Make sure they include all their full stops and capital letters.'

This is what she always did when the children were writing, so why was Julia saying it, thought Emily? Also, she noticed that Julia was fiddling with some pens on her table and not making eye contact with her classroom assistant.

'Very well,' Emily replied, a little curtly. Julia knew that Emily considered herself to be her friend and that she knew exactly what was expected of her in the classroom. And here she was speaking to her as if she was some kid from the comp, here for work experience. They had been working together for three years and Julia knew that Emily was bound to be feeling miffed.

'And after playtime what are we doing in maths?' asked Emily.

'Oh, we're continuing with the fraction work. You know the problems we were doing yesterday.' Julia thought it unwise to go into further details as Emily clearly knew what was expected. Although, she knew Emily would be dying to ask more about yesterday's outburst. she thankfully didn't, for that was a path that Julia was reluctant to tred. Sensing this, Emily nodded, took off her coat and hung it up in the cupboard.Just before she went outside to bring the children in, Julia saw Zoe's colourful shirt on the way to her own classroom and noted that she was wisely keeping out of her way.

As she collected her class, she said 'Good morning' to several of the parents and she wondered if any of the children had mentioned to them about her shouting yesterday. She hoped not, for there was still ample time for complaints to the Head to be made. All seemed normal so far, which was good. Though the children seemed unusually quiet, they all had their eyes fixed on her as they took their seats for the register. Julia actually wished there was more of the usual scuffles and problems to be addressed. But no, the class all sat meekly and waited for their names to be called. A sea of twenty four pairs of eyes stared from her head, to blue blouse, down to black trousers and shoes, and returned once more to her face. Julia was pleased she had made an effort with her appearance. Her shirt was new, she felt crisp, tidy and ready for the day.

While she went over what they had read so far about the characters in Robin Hood, the children continued watching and listening intently. When she asked for words to describe the two main characters in the book, nobody shouted out and they all put their hands up politely, waiting to be asked. They came up with sensible suggestions and they all had a good laugh talking about the nasty schemes that the Sheriff had planned to catch Robin Hood. Julia found she was quite enjoying this lesson and made eye contact with Emily for the first time that morning,

Just before playtime, while the children were reading out some of the very good writing they had produced, Ms Swan appeared in the classroom.
'Mrs Latimer,' Ms Swan spoke in her distinctive, deep voice. 'Could you come to my office at break time? I need to have a word with you about something.'
'Yes of course. Ms Swan.'
The head teacher scanned the children's books as she circumnavigated the classroom. 'Well done children. I can see there has been some excellent writing going on in here this morning.' Ms Swan only gave out compliments if she had some truly awful news to deliver and Julia dreaded what was to come next.

Zoe

Zoe thought she had better keep out of Julia's way and tried desperately to remember what had happened during the conversation last night. She was sure that Julia had actually hung up on her at the end and this wasn't a good sign. Most probably she had been rude about the precious Neil, but it was obvious that everything was far from rosy in that garden. Nevertheless, it was Julia's choice and only she alone could make the decision of when she should leave the rat. Zoe bit her lip while reckoning she had probably been too heavy-handed last night.

As she had walked past Julia's classroom earlier, everything seemed fine and she had seen her deep in conversation with Emily. Later on when she glanced through the window and watched her teaching, she and the children seemed to sharing a joke. That, she decided was a good sign. However, a few moments ago she saw Julia whizz past her in the corridor, before knocking on Ms Swan's door with a face a white as a sheet. This didn't bode well. One of the parents or maybe several of the parents must have made a complaint about the hullabaloo yesterday. Damn. That was the last thing Julia needed. She, Zoe decided, would wait where she was and check her friend was all right.

A few minutes later Julia emerged from the Head's office looking much calmer.

'Hi Zoe. How's your day going?' Julia smiled at her.

'I'm fine thanks. How about you?' She scanned her friend's face for signs of stress.

'Much better than yesterday…'

Zoe put a hand on Julia's shoulder.

'What's going on Julia? I saw you a few moments ago and you looked like a ghost. Are you in trouble with Swannie? What did she want you for?' She knew that Ms Swan had a way of getting rid of those she fell out with.

'Oh, it was just about one of the children.' Julia lowered her voice. 'It's Charlie, in my class, his grandmother's very poorly and she's in hospital…'

'Thank goodness for that.' Zoe pulled her hands through her hair in a desperate attempt to flatten it.

'What do you mean? It's serious – she might die.' She knew that Charlie would be devastated … what on earth is wrong with Zoe she thought?

'No, that's not what I mean … but I thought after yesterday, you know…'

'Zoe, I'm all right really. I just had a few things on my mind yesterday. I'm sorry if I was a bit offhand with you.'

Zoe was relieved that Julia didn't seem angry with her.

'As long as you are fine,' said Zoe. 'I know – let's go for a drink after school. We can have a proper chat, you know.' There are few problems that can't be solved by drinks and a good talk thought Zoe.

'Yes, ok. A chat would be good ... and a few drinks.'

It was good to see Julia smiling again.

'Drop your car off. We'll go to the pub near me. Neil can pick you up later or you can get a taxi home.' Zoe was looking forward to the end of the day now.

'Why not? Yes, Zoe that sounds like a plan.'

Two Weeks Earlier

Obadiah

Obadiah lived in the strict Orthodox Jewish Community in Bensham in Gateshead. In fact, he lived in the very house next to where he had been born, with his wife Bathsheba and their two little girls. His elderly parents, Solomon and Sarah, who were now well into their nineties lived in the adjacent house and the whole family ate together every Shabbat. Until recently, Sarah had done all the food preparation for their Friday feast but as she was becoming increasingly frail, responsibility was falling more on Bathsheba's shoulders.

Largely the community liked to keep themselves to themselves. Obadiah's successful career as an accountant had begun with him auditing the books for his father's small property-letting agency. Solomon owned eight properties nearby which allowed him a modest income. Then, Odadiah had taken on board the nearby kosher bakeries, schools and the Synagogue.

Everyone had been extremely pleased with the extensive savings he had made for them. Spreading his wings further afield, he began to search out other local businessmen, to whom he could be of service. Obadiah had taken to the business of accountancy like a duck to water. He had always had a flair for figures since a young boy and was proving himself to be excellent at his job. He worked efficiently, didn't procrastinate, and knew the most important loopholes to save his clients' money. Once people saw behind what they would consider his unusual appearance and odd eccentricities, they were only too willing to engage his services, especially when word of mouth told them how much money he could potentially save them.

Upon occasion, Obadiah had considered, whether he should tone down his appearance by straightening his ringlets and securing them into a pony tail. This he sometimes did but not too often, as not only might it offend his parents but it was really just too much bother.

Unbeknown to his parents, he had even joined the Heworth Golf Club. Although he had no interest in or idea of how to actually play the game, he could be often be seen in clubhouse propping up the bar and drinking cokes or soda waters. Obadiah was networking. He was forging friendship by striking up conversations and pretending to laugh at jokes. These he didn't really understand, as he hadn't been blessed with much of a sense of humour. In fact, he often guffawed in completely the wrong place in a joke, as he didn't recognise the punch line.

While at first, the local business men gave this weird, hyena-like person a wide berth, when they heard he could save them serious money, it was a different story. Indeed for Obadiah, this was an ideal place to make useful contacts and secure lucrative jobs. And this had been how he found himself in the company of Charles Lavender.

Charles had come into the clubhouse a week or so ago with his friend Neil. They had both been playing golf and it seemed that Charles was in very good spirits, as he had just beaten his friend. The two of them were at the bar ordering pints and Obadiah gave them a nod as he sipped his soda water, although he had never seen them before.

'Hey Charles, I've got a joke for you.' Neil gave a fleeting glance towards Obadiah and grinned at Charles.

'Go on then.' Charles rolled his eyes.

'A priest, a rabbit and a minister walk into a bar. The bartender asks the rabbit what he wants …' Neil's story was curtailed by the roaring laughter coming from Obadiah. His face went bright red and his glasses fell off. Charles and Neil looked at Obadiah and then each other not knowing what to say.

'Well I'm sorry Neil, despite someone obviously finding your tale hilarious, I wouldn't say it was one of your best.' Charles took a long drink from his pint and Neil gave Obadiah a cross look for spoiling his joke.
'It wasn't supposed to be a rabbit … he was only there because of auto correct.' Neil began but the moment was lost and nobody laughed, much to his annoyance.

Upon reflection, Obadiah thought it was one of the more amusing stories he had heard because a rabbit going into a bar for drink, was funny wasn't it? Or was there a tinge of racism lurking somewhere in this joke. Obadiah couldn't be sure, but he certainly hadn't taken to that Neil chap. As he drove along Bewick Road in his blue Volvo, he suspected that his father Solomon, would not be happy about all of this random fraternising of his. He thought that it was best to keep business within the Jewish faith, but Obadiah knew that this was limiting his options much too greatly.

Many years ago, Solomon had rented one of his flats to a weasel of young man who had mysteriously absconded and left owing his father a good sum of money. After neglecting to pay his rent for several months he had disappeared without a trace, taking with him a standard lamp and a set of dining room cutlery. From somewhere in the dim and distant past, Obadiah had some vague recollection of this despised gentile, which was surprising since he must have been very young at the time. This had been a lesson to Solomon and since then he had only rented his flats and houses out unfurnished to people of his own faith. Obadiah thought his father had limited his options too far, as such occurrences were bound to happen, no matter if the tenant was Jewish or gentile. Solomon wouldn't be told and once bitten twice shy became his much repeated motto.

However, if Solomon had knowledge of the amount of money his son had been dealing recently, it would have brought on a fit of apoplexy. Solomon must have lost no more than a couple of thousand from his disappearing tenant, while the thousands that had been siphoned off by Charles Lavender's thieving employee was in altogether different league. Tomorrow, he would present his final report to Mr Lavender and without any shadow of a doubt the man would see this was a big-time crook he had in his employ and that the police needed to be involved immediately.

Chapter 11

Twenty- Five Years Earlier

Trevor

Trevor imagined that the cheapskate Solomon Goldstein would have been more than a little annoyed by his sudden disappearance, leaving a backlog of unpaid rent. But Trevor justified himself by the fact that, he had been living in the dump for several years now and not once had the place been decorated. What did he expect? The pokey bedsit was barely habitable? The place was riddled with damp, it was dirty and in the winter he had to spent a fortune putting a mountain of pound coins into the meter, just to avoid freezing to death. No more cold nights for Trevor, in this toastie warm centrally- heated marital home to be. This winter, Trevor would be as snug as a bug, which was no more than a man like himself deserved.

He had been pleasantly surprised, as to how well the orange standard lamp had complemented the décor in the lounge at this, his new address. The Mason's front room was all beiges and muted pinks. His bright lamp brought a bit of much needed vibrancy, like a comforting candle cheering this dull bland room. It had been a touch of genius on his part, bringing a couple of things with him to put his stamp on the place. The mismatched set of cutlery, he told Julia, had been a precious keepsake from his parents. So now, when he and Julia ate with the disgusting implements at every mealtime, Trevor felt he was further marking his territory and making further progress.

Looking around, Trevor couldn't believe how easily the pieces of the jigsaw puzzle had slotted into place and he pushed his slippers smugly under the glass coffee table. Even he hadn't expected Julia to be so gullible. The silly cow had actually thought he was doing her a favour by moving in. Fortunately, she had never been able to see the hovel where he had lived before. She had mentioned how she would love to see his swish pad but fortunately, he had been able to fob her off: it was a terrible bus route, there was a dog in the flat below that bit people, the staircase to his flat was uneven and she might even trip up. The lies had just tripped off his tongue, when he described his plush black leather sofas, luxurious deep pile carpets and red satin bed sheets. Julia asked why he didn't bring them here but how fortunate they wouldn't match the decoration.

At this very moment, Julia would be scurrying around 'Safeways' buying those convenience foods to pass off as her own cooking. Well, once Trevor held all the purse strings, it would be a different matter altogether. Unbelievably, she believed him when he told her that the dreadful inedible offerings that she prepared for him were delicious. She was so stupid, that she imagined that the ready meal economy range of lame lasagnes, mediocre macaroni cheeses and horrendous hot pots actually tasted pleasant. Trevor felt sick at the thought of what awful salty presentation he would have to endure that evening. He was in no way fussy about food, but when he thought back nostalgically, to the wonderful home cooking of his mother ... still it was a small price to pay he reckoned. When Julia went to the supermarket, the imbecilic girl didn't realise that the reason he didn't accompany her was not because large shops brought on his agoraphobia, but so she had to pay for everything.

Already, his bank account was looking far healthier than ever before. He couldn't believe his luck. Once they were actually married, all her money of course would be his, as well as this house. Oh, his mother would be so proud if she could only see how well he had done for himself.

All was not yet a 'fait accompli'. The wedding was still a few days away. Trevor needed to remain on his best behaviour and not let the mask slip. There was still time for Julia to change her mind. Thank goodness he had convinced her to sever her friendship with that awful ginger-haired girl. Zoe – wasn't that her name? He was pleased that Julia had seen sense and given up on her. Although Trevor had the brainwave of throwing Julia's address book away, she was still attending college and would come in to contact with her. Well, at least he had the summer holidays to make her see sense and drop off that pointless course.

Also, there was the whole sorry bedroom business. He had insisted that it wasn't proper for them to be sharing a bed together, not before they were married, but she would have none of it. There was an inviting bedroom adjacent to hers and Trevor would have been much happier there, but for his plan to work he needed her to believe she was desired. Trevor felt a wave of nausea, like he was about to set foot on a roller coaster, pass over him. Unfortunately for him, Julia craved the security of being loved and having someone lie next to her to calm her night terrors. Since her parents had died, she had frequently woken up screaming and crying. She said it was much more bearable if he were lying next to her. Trevor hated having to feign concern, when all he wanted was a decent night's sleep. But it was a necessary evil. He needed to play his cards carefully to win the game and if that meant the inconvenience of not being able to sleep alone, so be it.

She had naively imagined that the compliments and affections he had showered on her at the outset were genuine. In fact, as he said many of the corny words, which had been lifted straight from the syrupy novels that his mother had read, he winced. For his part, they were just a means to an end but he hadn't realised he was such a brilliant actor. He guessed that was just another string to his bow, for Julia had fallen for them hook, line and sinker.

Although, he supposed she didn't look too bad when she was wearing a sensible outfit of his choosing, he certainly had no desire whatsoever to see her without any clothes. He could just about tolerate giving her a goodnight peck on the cheek and sharing the bed with her, while under his insistence, she wore her thick winceyette pyjamas, but that was about as far as he could go. Deep down Trevor knew he really wasn't attracted to grown women in the slightest, but his true desires were best kept to himself. Once this charade of a wedding was over, he would be moving into the spare room indefinitely and that would be the end of the unpleasant matter. The wedding night wasn't likely to be a pleasant occasion for either of them.

The Present Day

Julia

When Julia, dropped her car off back at the house, she found Neil sitting on the couch in the living room with Mabel, who with previous hostilities put to one side, was enjoying being stroked. She was making those familiar chirruping noises like a canary, as she did when she was happy or had got her own way. Julia had left Zoe sitting outside in the car, as she knew Neil and her didn't really hit it off. Her husband was dressed in his suit and was watching the end of The Chase, pretending he had just returned from work. Immediately, Julia noticed he had an angry gash down the side of one cheek but having neither the time nor inclination to discover its source she turned a blind eye.

'Hello love. Have you had a good day at school?' Neil by the sound of things, was trying hard to give the impression of having had a normal day fighting.

'Yes thanks.' Julia's reply was somewhat curt, as she delved in her bag for some make-up.' Look, I'm just leaving the car. Zoe is waiting for me outside. Is it ok if we go out for a couple of drinks? There's school stuff we need to discuss.'

'Of course – yes, you go out. Enjoy yourself.' Neil placed his hand across his cheek, in a futile attempt to hide the wound inflicted by Mabel, who was snuggling closely to him on the sofa.' A good chinwag will do you the world of good. Did you say you were going out with Zoe?'

'Yes, she's waiting in the drive.' Julia was hurriedly freshening up her make-up in the hallway window. 'Ok, I must dash.'

'Do you want me to pick you up later?' Neil appeared eager to get back in her good books.

'Please, if it's not too much bother. About eight, would that be all right?' Julia hurriedly straightened her hair with her fingers.

'Are you going to Zoe's dive of choice?' Neil actually liked Zoe's haunt, but couldn't resist a little dig.

'Yes Neil, I would imagine The Free Trade pub is where we'll be … but I'll text you if we are anywhere different.' Normally, Julia would have given Neil a kiss before leaving, but the mysterious gash just annoyed her further when coupled with his constant stream of lies. Fuelled by alcohol later, might be the ideal time for a few home truths to be revealed. Julia slammed the door shut and ran down the driveway to her friend's car.

25 Years Ago

Julia had not really known what to expect on the day of her nuptials, but as the two of them had sat in a less than mediocre Fish and Chip shop, on Gateshead High St, she couldn't help but feel a little disappointed about her wedding breakfast. In the apologetic café, there were green and white plastic tablecloths, brash strip lights and spillages of gravy on the linoleum floor. The middle aged women who had served them, had badly-dyed, bright, yellow hair, a filthy overall and when she plonked the plates on the table, Julia noticed she had dirty fingernails. She gave Julia a strange look, as she clearly appraised her wedding dress unfavourably, before smiling at Trevor and revealing nicotine stained teeth like small, over ripe bananas. In the brash lighting, she could see her husband's suit for what it was, cheap and nasty. Furthermore, he was making no effort to have a conversation with her, but just concentrating his efforts on eating his food.

She had been expecting something a little more out of the ordinary than greasy fish and chips, stale bread and margarine washed down with a cup of tea that had globules of curdled milk floating on the top. Although, she hadn't been expecting champagne, on this occasion surely a little extravagance wasn't an unnecessary indulgence. After all, this was supposed to have been the happiest day of her life but maybe that bit was still yet to come and she gave her new spouse a coy smile. He blanked her.

The wedding ceremony had been over in the blink of an eye. As they had no company with them, it had been necessary to hijack a couple of witnesses from the street. The first recruit, an elderly lady, seemed to be befuddled as to the purpose of their intentions towards her. She promptly hit Trevor on the arm with an umbrella, to make her response

to their proposal plain. Next, Trevor asked a gawky teenager on a skateboard if he could spare some time but Julia had queried if a youth of this age would be deemed suitable by the registrar for the task in hand. Finally, an obese couple both eating burgers, with a fat child screaming loudly in his pushchair, were persuaded to be of assistance. They were sitting on a bench and clearly had nothing better to do than make the street look untidy. While the man had a mullet haircut and looked as if he were about to burst out of his pale blue velour tracksuit, the woman's bouffant hair matched her equally ample ra-ra skirt, both being the colour of beetroot.

So the peculiar assortment of a wedding party hastened to the Civic Centre. The registrar, a middle aged woman in a crisp white blouse with a pussy cat bow and a stern expression, eyed them suspiciously. She proceeded with the ceremony in a quiet, controlled voice. The words she spoke were difficult to hear because of the child's constant bawling throughout the ceremony. While Julia tried her best to concentrate on the importance of what was being said and make sure she said her vows correctly, Trevor simply looked irritated. When it was time for him to make his responses, he demanded that the question was repeated as he couldn't bloody hear. The registrar pursed her lips, as if there was an unpleasant smell and gave the child a withering look. But he was purple in the face and so in the thrall of the most enormous paddy, that he was totally oblivious to her disapproval. Meanwhile, his mother shrugged her shoulders, as if to say what could she possibly do and the father looked at his watch every few seconds. He was only eager to get to the pub for a pint, as it was now twelve o clock.

Once it was declared they were married, Julia received a perfunctory peck on the cheek from her husband and he immediately grabbed her arm indicating they should leave. The registrar removed her spectacles and closed the large book, as if relieved that the class was dismissed. Before thanking the couple, Julia took her small Kodak camera from her bag and asked if the woman would mind taking a couple of pictures. She obliged, assuming her family would be invited to some slap up reception feast by this strange friendless couple. The newlyweds both posed awkwardly, in the car park of the Civic Centre for their photos. Flanking the uncomfortable pair, were a white Ford Cortina and a red Austin Allegra, adding gravitas to the shots as if they were a couple of random

bridesmaids. Julia thanked their witnesses before Trevor once more yanked her arm and they disappeared to sample the heady delights of Gateshead High Street.

Twenty five years later

Zoe and Julia were sitting in the Free Trade pub which was at the Ouseburn End of the Quayside in Newcastle. Upon visiting the place, many at first failed to recognise the charm of peeling paint from the walls, mismatched rickety furniture and gaps in the ceiling, patched up with random pieces of wood. But they soon did. It was like stepping back in time to the 1950's or even further. There, alongside current locals, sat the ghosts of shipbuilders, keel men and stall traders. Along with an unparalleled view of the Tyne, excellent selection of drinks and friendly, obliging bar staff, there was an ambience regarded by its champions as second to none. In Zoe's opinion, what was there not to like?

On that particular evening, the bright lights twinkled on both sides of the river. Julia thought they looked like two buzzing armies of fireflies and the diorama of the bridges; an epic stage back drop from a Tyneside musical. Zoe waved and greeted some of her friends a couple, who were sitting at the bar petting the tabby pub cat named Craig David before asking the bartender for some drinks. Then they both sat down at a window seat. Luckily, at that time of night on a Tuesday evening, it wasn't too busy and so they could talk freely.

'So you say he's got a big gash down the side of his face?' Zoe's eyes widened, she was enjoying this conversation already immensely. 'How do you think he's got that'?

'Well I know for a fact, that for the last couple of days, he's not been going to work.' Julia took a large sip from her double gin and tonic.

'I know Neil's hardly my favourite person but even I find it hard to believe he's been scouring the streets of Newcastle looking for fights.' But the idea of him doing so pleased her enormously.

'No, I've no idea how he came by that. That's just another incident in a long list of peculiar behaviours. But him lying to me and dressing up as if he's been to work is just weird.' After taking a massive leap of faith, Julia felt relief at the prospect of sharing at least some of her burdens.

'Do you mean he's pretending to be going to work for your benefit? Is he playing at being sick? Mind you, two weeks is rather a long time to be pulling a sickie.' When Zoe has had days when she can't cope she has always opted for two days rather than the one but two weeks was stretching it a bit far.

'No that's not what it is …' Julia gave her a worried look, and glanced around the pub to see if anyone else was listening.

'Julia … he's not really ill is he? He's not got cancer or some other awful illness.' Much as she disliked the man, even she wouldn't wish that on him.

'No I doubt it… Neil's always been as fit as a fiddle. But come to think of it , he hasn't been down the gym as much of late. And he's always looked after himself but maybe … ' Perhaps Neil was really ill and that mark on his face was some kind of awful cancerous lesion.

'Well, have you not asked him?' Zoe's mind was doing somersaults.

'No Zoe, I don't actually think he's ill. I think Charles has fired him.' There, she had said it. Although pretending not to, a nattily dressed man with a distinctive moustache, who had been working on a lap top was eavesdropping on the conversation.

'Why on earth would Charles do that?' Zoe lowered her voice as Julia put a finger to her lips. 'I mean, I know I'm not Neil's biggest fan but when all's said and done the silver-tongued bastard is an excellent salesman.'

'Yes that's what I always thought too. I don't think the company would be where it is today if it wasn't for Neil …'Julia sighed and went to the bar to get two more drinks for them, giving Zoe time to chew over what she had been told. And when she returned Zoe continued. 'So, Julia if that's the case he must have done something really bad.'

'You know I told you that Neil used to have a gambling problem.' Julia whispered and looked about furtively.

'No, I didn't know that Julia. Do you mean he used to bet on the horses?' Zoe nodded sagely.'My granddad used to do that till my nana put a stop to it …'

'No, it's casinos that are his thing. You know we used to go there together at one time. Sometimes he won hundreds and was high as a kite.' Julia gave a wistful smile thinking of happier times. 'It was great. We drank champagne and toasted his winnings. But other times …' Her face clouded over.

'Yes, the only people that really win in these places are the owners aren't they?' Zoe considered the massive list of flaws in the character of her own ex, but least he hadn't done this.

'Quite.' Julia's sombreness contrasted with the bright hair and loud shirt of her friend. 'When I realised how much of our money was being habitually thrown down the toilet, I refused to go.'

'That was the right thing to do, definitely. What about him? Did he stop?' Zoe had never known her friend to be so forthcoming before.

'Well not at first. He used to lie.' Julia looked so forlorn.

This, of the slippery Neil, she could easily believe. 'Well there's a surprise.' Zoe snorted and went to take a drink, before noticing that her glass was empty. She scuttled off to the bar once more to recharge their glasses. The bartender seemed a little alarmed by the loud, floral patterns on Zoe's shirt and speed at which they were knocking back the gin and tonics.

Soon Zoe banged two drinks down on the table, which wobbled precariously, then Julia continued. 'When I went to bed at night and this would be at nearly midnight, on a school night too.' Zoe was all ears as to what interesting information her friend would divulge next. 'He would sneak out on the pretext of going for a walk.'

'I suppose he claimed he was taking Mabel for a walk. 'Zoe laughed at the thought, then stopped herself, realising the severity of the situation.

'He didn't get back till well into the early hours … I couldn't sleep.' Continued Julia.

Zoe saw her friend's eyes were brimming with tears.'Oh, you poor thing. I can remember days when you looked terrible at school. I thought you must have been having a domestic the night before. And was he going to the casino?' Zoe wasn't sure which was worse. At least after an argument, no matter how nasty, the next morning your money was still in the bank.

'Yes but he promised me he has stopped. He's not been out at night for ages.' Julia's candid expression was child-like.

Zoe found this difficult to believe. 'But if he's not been going to work? Do you think while he's been off work that's where he's been going?' This would be the most likely explanation Zoe thought.

'Well, it's possible. But would Charles sack him for that? I mean the two of them are friends, surely he would just have a word.' Julia shrugged her shoulders.

'Maybe Neil has got himself into such a mess financially that he's been forced to *steal…*'

'From the company? Yes, those have been my thoughts exactly. But why has he said nothing to me, his wife?'

'Well firstly, he's embarrassed, isn't he? But most worryingly it must be the amount of money involved. I mean hasn't Charles Lavender had the police involved?'

Julia's face fell, as she hadn't even considered this and tried to put their involvement to the back of her mind, as her thoughts returned once more to the blasted rose bushes and the road. 'But this must have been going on for ages.' Zoe was picturing Neil with his piles of chips in the casino.

Pushing the even more unpleasant thoughts to one side, Julia concentrated on her errant husband once more ; this conversation after all, was about Neil not her. 'I would have spotted him sneaking off to the casino…'

'Julia there's more than one way to skin a cat.' Zoe said mysteriously and tapped her cheek with a finger.

'What do you mean?' Had Mabel got something to do with all of this? Julia was confused.

'What does Neil get up to on his *computer*?' Zoe stressed each syllable of the word..

And in Julia's head a light went on. 'You mean online gambling?' Now why hadn't she thought of that one?

Zoe

When Zoe arrived back at home, she poured herself another drink and was glad that Chloe was still at her gran's. Much as she loved her daughter's company, it was lovely to have some time to herself. She took off her shoes, stretched her legs and relaxed on the sofa with a large glass of wine. She didn't put the telly on. She needed to think. Zoe always enjoyed spending time with Julia, especially when in her favourite pub, but tonight had been a complete revelation. Yet she had been delighted that Julia had shared so much about her problems and she felt flattered. It seemed as if the revelations had sealed their friendship and it was as if they were young students once more.

Who would have suspected St Neil had a gambling problem and such a massive one. Imagine gullible Julia thinking he had just stopped, when he no longer ventured out to the casino in the middle of the night. Gamblers and addicts don't just sort themselves out, they simply become more devious. Once more Zoe, remembered her poor grandma. How could Julia have been so naive? Also, he hadn't been just sacked from his job over some trivial matter. Neil was clearly involved in some serious fraud and it was a wonder indeed that the police weren't involved. Maybe that was yet to come? Zoe pictured Neil incarcerated in a gloomy cell, wearing a convict's suit decorated with jaunty arrows and with thick metal bars in front of his face. The thought pleased her. Well, it was no more than he deserved.

When Neil had come to pick his wife up, he had dropped Zoe off at home and had clearly been on his best behaviour. He had fussed over the pair of them like an elderly aunt and asked if they had enjoyed themselves. Zoe had been unable to stop staring at the big gash down his left cheek. It was a deep wound and the blood was still congealing angrily on his cheek. She was sure this must have been some way connected with his gambling. Maybe, he had borrowed money off some loan shark and had been unable to repay him. Perhaps, some heavies had come round to the house and this was their doing. Quite clearly, Neil was in a lot of trouble and his wife was very worried. Julia was the sort of person who always played her cards close to her chest and tonight's disclosures were more than she had ever shared.

Zoe thought back to the time when she and Julia had met as young students. Although the two of them had spent great times together, there was always a secrecy and sadness about her. Zoe had guessed that this was connected with the loss of her parents. The young women had mostly shared gossip together. Julia had always been reluctant to discuss anything other than trivial matters but the two of them had been close. And despite Zoe having been delighted after all these years for their friendship to be rekindled, she couldn't quite forget how she had been discarded like an outgrown toy when that Trevor arrived on the scene.

Now when their paths had crossed all these many years later, Trevor had mysteriously disappeared and everything was all about perfect husband Neil. Neil was in property, Neil was so funny, Neil was so clever etc etc. Anytime, she had raised the matter of Trevor, Julia had changed the subject, which seemed very odd to say the least. Zoe didn't take to Neil, not one little bit. Neil with his sharp suits and smarmy ways. Now it seemed at last, that her shrewd judgements about the liar were proving to be more than justified. However, Neil was still nothing compared to the awful, controlling Trevor, who had just made her flesh creep.

All considered, Julia was just a terrible judge of men. Who knew what Trevor had done to her? But Neil's actions could see her lose her home. Julia's lovely house that had been left to her by her parents, with all its fancy fixtures and fittings, would have to be sold. This was terrible news and she could see how Julia would be worried. But there was something more. At the end of it all, these were Neil's problems and he would just have to sort them out himself. But there was something else troubling Julia. Zoe had the feeling there was more to all of this than Julia had told her. Something far worse, that she couldn't share with her friend or anyone else.

Chapter 12

Two weeks earlier

Charles

Charles had woken that morning, knowing that today was going to be one of those very difficult ones. The information that Obadiah was likely to present him with would be conclusive and damning, not only for Neil but for himself. Charles wasn't a man who made friends easily and even the most favourable of outcomes would mean severance of their long standing friendship. He poured himself another cup of tea and took a bite from his toast and marmalade. Once, Pamela had made him delicious breakfasts of bacon, eggs and sausages every morning. This was no longer, alas. Still, he suspected as he patted his waistline, it was for his own good.

'Everything okay? You look deep in thought.' Pamela put a little spoonful of her muesli into her mouth, like a bird pecking at a fat ball.

'No not really. It's going to be one of those days today. I'm afraid.' Charles nodded knowingly and put his head in his hands.

'Anything you want to share with me?' Sometimes Pamela wished her husband would take her more into his confidences.

'No …it's just one of those work problems.' Charles rubbed his bloodshot eyes, remembering that he had drunk more whisky than he had intended to last night.

'Well if there's anything I can do …' Pamela would love to have been of some help, if he would only let her.

'Pamela, just let it be' He slapped his hands on the table. 'Believe me … you wouldn't want to know about this one.'

Pamela knew better than to pursue this any further and indeed she should be grateful that he hadn't snapped at her as much as usual. Banging his hands was nothing compared to his usual tetchiness. This must be some big problem. If he couldn't even be bothered to summon up the energy to be rude to her, then something must be really getting his goat. Pamela went to get his packed lunch box and added some fruit to the wholemeal ham sandwiches she had made for him. She knew that the apple and banana would return in the box uneaten.

'Anything in particular you would like for dinner this evening?' Discussions about food usually cheered him up.

'It's a long time since you made steak and kidney pudding. That would be nice.' Charles couldn't remember when they had last eaten one.

'We'll see.' There was no way Pamela was making suet pastry with all that lard. She thought to change the conversation. 'Anyway … soon Max will be going to the office with you won't he?'

'Well you'd better get him into the habit of getting up. That lazy lout lies in bed far too late doesn't he? He needs to start seeing a lot more of the mornings you know. It might be happening a lot sooner than he expects.' And with that enigmatic comment, Charles drove off to work, leaving his wife wondering *what* the great mysterious problem was and *why* the sudden urgency for their son to be involved in the family business.

Once he arrived at the office, with a big cloud hanging over his head, Charles was given a cheery greeting from Tracy. She was wearing a tight white jacket and matching short skirt. Tracy informed him in a whisper, that Obadiah was already there. She pointed to a chair outside Charles' office, where sat the eager accountant, clutching his briefcase, as if his life depended on its contents. He was looking very pleased with himself, as he drank from a cup of coffee and stared at the ceiling.

Obadiah

Obadiah, much to the annoyance of his wife Bathsheba, had sat up for most of the previous night attacking the accounts with great zeal. His enthusiasm for the task had been further ignited, when he realised the culprit of the fraud, was none other than the joke-telling, buffoon sidekick of Charles that he had met at the Golf Club recently. Upon reflection, he was still unable to decide whether the rabbit/rabbi reference, had been a racist jibe at his expense. Still it had made his hackles rise and when he realise that the snappily-dressed Neil Latimer was the perpetrator of the alleged crime, he couldn't have been more delighted.

Scouring the files, he discovered the first appearance of the Personal Expenses Account over ten years ago.

At first small amounts of money had been taken out, in fact so insignificant they wouldn't have been noticed, unless someone like him was searching. And Obadiah was scrutinising every transaction and withdrawal in all the accounts with a fine-toothed comb. When midnight arrived and his wife shouted to him to come to bed, he didn't hear her as he was so wrapped up in his world of pounds, pennies and pilfering.

As the night gave way to the early hours, Obadiah's list of the unlawful transactions made by Mr N Latimer was veering towards the five hundred thousand mark and despite his personal feelings towards the vile individual, he couldn't fail to be a little impressed by his sheer audacity. When his disgruntled wife, who had not been pleased by the absence of her neglectful husband in the marital bed last night, brought him a begrudged cup of coffee, he ought to have been exhausted. But he wasn't. Obadiah was on fire, with an impressive nearly a half a million pound swindle itching to be revealed.

So eager was he to divulge his findings that he arrived a full ten minutes before any of the staff at OakElmAsh Residentials. He was forced to hover on the doorstep, checking his watch every few seconds, for his moment of glory to arrive. Eventually Tracy turned up, to open up the building and she gestured for him to take a seat outside her boss's office. Although suspicious to the purpose of his visit, she felt obliged to give him a cup of coffee. He had drunk so much caffeine throughout the night, that his hands were shaking like leaves and he spilt the brown liquid all over the light wood floor. Tracy watched him with distaste, thinking his carelessness would leave a stain. She felt glad to be drinking water and thankful she had sat him far away from her clean clothes.

Eventually, Charles Lavender arrived at the building and strode through the door. Obadiah instantly shot out of his seat. Charles saw him and shuddered.

'Mr Lavender, you won't believe what I …' Obadiah was drooling and the globules of saliva trickled down the sides his mouth.

'Mr Goldstein. Please step into my office.' Charles was aware of Tracy craning her ears in their direction. When the door opened Obadiah could barely get through fast enough.

'Nearly half a million pounds.' Charles slumped down in his set like a deflated balloon while Obadiah was far too excited to have a seat and was practically dancing a Charleston. 'Here is the final total of what he has stolen from you.' Obadiah produced a used envelope from his pocket. Until recently it had contained his council tax bill, upon this he had written with a red ball point pen and underlined twice, the sum of £497,256·02.

'Really, as much as that.' The usual florid colour slowly drained from Charles's face.

'Yes Mr Lavender. You must ring the police. Immediately.' If Charles hadn't known the man to be an Orthodox Jew, he would have sworn he was in the company of a born again Christian, gibbering in tongues.

'Mr Goldstein. Are you absolutely sure of this figure. It seems enormous.' Surely, the man had made a mistake with the decimal point, thought Charles, clutching at straws.

'Yes this sum is definite. I have checked many times. I couldn't believe it myself …'

'Thank you for bringing this to my attention.' Charles wished he had a pin to burst the man's bubble.

'But what about the police?' As he said the word police, Obadiah's eyes glowing like Belisha beacons behind the little round glasses, grew even bigger.

'Yes, yes. Not now. I need to think.' He held the envelope in his hand staring at the figure written in blood.

'But Mr Lavender. That man. He has stolen from you.' At last, Obadiah sat down, hoping to appear the voice of reason and force Mr Lavender to take immediate action.

'Yes, yes. I realise that.' He really hadn't thought his best friend, who he had known since they were lads, capable of such extreme or treacherous behaviour.

'The police need to be informed.' Obadiah was becoming like an irritating record, with the needle well and truly stuck on the cheesiest bit of the song.

'Well thank you Mr Goldstein. Your services have been greatly appreciated.' Charles moved to open the door. 'It's been a pleasure doing business with you.'

Obadiah remained in his seat. 'But what about the police? The police need to be informed.' He repeated, his voice sounding increasingly like that of a Darlek.
'You will find the sum we agreed in your bank account.' As Charles fully opened the door, all eyes were on an unsuspecting Neil as he sauntered into the showroom.

Twenty- Five Years Earlier

Trevor

Trevor had prepared for this day, as he realised that after the wedding ceremony certain unpleasant duties would be expected of him. This was an unfortunate inevitability of being married. Or maybe not, for Trevor had a few tricks up his sleeve. Working at a chemist's did have certain advantages and he knew that particular drugs had more than one purpose. Some of those that were used in palliative care for extreme pain relief and for severe depression had an entirely different function on the street. Here, they were used for recreation or even as a more sinister - means to an end.

While he knew that helping himself to particular drugs from the shop had its risks, Trevor felt he knew how to be discrete. Often, Trevor was first to open up the chemist's in the morning and frequently it was his role to lock up the place at night. Yes, there were CCTV cameras, but they weren't very reliable and he knew how easy they were to tamper with and bypass. Trevor had done his research.

After the fish and chip meal, which Trevor suspected would have been a disappointment to his new wife, the two of them took the familiar bus ride back to his new marital home. Trevor took pleasure in the thought that as from now, as he was the husband, it belonged to him more than her. Traditionally, everyone knew husbands had more rights than wives and her possessions were his. As they walked up his sizeable driveway, Julia was nudging her face at his shoulder like some pathetic cat. Obviously, she imagined she would be carried over the threshold like some precious cargo. Trevor pretended to have no inkling as to what she was angling for. He retrieved his key from the pocket and opened his front door.

'Well my dear. Now that's over with … we can relax can't we?' Trevor loosened his tie and thought for the umpteenth time that day, how ridiculous she looked in the awful makeshift dress. There were now grease marks down the front. Could his new spouse not even eat properly?

'Yes, I suppose so.' Julia was confused, (she had never been a wife before). She wasn't sure how she ought to be feeling at the moment but she didn't think it should to be like this. Something wasn't right.

'Well sit down wife. I have a little treat for you.' As Julia placed herself on the sofa, in front of her parents wedding photograph, she heard the unexpected pop of a cork from the kitchen. After some strange clunking of cupboard door sounds, Trevor came back into the room with a beaker in one hand and a green bottle of something fizzy in the other.

'Ooh is it champagne? I've never tasted that before.' Maybe everything was going to be fine after all and Julia heaved a sigh of relief.

'Well … it's just as good as.' Trevor gave her a strange smile, as he handed her the plastic cup.

'Aren't you having a glass with me?' Julia giggled nervously, imagining this was the beginning of the build-up of her being taken up to the bedroom.

'No Julia. You know my opinion, on intoxicating drink.' Julia thought that just for once, it would have been nice to see Trevor let himself go. She took a sip.

'Well, is that nice?' said Trevor.

Having never drunk champagne before, she had expected it to taste better than it actually did. While it was certainly fizzy, there was a strange metallic taste to it and she hadn't expected champagne to be cloudy like this drink. Then something started to kick in.

'Ooh Trevor, it's making me feel all whoozy.' Julia felt an unexplained euphoria engulf her, like a soft feathery cushion.

'Have some more, wife.' Trevor was watching her carefully, as if she were some bizarre biological experiment. He topped up her drink. Julia took another mouthful, grinning inanely, as she luxuriated in the numbing sensation that was ebbing and flowing through her body.

'I thought you would like my special bubbly.' He held the cup to her mouth, forcing her to drink more.

'I think I've had en … en …' Everything was swimming about the room. Trevor's face was leering and contorting in front of her eyes like an evil clown.

'Come on Julia, you and Zoe used to enjoy a pint of lager or two didn't you?' Julia felt sick. She didn't want any more of the wretched drink. As she slumped back on the sofa, her limbs froze and she could her feel her heart pounding double time inside her chest.

The Present Day

Neil

When Neil and Julia arrived back at the house, Neil could see imminent trouble brewing as his wife had a face like thunder. She had remained silent throughout the journey back, but he had seen her surreptitiously out of the corner of his eye examining the gash on his face. He wondered what she and Zoe had been talking about in the pub. Most likely he had featured largely in their topic of conversation and this could not be good.

Neil sat upright on a chair in the corner of the kitchen, preparing for a serious interrogation, when Mabel ran across the floor and jumped onto his lap. He pushed her off in annoyance, as the perpetrator of his wound needn't think he had been so easily forgotten.

'Neil, what are you doing to Mabel? What harm's she done?' Julia was standing by the sink watching him.

'Good question Julia. You've no doubt seen my mutilated face. Well it was her.' He pointed at the berated cat who was now skulking in the opposite corner of the room. 'She … that cat, she just lashed out at me.' Neil glared accusingly at Mabel, before pulling one of his well-practised, injured, little boy faces, which no longer sat so well on a man in his fifties.

'Well, I've never known her do that before. Mabel's not that sort of cat. You must have done something to her? What did you do? Stand on her tail? Give her a funny look?' Julia was mocking him now.

'No …the vicious beast just leapt up from nowhere and stuck her claws to my face.' Neil stroked the wound on his injured cheek and scowled at Mabel.

'And when did all of this happen?' Julia poured herself a large glass of wine, from the opened bottle in the fridge.

'It was around lunchtime to … day" He stumbled on the words and corrected himself.' I mean … it was just before you came home this evening.' Neil knew he had just dug himself into a massive hole.

'Ah, at lunchtime was it?' Julia, didn't miss a trick, despite having several drinks inside her.

'No, it was later.' Neil avoided his wife's eyes.

'Neil, do you think I am stupid?'

He thought if Julia hadn't been out with Zoe, this conversation wouldn't be happening. That cow must have been winding her up all night. 'No, why are you asking me that? Of course I don't think you are stupid.'

'Neil. You haven't been at work today have you? You haven't been anywhere near the place for the last couple of weeks have you?' Julia walked slowly towards him. She was now alarmingly, right in front of his face and giving him a Spanish Inquisition. He imagined her with a big gold cross, long red robe and a witch's hat.

'Well I …' Neil felt checkmate was fast approaching and he floundered for a get out.

'No more lies Neil. You promised me. 'Julia's voice was becoming more loud and shrill.

Neil had never known Julia raise her voice like that before. 'Yes, you're right. It's Charles he's … he's erm' Neil tried to find a plausible explanation,

'He's sacked you hasn't he?' The words just tripped so well off Julia's tongue, like the easily remembered lyrics of an irritating song.

'Well, not exactly.' Neil mumbled.

'And why has he done that? He's your friend … and the success of that business is down to you isn't it? So why in God's name would he sack you?' Julia's voice was once more gathering decibels.

'It's just a temporary misunderstanding over…'

Julia interrupted him and cut to the chase. 'Yes? This is about money isn't it?'

'Well, erm.' But Neil was still hoping to find an escape from her interrogation.

'This is about you and money. Have you been stealing money from Charles, Neil? That's fraud you know.' Finally, she'd hit the nail straight on the head.

'I only borrowed it Julia. I swear I haven't stolen. Not really. You have to believe me.' For he had meant to pay it all back, the next time he got lucky.

'Neil, are the police involved? This is a criminal offence you've committed. Please tell me we aren't awaiting a knock on the door.' Julia peered out onto the street where thankfully she could see no police cars.

'No, of course not.' Neil looked uneasy, as this was a real possibility he had been trying to push to the back of his mind.

'That's something I suppose.' Julia bit on her fingernails. 'Neil there is absolutely no reason for us to have money troubles but we do – don't we? And I think I can guess the reason –can't I?'

'But Julia, you know I never go to the casinos. I promised I wouldn't … and I have kept to my word.' Neil was telling the truth as he hadn't actually been inside a casino for years.

'In that case let's go upstairs.' Julia suggested in a matter of fact way. Really, thought Neil. He heaved a massive sigh of relief, Julia wanted to make things up in the bedroom. A most unexpected and favourable turn of events.

'Well of course.' He hadn't seen things going this way. He was half expecting her to throw him out and him having to spend a night in the old shed in the garden.

'You will open up your lap top and I want to see its history. Now.' No doubt the conversation had not yet run its course.

Two Weeks Earlier

Charles

Once Obadiah had finally gone, Charles was left sitting on his chair feeling bereft and wondering whatever he should do for the best. Obadiah's viewpoint was transparent; there was only one action to be taken to punish such duplicity. The man had hung around for ages, despite his company being obviously not wanted and Charles' not so subtle attempts to make him leave. Hoping to witness the arrival of the police, see retribution delivered and Neil arrested, Obadiah was itching to harvest his pound of flesh. His eagerness was both unsettling and repugnant in equal measures. Charles wished he could have dealt with the matter in a different way, but even he couldn't have predicted the treachery and the enormous sum of money involved.

Charles watched Judas, through the window in his office, in the showroom. Seemingly, without a care in the world, Neil was laughing and joking with Tracy. It was clear there was an easy rapport between the both of them. Neil was the type of person most people liked, both men and women. So, why Obadiah had such a downer on him was somewhat of a mystery. Tracy was clearly enjoying flirting with him and she was flicking her hair over her shoulders, as she was wont to do, when finding the person she was talking to attractive. In a few moments, Neil's world would come crashing right down. And despite all, Charles was dreading this looming, awkward conversation.

Charles opened his office door and called out.' Neil, could I just speak with you for a moment?' Charles was reluctant to break up the playful banter between the two of them.
'Yes of course, Charles. Is everything all right?' Neil was all smiles, as he breezed into the room.
'Sit down. I don't know if you noticed the visitor I had in with me just before.' Neil stretched out his legs and made himself comfortable.
'Oh yes. Obadiah isn't that his name? If I recall correctly. We met him at the golf club a few weeks ago, didn't we? Very strange sense of humour I remember.' Neil laughed,

bringing to mind the funny joke he had told and how that Obadiah had got completely the wrong end of the stick.

'Yes, well he's an accountant.' Charles said the words pointedly and Neil had his first inkling that something might be amiss.

'Very good … I believe there's plenty of money to be made in that line of business.' Neil wondered *why* Charles wanted a conversation with him about this Jewish accountant.

'Neil, is everything all right with you? I mean is everything tickety boo with you and Julia?' Charles looked very serious and Neil was becoming increasingly concerned.

'Yes, I think so. Why?' He wondered if Julia been complaining about him to Charles's wife Pamela?

'Well, when Mr Goldstein was looking through the accounts he found some …' Charles cleared his throat, 'He found some anomalies.'

'And you're telling me this because?' Neil was feeling increasingly hot and bothered. Beads of sweat were forming on his forehead.

'Neil do you know anything about an *expenses account*?' Charles over- stressed his consonants,

'I don't think so.' Neil couldn't meet his eye.

'But you see Neil, it has to be you that's set up this account. There's no one else could possibly have access.' Charles watched his long-time friend and wondered how he would react to this.

'Ah yes …' Neil looked up, as if he were plucking a recollection from the ceiling. 'I think when I have taken clients out for dinner, had to stay over in hotels … that sort of thing. I think I may have used an account I set up for such trivial matters.' He made a swish with his hand so to emphasise its inconsequence.

'Neil. I'm the only one who should be able to set up accounts such as this. You didn't even consult me.' Charles was becoming annoyed by Neil's attempts to worm his way out, even when there was clearly no exit available.

'Well Charles, I didn't think you would mind. It was only for the odd meal or so…' Neil was still trying to fob him off.

'Neil, you must have been eating some very lavish meals.'

Neil's feeble attempt at a smile failed to reach each of his terrified eyes .'Well you know how it is when you want to clinch a deal.' Neil cracked his knuckles.

'Bollocks.' Charles's face was now purple, he felt a pulse throbbing at his temple and he banged his fists on the table in fury. 'Do you have any idea of the sum of money I am talking about?'

'Charles … I can explain. I was going to pay it back. I promise.' A frightened Neil had now at last changed his tune.

'And exactly how do you propose to do that? I know you are good at selling houses but Jesus …' What exactly had this man spent all the money on? Even a heroin addict, with an acquired taste for luxury, couldn't have squandered all this. Neil simply beggared belief.

'Charles. I'm sorry. You will get your money back.' Neil was practically on his knees.

'Just go Neil. I can't bear to see your face.' Charles needed to collect his thoughts. Perhaps a long spell inside was just what the stupid man needed.

'Shall I see you tomorrow?'

Charles starred at him aghast at his very gall. 'No, Neil from this moment … you are sacked. Clear your belongings on your way out.' Charles pointed at the door. Twice in one morning, having to evict someone from his office, was not a usual event.

'But what will I tell Julia?'

He had never noticed the self- pitying whine in his former friend's voice before. 'You can tell her what you bloody like'. Charles was just wondering *if* and *what* to tell the police, but refrained from saying this out loud.

Chapter 13

Twenty Five Years Earlier

Julia

When Julia awoke, she found herself lying on the sofa in her living room. Her head hurt and she tried to remember the events of the previous day. Of course, she was still wearing her wedding dress, which was now torn and had yellowy brown stains of vomit down the front. Yesterday, had been her wedding day but something quite clearly wasn't right. What could have happened? She tried to piece together the events of the previous day.

There had been the disappointing wedding ceremony, when that awful child had screamed all through the proceedings. Then, Trevor had taken her for fish and chips. Imagine, fish and chips for your wedding breakfast! She had started to see him in a new light. No longer, the suitor who hung on her every word; he had practically ignored her throughout the whole day. What had she done? Images of a rude waitress with yellow hair, unappetising, greasy food, a dirty, gingham tablecloth and Trevor in his cheap suit, floated through her mind. For that matter where was Trevor, her husband? Also, why was she on the sofa and not in their marital bed?

As she moved to sit upright, not only did her head ache but her whole body hurt. It was as if all her limbs were made from lead. She tried to stay still and think what had happened when they got back home. When she looked to the table in front of her, she spotted a yellow beaker and an empty bottle. The label on the bottle revealed its contents to be Cava. Oh yes, recollections of a nasty tasting fizzy drink returned to haunt her and she was promptly sick once more. This time the contents of her stomach emptied themselves onto the cream sofa and she heard a noise, as Trevor appeared in the doorway.

'Oh, so we are finally back in the land of the living are we? Well, I hope you are pleased with yourself.' Trevor watched her with distaste, as if she were something nasty that had crawled out from under a stone.

'Trevor what happened? Why have I spent the night on the couch?' Julia just wished her husband would give her a hug and assure her that everything was all right.
'Because my dear wife, you have at last revealed your true colours haven't you?' He almost spat out the words.
'What do you mean? What have I done?' Julia pulled her sicky, sticky fingers through her matted hair.
'Well, it's a good thing you kept your drunken behaviour to yourself. Believe me, if I knew what you were really like … well, there's no way I would have married you.' Trevor exercised his moral high ground, from an upright dining chair.
'What did I do?' Julia remembered having a first drink and feeling on cloud nine. Then everything became fuzzy and unclear, as if she were a person with bad eyesight whose glasses had been lost.
'You really can't remember can you?' Trevor sneered and curled his lip at her.' Well I thought to mark the occasion, I would buy a bottle of champagne for you. As a little treat for my new wife.' His voice took on a needling tone. 'Having no idea the effect it would have on you. You just kept drinking and drinking until …well, take a long look at yourself in the mirror. Even now, you disgust me. Take a long look and see for yourself, the revolting creature I've had the misfortune to have married.'
Julia observed her sorry reflection in the mirror over the mantelpiece. Her face was so white it was almost green, her eyes had dark black rings beneath them and she frankly looked like a ghoul.
'I'm so sorry Trevor. Please forgive me.' Never before, not even when her parents had just died, had Julia felt so utterly wretched.
'Can you ever forgive yourself though? For spoiling our wedding day.'
Julia shook her head and a sorry tear trickled down her cheek.
'I will never be able to see you in the same light again.' He continued. 'Now, I suggest that you go and take a shower because you stink.' As Julia slunk out of the room, Trevor had to supress a little smile. Even he hadn't imagined events going so perfectly to plan.

The Present

Julia

Really, she ought to have guessed how Neil had been occupying the copious hours in his man cave. The amount of time he spent there was in itself highly suspicious. However, it was only very rarely that she ventured inside because she just couldn't stand the awful stale cigar smell. Her husband's lair reminded her of an unsavoury nightclub complete with its tacky posters, tasteless cocktail glasses and brash music from the 1980's. In Neil's head, he was still the man about town in his early twenties. Perhaps, he needed a light placed next to his full length mirror, for a more truthful reflection of what he had become of late. Qualities that had once seemed so endearing in her husband, were now more than a little pathetic.

For the past couple of years, she had just been relieved that he had stopped sloping off to those gambling dens of iniquity during ungodly hours of the night. Times when she had been left unable to sleep, worrying herself sick and then felt totally exhausted at school the next day. She had just felt relieved to know he was safely ensconced in his room close by. She had never really given much thought as to what he was doing. Ignorantly, she had presumed him to be content with his loud music, vile cigars and bottles of whiskey. Not for the first time in her life, Julia felt totally stupid, for leopards, as she well knew from bitter experience, never really changed their spots.

As Neil had sheepishly opened up his laptop and went back into his history, there was all the evidence like the insides of a pickpocket's purse. Casino Royale had been repeatedly visited today, last week and from as far back as his computer could reveal. Seemingly, Neil was loyale to the Casino Royale, when considering whose pockets he should generously line. There were plenty of other similar sites he could have visited, but no, Neil was nothing if not a creature of habit. Not for the first time that night Julia felt sick.

And when she asked as to how much money he had actually gambled away, he simply shrugged as if she had asked him a random question in a game of Trivial Pursuit. Julia felt even more furious, when it transpired it wasn't that he didn't want to tell her, but that he had simply lost count.

After having shared his burden, Neil was now sleeping like a baby in their bedroom. She could hear his snores reverberating from the next room, as if he didn't have a care in the world. Meanwhile, Julia was pouring over bank statements and the unopened mail that she had found stuffed into a drawer. Obviously, Neil had decided if the letters weren't opened, then they didn't really exist. How were they going to get themselves out of this mess? Now she realised why Neil had been so delighted about the prospect of the new road being built and the money from the council. Not that the figure would tackle much more than the tip of the iceberg, but it would provide a temporary reprieve at least.

However, Neil had no idea of what Julia had done and stirring that hornet's nest, would soon have the police dancing on their doorstep far more quickly than any allegations from Charles Lavender.

Charles

After his son's second day at OakElmAsh Residentials, Charles was in a belligerent mood, which was further compounded by Pamela producing a paltry, ham salad for his evening meal. He tossed the lettuce around on his plate and eyed the slices of cucumber with contempt. All day, he had spent pacifying angry customers, who had been dissatisfied with the service that had been provided by his son. As Tracy appeared repeatedly at his office door, to inform him of yet another unhappy individual, she wore her decidedly smug look with relish. It was like the most awful Groundhog Day imaginable.

Max had given the clients not only the wrong information, but also incorrect prices, and one elderly couple had even been shown the completely wrong property. To which of course he had no key. As a result two disgruntled pensioners, had been forced to stand for an hour in the rain, until they were dripping wet and hopping with rage. Meanwhile, Max had attempted to explain to the baffled owner, why three random people had come inexplicably to look round his home. At the end of the day, Charles was exhausted and he glared at his incompetent son who was toying with his food in a similarly disappointed manner. A stony silence hovered about the room, which came eventually to rest on Pamela's uncomfortable shoulders.

'Well is everyone enjoying their dinner?' Pamela's question was followed by a nervous, tinkly laugh.

'What do you think?' Charles' eyes glared like hot coals from beneath his corrugated forehead.

'Well I just thought as it was such a … lovely evening that we would have a salad for a change.' Pamela forced a smile and looked through the window onto the street where at that moment it was blowing a gale.

'There's nothing lovely about this evening is there? It's November, dark, cold … and after the day I've had, well I was expecting more than this rabbit food for my meal.' He harpooned a rolled-up piece of ham and shoved it half-heartedly into his mouth.

'What about you Max? What sort of a day have you had?' Pamela asked her son, who ignored the question and kept his eyes glued to his plate.

'Don't even begin to answer that one.' Charles slammed his knife and fork down on the table, to enable him to wag his finger aggressively at his useless son.' I've had to spend all day sorting your incompetent son's messes – all day!' He scowled at his wife as if the production of the faulty offspring was all her doing. 'I mean, how difficult is it… to take customers to the right property Max?'

'I'm sorry.' Max just wanted the meal to be over so he could retreat upstairs to the sanctity of his room.

'Just don't speak to me. I've had more than enough of your useless babble and its consequences today. Best thing you can do is bloody shut up.' Charles placed his knife and fork together, in the centre of the beastly meal, to show he'd eaten all he was going to.

'Charles, there's no need for swearing. Leave the poor lad alone.' Pamela wished for once, they could all just have a pleasant conversation together.

'And you can keep your gob shut too, woman.

'Pamela must have been expecting a reply of this nature, for Charles hated to be contradicted, especially by her.

'Well, Charles, you were the one who sacked Neil.'

Charles was astounded. Pamela must have been feeling particularly brave that evening. Charles wouldn't have been at all surprised, if the bloody chlorophyll in the lettuce hadn't given her gumption like it did to rabbits. The stupid ones who scampered across roads to be knocked over, after a belly full of grass.

She then twitched her nose and continued, 'I'm sure all of this would have been avoided if Neil had been there to show our poor Max what to …'

'Don't even go there. I can't bear to hear that man's name. 'Charles stood up to his full six feet, as if confronting the perfidious Neil once more. Yet there still remained a part of him that wished matters could have ended differently. He had given his friend so many get out clauses but all to no avail and once Obadiah had become involved … well the issue was then taken completely out of his hands.

As Pamela scuttled out of the room, he shouted after her, 'Now there had better be some decent pudding with custard to follow that.'

And eventually Pamela appeared once more from the kitchen bearing the unwelcome gifts of three fresh fruit salads. She announced, 'Sorry I didn't buy any cream.' As she placed the unappetising offerings on the table Charles wondered what time the fish and chip shop closed.

The Next Day

Pamela

Understandably, Pamela was feeling disappointed by the reaction to the healthy option she had prepared for last night 's meal and thought she had better to return to some less controversial food for this evening's choice. Pork chops were a tradition on Wednesdays, so a trip to the supermarket would be needed.

The morning had been largely taken up with her usual housewifery tasks of hovering, dusting and cleaning. She loved the fact that now both of her boys were away at work, she had the place to herself. Much as she loved Max, it was a relief not to feel the aura of his gloom seeping from his bedroom and cramping her style. Pamela wafted contentedly through the house, listening to the radio. She was singing along in her rasping off-key voice, with some of the songs that she knew. Soon, all the surfaces were shining, dust obliterated and carpets vacuumed until pristine . Pamela smiled, made herself a coffee and opened the new jigsaw puzzle of Alnwick Castle that had arrived through the post yesterday. As she opened the box, she felt a familiar flurry of excitement, from the smell of the virgin pieces itching to be interlocked and the fortress waiting to be conquered.

Once Pamela had completed the outside edge, she realised the time was now nearly two o' clock and she needed to pay that visit to the shops. So, she went upstairs, and noticing the persistent rainfall outside, noted that an outfit to banish the weather blues was called for. She selected a primrose coloured dress with little lilac flowers and a Princess Diana ruffle round the neck. This would sit well with her long cream mackintosh and the shoes with the smart bows on the front. Pamela had been taught by her own mother that it was important to dress carefully for any occasion and a trip to the supermarket fell snugly into the shopping-attire category. She wouldn't dream of patronising the sort of establishment where the patrons rocked up to shop still wearing their pyjamas. Heaven forbid. Pamela appraised her appearance in the mirror favourably, before picking up her car keys and leaving the house.

Driving along the High Street, in the silver Toyota Yaris her husband had bought her last year as a birthday gift, she headed down to the Team Valley trading estate. She was looking forward to returning to her puzzle. Imagining that completing those crenulation's would prove a particularly satisfying challenge , she pulled into the Sainsbury's car park. Walking towards the main door, she spotted a familiar figure. It was Julia, with a full trolley laden with groceries including several bottles of wine. Pamela wondered why she wasn't at school, as it wasn't yet three o' clock.

'Julia. How lovely to see you.' Pamela trilled across the car park, to catch her attention

'Oh hello Pamela. How are you?' Julia looked at first, as if she was trying to pretend she hadn't heard or seen her but realised that Pamela's loud voice and strident, yellow attire were pretty impossible to miss.

'I've just come to do a little shopping.' Pamela fussed with her neckline, so the ruffle sat smoothly on the collar of her mac. 'If you don't mind me asking why aren't you at school?' Pamela posed bluntly, wondering if Julia was so upset by her husband's lack of a job, that she had been forced to take time off school.

'Oh it's Wednesday afternoons. It's my PPA time.' She answered in annoying code, as if she was talking to one of her teacher friends.

'Oh that's nice.' Pamela clearly had no idea what she was talking about.

'It means planning, preparation and assessment. When I get to do my marking and other stuff.' Julia explained condescendingly, as if Pamela was one of her wretched pupils.

Pamela continued to smile vacantly, clearly none the wiser. If this was how Julia introduced new information in lessons, she was obviously not passing muster. 'How's Neil doing?' Pamela asked.

'He's fine … thanks Pamela. 'Julia checked her watch, looking very uncomfortable. ' Look Pamela, I really need to get going ….'

'I'm so sorry about what happened.' Pamela searched Julia's face for clues.' I don't know what could possibly have happened between them but I'm sure Charles will soon see sense. I mean him and Neil have been friends for years. I'm sure that soon … '

'What are you talking about Pamela?' There was no way, Julia was thinking, that this nosey parker was going to get her salacious gossip fix from her.

'Well, about Charles sacking Neil.' Pamela persisted, hoping for some clarification.

'Neil left … he wasn't sacked.' Julia couldn't hide the look of contempt for this woman from her face.

‘Oh that’s not what I understood had happened.’ Pamela was now confused, Charles had given her distinct impression he had been forced to sack Neil, and she was desperate to find out why.

‘No, I think Neil just thought he had outgrown OakElmAsh. I think he has bigger … aspirations.’

Pamela was convinced that Julia wasn’t telling the truth and was probably just embarrassed by whatever had transpired between their husbands. She could see Julia was trying to make her escape, as she edged her trolley in the direction of her own car.

‘And I for one am hoping he’ll return soon.’ Pamela didn’t want Julia to slip through the net with so many questions she needed answers to. ‘You know poor Max has been really thrown in the deep end …’

‘Well I’m sorry about that but I must fly. Bye bye Pamela.’ And Julia started to run.

‘Bye Julia. Was lovely to see you …’ But Julia was already in her car, driving away and soon to be a speck on the horizon.

Chapter 14

Twenty- Five Years Earlier

Trevor

As Julia slunk out of the room, Trevor had been delighted. It was as if the script he had written had been executed with such precision, that the performance deserved an Oscar. Now that the charade of a wedding was over, Trevor thankfully no longer needed to pretend. After his wife's sorry performance last night, his role as the protagonist in this matrimonial drama was finalised.

From the moment she stepped off the bus, wearing that horrible dress and simpering smile, any respect he had for her had just flown out of the window. What sort of a woman would agree to wear that tatty pillowcase of a dress disaster for their wedding? Who would spoil their sorry ensemble further, by attaching to the hemline, half of an old table cloth in big red stitches? Was the sad cow really so blinded by love, that she couldn't see her own ridiculous reflection? Yet the costume was quite fitting for their soon-to-be sham of a wedding. Nevertheless, Trevor was pleased that his mother couldn't witness his pathetic specimen of a bride or pantomime of a wedding.

The perfect congregation for their nightmare nuptials, had been provided brilliantly by the choice of witnesses. Even Julia didn't look quite so hideous when compared with that obese couple with their rough Geordie accents and terrible clothes. In fact, the woman with her short maroon dress and matching fat corned beef legs, made the ideal bridesmaid for his new spouse. And the musical backtrack, supplied by the persistent bawling of the son was the additional icing on the cake.

While Julia had watched him all dewy-eyed in the café, Trevor had pretended not to notice. He was further amused and repulsed by the mutton-dressed-as-lamb waitress. The old peroxide tart had attempted to flirt with him as he tucked into his fish and chips. After all those dreadful meals prepared by Julia over the past few weeks, this food was indeed a rare treat.

Soon he thought, it would be time for Julia to be confronted with a few more unpleasant home truths. Trevor shuddered as he thought of his wife's naked body in the shower. He hoped the water was boiling hot and that she was trying hard scrub away all of her evil. Then he imagined her as a stone cold statue and that in his hand he held a chisel. Once Trevor made it plain that the slop she served him as meals was almost inedible and that he knew they were just ready meals, she would be gutted. With the chisel he tapped away a piece of the rock. When he told her that their house was as filthy and untidy as a pig sty she would be ashamed of her slovenly ways. Next he cut away a portion of her leg.

After the drunken slut exhibition she had made of herself last night, she would realise that there was no way he could have find her attractive last night or ever. Any bedroom shenanigans would be thankfully out of the question, so the removal of himself to the spare room would be completely justifiable. Next, Trevor removed a chunk of her brain and his lips curled upwards. Very quickly, Julia would recognise herself as an incomplete woman and total failure of a wife. She would understandably give up this ludicrous idea of being a teacher. For if she was unable to even fulfil her role as a wife in catering for her husband's simple needs, how could she possibly be left in charge of a class of children?

Once Trevor realised that the shower had stopped running, his mind clicked back to the present. Shortly a forlorn looking Julia appeared in the doorway, wearing a pink dressing gown and a miserable face.

'I expect you'll be feeling a lot better after that.' Julia nodded and slumped down on the sick stained couch. 'What about a nice hot drink? Can I get one for you?' Trevor resurrected one of his old smiles for a brief visitation.

Julia's face brightened, imagining that things might not be as awful as she had imagined. Trevor disappeared into the kitchen and looked in the cupboard. 'What about a nice mug of hot chocolate?'

'Yes please.'

Trevor could hear noise from the television and Julia had obviously put one of her annoying programmes on. As the kettle came to boil, Trevor heaped two large spoonful's of chocolate from the tin and poured in the water. Then, stepping on his tip toes he reached for packet of powder from the back of the top shelf. Before he took the drink through to his wife, he sprinkled a generous amount into her cup. She wouldn't be watching that programme for long, he thought with some satisfaction.

The Present Day

Zoe

Zoe looked at the clock. How could it only have been quarter past two? This afternoon was stretching into eternity. She swore if the minute hand moved any slower, it would be going backwards. Since the meeting with Julia last night, there were a thousand questions she wanted to ask her friend. Unfortunately, Zoe had been stuck in traffic and it was about time the council built that bloody bypass. She had only just made it to school on time this morning and Wednesday was the day she ran the lunchtime chess club. So there was that been no available opportunity for her to speak with Julia until the end of the day. Suddenly her eyes were alerted to a rubber flying across the room and hitting the side of a girl's head before landing on the floor.

'Aaaargh.' Screeched Amelia , 'It was Cameron. Miss … Cameron chucked the …'

'It wasn't me Miss.'

Quite obviously the rubber had come from Cameron's direction, despite the look of mock innocence on his face.

'Get out Cameron.' It was definitely him. He was always throwing things, if he thought no one was looking.

'But Miss I didn't …' Cameron protested.

'My head hurts' Wailed Amelia, 'I'm gonna tell my Mam.'

'I saw him.' Henry was the sort of boy you could rely upon to tell the truth.

'Just get out and stand in the corridor.' Zoe wasn't putting up with any more nonsense.

'Amelia, calm down. Do you need to see a first aider?'

Amelia shook her head and rubbed it, as the surly boy scraped his feet across the classroom floor, muttering about unfairness, before slamming the door. And so, the afternoon continued. Zoe watched and saw that out of twenty four pairs of eyes, only six seemed to be on task. The rest were either gazing out of the window, fiddling with their pencil cases or looking around the classroom for ways to make mischief. This class, honestly, it was like sitting on a time bomb. If you took your eyes off them for one second, all hell broke loose.

Eventually, quarter past three arrived and the children bolted out of the door, closely followed by their teacher. Just before she barged into the Year 4 classroom, she noticed that Julia was speaking to a mother and Emily was shaking her head at her through the door window. It was Charlie's mum, the one whose gran had just died. Julia had her back to the door, so Zoe couldn't see her face but she was deep in sympathetic conversation with the bereaved mother.

Once the meeting was over, Julia followed Mrs Stevenson to the door and only then could Zoe see the tell-tale dark shadows beneath her friend's eyes. Clearly, Julia hadn't slept much last night and had struggled to get through the day. Waiting for Emily to leave, Zoe sat down at a desk and flicked through a child's English book feigning to show some interest. Emily could obviously sense something was amiss and seemed reluctant to leave. As she sharpened some pencils, the three women sat in stony silence, until Emily picked up her belongings and headed for the staffroom.

Immediately, Zoe jumped out of her seat. 'Well, was it what we thought? Has Neil been gambling on line? Has he stolen money from his boss.'

'Yes to all three I'm afraid.' Julia's eyes filled with enough tears to make a small pond.

'Oh my God … how bad is it? Zoe realised the problem was clearly far more serious than she had thought.

'Very. Much worse than I could've possibly imagined.' Never had Zoe before, seen such despair on her friend's face.

'How much money are we talking here?' Julia had a decent job. Surely if worse came to the worse she could take out a bank loan.

'Oh, Zoe. You really don't want to know.' Obviously not thinking straight, Julia began chewing on a pencil which had probably been in some child's mouth earlier that day. Zoe thought it best not to mention this. 'I'm sorry, I'm not in a position to lend …' Zoe's bank account was perpetually overdrawn from one pay day to the next.

'It's all right Zoe. A few hundred wouldn't make much difference anyway…' Julia's cheeks now had black spider's legs trickles, on them from where her mascara had run.

'Julia how much money do you owe?' Zoe was curious to know.

She didn't answer the question, 'Yes that's the thing with bloody marriage. It's not just Neil's problem. It's my problem too.' She attempted to wipe the black wet smudges from round her eyes but just made them worse.

'Julia. You'll get through this. I mean it's only money isn't it? Really … what's the worst that could happen?' Zoe knew that Julia had overcome troubles before and if anyone could handle this mess, it was her.

'Prison, I suppose.' Julia said bleakly.

Zoe gulped. 'Well, maybe for your thieving husband. Perhaps a spell inside wouldn't do him any harm. Open his eyes up to the real world. Julia, you'll deal with this. I know you will. She held her friend's hand. 'Julia, you can get through anything. I mean after what you went through with Trevor ...'

'This is nothing like that.' Julia, like seasoned politician book, quickly changed the topic of conversation. 'Anyway there may be a way out.'

'Really?' This should be interesting thought Zoe, because she was sure she couldn't think of one.

'Well, the council are talking about building a new road and they are planning for the route to cut through our garden.' Julia's voice was deadpan, as if this in itself was yet a further obstacle to be dealt with.

'Of course, they'll be some compensation.' Zoe guessed that this must be either a very small amount or the amount of money owed must be colossal, as it seemed to bring Julia no relief whatsoever.

'Yes. They'll give us some compensation. So that will buy us some time with the bank.' Although Julia tried to muster a smile, this new information obviously provided little recompense to rectify the dreadful situation. Zoe had thought to delve a little more into her friend's past with Trevor but now was just not the time. Clearly another visit to the pub was needed and very soon.

Obadiah

It was now two weeks since Obadiah had completed his auditing at OakElmAsh but there were certain matters that he just couldn't get out of his head. Now, he was working on the accounts of the Rosenberg Kosher Bakery, from just across the road from where he lived. This was all pretty routine auditing, and everything, much as he would expect, was in order. Having had a taste of excitement he was finding it difficult to concentrate on meagre profits from mundane breads and pastries. Bathsheba, his wife, was busy singing in the kitchen and although she had a pleasant enough voice, her incessant warbling was beginning to grate on him.

Obadiah removed his little round glasses, polished them with the white handkerchief he kept next to the prayer book and menorah candlestick on his desk, before placing them back on his long aquiline nose. Then, he stared at the foreboding portrait of his namesake, the first Obadiah Goldstein. This hung purposefully, next to a splendid picture of the city of Jerusalem, hurling the golden spires and domes from its rooftops towards heaven, like Hasidic weapons of retaliation.

His grandfather Obadiah, had died in tragic circumstances just two days before Obadiah grandson, had been born. As the television aerial had been faulty and spoiling the family viewings of Family Fortunes, Bull's Eye and Blankety Blank, the intrepid grandfather, Obadiah had ventured out of the window to fix it. Unfortunately, this was during a thunderstorm and the screening of an old episode of 'The Golden Shot'. After the slick but smarmy Bob Monkhouse had listened to the current contestant's instructions of 'down a bit, left a bit', on the came the order of 'fire'. And on this particular occasion it was accompanied by an almighty clap of thunder, followed by an enormous flash of lightning. The shocked family Goldstein heard a piercing scream and watched in horror as Obadiah's body fell past the window to land in a crumpled heap on the pavement.

As the late Obadiah Goldstein had met his unfortunate end on a Saturday, neighbours drew their own conclusions as to why this had happened. There were whispers of divine retribution. However, never again within the community, was tampering with the television aerials on the Sabbath openly mentioned. Nevertheless, quite often when Solomon walked along Coatsworth Road, he was almost certain he heard mutterings of 'It's a hit' or 'Bernie get your bolt'.

x 2

Obadiah the elder's steely gaze watched him from within the frame as if in warning, and Obadiah the younger returned to the sale of bagels. Yet persistently, images of the smug Neil, his inappropriate jokes and heinous crime would not leave him alone.
Persistently, he had searched online and listened to the news for the mention of Neil Latimer's arrest, but there had been nothing. Surely by now, Charles Lavender must have reported the shocking embezzlement to the police and if not, why not? Obadiah was chomping at the bit for further involvement in the case and he felt as if he were Inspector Morse in his favourite crime programme. Misdemeanours of this nature, needed to be punished, and by gathering momentum from the message proclaimed by the nearby Jerusalem painting and the unfortunate demise of his grandfather, he girded up his loins to make a phone call to Charles Lavender. Obadiah sat bolt upright in his seat to metamorphosis into an avenging angel of retribution.

Max

While sitting in his bedroom after another beastly day at work, Max was feeling extremely sorry for himself. It just wasn't fair. He hated the job, his dad, and his life. Just because the company belonged to his father, there was absolutely no reason why he should have any aptitude or interest in selling houses. It obviously wasn't a trait that the Lavender gene pool had been generous enough to share with him, but then the flowing sales patter was also lacking. Yet, it was all within the forte of the mysteriously absent Neil. Closing deals was nothing that the bully Charles Lavender could take any credit for and Max felt like a rogue piece from one of his mother's wretched jigsaws that had been shoved in the wrong puzzle box.

Max had never been particularly fond of the smooth-talking Neil, who seemed to have an uncanny chameleon-like ability to adapt his manner to whatever the occasion or company. He could flatter and flirt with an unnerving ease, any women from giggling teenager girls to simpering octogenarian widows. Likewise, his amusing delivery of anecdotes and jokes made him 'one of the lads' and a drinking buddy to prop up a bar with. In most situations Max became tongue-tied and embarrassed, feeling himself a sorry fish out of water. This opinion was clearly shared by the horrible Tracy, who managed to find time to look down her thickly powdered nose at him, several times a day. This was despite him being a good foot taller than her. Nevertheless, he had been giving the job his best. Granted, in three days he had made no sales whatsoever, or had any potential buyers wishing to arrange a second viewing. But at least he had managed mostly to find the correct locations of the properties and today he had only been late twice. Not that his father appreciated any of this.

A peevish Max logged on to his computer, to check out his Facebook page. He had 2,345 friends, although only about six of these that he actually knew in person and only Nigel who was truly any more than at best an acquaintance. Some Lucy Phillips in a leopard print jumpsuit had been having a drunken night out in Manchester with the girls. An Oscar Gordon was bestriding his new red Harley Davison motorbike, clad in a peculiar fetish-like leather ensemble, in which he resembled Spiderman. And a Toby Mackintosh was in Thailand. Grinning Toby, with his bright carrot hair and badly burnt skin, was posing with his surfboard on a golden beach in Phuket. The cloudless sky was the most bewitching blue Max had ever seen and the seductive sea beckoned him. Outside his window, what had been dull grey all day was now a smothering black blanket of darkness. Max sighed.

On top of the wardrobe, Max spotted his old skateboard. He remembered when Nigel and he had tried to hang out with the cool boys in Exhibition Park at the weekends. He had spent hours in front of the mirror perfecting his sulk and hacked at his new jeans with his mother's bread knife for the obligatory rips, but all to no avail. Although, they sported their matching menacing hoodies emblazoned with skulls, their tentative wobbles round the concourse were met largely with sniggers and disparaging stares. Then, when Nigel's oscillations had finally resulted in the indignity of him tumbling awkwardly from his board, an inglorious visit to the Royal Infirmary was required. A twisted ankle was pronounced and heralded the end of their skater-boy days.

However, this sorry demise had been Nigel's fault not Max's. If he had persevered, who knows how different his life might have been. A skateboard wasn't that much different to a surf board and he looked once more with envy at the post from the ginger Toby. Max had dark brown wavy hair and his skin always tanned with ease, much to the annoyance of Pamela who had liked to fuss over him with her expensive, unnecessary sun creams while on family holidays. With little difficulty, Max imagined himself as the golden beach boy in Phuket. He pictured himself riding the waves with his toned physique and muscles rippling in the waves. Max, flanked by two beautiful girls, all three baring sparkling white teeth. His post on face book would show Toby bloody Mackintosh a thing or two, and he began researching the price of flights.

Charles

Earlier that day, after dealing with yet another phone call complaining about his son's complete incompetence and total rudeness, Charles Lavender wasn't feeling in the finest of fettles. What was wrong with the lad? All he had to do was put the post code into the SatNav and follow its directions. It was hardly rocket science. Why did it seem to take him so long to find these properties? Also, there was even a script for him to follow, prepared by the ever efficient Tracy, outlining which features best to emphasise and those which to avoid. Obviously, if the house had an ancient central heating system and needed double glazing, this was not best drawn attention to. Yet, the numerous phone calls, from people voicing their displeasure at being shown such awful houses, with so many glaring faults highlighted the fact that his idiot son must have been doing so.

All he had to do was add in the odd, effusive adjective and superfluous adverb to his estate agent spiel. Surely, his expensive schooling had provided with at least the basics of an English education. Neil was hardly the fizziest can of pop in the fridge but even he was able master these essentials. Although he wasn't the brightest of men, it had to be admitted that he did possess that savvy manner of a cockney wide boy. He clinched deals effortlessly, fast and with maximum profit. Charles couldn't deny he had a gift. Charles was loathe admit it, but if it hadn't been for streetwise Neil, his company would most likely be no longer operating. On more than one occasion when close to being butchered by debts, Neil had saved their bacon. Through the past twenty odd years when other estate agents had sprung up and closed, only OakElmAsh had remained as a constant.

Unfortunately though, Neil had demonstrated his stupidity in the very worst way by his complete betrayal. While he had had his suspicions, Charles had always hoped that he was mistaken but when Obadiah Goldstein had exposed the full extent of the fraud … well, he'd had no choice. To count how many times Charles wished that events had not taken this particular turn, would be like keeping a tally of the number of breaths he took in a day. He prayed frequently that he could just turn back the clock and save Neil from himself. For without Neil, he feared all their days were numbered and futures unsecure. Left with these worrying thoughts, once more Charles heard his phone ringing.

Expecting another call of complaint he was surprised to hear Obadiah Goldstein's distinctively nasal voice.

'Good afternoon Mr Lavender. How are you today?' Obadiah enquired casually.

'I'm very well thanks and what can I do for you?' Charles wondered what he wanted as he knew he had paid the man and the transaction had been cleared.

'Well, I was just wondering what had happened with Mr Latimer. You know … after certain matters came to light.'

So in other words Obadiah, was just being nosey, Charles instantly realised. 'I expect you'll be pleased to know that Neil Latimer no longer works here.'

'Well, I would have assumed that but … erm …What else has happened?' The thirst for punishment in Obadiah's voice was repugnant.

'What do you mean Mr Goldstein?' Charles felt weary and much older than his fifty three years.

'Well, I have been listening to the radio and looking on the internet … erm … for some sort of announcement …' Obadiah spoke so matter of factly, as if they were waiting for news about the daily pollen count.

'Announcement! Announcement of what?' This man just took the biscuit.

'Well, considering the sum of money involved … I would have assumed that by now …'

'Mr Goldstein.' Charles cut him dead. 'You can keep your bloody assumptions to yourself. I'm a busy man.'

'So, what did you tell the police?' Obadiah's voice was becoming increasingly snakelike and was now almost hissing.

'Mr Goldstein! I have paid you for your services. Goodbye.' Charles slammed down the phone.

Chapter 15

Thirty Years Earlier

Julia

Dragging her head up from the pillow, Julia looked at her alarm clock with horror, as the time was already quarter to eleven. She looked around the room, at the once pretty but now faded yellow wallpaper, chosen once by her mother, and the threadbare beige carpet, that her father had fitted himself. Her mother had been so pleased with this bedroom all those years ago, when it had been newly decorated and the fancy, new dressing table had arrived, to be kept in pride of place under the window. The once lovely rosewood piece of furniture with its elaborate triptych mirror was now shabby and stained with shoe polish. This was now where Trevor kept his shoes and cleaned them regularly, while sitting on the matching stool whistling and admiring his own reflection in triplicate. The keeping of his footwear here was odd because Trevor kept all of his other belongings next door in his room. But it seemed his shoes, with their untidy appearance and unpleasant odour he liked to keep near to where Julia slept. It was as if they were his way of keeping a watchful eye on her, without having to suffer her company in the bedroom.

Trevor was right, she was lazy and useless. How could she allow herself to lie so long in bed when there was such a lot of work to be done? It was now the middle of August and only a few weeks until the new term would begin at University. How on earth would she be able to cope? It was becoming increasingly unlikely she would ever finish the course which would be no loss to the country's educational system. Julia felt like a slug; a fat lazy bloated creature lying beneath the covers of the bed. She wished someone would put some salt on her tail and be done with it.

She took a sip from her tea, which as usual made her almost gag. Trevor had made it for her half an hour ago and would be up soon she guessed, to see if she had drunk it. Whenever he made her a drink and she neglected to drink it, he was always furious. When Trevor was angry, his face turned a most unpleasant colour and little, clear maggots of sweat trickled down his forehead. This disturbing sight, which was all of her making, was something that she wanted to avoid at all costs. Trevor wasn't a bad tempered person, as he constantly reminded her, but her slovenliness and ingratitude just brought out the worst in him. Julia was sad that she had become such a despicable person. This tea tasted so terrible though, in fact everything she ate and drank just didn't taste right.

Trevor had said it was wasteful to buy the coffee and tea brands that she was used to, as the economy ones were just as good if not better. Julia had always bought the same labels that her parents had, as it was just what she was used to. But as Trevor had wisely pointed out to her, there were some people in the world that didn't even have fresh water to drink and Julia was just behaving like a pampered princess, thinking that she deserved the best. But these drinks, to her they tasted truly dreadful. Trevor had said that it was just her being over pernickety and spoilt, which must be true because he drank the same drinks and never made a fuss.

After Julia had heaved herself out of her bed, as there was work which needed to be done, she pulled on the same clothes she had worn the day before. Trevor said it didn't matter how she dressed, as she had really let herself go and she looked awful in whatever she wore. When he had married her she had been no oil painting but now … she was just hideous. If truth be known, these were the only clothes that still fitted her as her weight had ballooned out of all control. Trevor said to waste food was evil and always made her finish not only her own meal but his as well. If she left anything on the plate, he would scrape it into a bowl and make her eat it on the floor like a dog. This he watched with a curious smile hovering round his lips and despite all, Julia was happy she had in some way pleased him.

Yesterday, after Julia had finished hoovering the room, Trevor had been horrified to find some crisp crumbs behind the sofa and insisted she did the whole room again. Julia noticed a crisp packet sticking out of his trouser pocket but thought better than to mention this. Then he pointed out a greasy mark on the mirror and as he prodded the mirror several times with his smeary finger, so the mirror became completely covered with marks. Obviously none of this made any sense, it was just a manifestation of her nasty nature in doubting her husband and yet a further indication of her worthlessness as a wife and human being.

The Present

Tracy

Tracy was back from the gym and being satisfied with her efforts that evening, she locked the door to her neat little flat with a certain smugness. Her compact lounge/kitchen was painted white and had mirrors in every available space. Tracy always professed that this was to make the small room seem larger, but as she spent an inordinate amount of the time there contemplating her own reflection, they were well used.

That night, she had prepared chicken breast and salad for her evening meal. She wished that she was about to tuck into something a little more substantial, but as it was said,' no pain, no gain', so she took pleasure from her own self-discipline. As she chewed on a mouthful of limp lettuce and bland cucumber, she imagined that her boss would be eating somewhat differently. She thought of Charles's stomach straining unattractively and pulling tight across the buttons of his shirt. When Charles spoke, the skin beneath his chin wobbled and even as winter was approaching he continued to sweat profusely. Such thoughts made Tracy's food seem much more palatable.

That day, Tracy had been very surprised to hear that Jewish accountant's distinctive voice on the phone. As she transferred the call through to Charles, she wondered what his business could be. More than likely, it was something connected to his fee and was requesting more money from her boss. This wouldn't please Mr Lavender, who seemed more than usually hot and bothered. He had been huffing and puffing around like an old-fashioned steam engine. The reason for this to Tracy was no mystery. That son of his was just a liability and the sooner he realised that the better. Since he had come to work there, not one single sale had been made and Tracy was actually becoming fearful for her own job. These were not good times for businesses, in particular estate agents, and with the sizable mortgage she had to pay on her small flat, Tracy could not afford to be out of a job. The sooner Charles saw sense and reinstated Neil, then everyone would be able to sleep more soundly in their beds.

Tracy poured herself a gin and slim line tonic. Well, she deserved it. After all she was only doing what she was doing for the sake of the company. She pulled her laptop out of her bag, placed it on her table and searched for the particular file she needed. This was the one with all the new properties that had come onto their books recently. Ah yes, here it was Cherryburn Gardens, a semi-detached house. It was said to be reasonably priced due to its small overgrown garden and tired decorations. The previous owner was deceased and the vendor was hoping for a quick sale. Tracy began typing 'delightful, well-maintained established garden' and 'tasteful modern furnishings throughout the property'. A smile flickered on her lips as she imagined Max's inept bumblings about the house with his confused viewers. That was if he even found the address. She altered the NE6 Wallsend postcode to that of NE3 which was Gosforth, an entirely different area. Tracy knew she was playing a dangerous game but it was well worth the risks involved.

Julia

After school, Julia was sitting down at the bottom of the garden next to the perturbing flower bed. The roses were now past their best, as it was November. Being late in the day, the shadows falling across the lawn were elongated and the sun was slipping behind the trees like a melting globule of butter. There were still a few tenacious flower heads clinging onto the bushes for dear life. Julia's eyes glazed over, staring at the fading red, pink and yellow rose petals. Her mother had liked the yellow roses best but Julia hated them all because of what they represented. She imagined that Neil thought she was protective of the rose garden, as it brought back cherished memories of her parents. This it did to some degree, but they were overshadowed by other, more sinister recollections.

Now, this wretched road and its proposed route through their garden, had created a problem, that she didn't have the possibility of being able to share with her husband.

When she had arrived home from school, she could hear her husband singing upstairs like a bloody canary. Obviously, as he had unburdened himself the night before, it was as if he didn't have a care in the world. Julia could imagine how the idiot's mind would be working: she would sort out the money; he would soon find another job; if Charles was going to tell the police he would have done so by now and the new road's benefits were the solution to all of their problems. As if.

Still she needed to pull herself together and work out what needed to be done. Once, long ago, she had been in a far worse position than this. Feckless and stupid husband number two Neil might be, but at least he wasn't evil. Snapshots appeared in her mind of the cruelties that Trevor had once inflicted on her. First came the picture of her on her wedding night lying in a vile pool of vomit. Then, she saw her younger self being forced to crawl on the floor like an animal. Finally, there was her first husband, wearing his familiar sneer of contempt like a badge of honour and reminding her just how useless she was. Twenty five years ago, Julia had somehow managed to release herself from this hell. If she had been able to that then, surely there was some way to salvage herself from all this.

Julia ran round to the front of the house, marched across the drive and just carried on walking. Although it was getting dark, she was on a mission. She continued out of her estate and crossed over the main road. Following a path that led into a wood, she continued. It was hard to see, as the light was fading and the trees growing denser. Somewhere near here there had to be just the place she was looking for.

Pamela was cooking the pork chops in a cider sauce : Somerset Pork. She was going to serve the meal with creamy, mashed potatoes, broccoli and savoy cabbage. After last night's disparagement of the salad, she was trying to make something Charles would like but still was quite healthy. There was no way that a suet pudding was on the cards. She shook her head knowingly as she chopped an onion, thinking that despite her husband's belligerent manner, she was fortunate in many ways to have him. It was in Pamela's own interests to keep Charles fit and healthy.

Pamela thankfully never had to worry about getting a job and now her son was grown up, well, she had plenty of free time to do as she pleased. Perhaps she should think of joining some clubs, although quite what she couldn't think. Some of the women she knew seemed to be in book groups, but reading wasn't really her thing. Likewise exercise classes were popular, but she couldn't really see herself prancing around in lycra like an ageing member of Pan's People. Maybe, she and Charles should think about joining a rambling group, but as images of thermos flasks and indecipherable maps flashed through her mind; no both of them would hate that equally.

At least Charles had his golf club, but any exercise there was counter balanced by the copious pints afterwards. In fact jigsaws puzzles were really her only interest and she had never come across clubs relating to these. She supposed a jigsaw club would swop puzzles but she would hate that, you never knew where people's fingers had been. Pamela liked her puzzles new. And gossip, yes she had to admit she enjoyed that. Although Pamela didn't have many close friends, she knew plenty of women who lived locally and depended on her to keep them informed with what was going on. If anybody's marriage was on the rocks, having financial problems or children getting themselves into trouble, Pamela was the *go to* person and it gave her a feeling of power.

After all, she spent a lot of time wandering up and down Low Fell High Street; close by to where she lived. This was a busy place, particularly on a weekend evening with its preponderance of rowdy pubs filled with gangs of young and not so young lads and lasses out for a good time. However, during most daytimes there was just a congenial buzz, as shoppers flitted between the butchers, greengrocers, small supermarkets and shops selling gifts and random bric a brac. This was the perfect place for Pamela to prowl to find both sources and recipients for her tittle-tattle. It was amazing how loudly some people spoke and what information could be gleaned simply by keeping one's ears open. For example, the Taylor household opposite had been in a state of disrepair for years and had been totally letting the street down. Their Christmas decorations, it went without saying, were generally pathetic and had become increasingly so during the last couple of years.

However, just in the last few months, doors had been painted, window frames replaced, an extension added and even a new mobile home appeared out the front. Now, she knew Mr Taylor had lost his job last year, so the source of these home improvements was a matter of great speculation. She had kept asking Charles how they could be affording it but he was indifferent to the subject. However, from keeping her ears peeled, Pamela had heard their twin teenage girls, both with bad acne, boasting how their parents had recently won the lottery. Mystery solved. And well, Pamela, she couldn't believe her luck but had thoroughly enjoyed sharing this juicy knowledge with all and sundry.

This, was why she had been so annoyed when she had bumped into Julia, who she regarded as one of her closest friends, earlier that afternoon. If anyone knew what the reason behind the sacking of Neil was, it was her. Although she had tried her very best, no information was to be disclosed. She could have sworn that at first Julia, had tried to pretend that she hadn't even seen her. Then she had tried to bamboozle her with all that teacher jargon which Pamela had found very rude. But to cap it all, she had denied any knowledge that Neil had been sacked, professing that he had just resigned and got a better job. This was quite clearly lies.

Furthermore, Julia was wearing an unbecoming, puffy, quilt-coat that she had probably been wearing for yard duty that day. Pamela was pleased she didn't have to wear such abominations of clothing. Also, the wind had been blowing her usually dark immaculate bob all over the place, so it looked like a burnt haystack. How Charles could ever have suggested that she dressed better than his wife merely added insult to injury. Pamela was becoming less fond of Julia each time she saw her. She was determined to find out the cause of Neil's sacking but until she did, she could spread a few possible rumours. Pamela popped the casserole into the oven and went back to concentrate on the crenulations of Alnwick Castle.

Charles

Charles was in a quandary, and he just didn't know what to do for the best. He wished that there was somebody he could talk to but there wasn't. Neil had been his only friend really and now look what the Judas had done to him. If he could turn back the clock and speak frankly with him at some earlier date, then all this unfortunate business could possibly have been avoided. What had Neil needed money so desperately for that he had been forced to steal nearly half a million pounds off his employer and more importantly – chum? *That* Obadiah was insistent that the police ought to be involved in the fraud, but hadn't he done enough to his friend already? Although the stolen sum sounded at lot of money, which it was, how many millions had Neil made his company over the years?

If Neil had required that money, then there must be a very good reason. Was Neil on drugs? Well he knew from experience that Neil was fond, as he was himself of a drink or two … but was it more than that? When Neil was clinching deals, he was hyper, animated – almost unnaturally so. He pictured Neil, with his amber eyes glistening like fire and his tail slowly wagging, as if he were an agitated fox about to attack a chicken coup. But maybe this wired state was artificial, because for Neil to be able to do this perhaps he needed pharmaceutical assistance. What if Neil was taking drugs? Heroin? LSD? Cocaine? Charles knew these were very expensive but he himself had never dabbled in drugs – not even as a young man.

But, he had been led to believe that cocaine gave people a feeling of omnipotence. Oh my God, the bloody idiot must have allowed himself to become a cocaine addict. He could easily picture Neil on the floor in the toilet desperately, snorting wadges of the evil, white powder through a rolled up ten pound note into his nose. He recalled recent conversations with his troubled friend to see if he could detect any deterioration in his nostrils. Were they bleeding or rotting?

When Neil had a cold a few months ago hadn't he exhibited a definite reddening around the nostrils? Charles read that this was what happened to cocaine addicts. Poor misguided Neil.

What if Neil was having to pay for cosmetic surgery, that he had been forced to have, to appear normal and continue to sell property with his decaying nose. Charles felt dreadful. He had reduced his friend to this by his stupid motto of "Sales make your Salary". This was all Charles' fault and his mind was turning somersaults.

Somebody else might have found out about Neil's problem and was blackmailing him. Poor Neil, that person could have been have been exhorting money from him for ages and this was the reason for his reckless embezzlements. For all he knew, it might even be somebody who worked here. He looked through into the main showroom and there he saw Tracy with her false laugh and affected mannerisms. She always had plenty to say to Neil didn't she? He knew that he paid her a good salary, but she always had the latest designer clothes didn't she? And he remembered Neil always smiling and full of bonhomie, especially when speaking to her. This had all just been an act. Charles should have recognised earlier that his poor drug-addled, blackmailed, friend needed his help. He pictured Neil of Christmas Past, enjoying festivities on the beach in glorious Florida, Neil of Christmas Present eating a tiny turkey portion in silence with Julia and Neil of Christmas Future, dead under the Tyne Bridge with a syringe lying next to his wasted body. Charles felt his eyes fill with tears.

There was nobody he could talk about this with. He wished he could with his wife, but the silly woman would just broadcast this to everyone as a piece of idle tittle-tattle. Why could that woman not keep her mouth shut? If anyone was a suitable candidate for a scold's bridle it was his wife Pamela. Why couldn't she be more discreet like Julia? Julia – of course. He must speak with her. If anyone knew the truth of the matter it was Julia.

Chapter 16

Julia

When Julia returned from her walk in the wood, she could hear Neil still playing loud music upstairs, and oblivious to her return. She poured herself a glass of wine from an opened bottle in the fridge and sat down at the kitchen table. She had a full bag of marking to be done, but that could wait until later. Mabel was brushing against her legs and walking backwards and forwards, to and from her empty feeding bowl. Julia knew the greedy girl would have plenty to eat already with Neil all day at home, so she ignored her.

Julia was feeling very much all of her forty-seven years, if not more so, and she let her mind drift back to earlier days. She remembered holidays as a child in the Lake District when she and her parents had gone camping. Smiling, she remembered the happy times she had enjoyed there. Her mother had always been laughing and exuded such *joie de vivre*. Whether in the car, or elsewhere, the radio seemed to be perpetually playing and her mother had liked to sing along with all the latest songs. The two of them would sing together whilst her father listened lovingly to his cherished wife and daughter. It seemed the most idyllic childhood.

While in the Lake District, she remembered the weather was perfect every day with the blue skies and beautiful lakes. As they enjoyed long walks around lakes and on mountain footpaths, it seemed like life couldn't be any more halcyon. Then they would come back to the tent and cook sausages, bacon and fried eggs. That was all she could remember eating delicious food, washed down with lashings of milky tea.

She pictured Carol, her mother in tiny yellow shorts, halter-necked tops and floppy hats, looking beautiful. Her dad, Michael in his cheesecloth shirt and flared trousers would be gazing at her in adoration. They were the perfect couple from a Freeman's catalogue. The three of them had been so happy and it seemed so unfair that that cruel accident had stolen them away from her. This family life, had been all she had aspired to, but it was not to be and Julia had remained childless. This had been a blessing regarding her first choice of husband, but her hopes had been high with Neil. Nevertheless, no child had arrived and despite all the previous good times together; their current predicament was disastrous.

Julia caught sight of an envelope on the table. It was from the council and had already been opened. The letter had been left in a prominent position where she couldn't fail to see it. She knew what the contents would confirm – her worst suspicions. As she went to open a can of food for the now, loudly chirruping Mabel, she heard a loud whistling coming down the stairs.

'Hello love, when did you come home?' Neil was looking very pleased with himself.

'Well I came back about an hour ago … but I've been out a walk.' Julia placed the salmon-flavoured cat food into the bowl and Mabel began wolfing it down.

'Why don't we celebrate and get a take-away tonight? I fancy a …'

Neil was cut short by his furious wife. 'Neil stop it! What exactly have we got to celebrate?'

'Well, I thought you might have read that letter on the table there. 'Smug Neil, removed the contents from the envelope. 'They are going to start building the road in two weeks' time and if you look inside there's a cheque for £10,000 pounds.'

'And how much exactly do *you* owe Neil?' Julia knew this to be a mere tip of the iceberg, but that was not what was really freaking her out.

'There's more good news though.' Neil wasn't to have his parade rained upon.

'And what exactly is that?' Good news? How dear God, was the impending road works anything to be happy about?

'I have a job interview lined up for tomorrow.' Even Mabel looked up from her meal in shocked surprise and Neil went to the fridge to pour himself a glass of wine.

How's he pulled that one out of the bag thought Julia. 'What? How have you done that? Surely Charles wouldn't have given you a reference. Anyone in the property world will know all about you and your misdemeanours now. Who in their right mind is going to give you a job?'

‘It‘s not selling property. It’s selling cars and the jobs practically in the bag. Chink, chink.’ He clinked his wine glass with hers.

‘What do you know about selling cars Neil? You’ve never been particularly interested in them. When you turn up for an interview in your clapped out old red Corsa you’ll get laughed out of the showroom.’ Julia’s mind returned once more to the problem of the road and flowerbed.

‘Ah well. You wait and see. I was down the golf club today and I got chatting to an old pal, Geoff Armstrong.’ The Neil of old was back, and twice as large as life.

‘I don’t remember any Geoff Armstrong.’

‘Yes, you must remember him, he’s balding, with a beer gut and drives a pewter BMW. His wife’s about twenty years younger. You know she used to be a model and has a pronounced lisp.’ Julia had no interest in any fat car salesman and his vocally challenged wife.

‘Sounds vaguely familiar, go on anyway … what about him?’

‘Well I told him that Charles and I had recently had a few disagreements and |I had quit my job there. And knowing of my excellent sales reputation, he offered me a job there and then.’ Oh yes, the old boys club, thought Julia but it would take more than this for Neil to come up smelling of even dandelions.

‘I thought you said you had an interview tomorrow. What about references?’ This all sounded wrong, thought Julia, but she had her own problems to solve.

‘I told you … it’s a formality. The job’s mine.’ Neil emptied his drink and slammed the glass on the table.

Max

Max was sitting with his friend Nigel in a dubious pub on Percy Street, in the centre of Newcastle. As loud, heavy metal music was playing on the jukebox, they were having to shout at each other to make themselves heard. Curious red lighting cast a demonic glow across the black and white tiles on the floor, bringing to mind playing chess with the devil in The Seventh Seal film. Two skinheads snarled at each other from across a pool table and it looked as if their game would likely end in a brawl. Two women with big inky-coloured hair and sprayed-on leather pants, shook their heads and went outside for a fag.

The belligerent landlord watched with a look of well-practised contempt. He was rumoured to have a police record, keep a set of knives under the bar counter and had several deep scars on his face. Most of the tables around were occupied by menacing-looking bikers and serious, thrash devotees. Despite their leather jackets and ripped jeans the two lads looked a little out of place.

'You know dude. This property business, it's just not me.' Max complained to his friend, trying to scrape his hair behind his ears.

'Well, I didn't really think it would be.' Nigel nodded sagely, suspecting this would be the case. 'You are too much like me. We're just free spirits, you know.'

'Yeah, but Nige, you can't believe how awful it is …' Max had big rings under his eyes, as if he hadn't been sleeping.

'Hey Maxi … can you believe that my dad wants me to go work in his business … if I don't sort myself out by Christmas.' Nigel looked aghast at the thought.

'Don't do it Nige … work stinks.' Max shook his head.

'What am I going to do? I mean, dad's business is a building firm. I mean, can you imagine me as a hodcarrier or bricklayer?' Nigel looked down in horror at his smooth, white hands.

'Sure no. It's def not you … but I have to sell houses to people. Imagine. I can't do it. I'm gonna bankrupt the firm.' Max was actually now starting to worry about those other than himself, especially as Tracy never missed any opportunity to remind him of his own shortcomings.

'Bloody parents … I mean, we didn't choose to be born did we?' They took big sips from their half pint glasses of Newcastle brown ale in synchronicity. 'There's got to be a way out of this Maxi.'

'Believe me Nige, I've been racking my brains and I've actually come up with an idea.' Max enigmatically cocked his head to one side.

'Go on…' Nigel's eyes grew round.

'Well, do you know how we used to do skateboard?' Max leant in closer to his friend and got a contemptuous look from the giant sitting at the next table drinking a Guinness with a whisky chaser, bloodshot eyes and a big black beard.

'What about it?' Nigel didn't really want to be reminded of this humiliating experience.

‘Well if we went to Thailand we could become … surfer boys. It’s all the rage there … imagine golden sands, shooting the breeze, bikini clad girls falling at our feet …’ Blackbeard, the pub regular sitting nearby, listened closely in disbelief at the tosh he was hearing from these two jerks invading his pub of choice. In his opinion, these daft clowns clearly had no business being here at all.

‘Thailand that’s a little random isn’t it. Are you mad, Max? How’re we gonna do that?’ Unfortunately Max’s voice started to squeak and Blackbeard rolled his eyes.

‘Look, what’s the wi fi code in here.’ Max fiddled around with his phone and found the post he was looking for on Facebook. ‘Look at this, Toby Mackintosh. He looks like he’s having an awesome time. And look what a weed he is.’

‘Yeah but… Max dude, like I say, how’re we gonna do that?’ Nigel was dubious but nonetheless becoming quite excited.

‘Are you in for it mate?’ Max felt like an evil drug pusher.

‘Well… I might be – but how?’ Nigel’s eyes were now as round as saucers.

‘Just leave it to Maxi.’ He tapped his nose and gave his friend a wink, feeling very pleased with himself..

Tracy

Tracy had noticed a peculiar atmosphere in the office that day. At first, Charles had been his expected self and given her his usual morning greeting, but as the day progressed, she noticed a change in his manner. Whenever it had been necessary for her to make contact with him, he had seemed unusually aloof and distracted as if she had offended him in some way. Tracy couldn’t understand this and she racked her brains to recall a disparaging remark she might have made about his greediness, but drew a blank.

She had always thought she got along well enough with her boss, and like most men she knew, she assumed he fancied her. Tracy imagined that not only did he appreciate the daily efforts she went to her with her appearance and professional business-like manner, but most importantly she thought he valued her ability to run a tight ship. Yet, he had failed to return any of her most charming smiles since his morning break, which was quite unknown. And she was almost sure that she had seen him watching her, and not in a good way, when he thought she wasn't looking. Well she *had* seen him, several times and Tracy was worried.

Tracy wondered if she gone too far? She would have thought by now that Neil would have been reinstated in his role and she wouldn't have been forced to keep setting Max up for failures. Over the past few days, complaints about Max had been flooding in thick and fast: why had he been late; why had he not known the facts about the property; why had he met them at completely the wrong address and why had he been rude? Well, Tracy knew well enough the answers to these and she had felt, it had served both father and son right. What gave Charles the audacity to think his incompetent son could just breeze into Neil's job and expect everything to be tickety boo? Likewise, how did Max have the gall to imagine that his attempts at property sales could result in anything not downright tickety bad? Tracy's interventions were merely a *kind* act on her part, to ensure that everything returned to the status quo as soon as possible.

At first, when she had directed the calls through to Charles, she had taken a certain pleasure in watching him wince and give effusive apologies to the offended parties on the phone. However, now it seemed he couldn't care less and pretended that he was elsewhere when those difficult calls arrived. So, poor, reliable Tracy had to take all the flack and when she reported back to Charles, he seemed to feign indifference to his son's ineptitude. Did he no longer care about his business? Tracy was baffled and was beginning to fear for the future of the firm and most importantly, her own job.

Also, even more disturbing was that Max had started to behave rather differently towards her too. She detected a change from his initial wariness of her, to a distinct hostility. It seemed he no longer cared about her opinion of him. Rather than asking her for the list of appointments each day, he went to check them himself on the system and didn't even bother speaking with her. How dare he? But although she was loathe to admit it, she had to give him some credit on picking up on a few of the anomalies. As yet he hadn't spoken to her about any of this, but of course she would deny all knowledge. Much to her chagrin, as from yesterday the complaints were becoming less frequent and he had even managed to persuade two clients to make an offer on a house. This was not a turn of events she had anticipated. Tracy wondered if he and his father had been talking, and she was worried. Tracy didn't like this, not one little bit, and she could feel she was losing her power.

Furthermore, each time she had rung Neil lately, he had failed to pick up the phone. Tracy bit her lip and called the number one more time. Bingo. This time he picked up.
'Neil is that you?' She asked loudly.
'Well it's my phone who else would you expect it to be?' He really didn't have the time to be gossiping with Tracy, as his appointment with Geoff Armstrong was only half an hour away.
'Oh it's lovely to hear your voice. Everyone is missing you so much here.' Tracy fawned and he imagined her fluttering her lashes at him, in what she assumed was an alluring manner.
'Well I doubt that is the case …' Neil checked his watch and sighed in irritation.
'When are you coming back Neil? The place just isn't the same without you. You know nothing has sold. There has not been one house, flat or even hovel sale since you…'
'Look Tracy. I won't be coming back and if you don't mind. I'm really rather busy so …'
'Busy? Busy doing what? Making Julia's tea and doing her ironing?' Now, at her mention of Julia's name, it was Tracy's turn to feel angry.
'Tracy. I haven't got time for this now and I really need to get going. Bye.'
But from Tracy's point of view this conversation was by no means over. 'Wait Neil …'
But Neil had already put the phone down much to her annoyance.

Watching from his office, Charles had noted the fury on his receptionist's face and he had heard her mention the name Neil more than once. Judging the by her expression, this phone call had not gone according to plan. Well he now knew what the sly bitch was up to didn't he? From now on her card would be well and truly marked and she would be being watched very carefully. Perhaps a replacement for Tracy would soon need to be considered and he pictured Pamela behind the desk, but somehow the image of his wife with all her fussy frills did not sit so well.

From his seat in the corner of Heworth Golf Club, Obadiah sipped from his soda water and read the Financial Times. Although he was currently busy auditing the accounts of the Kosher bakeries and other small businesses of the Jewish community, he had so particularly enjoyed the work he had done for Mr Lavender. Aware that his rather extreme appearance might discourage some clients, he had tied his ringlets into a neat ponytail and given his attire an infusion of colour with a chunky charcoal sweater. While pretending to be ensconced with some movement of stocks and shares, he heard a familiar voice booming and laughing. Surely that couldn't be ... but yes it was. There to his horror, not six meters away, was that disgraced fraudster, Neil, his nemesis, Latimer holding court like some ridiculous jester. Slinking further down in his seat, Obadiah slid down to hide behind his newspaper with his blood boiling. How could this be?

'Oh that's a good one Neil. Have you got another?' A red-faced wide-boy with a large paunch, traces of food lodged between his teeth and a bald head slapped Neil on the back.

'Well there were these three undertakers and they….' Neil lowered his voice so his audience had to draw closer to hear.

Oh what a surprise the joker's at it again, thought the seething Obadiah peering from behind his paper …

'Ha ha. So Neil, How are things in the property world these days?' An unpleasant-looking, short man with a moustache and pin striped jacket asked the fraud.

'I'm having a break from that.' Replied the monster, cool as a cucumber. 'The bottom's fallen out of the market. I kept telling Charles - but you know him.' Neil smirked triumphantly, as if he knew Obadiah was watching and took a long gulp from his drink.

'Yes Charles. How he's still in business is a mystery.' The fat man with the red face, shook his head and his plethora of chins wobbled.

'Well, I think we all know how Charles has kept his business afloat all this time.' Shifty pin-stripe jacket looked towards Neil and they all made appreciative noises in the bastard's direction. Obadiah was gobsmacked. How could this be happening?

'You are too kind gentlemen. Anyone for another beer?' Neil swaggered over to the bar like he was the cock of the walk.

'So is that right? Neil's no longer working for Charles Lavender?' Fatty seemed much too interested in all of this for Obadiah's liking.

'That seems to be the case. He'll not be out of a job for long though. Not Neil.' Shorty tapped the side of his nose with his little finger.

'Here you are lads.' A beaming Neil handed out the drinks. 'Now where were we?'

'So Neil, is that right. You and Charles have parted company?' Obadiah didn't like where this conversation seems to be going, not one little bit.

'About time don't you think? Only got one life. This is no dress rehearsal and all that…' Neil splayed his fingers into jazz hands as if he were a white-gloved Al Jolson.

Bloody clichés thought Obadiah.

Neil was interrupted by the fat baldy. 'Have you ever thought about cars?'

'Well I wasn't looking to get a new one at the moment…' Sly Neil was pretending he couldn't guess where this one was going.

'No selling them, you plank.' Baldy slapped him on the back once more.

'Well my line of business, has been mostly dealing with properties,' said Neil seriously, as though carefully considering his choice of words.

You liar, scowled Obadiah to himself. Your line of business has been embezzling other people's money.

'Neil my pal, they're all commodities.' Fat man leered. 'If you can sell one, you can sell the other … and your track record is proven.' There was more ribald laughter and Obadiah was feeling increasingly nauseous.

'Well …'

Obadiah could see from his face that the con man was flattered.

'Look come and see me. Armstrong Automobiles tomorrow. Geoff Armstrong, here's my card.' He foraged in his pocket. 'Shall we say eleven, and there's a vacancy with your name on.'

Obadiah wanted to vomit.

'Well I'll have to talk it through with Julia but…' Neil couldn't believe his luck.

'No buts … see you tomorrow. Now who's up for another drink?'

Once more the party erupted into laughter, guffaws and backslapping. Obadiah was in no mood for any networking today. As he slipped out the side door of the club, he felt too hot in his sweater, his curls were escaping from their constraints and he was eager to be back home with his wife and family.

Chapter 17

Thirty Years Earlier

Trevor

Trevor was quite pleased to get out of the house and get into his car to go to work on this Monday morning. Although he had passed his test years ago, he had never been able to afford to run a car up until now. A couple of weeks ago, he selected an almost new VW Golf in racing green and was enjoying driving his new purchase enormously. It really was an essential, as it was far too tricky relying on the buses to get from Washington Village all the way to the pharmacists in Bensham. He felt no gratitude towards Julia because the money was his now and he could do with it as he pleased. Also, with his new freedom, he had full intention of exploring the locality and beyond. He'd always had a fancy to visit Scarborough, Whitby and perhaps even Great Yarmouth. Really there was nothing to stop him going wherever he fancied. What a pity his mother wasn't still alive; how she would have enjoyed being ferried about by her son in his smart new automobile.

There was no point in taking Julia anywhere. As each day progressed, she became more pathetic and useless. Pretty soon, she would have to face the inevitability of the unlikeliness of her ever returning to university. In fact, she was hardly capable of the simplest of household chores. Each menial task she attempted had to be redone again but this time properly by Trevor. If it wasn't for him, the two of them would live in a pigsty; she really was disgusting. He imagined her lying in her sweaty bed with its foisty sheets, in bad need of a shower. Was it any wonder that he slept in the other room? The thought of sharing a bed with her made him feel bilious. The only belongings of his which he kept in there were his shoes, which he knew didn't smell very pleasant, so they were in good company.

He hoped the lazy cow had bothered to drink the tea he had made for her before he left. She didn't appreciate half the bother he went to for her sake. With that on his mind, he had noticed that his supplies of Ketamine were getting low and hoped he would have opportunity today to replenish them. He had a feeling that Nick, the senior chemist, would be out, but he still needed to be mindful of other prying eyes. Really, it was ridiculous, he had been working in this pharmacists for nearly twenty years and knew how to make up prescriptions like the back of his hand. Still, because he didn't have that stupid certificate, he was given no real responsibility other than opening and locking up the building. For the rest of the day he was just at the beck and call of the qualified chemists. It made him sick when the new graduates began: they were wet behind the ears and knew virtually nothing. They asked for Trevor's advice then didn't they? Still, within a matter of weeks they were trying to lord it over him. It was so unfair. This wouldn't be the case for much longer though would it? Not now.

Luckily, there was a little car park in the street behind the chemist's, providing a perfect spot for Trevor's new VW. As he pulled up, he noticed that the shop was in darkness which meant he must be the first on the premises. He had set off early for this specific purpose, but still one never knew. The early bird didn't necessarily catch the biggest worm. It was essential that Trevor kept his wits about him and his eyes peeled. Ketamine was kept locked up in the special cupboard underneath the till, along with the narcotics like morphine, heroin and codeine. If a chemist's was to be burgled, these were the drugs that would be targeted. For as well as bringing pain relief, their recreational purposes were well known to smack heads and such like. He supposed his wife Julia, must now also fall into this dubious category.

All the qualified chemists had their own keys to the cupboard, but this of course didn't include Trevor. Strictly speaking he had no business whatsoever going into the cupboard, but it was common knowledge that the spare key was kept in an old Strepsil's throat lozenge tin next to the sink. Nevertheless, he needed to be careful, if he was caught going into the cupboard he would be in trouble enough. But if he were discovered to be helping himself to Ketamine, even if the purpose of the theft wasn't known, he would be facing dismissal and the involvement of the police. Really, Trevor went far beyond the call of duty for the sake of his burdensome wife.

Zoe

The Present

Zoe was sitting watching the television, with her daughter Chloe. David Attenborough was presenting a programme about penguins and although Chloe was glued to the screen, Zoe wasn't particularly interested. They had eaten carbonara with tagliatelle for tea; Zoe had eaten rather too much and felt a little sick. Chloe had picked unenthusiastically at hers. Granted, the bacon was a little burnt but Chloe had reached that age when she had become obsessed with eating, or not eating to be more accurate; being in a perpetual state of hunger was the all-important goal. Before Chloe had a chance to scrap the leftover meal into the bin, Zoe had grabbed the plate and finished off the remains. At the best of times, carbonara could be a sickly meal but now, Zoe couldn't even stomach a glass of wine.

The details of the conversation she had with Julia earlier kept running over in her mind, like a stuck needle on a vinyl record. There was something that deeply disturbed her but Zoe couldn't quite put her finger on what it might be. Yes, she and Neil were obviously having some serious money troubles, as a result of his stupidity but Julia had been through worse in the past. The money that the council would be providing would keep them afloat , at least for the time being, but there was something else. It was connected with the building of the new road, yet how could that possibly be of any cause for concern?

Zoe thought back to all those years ago and when Julia had completely disappeared off the radar, once she had taken up with Trevor. At the time Zoe, had been offended by her friend's desertion, and it was as if he had some evil hold over her. Goodness only knew what had happened there, as the man obviously had sadistic leanings, upon which Zoe didn't like to dwell. Julia must have been forced by Trevor to abandon her teaching course, because at the end of the first year Julia had quit the university altogether. While Zoe had been teaching now for twenty five years, Julia had only been teaching for twenty.

Three of those years she would have been doing a further training course and that left a further two years unaccounted for. What had Julia suffered in those two missing years?

Zoe assumed that in order for her to have done that second course, she must have somehow got rid of Trevor. How had she persuaded him to give her a divorce? That can't have been easy. It seemed to Zoe that in marrying Julia, Trevor must have quickly realised where his bread was well and truly buttered. Zoe just couldn't see him forgoing the comfortable circumstances that his marriage provided him with, without at least some very good incentive. What could that have been?

The fact that Julia was loathe to speak about her evil first husband Zoe guessed was because she had been scarred by the awful memories. But just maybe there was more to it than that. Where exactly was Trevor? Unwanted husbands didn't just obediently crawl under stones. Perhaps Julia didn't want to speak about him as it might jeopardise her relationship with new husband, Neil. Maybe she didn't want to mention husband number one because that was what he still was. Number one – Trevor, number – two Neil; Julia was obviously a bigamist. Yet, what did that have to do with the new road coming through her garden?

There was only one way that this could be sorted. It was down to Zoe to discover what had happened to Trevor and where he was now.

'Mum…mum. What do you think?'

The nature programme had obviously finished and Zoe realised that her daughter was asking her a question. 'Sorry…what do I think about what?'

'About the penguins and polar bears.' Chloe was sounding exasperated with her mother.

'Erm, I'm sure they are very nice but we can't have them as pets.'

'Honestly Mum weren't you watching the programme. It's about global warming.'

'Yes it's dreadful dear.'

But Chloe could see her mother's mind was clearly elsewhere.

Charles was wondering when the best time would be to bite the bullet to go and visit Julia. It was now four o clock, so she would have most certainly have finished her teaching, but was more than likely still at the school. Without a doubt, he couldn't just turn up at their house unannounced, and now definitely wasn't the time for him to be crossing paths with the disgraced Neil. He had always been fond of Julia but he knew her and Neil as a couple, and could hardly consider Julia as a friend of his own. She would obviously think it very odd for him to be contacting her at all, but needs must. It was a great pity that this couldn't have been done through his wife Pamela but this wasn't information that she could be trusted with. He imagined his wife having a field day on the High Street, almost bursting with delight as the words embezzlement, blackmail and police investigation exploded from her mouth like shook up cans of coke. Once again Charles made comparisons between the two wives and as usual, Pamela came out rather badly.

Charles was worried about Neil and Julia as a couple and he wondered what Julia actually knew about her husband's recent misguided actions . He felt that she needed to be put in the picture, but also be made aware that all of this might not be entirely of his own making. There were other agencies involved, of that he was now certain and he was convinced that Tracy was responsible for him being blackmailed. It was all such a mess which he could make a million times worse if he did what Obadiah wanted and contacted the police. Not only would it land Neil in prison, but also Tracy and God knew how many other OakElmAsh employees. No doubt himself as the owner of the disreputable establishment, would be arrested and found to be guilty by mere association of some crime or other. Charles wished he could turn back the clock and the problem could have been nipped in the bud before it had escalated into such massive proportions.

Thinking it to be inappropriate to contact Julia through the school telephone landline, he needed to hunt through his employee records to find the number of Neil's next of kin. Much as he wished to avoid unnecessary contact with Tracy, he knew she would find

Julia's phone number much more quickly than he would. Unusually for Tracy, she made no comment about why he wanted it and within seconds had the information scribbled down. He decided to strike while the iron was hot and rang Julia's phone before he could think of a reason to wriggle out of the difficult conversation.

'Hello. Is that Julia?' Charles felt nervous.

'Yes. Who am I speaking to? If you are trying to sell me something …' Julia recognised neither the number or the voice.

'No it's Charles. Charles Lavender.' Charles cleared his throat uneasily.

'Oh … hello Charles.' Julia was extremely puzzled and wondered why he wanted to speak to her, of all people.

'I was wondering if you had the time to meet with me. Maybe for a coffee or…' Charles didn't know where he was going to begin explaining everything to Julia.

What was going on here Julia wondered? 'Charles I'm not being funny or anything but after the recent events … well I can't think of anything that we can possibly have to say to each other.'

'Julia … this is all very awkward, but you see *that's* what I want to speak to you about.' He could totally understand why Julia would be reluctant to meet him.

Maybe she ought to find out what this was all about. After all Charles had been good enough not to contact the police … yet. 'Well, I shall be leaving school in about half an hour… so if it's that important why don't you just come round to the house.'

'I don't think that would be a very good idea.' Charles couldn't face seeing Neil.

'Neil won't be there.' Julia could guess why he wouldn't want to come to their house.

'All the same … I think it would be better if we met in a more neutral place … with all things considered.' Charles was thinking of the coffee shop in Sainsbury's on the Team Valley.

'Charles, Neil won't be here for at least another hour.' There was a pause in the conversation, and Julia knew Charles would no doubt be wondering where his ex-employee could possibly be. 'He's got a new job and he won't be back home until at least after six.'

'Ok Julia. Shall we say just after five.' So Neil had managed to get himself another job. Well that was a turn up for the books. Charles couldn't decide whether he was pleased for him or not.

As it was an unusually bright day in November, Max decided rather than stay in the office, he would go to the nearby Leazes Park to eat his lunch. The horrible Tracy seemed to be in a particularly bad mood and had extended her surliness to the customers, whom she had been snarling and scowling at all morning. Max thought it best to keep as well away from her as he could before her nastiness became aimed once more in his direction.

Without a doubt, the park with its copper-coloured leaves and shimmering sunlight reflecting on the lake's surface during this contemplative season looked splendid. These juxtaposed impressively with the gigantic, metallic St James' Park football ground which dominated the sky-line like a modern day Tyrannosaurus Rex. Max sat down upon a bench somewhat baffled by his own eloquence. Where had these words come from? Was Max starting to actually think like an estate–agent? Something very odd seemed to be taking its course.

Nevertheless, this was definitely a preferable place than the office to eat his mother's ham sandwiches. They didn't actually taste too bad, although as usual Pamela had spread too much butter on the bread and she had cut off crusts for him, as if he were still a pampered little boy. Well not for much longer. Max took a bite out of an apple, before throwing it, in a devil may care manner, into a nearby bush and taking the laptop out of his man bag.

Let's see, thought Max, as he searched through the flights to Thailand. £555 seemed a good price for a one way flight leaving next Thursday from Newcastle Airport and arriving the following day. One change, at Amsterdam Schipol, with a wait of three hours. Well that looked perfect. He would ring Nigel after work, feeling sure that his pal wouldn't be able to resist keeping him company on the forthcoming adventure. He looked on Facebook, to see two further posts from Toby Mackintosh, who was with two blonde Australian girls, sipping a Blue Lagoon cocktail in one photo and hugging a Chinese girl in another, whilst eating a gigantic burger. Max watched two skater boys in action on the other side of the park and imagined him and Nige, as two cool dudes surfing the waves.

Funnily enough, that morning at work hadn't actually been that bad. He had shown a smart young couple around a flat on the Gateshead Quayside. It had a lovely view of the bridges, Baltic Art Gallery and Sage Music Centre, which were looking particularly splendid that morning. Max thought the apartment itself was a pretty good price considering the plush fixtures and fittings, combined with its excellent location. In fact, he told his clients that he wouldn't mind living there himself, if he hadn't got some travelling plans up his sleeve. This piqued the young couple's attention. It transpired, they had been to Phuket, only a few months ago and they showed him some great pictures of the beaches and bars on their phones.

Next, Max showed a rather stout man in late middle age, wearing a loud checked suit round a semi-detached house in, Cochrane Park in Heaton. It seemed the vendors were hoping for a quick sale, so they could go travelling around the world and the money from the house would allow them to do this in some style. The house had two bedrooms and a large garden, which seemed to impress Mr Blackburn and his cocker spaniel, Duncan. Eventually, Duncan stopped barking, once he was allowed to run around outside and dig holes in the flower beds. Apparently, Mr Blackburn was looking to buy a house because of his impending nuptials. He proudly produced his phone to reveal a picture of a stunning young Asian girl called Delores, whose arrival he was awaiting from would you believe …Thailand.

Upon reflection, Max took these both to be positive affirmations relating to the wisdom of his plans and he returned to the office with a spring in his step. Tracy was sitting behind the desk with a face like a gorgon. She grunted at him when came through the door. x he

'Well I suppose some congratulations are in order.'

The face didn't match the words.

'Sorry. Are you speaking to me?' Max thought he must be hearing things.

'I can't see anybody else here. So, I suppose I must be.' Tracy looked deadpan.

'What are you congratulating me for anyway?'

This was seeming a most unlikely conversation.

'That flat on the Quayside and the house in Heaton.' Tracy was flicking through a magazine.

‘What about them? The fact I managed to find them or that I arrived on time.’ Max was pleased with his attempt at sarcasm.

‘They’ve both have had offers on them and above the asking price too. Yes I thought I saw a pig flying about outside the window too.’

Julia

Julia had been most surprised to receive a phone call from Charles. She couldn’t imagine whatever he wanted to talk about. Neil had stolen lots of money off him, end of. No doubt, he was wondering how the money was going to be paid back or he was going to warn her about a visit from the police. Either way, it wasn’t good news. The only reason she had agreed to meet him was that so far, the Law hadn’t been involved and she hoped that it would remain that way. Remembering that Charles had a fondness for sweet things, she put some Penguin biscuits onto a plate in the middle of the kitchen table and Mabel eyed the shiny foil wrappers with some interest.

Shortly, there was a knock on the door and Julia opened it, to see a sheepish-looking Charles standing on the doorstep. She hung his overcoat up in the hallway and gestured for him to go through to the kitchen.

‘Thank you for seeing me Julia. You are probably wondering why I am here.’ Charles sat himself down at the kitchen table while Mabel watched him suspiciously from the other side of the room.

‘Well I imagine it is about Neil.’ Julia felt really uncomfortable about Charles being in her house, as it all seemed a little odd. ‘I can only apologise for my husband … but I’m sorry I simply don’t have the money to pay you back.’

‘No, that’s not why I’m here. But first how are you?’ A look of genuine concern was evident on Charles’s face.

‘Well not great as I’m sure you can imagine.’ Charles didn’t know the half of it thought Julia.

‘So you do know what Neil did?’ He wondered how many of the details she was party to.

‘Yes, as I said I can only apologise.’ Julia couldn’t think what she was expected to say.

‘The thing that I don’t understand is … why he needed to take that money in the first place?’ Charles looked at the biscuits and was surprised that he hadn’t yet been offered a cup of tea. ‘I mean the pair of you can’t be that badly off.’

‘It’s gambling Charles. Neil has a problem with gambling. He just can’t stop himself.’ Julia shook her head woefully

‘Ah … I must confess. I hadn’t considered that one.’ Charles reflected upon this information.

‘I‘ve just made a pot of tea would you like some.’

Charles nodded, as Julia poured out two cups of tea. And before being offered, Charles began removing the wrapper of a biscuit. ‘Why to be honest Julia. I thought he might have been taking drugs. So to some extent gambling is a …’

‘It’s the same. Gambling is an addiction, just like taking drugs.’

Charles took a generous bite from the biscuit, enjoying the sweet chocolate taste, then continued. ‘Well I’ll tell you why I thought that. You see, I think that somebody has been blackmailing him. If it were drugs you see …that would make more sense.’

‘Blackmailing. Who’d do that?’ Was there a chance of salvaging some measure of innocence for her husband. Julia was desperate to grasp at straws. ‘They might still be … If Neil has been blackmailed then surely that’s a matter for the police.’

‘Police Julia?’ Charles shot her a look. ‘Do you really want to get them involved?’

‘No I guess not.’ Julia paused to gather her thoughts.’ And thank you so much Charles for not getting them involved.’ Julia cast her eyes downwards.

‘It might be against my better judgement, but we go back a long way. Neil and me.’ Charles took a drink of his tea before helping himself to a further biscuit. ‘So you said on the phone he’s got himself another job. How’s he done that? I mean I’ve had no one asking me for any references.’

‘He’s not selling property. Its cars, that’s the job. Car salesman.’

‘Let me guess.’ Charles smiled to himself.’ Geoff Armstrong? Does that name ring any bells?’

‘Yes I think it does … Armstrong Automobiles?’

‘That figures. He’s a keen golf player.’ And a con merchant, thought Charles, remembering a dodgy car he had once bought from the man years ago. Oh well, birds of a feather, he surmised .

'But you said earlier that you think Neil's being blackmailed.' Julia returned to the one ounce of hope that this meeting had revealed.

'Well I thought Neil was on drugs which gave more credibility to the blackmailing … but it's still possible.' Charles realised this meant a lot to Julia.

'If Neil is being blackmailed and you know *who* it is. Then maybe we or you could get at least some of the money back.'

'That had crossed my mind too Julia but let me see … I must get going. Neil will be back soon and you know …'

'Yes of course and thank you once again Charles.' Charles had indeed given Julia food for thought.

'I know none of this is your fault Julia. I'll be in touch, if I find out anything.' Before he left, Charles slipped two more of the Penguin biscuits into his pocket.

Chapter 18

Julia

Thirty Years Earlier

The day had finally arrived and Julia knew that she could no longer bury her head in the sand. Now, it was practically the end of August and she needed to inform the University that she wouldn't be returning. Considering the pathetic state she had become reduced to, it was the only possible decision to be made. Julia didn't feel so much sadness for herself it was more for her parents who would have been proud as Punch to see her graduate with a teaching degree.

However, she wasn't the same Julia she had been even a few short months ago. Circumstances had reduced her to a pale, albeit larger shadow, of her former self. She thought back over the fun times that she had spent with Zoe and wondered what her friend was doing now. No doubt, Zoe would have found a new best friend to hang out with, but Julia couldn't help but feel sad and guilty when she thought how abruptly she had cut all ties with her. That was all down to Trevor; he had taken an instant dislike to Zoe and Julia had been so besotted with him that whatever Trevor wanted, Trevor got.

Frankly, it was just as well that Trevor wasn't here at the moment. She looked at the cup of tea by the side of the bed which she had neglected to drink. Her husband always became so angry when she didn't finish whatever drinks he prepared for her. Julia assumed this was due to him hating any sort of waste, but the tea and coffee always tasted so awful to her. She understood that these economy brands were so much cheaper to buy, but was it really necessary for them to make such huge sacrifices? They never really went out did they? Not for meals or to the cinema or anywhere. Most people had mortgages to pay for, but her parents had left the house to her with plenty of money. She wasn't sure how much Trevor earned, but she was sure that chemists must receive a decent wage.

Julia looked at the clock and saw it was midday already. It seemed to her that Groundhog Day was on a constant repeat, and each time she had to part company with her bed was the very worst moment of the day. Within the cocoon of her duvet she at least had some sanctuary. She felt like a sloth, with no energy whatsoever, but if this letter to the university was to be written she needed to get motivation from somewhere. The bed sheets smelt like sour milk and she sighed, unable to remember the last time she had changed them. First thing though, must be for her to have a shower. Unsteadily on her feet, like a new born calf, she staggered to the bathroom.

After having had a shower and putting on some fresh clothes, Julia felt a little better. She went downstairs to make herself a horrible cup of tea. While the kettle was boiling, she sniffed the packet which smelt totally ordinary. Then she made herself a drink and took a reluctant sip. This didn't taste the same as the usual drinks. It tasted of tea. How peculiar she thought and began to feel a little more like the Julia of old. Usually, Trevor prepared her a flask of tea for her to drink throughout the day. It was thoughtful of him, so she wouldn't have the bother of going downstairs but for some reason today he had forgotten. Well, this tea tasted as it ought to and Julia enjoyed the moment imagining herself as an exotic geisha in a tea drinking ceremony. She couldn't remember the last time she had been able to partake in such pleasant, fanciful thoughts.

Slowly, Julia went back up the staircase, opened the bedroom window and struggled to strip the bed. After some time, she managed to get the crisp clean bed linen in place and put a fresh nightie under the pillow for herself. What a luxury slipping into fresh sheets was going to be that night. She almost felt tempted to get back into bed herself but no … it felt as if some progress was at last being made. There was still an unpleasant smell in the room, most likely from the pile of Trevor's shoes stacked up on her mother's dressing table. Julia, for the first time began to wonder if the situation she was in was completely of her own making, because before Trevor, she had very rarely been ill.

Julia opened the backdoor and ventured outside for the first time in weeks. As she inhaled some of the summer air, it felt surprisingly good. Then she looked about her and saw the full state of the garden's disrepair. For, not only did the grass need cutting; some of the blades must have been almost a foot tall, but ivy had spread everywhere like some virulent epidemic had taken hold and the poor flowers, unsafe in their beds, had been strangled by weeds. Since her parents had died, this once lovely place had become sadly neglected. Although she had at first had tried to keep on top of things as best she could, recently this was not the case and it didn't looked nowhere near the way it once did. She thought of the once immaculate lawns, profusion of colours, and her parents using the ancient tools kept in the shed. It was a long time since anyone had been in the shed and her eyes filled with tears as she looked at the sturdy padlock attached to the door. She imagined any burglar would be greatly disappointed by the booty held there.

Trevor behaved as if he had never had a garden before and showed no interest in it whatsoever. It seemed that he thought, if he didn't look at it, then it wasn't a problem, and Julia suddenly felt a great sadness weighing upon her, as once more, she had let her parents down. This was just another example of her uselessness in letting matters slide and allowing this once lovely garden become a disgusting jungley mess.

As she wandered down to the bottom edge, she noticed the distinctive sickly perfume of the roses. The smell had always reminded her of old ladies' talcum powder. Despite the fierce battle the flowers were having with the dandelions and nettles, the resilient blooms were still somehow holding their own. They formed a defiant rectangular barricade around the outside of the flower bed, as if protecting what lay beneath, while the centre had given up completely by surrendering and running to the wild with weeds. Julia shuddered. She knew that some serious cutting, digging and weeding needed to be done. Without doubt people's tongues would be wagging at this wanton neglect. And any derogatory comments or neighbourly attention paid to this particular garden was most definitely unwanted.

'Julia … Julia. You surely can't be out here.' The angry voice of her husband cut through the air. 'Julia, what in God's name are you doing out here?'

'I was … just getting a little fresh air.' Julia was startled and she glanced at her watch astonished that it was already time for his return from work.

'Fresh air? You aren't well. Come on, look at the state of you. Get yourself inside before the neighbours see you.' Trevor's voice bleated at her like an agitated ram.

'But Trevor … it's lovely sitting out here in the garden.' Julia stared, as if mesmerised by the roses and their vicious pointed thorns, imagining them tearing her husband's skin.
'I don't see what's at all lovely about this dump.' Trevor really didn't see the point in gardens and roughly grabbed her arm.
'Just let me stay here a few more moments.' Julia couldn't take her eyes of the patch of weeds in the middle of the rose bed.
'Julia, let's just get you indoors - this minute.' He grabbed the other arm, to pinion them both behind her and frogmarch her indoors.

Zoe

The present day

Zoe had put the name of Trevor Squires into the search bar of her lap top, but so far nothing seemed to connect with Julia's Trevor. There were two obituaries, one for an eighty-seven year old Trevor Squires in Oregon and a forty-four year old Trevor Squires in Plymouth. She wasn't sure of Trevor's age, but he was definitely much older than her and Julia. Zoe reckoned that he must have been close to forty at the time. That would make him about sixty-five or so now. So, Oregon Trevor was much too old, and Plymouth Trevor, who died five years ago, was much too young to fit the bill. So, it seemed unlikely that this Trevor was dead. Or if he were, nothing had been recorded which was peculiar. Zoe deduced from this that Trevor was most certainly still alive and causing mischief elsewhere.

Zoe was sitting in her bedroom, as Chloe was downstairs and she didn't really want to explain to her daughter what she was doing. While Zoe considered herself carrying out research, Chloe would more than likely accuse her of snooping. She couldn't find any Trevor Squires on Facebook either which wasn't surprising as she couldn't really see that being his bag. Here there was a Carl Squires who looked to be round about the right age,

and he lived somewhere in County Durham. That sounded promising. But this Trevor sported a white handle bar moustache, checked cowboy shirt and a Stetson hat.

Apparently, he had recently won an award in an over sixties line-dancing competition. Judging by the smile he wore on his face as he held his trophy; he was extremely proud of himself. This couldn't possibly be the Trevor she was searching for. Zoe's project wasn't going too well and she was glad she had brought the bottle of wine up to the room with her.

So, she had covered obituaries and Facebook, both to no avail so which other possible avenues could she explore? Missing persons she thought, maybe that was a possibility and … Bingo.

" Trevor Squires (36) of Lowfield Avenue, Washington Village on the 31st August 1995, was reported missing by his wife Julia Squires (19). The couple had not long been married. Trevor a Pharmacist's Assistant in Bensham, was last seen wearing a light blue anorak, beige corduroy pants and black slip-on shoes. Trevor's vehicle, a green VW Golf is also missing. If anyone knows anything about his whereabouts please contact the police."

There was no mistaking: the picture of him was exactly as Zoe remembered. She would have thought him more elderly than thirty six, but that was more than likely due to the clothes he wore. Oddly though, there were no threads following this up. It seemed as though Trevor had completely disappeared without trace, and even now, after all these years nobody knew what happened to Julia's husband. That was unless Julia knew more than she was letting on. The plot was thickening. Did this have some connection with the construction of the new road Zoe wondered? Possibly, but she couldn't think how.

Neil

Neil had enjoyed a highly successful day, after selling six cars and making several new chums at the car showroom. He thought he was going to enjoy being a car salesman and without shadow of a doubt, he felt he possessed an exceptional flair for the job. Neil had taken to selling cars like a duck to water. It was a testosterone-filled, masculine environment with only poor old Bridget, as the token female on the reception desk. And with her mad curly perm, thick black framed glasses and penchant for bright, hand-knitted sweaters, she wasn't a patch on Tracy. There were three other alpha male salesmen alongside himself and six burly mechanics who worked in the garage behind. Laughter, cups of strong tea and joke telling were in abundance. And to round the day off nicely, Geoff Armstrong had provided him with an Alfa Romero, sporty- red company, car and taken him for a couple of pints at the Golf Club. Success at last, Neil thought. Had the phoenix risen or what?

When he arrived home, beaming and full of himself, he found his wife in rather a pensive mood. 'Julia, how's your day been? Mine's been fantastic.'
'Actually my day's been quite interesting.' Julia said but Neil wasn't listening.
'My day has been brilliant. Charles can stick his property business where the sun don't shine, as far as I'm concerned.' Neil was riding high.
'It's interesting that you should mention Charles because…'
'Go on … guess how many cars I sold today?' Neil was practically skipping round the kitchen.
'Neil I've just had a visitor and …'
'Look outside.' Neil pointed at his favourite new toy in the drive. 'Geoff has given me a company car. And it's an Alpha Romero. Come on Julia, let's go for a spin.'
'Neil, have you been for a drink?' Julia was the voice of reason.' It certainly sounds like you have. I'm not sure that going out for a spin is such a brilliant idea.'
'Yes, maybe you're right' Neil certainly wasn't going to allow Julia to spoil his party. 'I've just been down the golf club with Geoff and the lads. They're a great bunch. Well, come outside and see the car and sit inside of it. It's really awesome. In fact Julia, why don't you drive it? The engine purrs just like … Mabel actually.' Mabel at the mention of her name ran under a chair; fearful of the overly-exuberant Neil.
'Neil, will you just listen to what I'm trying to tell you. Charles Lavender has just left. He came round to see me.'
'Charles … Charles has been round here. Why? What did he want?' It was as if a pin had burst Neil the balloon, and he quickly sobered up.
'To be honest you should be very grateful to him.' Julia couldn't believe she had finally got her husband's attention. 'Any other person would have been straight on to the police.'
'Did he say anything about that?' Neil had, up until this point today, put these matters to the very back of his mind. 'What did he want?'

'He wanted to know what you 'd been spending his money on.' Julia raised her eyebrows and looked at her husband straight in the eye.' He thought you were on drugs and he actually had the decency to look relieved when I told him about your gambling.' She spat out the last word as if it were a nasty piece of gristle, spoiling a lovely Sunday dinner.

'He thought I was on drugs … I mean really do I look the type.' Neil's' innocent little boy face no longer worked on Julia, as it once had.

'And there's more. He was worried that someone might be blackmailing you. Tell me – *is* someone blackmailing you?' Julia looked for a clue in his face, hoping that this indeed was the case.

'No, nobody is blackmailing me.' Deflated, Neil sat down on a chair. Typical that after his brilliant fresh start today, that his bloody chickens should come home to roost.

'Are you sure because he implied it was somebody he actually knew? Maybe someone at OakElmAsh . 'Tracy was the only person that sprung to Julia's mind and she wouldn't put it past her at all.

'No I'm not being blackmailed.' Neil shook his head and Julia's face fell.

Tracy

Tracy, as usual was the last person in the office because everybody else had left for home. As she watered the pot plants and placed some cups in the sink, thoughts like deranged fish swam round in her head. She was confused about Neil and was beginning to wonder whether her allegiance to him had been misplaced. The last few times she had tried to contact him, it was clear that he could hardly be bothered to give her the time of day. Gone were their flirty chats and he seemed to have completely lost his sense of humour.

Whatever the fallout had been between him and Charles; it clearly wasn't going to be blowing over in the near future.

And if Charles could dispense with the services of his long-time friend in such a blasé manner, that made her position at OakElmAsh a lot less secure than she had led herself to believe. Furthermore, she had noted a distinct frostiness in Charles' attitude towards her that day and wondered if he suspected her of deliberately misleading his son. Tracy bit her lip.

Despite all of the false information she had supplied Max with, the boy clearly wasn't as stupid as she had first thought. Pretty soon he had got wise enough to look up the days viewings for himself and not ask her for any advice. Also, he had actually managed to sell a couple of properties that day. It seemed that his appointment might not be the temporary glitch that she had at first thought. And, if Max was going to be a more permanent fixture, then she ought perhaps to make an effort with who was after all, the boss's son. Tracy wished she could take back her earlier snide comment about the flying pigs. If Tracy wanted to get back into Charles's good books then being nicer to Max was a prerequisite.

Was it possible that Charles knew about her leading Max a song and dance? She thought back to all those complaints and angry customers on the phone. Maybe it hadn't been her smartest move to fiddle with the times and post codes. But even now, picturing those angry faces grumbling about him brought a smile to her lips, which she quickly suppressed. After all, Max seemed to have cottoned on pretty quick and no doubt must have mentioned it to his father or maybe his mother. The lovely Pamela, oh yes, she had some information about her husband that she perhaps needed to hear. Once more, Tracy's lips set into an upward curve.

That day had certainly been very strange. At first Charles had skirted around her and kept his distance, as if she was creating some bad smell. Then all of a sudden he was bothering her for phone numbers. Well one number in particular. Why had Charles been so desperate to have Julia's number? Tracy knew there could only be one plausible explanation. As soon as he had the paper in his hand, he was straight on the phone to Julia arranging what could only be a rendezvous. Charles and Julia, now there was an interesting thought. When Charles had left the office that afternoon, Tracy knew exactly where he was going and with whom he would be meeting. Was this to become a regular occurrence Tracy wondered? Personally, she couldn't see what Charles, Neil or anyone would find attractive about dowdy Julia but then compared with Pamela …

Pamela was surprised that Max had come home by himself and not with his father. When the white company van had pulled up outside the house and her son got out, she automatically assumed there had been some accident. She imagined Charles bleeding and lying on a stretcher, or worse. If something dreadful had happened to her husband however would she cope?

Pamela anxiously ran to open the door. ‘Max … where‘s your father? You always come home together.’

‘I don’t know. He wasn’t in the office.’ Max removed his jacket and didn’t seem in the least concerned about Charles’s whereabouts.

‘Wasn’t in the office. Didn’t you find out? Oh my God … he’s ill isn’t he? Max where is he?’ Pamela was becoming hysterical.

‘Well, I asked Tracy and she said he’d gone to a meeting.’ Tracy had that familiar glint of mischief in her eye he recalled, as if *meeting* was some type of saucy euphemism.

‘A meeting? Meeting with whom. It’s after six and it’s getting late.’ Pamela looked at her watch to further verify this fact.

‘I don’t know. Maybe he’s gone to the golf club.’ Max thought this the most likely place.

‘No it can’t be … he would have rung me. Where’s my phone?’ Pamela ran to the lounge to scour likely phone places.

‘I’m sure he’ll be back soon.’ Max shouted from the hallway.

‘I’m not sure. This isn’t like your father. He’s always ready for his dinner and I’ve made steak and kidney pie.’ She dashed into the kitchen to see if that’s where she left it. ‘Ring your father now.’

‘He’s here. Look his cars pulling into the drive.’ Max watched his father’s car through the window.

‘Thank goodness.’ Pamela straightened her hair in the mirror.

‘Sorry son. Did Tracy tell you I’d gone to a meeting,’ Charles said nonchantly, as he came through the door.

'A funny time for a meeting Charles.' Pamela looked at him accusingly. 'I was worried sick. Why didn't you ring me to tell me you'd be late?'

'I'm only a few minutes later than normal … I'm hardly late. What's all the fuss?' Charles raised his hands to signal the conversation was over.

'Who were you meeting?' Pamela's nose wrinkled and though she had smelled a decaying rat.

'Just a client. Nobody special.' A hint of annoyance crept into Charles's voice.

'What client? What was it about?' Pamela was becoming alarmingly screechy..

'I'm a bloody estate agent. What do you think it was about?' He threw his coat on the sofa in anger. 'Anyway Max, well done to you.'

'Thanks dad.' For once Max felt pleased with himself.

'Pamela you should be proud of your son. Two offers on properties today. Excellent work.' He patted his son on the back.

'But who was this meeting with?' Pamela persisted.

'For Christ's sake woman, be quiet.' Charles sat at the table waiting for his food and refused to say another word.

Chapter 19

Julia

Forty Years Earlier

It was a warm day in late July and it was the first morning of the Mason family's summer holiday in the Lake District. Up above was a cornflower blue sky, which the clouds scudded across in herds of fluffy white sheep. Julia had fond memories of this place from last year and she hoped the day wasn't going to be spoilt by rain. She had remembered:the long walks over hills and round lakes; delicious meals of sausages and bacon cooked on the little primus stove and the laughter the three of them had shared together. Mum, dad and Julia, on camping vacation and having the very best of times. Last year, she had been only eight years old and now she was a much more worldly-wise nine; it could only be better. They had even come to the same campsite at Hawkeshead.

They had arrived last night because dad had been at work, so they hadn't been able to begin their journey until quite late. Julia had waited in the car, while mum and dad were putting up the tent. It was raining and it seemed to take them ages. Neither of them had very happy faces and they were speaking to each other in surly, loud voices. The poles and orange canvas kept collapsing into muddled heaps on the floor. Julia was pleased when the task was accomplished, as she was very tired and wanted to get inside her little blue sleeping bag.

Once they had finished, she happily went into her compartment in the tent. As she fell asleep, she could hear her parents whispering outside and before she knew it morning, had arrived.

'Come on sleepy head.' Her mother opened the zip on the tent and was her usual cheerful self. As always, mum looked lovely in denim shorts, a flowery tea shirt and blue flip flops. Julia could smell the bacon and sausages cooking and dressed as quick as a flash in her blue shorts and top.

'Morning love. Are you ready for something to eat?' Her mother asked and Julia nodded. She sat on the tartan blanket that was spread out on the ground, to admire the scenery. Her father looked more relaxed than he had of late, and he was wearing his jeans and a t shirt. Julia liked her father dressed like this, as he looked somehow more approachable than when he was wearing a suit and going to work.

'Did you sleep alright dear?' Her father didn't look at her but continued reading his newspaper.

'So what are we going to do today?' Carol gave both Julia and her husband plates laden with the usual eggs, bacon and sausage. Julia was hungry and began eating hers immediately, as meals always tasted so much better out of doors. ? outdoors

'Well,' answered Michael, after a few mouthfuls of food. 'We are in the Lake District, so a walk might be a good idea.'

'Yes, a walk would be lovely.' But Julia noticed that her mum wasn't eating any breakfast and her eyes looked wet.

'And do you have any suggestions where we might go to? I seriously hope you aren't thinking of wearing those shoes.' Dad didn't sound very happy and he pointed at mum's little blue flip flops with their pretty shiny sequins.

'No, of course not.' Mum sighed.' I have my boots in the tent.'

'And your proposition is? As to where we should actually go?' He jabbed at a sausage on his plate.

'What about that nice circular route around Buttermere.' Carol looked at her husband searching for approval of this idea. Julia could remember this walk fondly from last year, as it hadn't been too tiring and there had been none of the really big hills to climb. But best of all was the lovely ice cream she had eaten at the end.

'And that's your best suggestion is it?' Her father rolled his eyes and opened his book on strenuous Lakeland Walks . 'We did that one last year. What about this one on *The Old Man of Coniston.'*

'Won't that one be difficult. I mean Coniston's a big mountain and Julia is only little …' Carol sounded uncertain.

'I'm nine years old.' Julia announced proudly.

'You see Julia's up for it. Got more gumption than your pathetic mother haven't you?' Father and daughter shared a conspiratorial smile.

'Listen, it sounds perfect *At over 2,600 feet, the mountain Old Man Coniston is an excellent walk for those with a bit of stamina. It's a pleasant walk at first but does become more challenging as the hike progresses.*' Michael waited for his wife's reaction.

'How long does it take?' Carol noticed her watch said eight o'clock.

'Six hours. And don't worry we have plenty of time before dark.' Michael was gleefully tracing the route, with its closely spaced contours, on the Ordinance Survey Map.

'That's a long time and I think it's too much for Julia.' Carols lower lip was quivering.

'Now come on my dear. It's not really Julia you are thinking of, is it?'

Trevor

Ten Years Later

Trevor had been very shocked when he had discovered his wife in the garden when he came back from work. For the past few weeks, her most strenuous unassisted journey had been from bed to bathroom. It was obvious that the effects of the ketamine were wearing off and it was essential that he got his hands on some of the drug today, otherwise all of his good work might well come undone. The fact that she had deluded herself that there was anything at all pleasant in that weed-infested mess of a garden, was proof that her brain was still befuddled. But if she was without the drug for much longer, she might become capable of rational thought. She needed to write that bloody letter, so there was no chance of her returning to the university.

Realising that his best chance of gaining access to the cupboard was by getting to work even earlier, at half past six he had left from home. There was just a little of the ketamine left, so he been able to make a flask of tea for Julia, but that was the last of it. He shouldn't have been so negligent and allowed his supplies to get so low. Once he was inside the building he placed his coat over the C.C.T.V. and went to the throat lozenge tin. When he opened the cupboard, there were the bottles of ketamine lined up next to the codeine and heroin. Carefully he opened one and poured some of the powder into an old coffee jar. He didn't like to take too much at once. Little and often that was the way. Suddenly, he heard a noise from the door. Quickly, Trevor locked the cupboard then squashed the tin and key into his trouser pocket.

'Is somebody there?' Nick, the manager of the pharmacy came in through the door and was surprised to see Trevor. 'Why Trevor, what on earth are you doing on the floor down there?'

'Morning Nick.' Damn, Trevor needed to think quickly. 'I thought I heard a … scuffling noise down here and thought it might be a ... rat.

'A rat? Gracious me I hope not. Still it wouldn't be surprising with all of the bakeries and such like around here. Did you find any trace? Any droppings or such like.' Nick observed his assistant on the floor almost appearing like some weird giant rodent himself.

'No not as yet but I'll keep looking.' Trevor scratched his fingers across the floor, as if trying to make himself a burrow to hide in.

'Trevor. Why are you here?' Nick thought there was no reason for him to be at work so early.' It's only half past seven and you don't begin work for another hour.'

'Erm … I couldn't sleep. So I thought I'd get myself here nice and early.' Trevor stretched his arms as if he had just got out of bed.

'Having dreams about being a rat catcher were you. Ha ha.'

Nick didn't look very amused.

'Must have been ... something like that.' Trevor felt very awkward and wished the ground would swallow him up.

Nick left Trevor crawling about the floor but he thought it very odd. There was something about the man that he couldn't just bring himself to like. Trevor had worked here longer than him, and in accordance with his position was always deferential to his boss, but it seemed he was almost excessively so. There was something creepy about the man and he reminded him of Uriah Heep in David Copperfield. He gathered that Trevor had not been long married and he found it very strange that he should want to tear himself away from his matrimonial bed so early. However, Nick wondered what sort of odd creature would want to marry Trevor. Nick had come in early to send an order for some drugs and had expected to find the place empty. There was definitely something very peculiar about Trevor's presence and then he caught sight of the black coat covering the C.C.T.V. camera.

Zoe

The Present

Zoe knew that Julia wasn't going to like it, but she felt compelled to ask her about the information she had found out about Trevor being a missing person. What she found really odd was, after the initial report there was no thread to follow this up. Had Trevor been found? Was Trevor dead? Was Julia a bigamist? This wasn't going to be an easy conversation but her friend was clearly troubled by something and once the whereabouts of Trevor were cleared up – well it could only help surely. At the end of the day, Zoe went along to Julia's classroom where she was deep in conversation with her classroom assistant Emily.

'Hi Julia have you had a good day?' Zoe plonked herself onto one of the classroom tables.

'Yes fine thanks Zoe. What about you?' Julia looked much calmer today.

'Julia, I'm in a bit of a rush.' Emily put on her coat.' My son's got a dentist's appointment.'

'Yes Emily, you go. I'll fill you in with tomorrow's details in the morning.' Julia straightened the pens on her desk.

Zoe was pleased that Emily had been got rid of so easily. 'Julia, I've got a few questions I need to ask you.'

'Go on.' Julia thought this sounded ominous.

Zoe bit the bullet. 'It's about Trevor. You know your *first* husband.'

'Yes I knew who you were referring to.' She really couldn't be bothered with this again.' But really Zoe, it was such a terrible time in my life, I can hardly bear to think about it all.'

'I know but Julia, you clearly have something on your mind which is troubling you.' Zoe wasn't going to give up on this one.

'Zoe you know I've had problems with Neil, but they seem to be resolving themselves.' Julia nodded and forced a smile.

'Julia, 'Continued Zoe. 'I looked up Trevor … Trevor Squires on the internet … And he's a *missing person.*' Zoe looked around to see if anyone was listening but nobody was.

'Yes Zoe. That's right he is.' Julia confirmed.

'But Julia that was over twenty years ago and has he never been found?' Zoe was confused, because while she was shocked by this puzzling discovery, Julia was as cool as a cucumber.

'Well Zoe, I don't know where he is. He might be alive or dead. I really have no idea.' And she shrugged her shoulders.

'But Julia you could be a *bigamist.*' The horror of this idea was transparent on Zoe's face.

'No I'm not a bigamist. Once someone has been missing for seven years, they are presumed dead and you are free to marry again.' Zoe was flabbergasted, as Julia reeled off the information like a passage from a dry school textbook.

'I see. And do you think he is dead?' This wasn't what Zoe was expecting at all.

'Well it certainly seems more than likely. I mean toads don't just crawl under stones and never emerge do they? Do you imagine if he were alive, he would have been pleased to see me happy with Neil? If Trevor could possibly cause me any trouble, he would. Don't you think?' Julia had not expected to be having any conversation about her detested former husband with Zoe or anyone else for that matter.

'And are you happy with Neil?' Zoe couldn't possibly believe that Julia could possibly be happy with her second lying, cheating husband.

'He's got another job.' She said matter-of-factly.

'Really. How's he done that?' Zoe was aghast.

'He's not in property anymore … he's selling cars.'

Zoe couldn't understand how Neil had pulled this one off. 'Wow. Well that's a turn up for the books. So that must mean you'll be all right.'

'Yes, I guess so.' But there was an uncertainty in her voice. Julia picked up her bag and although this conversation was over for now, there was something her friend just wasn't telling her.

Tracy

The next day, during her lunch hour, Tracy decided to do a little shopping. There were a few essentials that she really needed to buy from Boots; her best mascara had become all claggy and she needed a new bottle of nail vanish remover. She glanced down with distaste at the chip in her ice white nail varnish, seeming to her like a massive crack in a pane of glass. After crossing over Newgate Street, she entered the busy Eldon Square shopping centre through Debenhams, where she noticed one of her favourite perfumes; Paris by Yves St Laurent, was on special offer. Usually Tracy could never resist a bargain, but as her relationship with Charles still seemed decidedly shaky at the moment, she decided against the unnecessary expenditure.

She was puzzled about Charles' strange behaviour towards her, because if it had been brought to light that she was setting up his son to failure, then surely it would have been mentioned to her earlier. Even Max, who wasn't the sharpest tool in the box, had suspected something was amiss. Also, she had felt that her orchestration of Max's poor performance, at been in the best interests of the company. For if Charles were to reinstate Neil, she had thought at the time, then it was to everyone's benefit.

Tracy was annoyed and she felt that she was being poorly treated. She had never known a time before when she had to think twice about buying what was clearly an excellent bargain. Whether she was more angry with the indifference of Neil or the attitude of Charles towards her, she just couldn't decide. Catching sight of her reflection, she noticed the bright lights in the shop illuminating the scowl on her face, the corrugated lines on her forehead and spiders webs at corners of her eyes most unattractively. This wasn't good, she was forty eight and still single. Throughout the years her penchant for married men had certainly not paid any dividends, and Tracy, ever the party girl wasn't having so much fun. Switching her thoughts back and forth between Julia and Pamela, she couldn't pick which smug wife she disliked the most; dowdy, boring Julia or prissy pathetic Pamela.

Then across the department shop floor, she spotted a familiar figure dressed in a peculiar shade of lavender, who was non-other than Pamela herself. As usual, Tracy found the fussy flowery dress, accompanied by a vivid purple jacket she was wearing awful. On her feet were little cream ballet type pumps and round her neck she wore a string of pearls. Who in this day and age dressed like that? An unkind image of Bette Davis in *Whatever Happened to Baby Jane* flashed through her mind. Pamela was engrossed in testing various vibrant lipsticks on the back of her hand, until Tracy marched over.
'Hello Pamela … I mean … Mrs Lavender. How are you today?' Pamela in confusion scanned Tracy up and down, from the bleached platinum tresses to the tarty white stilettos shoes, before eventually recognising her.
'Oh hello. It's Tracy isn't it?' This woman wasn't somebody she usually held conversations with.
'Yes that's right. I was just wondering how your husband has been at home recently?'
A very odd question, and what business is it of yours anyway thought Pamela. 'Charles? He's been fine? Why do you ask?'
'Well it's just with everything being so busy with the … comings and goings there.' She said pointedly.' You know with Max *coming* and Neil *going*.'
'Yes, well, Charles has always been very good at handling tricky situations.' Pamela was starting to feel a little uncomfortable and couldn't see where this could be leading.
'So I gather. Well he would have to be wouldn't he? Especially at the moment.'
There was a certain glee in Tracy's voice that Pamela found unnerving and she couldn't understand why on earth Charles employed this brash, common woman. 'What do you mean?' She asked warily.
'Well now he has all these extra *meetings* to attend to.' Tracy stressed the word meetings, to imply something distasteful had been taking place.
Pamela had a feeling of foreboding. 'Yes, he was late home last night … because of a

meeting with some client or other.' The anxious feelings of last night were returning but keeping even worse company.

'Really, that's very interesting because I know for a fact, this meeting was with a most unlikely client.' Tracy was enjoying herself enormously.

'Who was it with?' As the conversation unravelled, Pamela was visibly shrinking.

'Not that I'm one to spread gossip but …' Teasing this tittle-tattle merchant was such fun thought Tracy and no less than she deserved.

'Tell me Tracy. I felt there was something amiss last night. Who was he meeting?' Pamela was almost down on her knees scraping and bowing to this horrible woman.

'Well I must admit I was quite surprised myself. I couldn't for the life of me think what those two would have to talk about. I mean after everything that had happened recently…' Tracy felt like a cat playing with a feeble mouse.

'Tracy I think this is something I deserve to know.' Pamela's eyes were welling with tears.

Had the woman no dignity thought Tracy, and after a long pause she pronounced. 'Very well … it was Julia.' And she pronounced each syllable of the name with a distinct note of pleasure.

'Julia Latimer … Neil's Julia?' Julia who always wore such elegant clothes, unlike her? Pamela hadn't been expecting that. Her confusion turned to anger and then to fear.

'Yes I thought it was very peculiar.' Tracy's face wore a mask of mock innocence, as if unaware of the damage she was doing.' He was on the phone to her nearly all afternoon. I have no idea what that was all about. And then for some reason, he went round to her house.'

'Oh well, Neil must have been there too.' Relief flooded across Pamela's face. 'Maybe they are sorting work related things and … Charles is going to reinstate Neil.' The tone of Pamela's voice became fifty times lighter.

'I must admit, I thought that myself too but … Neil couldn't have been there because he's got a new job.' Tracy delivered this piece of information as if accompanied by a triumphant crash of cymbals.

'Well that means …' Pamela's voice trailed off. Charles must be having an affair with Julia and that's why he was so elusive with his whereabouts last night.

'Anyway, talking of jobs. It's time I was on my way to mine or your husband won't be too happy with me. But please, Mrs Lavender… Pamela, don't mention that you heard all this from me.' And after opening this Pandora's Box, Tracy disappeared behind a display of suitcases and carpet bags.

Julia

Julia realised that after forcing Neil to confront a few home truths last night, more than likely he wouldn't be home early but in the Golf Club with his new drinking buddies. She could picture him there vividly, downing the pints, laughing and telling jokes. Julia shook her head. Her conversation with Zoe, had made her see that it was imperative to take action now. At any time it was likely that work would begin on the new road, diggers would arrive, land would be upturned and the ghastly contents of the rose bed would be revealed. She shuddered to think how her world would be turned upside down upon this discovery. She imagined her immediate arrest, brutal interrogations from police, lawyers and judges, followed almost certainly by her lifelong incarceration. Julia just couldn't bear the thought. Additionally, the problem with Neil and his stupid embezzlement still wasn't settled, but that one was out of her hands and if he made a success of this job maybe he could pay Charles Lavender back the money he owed.

As Zoe suspected, Julia did have other plates to spin and to maintain control, action was needed immediately. With that thought in mind she set off for the woods, to find a suitable burial spot. Yet was this only delaying the inevitable? The contents of the flower bed were far much safer in the back garden and less likely to be discovered there than any place she could find in the woods. Nevertheless, their finding would now be imminent and the connection with her obvious. At least, if they were elsewhere, their detection might take some time and after all everyone only lives for so long. So with a little luck they might lay undisturbed until years after her death. How awful it was to have this hanging over her, but this terrible burden was now so much part of her, without it she would no longer be herself. Any Julia, without her Sword of Damocles, just didn't exist.

As she walked through the nearby woods, she found children playing and people walking dogs everywhere. How on earth was she going to dig a deep enough hole for a grave without being detected? After some time moving deeper into the more densely packed trees, she came upon some boulders by a thick clump of bushes. This spot might be the place. She could move the boulders to dig underneath where they lay and then cover up the hole with them. But, even from here she could hear voices. There was only one possible time this deed could be done and this was during the dead of night. How could she explain her strange nightly sojourns to Neil though? Perhaps she could persuade him that his gambling peccadillos had proved contagious and she was now compelled to visit the casino each night. This of course was a ridiculous idea. However, she needed to think of a plan and time was not a luxury she had. Neil would no doubt becoming back for his tea well tanked-up. All she had to do was ply him with more drink until he fell asleep unconscious and she could go out to accomplish her mission in the woods. Although she didn't wish alcoholism upon her husband, he wasn't far off that anyway … and needs must.

Well, there was no time like the present. So Julia went to search out a tempting collection of whiskies, gins, wines and beers for her new project. The most convenient place was the local shop she often visited, when she had run out of small items like milk or bread. The owner, Mr Singh, was a middle-aged Sikh man sporting a purple turban. At first, he raised his eyebrows at her decadent purchases but soon his eyes lit up like Diva lamps when he realised just how much money she was actually spending in his humble establishment.

As she was walking home, having left her car back at home, the two carrier bags filled with the various bottles were a struggle. The bottles clanked together noisily, as she passed a couple who tutted at her with judgemental disapproval. Julia ignored them and continued on her way.

When she arrived home Mabel was watching her curiously and listening to the clinking sounds, as Julia plonked the bags on the floor with great relief. By now it was dark, after seven and there was still no sign of Neil. Julia poured herself a glass of wine, just the one though, as she needed to keep her wits about her for later. Then, she took a couple of steaks out of freezer to prepare Neil's favourite meal. Mabel was being at her most annoying as she kept purring loudly and trying to jump up onto the bench, as she was also fond of sirloin.

'Mabel, behave.' As Julia picked up the large furry creature for the umpteenth time, Neil appeared at the door obviously the worse for wear.

'Hello dear. Have you had a good day? And before you say anything … I've left the car ... car at work and I've just got a taxi back from the golf club.' Neil was staggering across the kitchen floor, slurring his words and Mabel took this as her cue for a sharp exit.

'That's ok dearest. I knew you wouldn't be silly enough to drive after a few drinks. Yes, my day's been fine thank you and what can I get you to drink?' Neil slumped himself onto a chair and clocked with delight the selection of drinks lined up on the side.

'Mmm … I think I'll have a whisky if that's ok.' Neil wondered what this was all about, but in a good way.

Julia threw a couple of ice cubes in a glass, and then filled the rest of the tumbler with whisky. 'There you go Neil.' She handed him the drink. 'Now I hope you are hungry because guess what I'm making for tea.'

'I hope it's something good because I'm starving.' Neil patted his stomach, which contained several pints which needed soaking up, took a large gulp of whisky and smacked his lips.

'Your favourite … Steak Diane.' And Julia placed a bowl of salad on the table, knowing full well Neil wouldn't be touching any of it.

'Well Julia, this is a welcome turn up for the books. What have I done to deserve all of this?' Neil couldn't believe his good fortune.

'Neil, you have been through such a horrible time … and now you have your new job.' Julia gave her husband her sweetest of smiles. 'Well I thought my husband deserved a little pampering for a change.' She reached for the bottle and topped her husband's drink up, before returning to the steaks.

'Well I'm not going to argue with that one.' Neil felt like the king in his castle.

'So who was there at the golf club?' Julia watched him closely while adding the cream, mustard and a little brandy to the pan.

'Oh it was just Geoff and the gang … you know.' Neil grinned to himself like Cheshire

Cat, remembering proudly all the hilarious jokes he had told, that had made everyone crease up with laughter.

'Right well drink up, your food's just about ready.' Neil needed little encouragement and downed his second large glass of whisky. Julia placed two plates on the table and opened a bottle of Chateauneuf-du-Pape. She brought her glass of white to the table, that she had poured herself earlier and filled husband's glass to the brim with the red.

Neil attacked his steak with gusto, which he washed down enthusiastically with the expensive wine. 'This is the life Ju … Julia. This is like the old days on holiday, isn't it?'

'Well perhaps if your new job goes well, we can have a holiday soon.' Julia took a conservative sip from her drink, added some salad to her plate. She thought this unlikely considering their debts, but didn't mention it as she wanted to keep her husband sweet.

'So, where … where would you … like to go?' Neil was now slurring very badly and his eyes had a peculiar glaze.

'I wouldn't mind going back to Sorrento. We had a lovely time there didn't we?' Julia thought briefly of the lovely blues of the sky and sea at the Amalfi coast, before concentrating completely on the task in hand; rendering her husband unconscious.

'Is that where we went to Pomp…Pomp Pomp…' Neil had blurry recollections of the people's preserved bodies, like the snake woman had turned them to stone.

'Yes, Pompei, and remember we went to Herculaneum and Naples too.' Julia filled up Neil's glass generously once more and she could see he was beginning to struggle with his food. She needed to keep the conversation going, to make sure he drank more and went out like a light.

'When we went to Crete that was great too. That must be a few years ago now. We saw where the Labyrinth, which was where King Minos kept the Minotaur.' Julia held the drink to his lips and the red liquid dribbled down his chin.

'Minotaur.' Repeated Neil, slavering like one of Pavlov's dogs and struggling to keep his eyes open.

'Do you remember in Barcelona when someone tried to steal your wallet on the train? And then in Rome, I had my purse stolen on the Spanish Steps?' By this time Neil was loudly snoring like a pig and Julia guessed she had better help him to bed.

Chapter 20

Julia

30 Years Ago

Julia had just finished writing the letter to Newcastle University, to inform them that she would not be returning to complete her teaching degree in September. Although she felt a great sadness about this, she also felt a massive relief, as if an enormous weight had been lifted from her shoulders. The cup of tea that Trevor had left her in the morning had been left to go cold and untouched. The thermos flask next to be bed likewise remained unopened. Julia had drunk three cups of tea, which had all tasted marvellous and actually like tea. She herself, was feeling better than she had done in weeks. Although she had gone to sleep the night before in her usual groggy state, she had nevertheless appreciated the clean sheets on the bed. Almost as soon as she had woken, she had showered and made herself a drink and was proud with herself to be actually doing something purposeful for once.

Despite the fact that when Trevor had dragged her back into the house, the usual humiliations and criticisms continued, she was beginning to feel just a little less worthless. It was almost as if her visit to the garden had provided her with chain mail and some of his hurtful words were just bouncing off her like arrows. She wasn't useless; she'd had friends like Zoe and was successfully pursuing a teaching degree before she met him. She thought back to her hideous charade of a wedding and that pitiful dress. Then there had been the catastrophic aftermath, for which she had been blamed.

For the first time she was beginning to see the situation as it really was. It was as if some curtains had now been opened. There were still thick, lace ones in place on the windows, but they were not opaque and slowly, she was beginning to see blurry images through them. The Trevor she had met was not the Trevor she had married. Similarly, the Julia she had been, was not the Julia of now. But beneath the ugly cocoon of weight gain, the real Julia lay there dormant but waiting … waiting to emerge from the ugly chrysalis and fly. For the first time Julia could see that the charming, thoughtful Trevor who had wooed her, had just been a clever act.

From the moment they had married, even at the ceremony and disgusting fish and chip wedding breakfast, Prince Charming had revealed himself as the true frog he actually was. Their marriage had never been consummated because he had plied her with drink on that very first night. He had done it deliberately so he didn't have to fulfil his husbandly duties. It was now plain that he had never wanted to and the forcing of her to drink all the disgusting cheap cava had all been a deliberate ploy.

If truth be known, what did actually know about the monster she had married? It suited him perfectly to sleep in the other bedroom because he had never considered her sexually attractive in the first place. So what had he wanted from her?

In hindsight, she ought to have found it strange that he had never shown her where he had lived and for that matter he had never taken her to his place of work. Was he even a chemist? She was sure a chemist would earn a decent wage but as far as she could see her financial circumstances had reduced considerably since her marriage. In fact, she felt like a pauper while Trevor held the purse strings, owned her parents' house and kept her as a prisoner. And why had she allowed herself to become so fat, useless and pathetic. Julia poured the contents of the thermos flask down the sink and went outside to begin tackling the garden.

Max

The Present

Max was glad to be escaping from the house. Something was clearly amiss with his mother, who had been even more jumpy than usual and had prattled relentlessly throughout the meal about the most absurd rubbish. She had actually been talking about all the items that she had bought, first in town and then at the supermarket. The list was endless but as if that wasn't bad enough, she proceeded to describe each one in detail to assess the quality and value of each product. His father had switched off and he had just tried to eat his meal as quickly as possible to escape.

He was going to meet his friend Nigel in town to discuss their forthcoming trip to Thailand. Neither of them had booked their flights as yet. However, each time he had spoken to Nigel recently, it was clear that whilst he was becoming more excited at the prospect, Max was starting to have his own reservations. A large part of this was due to him beginning to make a go of things at OakElmAsh and he was beginning to actually enjoy himself there. Some of this was a result of the offers on the properties that he had facilitated yesterday, but an even bigger level of satisfaction he was gaining from getting up one on that mean cow Tracy. He now knew full well what her little game had been about. Now he was looking forward at her getting her comeuppance and seeing that smug smile wiped from her face for good.

This time their meeting was in the Mean-Eyed Cat bar, on St Thomas Street, which wasn't actually that far from his place of work. He hadn't been there before but he had spotted it on one of his lunch breaks and liked the sound of the name. Although the outside had the appearance of a pre-fab classroom, when he walked in he was greeted by the warmth from the yellow and terracotta walls, jauntily-tiled tables and a cacophony of colour. There were some frenzied instruments playing in the background, as if a collection of drums, conches, flutes and trumpets had been randomly placed in a sack and were being persistently rattled. The clientele, largely a mixture of students and the recently-retired were deep in conversation and obviously enjoying themselves as their laughter soared above the sounds of the music.

Max spotted his friend sitting beneath the framed picture of a ferocious-looking tabby, sporting a sombrero and a scowl. The place had a cool, Mexican feel to it. Max nodded to his friend before going to the bar to order a Sol, with a slice of lime in the neck of the bottle.

'Hi dude. How's it rolling?'

Max pulled up a blue, painted chair at the table next to his friend.

'How's it going with the flights?' Max had never seen his friend looking so fired up and animated; it wasn't a good look.

'Well … those I was looking at the other day… well, they seem to have all gone bruv.' Max twisted his face into an apologetic grimace.

'Damn, just think though. This time next week we could be surfin' the waves.' Nigel wasn't picking up on any negative vibes.

'Actually, all the flights I've seen seem to have increased massively in price.' Max stared fixedly at the yellow wall in front of him.

'Never … how much are you talkin'?' Nigel didn't think the odd couple of hundred made much difference, as his mind was now a full conglomerate of sun, sea and sand.

'I've not seen anything under two grand.' Max took a drink from his beer and avoided eye contact with Nigel.

'Shit. That's more than four times the price.' Nigel felt his crest beginning to fall.

'I know. It's a bugger, isn't it?' Max shook his head sympathetically.

'But does it matter? I mean we're just sticking it on the wrinklies' credit cards, aren't we?' Nigel would not let his dreams be so easily shattered.

'Yes, but … if we just hold fire. These flights change on a daily basis.' Max hated lying to his best friend but what else could he do?

Nigel took his phone out of pocket, switched on his mobile data and began searching on Google. Max knew what he was doing and winced, while staring at his empty drink for some help'

'I'm going to the bar Nige. Do you want another drink?'

Nigel shook his head as he had been far too excited to hardly touch his pint.

'Max what you on about?' Said Nigel'

Max came back to the table, this time with a pint, looking sheepish. 'There's one here for £876. It goes next week and changes at Paris and Dubai.'

'I'm not sure.' Max wriggled uncomfortably in his seat and the mean cat on the wall watched him judgementally.

'What do you mean? This was all your idea. You said you were sick of all the wasters here. You were the one who wanted to seize the moment. What's wrong with you? You're not having second thoughts, are you?' Nigel was becoming agitated and as he pulled his fingers through his unruly blond hair it stuck up in spikes like pitchforks.

'No it's not that at all.' Max wasn't ruling out the idea completely, he just needed a little time. 'I mean, Newcastle in the winter or Thailand in the sun. I mean, there's just no comparison is there.'

'Exactly, so what's all this shit about expensive flights?' Nigel voice was getting louder and his bottom lip was well sticking out.

'I dunno. Guess I just must have been … looking in the wrong places.' Max notices the barman eyeing them suspiciously, hoping there wasn't going to be any trouble from them.

'Well what about this one? We could book it now …' Nigel persisted.

'I haven't got that card with me.' Max told yet another lie and felt the plastic in his wallet burning a hole in his pocket.

'Well … I've got mine. 'Nigel slammed it on the table triumphantly.' I could book them and you could pay me back. Just imagine us shootin' the breeze in the sunshine.'

Max had never seen his friend with what he assumed was a seductive glint in his eye before, and it was unsettling.

'No Nige. Just hang fire. Not now.' Max was aware that everyone in the pub was listening to their conversation with interest.

'I knew you were having second thoughts. Stop lying.' Nigel banged his fist down hard so both his phone and card fell off the table and clattered on the wooden floor.

'I'm not having second thoughts. I just need a couple of weeks to sort a few things out.' Max wasn't sure if this wasn't even worse than being at home. He had never seen laid back Nigel like this before.

'What sort of things? Have you got a girlfriend or something?' Nigel, sick with sour grapes, couldn't think what else it could be.

'No … it's nothing like that.' Max wasn't even sure he ever wanted to go anywhere again with Nigel, after this unbecoming display.

'Well?'

Nigel just needed a silly hat to be the double of the cat in the picture above him.

'It's connected with work.' Max knew Nigel would hate this.

'You said you hated work.' He spat the words out as if they were poisoned darts.

'I know. But it's not as bad as I thought.' Max looked sheepish.

Nigel looked incredulous. 'Really? Look, just tell me the truth. This isn't fair. If you don't want to go, just tell me.' Nigel stood up.

'Dude come on, of course I want to go. I just need to sort a few things out first.' Max wished he'd never mentioned it to him in the first place.

'Whatever. Oh just do one.'

With half of his pint still on the table, a furious Nigel left the bar.

Charles

Charles couldn't think whatever had got into his wife that evening, as she had been twittering even more inanely than usual and he wished that he too had gone out for a drink with a friend. Yet, since the situation with Neil, he now had nobody to meet for a few beers. This saddened him greatly. He was wary of going to the golf club, in case he should be questioned by anyone about the embarrassing sacking situation. Also, there was a likelihood he might actually bump into Neil or even worse, the self-appointed angel of retribution; Obadiah.

So, he had the dubious pleasure of spending another lovely evening in the company of his dear wife. Currently, Pamela was pretending to be engrossed in a jigsaw puzzle of an old castle that she had been working on for several days. Yet, during the past half hour, she appeared to have added no new pieces whatsoever to the picture and he was aware of her giving him sidelong glances, when she thought he wasn't watching. Her constant sighing was a source of great irritation, especially as he was trying to watch an old episode of Vera on the television and the plot was even more complicated than usual.

Normally, he would just tell her to be quiet but he could see that something was deeply bothering her. As he could think of nothing that he'd done wrong recently, he assumed it must be down to women's problems. The menopause was a mystery to him which he had no desire to investigate. So any conversation with his wife at this time was best avoided, as this was an exclusively female road, down which he did not wish to travel.

'Would you like a cup of tea Charles?' Pamela asked, knowing full well he was fully occupied drinking whiskies and soda.

'No, you're all right thanks.' Charles was intently watching Vera's bulky frame running down a street.

'It looks like Vera's in Tynemouth, doesn't it?' She tried to engage her husband in conversation.

'Yes that's where she is. She's just had a meeting with one of the murder suspects.' Charles was enjoying looking for places he recognised.

'Have you had any meetings today?' Pamela's affected nonchalance didn't quite work and Charles remembered her earlier ranting on this matter.

'A couple. Just the usual stuff.' Charles rolled his eyes and refilled his glass generously from the Jameson's bottle.

'Who were your meetings with?' Pamela hovered in the doorway.

'Nobody you know. Just people interested in buying houses.' Why was she prattling on about again about meetings wondered Charles in irritation?

'What were their names? I might know them if they are local.' She continued, and the manic note once more crept into her voice.

'I can't remember their names. I would have to check in my diary.' Whatever was the matter with the crazy woman? Charles just wanted to be left in peace to enjoy his programme.

'Well go on then.' She persisted.

'I left it at work. Why are you so interested anyway?' Pamela rarely had any interest in the business and he couldn't fathom what this was all about. The other night he had felt a little uncomfortable about seeing Julia and didn't like to mention it. But his wife wasn't to know this and he hadn't seen anything of Julia since.

'No reason.' Unable to decide where she wanted this conversation to lead and aware she was skating on thin ice, she disappeared into the kitchen to regroup her thoughts and consider her next move.

Charles turned his mind to Julia and wondered what she and Neil were doing at this time. No doubt Neil would be out boozing in the golf club with his new best friend Geoff Armstrong. Charles had never liked the man, there was something definitely shifty about him and his eyes were too close together and An alliance with him, more than likely would get Neil into further bother and it was a well-known fact that Geoff had form. It was rumoured he had spent a considerable part of his younger days *inside* and an association with slippery Geoff could only take Neil further down the rocky road. If only, this had been nipped in the bud … Julia had said that he was a gambler, but to get through that amount of money was gambling in a very serious league. There had to be more to the matter than Julia knew and he was sure that Tracy was in some way involved.

He had thought that Tracy was an asset to the company, with her winning looks and efficiency, but recently he wasn't quite so sure. Certainly, she had seen her giving Max snide looks and speaking to him with a very patronising tone. Considering that he was her boss's son, this didn't sit easily and he would have thought Tracy canny enough to realise on which side her bread was actually buttered. Also, he knew she was unhappy that Neil had been sacked. He had assumed that she missed the pathetic flirting with him and that she had no notion of his crimes whatsoever. But, maybe this was simply not the case. If she had been fully aware of Neil's penchant for risk taking, gambling and theft, then she could quite possibly be equally guilty. Tracy, with her platinum hair and glistening teeth was not quite the lily-white employee she would have him believe. She was clearly not a team player and her blackmailing of that numpty Neil was clearly more of a certainty than inkling. Despite Julia having no knowledge of this, Tracy clearly played a major part in this whole sorry drama.

Pamela back, and armed with a cup of tea, was staring woefully into space.

'Pamela, what do you make of Tracy?' Charles was curious, as to his wife's opinion of the woman as the two of them were clearly as different as chalk and cheese.

Pamela almost spat her tea out over Alnwick Castle. Was her husband reading her mind

as the conversation with that woman was on permanent replay in her head. 'Tracy … you mean the Tracy your receptionist?'
'Yes that Tracy. What are your thoughts on her?' He doubted Pamela held her in great esteem and Charles was looking for further ammunition to engineer her dismissal.
'Well I don't really know … I have never given her much thought.' Pamela lied as her brows knitted together a horrid, white, Tracy jumper in her brain.
'I just wondered. When people come into the showroom, do you think she projects the right image?' Charles couldn't read the strange look on his wife's face.
'Well now that you ask. No. She has a very … I would say she looks cheap. She looks like a tart now that you ask. But worse than that. She looks like a … ghost. All that white hair, clothes, teeth, shoes … it's too much. She must scare people away and give them recurring nightmares.'
'Really? But I thought people liked her.'
'No, everybody I know hates her. She looks like a prostitute and she has a common voice.'
Charles chuckled to himself. 'So I guess, you wouldn't mind if I let her go.'
And Pamela felt a wave of pleasure wash over her, for the first time in days. Now why didn't Charles ask her about Julia, she could put him straight on a few facts there too.

Neil

Neil woke up with a splitting headache and was aghast when he saw that it was ten to nine. Julia had long gone to work and the cup of tea by the side of the bed was stone cold. He groaned, his mouth tasted of cardboard and when he looked in horror at the mirror, his bloodshot eyes told the sorry tale of last night's exploits. He was never going to drink again. This was only his third day at work. Being late and hung-over was not the impression he wanted to give. Armstrong Automobiles was located at the Silverlink Retail Park in Wallsend. That was at least a forty minute drive from his house and that was when the traffic was good. Then to his annoyance, he remembered that he had left his car at the golf club and rang for a taxi.

When he staggered into the shower, the droplets of water bounced off his head like hailstones. There was no time for a drink of coffee or tea and while still half-wet, he dressed hurriedly in his grey shirt and blue suit, making his clothes all uncomfortable and damp. Even after brushing his teeth, he was sure his breath smelt of whisky and he swallowed half a packet of peppermints before jumping into the taxi waiting outside. After a fifteen minute drive with an unusually silent taxi driver, who kept giving him disapproving looks, he was delivered to his new Alpha Romeo. He had better take it easy, for if he were pulled over by the police, the outcome would not be good.

As the traffic lined up bumper to bumper over the Tyne Bridge, he thought about how strange last night had all been. He would have thought Julia would have been angry with him for arriving home drunk – but no. She had been all sweetness and light. He remembered that she had made his favourite meal, Steak Dianne but he couldn't actually remember eating very much of it. In fact the whole of the evening once he arrived home had all been a bit of a foggy blur. Neil went through the chronology of last night's events, as his car crawled along to join the Coast road.

He called to mind holding court in the golf club, as he entertained the gang with his funny jokes and clever repartee. There was lots of laughter, pint downing and back slapping, as another day of successful car selling was celebrated. He was sure he had seen that miserable accountant, Obadiah Goldstein sitting alone in the corner, with a face like he was sucking lemons. He needed to get a life. Anyway, yesterday, Neil had sold seven cars and Geoff had been delighted. Still he couldn't see himself matching that figure today. His head was still pounding like it was a thrash metal player's drum kit and he felt sick.

When he had arrived home last night, Julia had been busy cooking but she had been eager to pour him a whisky, almost as soon as he walked through the door. This at the time had pleased him immensely but upon reflection was slightly odd. She must have been able to tell he had indulged in several drinks already and for him to have more wasn't something she normally encouraged on a school-night, especially now they were both working. Also there was a selection of new bottles in the kitchen that must have cost quite a lot of money. Considering recent conversations about frugality; this was very odd.

As Julia recharged his glass, very generously, Neil had felt very pleased with himself. It was like the old days when they had first got together and they were reminiscing about past holidays in Italy and Greece. But Julia kept filling up his drink repeatedly. It was as if she were deliberately plying him with alcohol. But why would she do that? It made no sense. He remembered seeing his favourite meal on the table but he was sure he couldn't remember eating any of it.

Next thing he recalled was the horror of waking up and realising it was ten to nine. It was now quarter past and he was going to be well and truly late. There were traffic works and hold ups. Plausible excuses tumbled round in his mind like laundry. Then he thought about when he had got up in the early morning to go to the bathroom and Julia had been snoring contentedly next to him. But he had also woken up briefly earlier and he was sure she wasn't there then. Her side of the bed was all cold. Maybe she was just in the bathroom and he hadn't worried because pretty soon he was sparked out once more.

Chapter 21

Julia

36 Years Ago

Julia and her parents had just returned from their annual camping holiday. They had once more, chosen the familiar camp site at Hawkeshead in the Lake District, hoping to recapture the magic of earlier times spent there. Despite the fourteen year old Julia's best efforts to remain upbeat, the only mutual enthusiasm shown by her parents, Carol and Michael was for the curtailing of the whole ordeal rather sooner than planned. During the last few years, vacations had been spent in Yorkshire, The Peak District and Wales, had been quite difficult and they had thought that a return to their earlier stomping ground might rectify matters. But sadly, this didn't seem to be the case. While at home, Carol and Michael were able to avoid each other when they wished; this was not obviously possible while living under canvas.

From the moment the journey began, Michael was particularly surly and snapped at his wife at every available opportunity. Meanwhile Carol, spent most of the car journey, looking out of the window loudly sighing and showing her irritation by grunting at her husband. Julia had asked if they would be going on the lovely walk round Buttermere but her father merely growled and her mother didn't even bother to reply.

Each day, when Julia and her father poured over maps to finalise the walking route for the day, Carol dramatically held an upturned wrist against her forehead, as if in great pain and claimed to not to be very well. Wearing on one occasion, a short ra ra skirt, high heeled shoes and the obligatory, large, 1980s-bouffant hair, she certainly didn't seem suitably attired for a mountain hike. She claimed to have suffered the days looking in the gift shops and sitting in cafes. Options for doing this were somewhat limited in Hawkeshead, so she must have been going further afield. One day, when they were setting off in the direction of Grizedale Forest, they saw Carol disappearing into a phone box.

However, while Julia and Michael were alone together, he visibly relaxed and father and daughter enjoyed each other's company. Michael had a keen interest in ornithology and was delighted when he spotted a Barn Owl, a lone Osprey circling the sky and two Herons balancing unsteadily on their pipe cleaner legs, in a small lake called Angle Tarn near Hartsop. As he made notes in a little yellow book, Julia had never seen him so happy in ages or known them to have such great rapport.

Yet when they returned once more to the tent, daggers with his wife once more were drawn. Voices were raised and faces set in scowls, resulting in him retiring to the Red Lion or King's Arms to spend the evening. This was unusual because Michael wasn't much of a drinker and hardly ever went to a pub at home. Julia and her mother spent the evening sharing a can of soup, lying on their sleeping bags reading and were fast asleep long before Michael returned.

After four long days Michael and Carol mutually agreed, that the holiday should be terminated and for the first time in ages Julia saw her mother smile. In fact, on the journey back Carol seemed much brighter than she had in ages and even sang along with some songs on the radio. She was even dressed in some sensible clothes. Julia was disappointed, as she had nursed high hopes of this special family Lakeland break. In a few years, she would be too old for such holidays and they were precious times to be treasured. Although she had enjoyed the walks with her father, she felt cheated and was angry with her mother, as it was her fault the holiday had been spoilt.

Zoe

The Present

Although Zoe, who had her time out from the classroom on a Thursday afternoon for planning lessons and marking books, should have been concentrating on school matters, she was finding it difficult to concentrate. She knew there was more going on in Julia's life than she had admitted so far, but she could hardly prise the information out of her at gun point. So, Zoe focused upon the facts as she knew them. Firstly, Neil was a gambler who had recklessly stolen from his employer. As yet, he hadn't been arrested but it could still happen and he nonetheless burdened them both with massive debts. Fortunately, the council were giving them some compensation money due to the new road cutting through their garden. Admittedly, this would give them some money to keep the wolf from the door, but for some strange reason Julia didn't seem happy with this. Why could this possibly be? Also somehow, Neil had managed to acquire a new job as a car salesman but seemingly without any references. How had Mr Smarmy managed this? Another mystery for Inspector Zoe Jackson to solve.

Julia could certainly pick her husbands. Not that Zoe could profess to particularly successful at this, but at least she had only made the marriage mistake only once and which had at least produced some fruition; Chloe. Zoe loved her daughter dearly. She felt a pity for Julia who was childless and probably of the age when she would remain forever so. Zoe reflected on both their positions and concluded that she was the one with the least empty glass. Especially when considering that Julia must have gone through even worse in the past.

This brought Zoe onto the unsavoury matter of Julia's husband number one; Trevor the chemist. A man who it transpired that Julia had never actually divorced but after he had been missing for several years, the marriage had been conveniently declared null and void. Zoe had been surprised but relieved when Julia had told her this piece of information. So where had Trevor Squires mysteriously disappeared to? This had to hold the key as to what was troubling Julia. It was time for Zoe once more to play detective.

What did she know about Trevor? Well he was a creepy bastard, but that was not very useful for her purposes. He had married Julia disturbingly quickly and had almost immediately moved in with her when they first met. If Julia had not been avoiding Zoe at that time, she would have made her see sense. Anyway, where had he actually lived before? He worked as a chemist somewhere in Bensham. That was the place in Gateshead with the strict Orthodox Jewish community wasn't it? Well, there can't be many chemists there. So, maybe she could track down where he worked. Someone might remember him and perhaps Zoe could make a start in solving this mystery. In which case, she might as well strike while the iron was hot.

Zoe, all thoughts of schoolwork forgotten, wrapped herself her orange tartan coat and left her home in St Peter's Basin. She sped along the quayside in her yellow Fiat 500 and crossed over the swing bridge. Pretty soon she arrived in Bensham, which was a place that she wasn't really very familiar with. Finding a suitable place to park in a side street, she wandered along Coatsworth Road, to get a feel of the place. The street seemed to be lined with Kosher bakeries and populated by people wearing mostly black. Zoe drew a few surprised glances, as in her colourful attire amongst the very sombrely-dressed, she looked like a firework .Oblivious to this, Zoe felt excited because she had the thrilling sensation of being in a different country and it was a long time since she had been on holiday. The men sported wide brimmed hats and long ringlets, while the women wore demure calf length skirts, plain black shoes with sensible heels. It seemed as if all the ladies had almost identical brown haircuts. A notion of a strange remaking of the Stepford Wives passed through Zoe's mind. She smelled the baking of bagels and was happy to step back and watch this different world, so removed from her own experience.

While children played in the street, paying no heed to the traffic, the mothers chatted oblivious to any dangers to their offspring from careless driving. Zoe could see this was a place popular with learner drivers. There was one across the road precariously mounting the pavement, while attempting a reverse turn and Zoe wondered what the young Jewish wives were talking about. As tomorrow would be their Sabbath, the focus of their conversation might be what was on the menu for Friday night's dinner. Zoe smiled with thoughts of the greeting Shallom, and wondered if these people watched the comedy programme with the same name.

they

Further down the street, it seemed to be less obviously Jewish and a plump lad with ginger hair was playing on a skateboard. Then she spotted a chemist's. It was a Lloyds Pharmacy and it looked as if the business had been there for some time. The paint was flaking off the window frame and there were weeds growing round the doorway. As Zoe opened the door, a bell jingled loudly, to alert the staff to her presence. Well, Zoe guessed there would be plenty of what would be considered by some to be very desirable commodities : Class A drugs.

A young woman with impossibly long eyelashes and unbelievably puffy lips appeared behind the counter.

'Can I help you?' asked the girl. As she opened and closed her mouth, Zoe was put in mind of a goldfish.

'Yes I was wondering if you knew anything of a chemist called … Trevor Squires.'

The girl shook her head. 'There's nobody of that name working here.'

This must be long before this girl was even born thought Zoe. 'No, he used to work here some time ago.'

'Well I've been here nearly … let me see.' The girl did some elaborate calculations on her fingers.' About eighteen months now and I've never come across any Trevors.' Her thick lips mouthed the word Trevors, as if they were some particularly nasty variant of a tropical disease.

'No this must be more than twenty years ago. You won't remember.' Zoe sighed in exasperation.

At first the girl looked a little perplexed, as to why she was being asked this bizarre question. Then a light went on. 'Mr Stewart's been here a long time. He might know. He's been here ever since the last century I reckon … Mr Stewart.' She called as she floated into the room behind, with a long scarf trailing behind as if it were a swishy tail.

A grey-haired man, in his early sixties, with a twinkle in his eye came into the shop.

'Who were you looking for?' Mr Stewart put some bottles into white paper bags.

This looked more promising thought Zoe. 'Well it's probably a long shot…this was a long time ago. I was wondering if there was a chemist called Trevor Squires who used to work here.'

'Well that's a name I haven't heard in a very long time.' Mr Stewart's eyes scanned the ceiling for clarification, as if a Trevor file was suspended there.

'So you do remember him?' Zoe felt a flutter of excitement.

'I remember a Trevor Squires working here but… he wasn't a chemist.' Mr Stewart scratched his chin.

'Really? What was he then.' Zoe lent on the counter and was beginning to find this Mr Stewart quite attractive, in a quirky Father Ted sort of way and she imagined him in ecclesiastical vestments.

'Trevor was a chemist's assistant. He was a peculiar chap … about my age.'

Mr Stewart must have been quite a looker then surmised Zoe.

'He wasn't qualified as a chemist but he liked to think he was.'

'What do you mean?' Zoe was back on track as to the purpose of this visit

'Well it was very odd. He just went. One morning he just disappeared from work which was most unlike him. One minute he was there … and then he was gone.' Mr Stewart was enjoying this conversation with this brightly-dressed woman on a matter that had always intrigued him.

'What was Trevor Squires like then?' Zoe wound a strand of her ginger hair round a finger.

'He was always punctual … but there was something a little creepy about him.' Mr Stewart wrinkled up his face in distaste.

That was a spot on assessment; Zoe's thoughts exactly and she was liking this man more by each moment. 'Yes, that's exactly what I thought… and did you know? He's been a missing person for many years.'

'I suspected as much … but there's more to this. You see, it was never proven but I had my suspicions that he was guilty of gross misconduct.'

'In what way?' What a fortunate meeting this was proving to be thought Zoe and she wondered if this man had a wife.

'Well' Mr Stewart paused briefly for dramatic effect. 'Large quantities of a Class A drug called ketamine had been mysteriously disappearing over a considerable length of time. Then I caught him in the *special* locked cupboard used for such class A drugs. He'd no business in there and I had caught him red-handed. Goodness knows how many more times he'd been in there before. You see he always arrived at work early… long before me. Which was strange, because he'd no reason to be here, and he'd not long been married. I mean you think he would want to spend time over breakfast with his new wife' He gave Zoe, a knowing look, as he noticed with pleasure, that she was hanging on his every word. 'But you see, that particular morning there was an order I needed to chase up. And there he was crawling about on the floor … pretending he had heard a rat of all things. It was transparent what he'd been up to. You see I'd seen him slam the door shut and he was looking very furtive. Also, he had put a cloth over the cctv camera, so he couldn't be seen on any footage.' Mr Stewart pointed to an ancient security camera on the ceiling.

'So what would have happened?' Zoe had a very pleasing image of Trevor locked up in a prison cell.

'Well, I was going to confront him about it. Obviously, I would have had to have got the police involved. This was very serious.' He straightened his tie properly, to emphasise to this likeable woman that he by comparison, was an upstanding member of the community.

'So do you think he was a drug addict?' This was getting better by the moment thought Zoe.

'I don't know … but he always seemed very much in control of himself so this is unlikely. I guess he was using the drug for his own ghastly purpose on some other poor unwitting soul.' Mr Stewart shook his head. 'Anyway why are you interested in all of this?'

'Well my friend Julia Latimer … she used to be Julia Squires and before that, when I first knew her she was Julia Mason …' Zoe bit her tongue, wondering if she was revealing too much information about her friend. 'She was his wife and there is something troubling her and I'm sure it's connected with this Trevor.'

The chemist wondered what sort of weird creature would have married Trevor. This jolly woman seemed so normal and she was this unfortunate Mrs Squire's friend. 'Well, if he hadn't disappeared like that. No doubt he would have been facing criminal charges … unless I was mistaken of course. As I say, nothing was ever proven.' It was clear from his face that he thought Trevor guilty of stealing drugs and possibly even more deplorable crimes.

'Well thank you Mr Stewart. This has been very interesting.' Mr Stewart had given her plenty to think about.

'No problems. Call me Nick please.' He reached for his mobile phone. 'And if you discover anything else about this man please let me know.'

"Yes and likewise you. And by the way, I'm Zoe. Zoe Jackson." And as she gave him a conspiratorial smile, he thought how lovely she looked with the autumn light shining on her red hair.

As they exchanged numbers, they were unaware of an elderly Jewish man, who was looking at some corn plasters and taking a very great interest in the conversation.

Obadiah

It was Friday night, and Obadiah was trying to banish all poisonous thoughts of that thieving braggart, Neil Latimer, from his mind. While he was in the shower, he worked the soapsuds into such a furious lather, he imagined that he was manufacturing a toxic, radioactive cocktail to destroy the man. However, it merely made his own skin red and chapped, so it really hurt when he tried to dry himself with a towel that felt like sandpaper. He knew he needed to get a grip and just let matters be, but he couldn't. Since his last visit to the Golf Club, where his nemesis had been holding court with his new set of clowns, he just couldn't face it. He knew as a result, he was forgoing valuable networking time and he would be limiting himself to the less lucrative auditing assignments, restricting himself to within the Jewish community.

Downstairs, he could hear the familiar sound of Bathsheba's annoying singing, as she prepared for the night's dinner. Soon his father and mother would be arriving and they would be all sat around the table for the most special meal of the week. He could hear his young daughters creating a fuss and he supposed he ought to go and help Bathsheba out by reading them a story.

As punctual as ever, when the sun begins to set, there was the expected knock on the door. Although his elderly parents were smiling, they both appeared frailer each time he saw them. Unfortunately, Sarah's back now formed the unfortunate question mark shape of a Dowager's Hump and poor Solomon found it impossible to walk without his stick. Still thankfully, despite both being in their nineties, they were as still as sharp as tacks. They observed like unblinking owls, the carefully prepared Sabbath table with its crisp, white cloth, shining plates and sparkling glasses winking in the candlelight. Upon entry to the house, Obadiah had bade them both a hearty 'Shalom', as his wife in her best blue dress, took their warm winter coats and he concentrated upon drawing the thick purple curtains closed for the Shabbat to commence.

While Sarah struggled to manoeuvre herself onto a dining chair, Solomon moved awkwardly, leaning against the table as a support, to find his place. Obadiah's two young daughters Esther and Ruth in their best attire sat down obediently, knowing they must be on their best behaviour in front of their grandparents and looked forward to returning to their PlayStations.

After the Kiddish Wine, Challah Bread and Gefitle Fish, Obadiah was now looking forward to the main dish and was pleased that his wife has made his favourite lamb stew. Until this point in the evening, the conversation has been quite mundane regarding the weather getting colder and some neighbours who had painted their front door an ugly shape of red. Then Solomon announced in his croaky voice, 'I heard an interesting conversation in the chemist's yesterday.'

'Oh what was that about?' asked Bathsheba, not really very interested. 'Is everybody enjoying their food?' Everyone nodded and made appreciative noises.

'As my usual chemist was closed for some reason, I was forced to trek further along the street. This was not ideal as my feet were hurting and I was wanting some corn plasters for them.' Solomon paused and looked around the table to check that his audience was listening.

Obadiah doubted very much that this would be one of his father's more interesting stories and he was wondering what Neil was now doing. Solomon continued with his tale. 'Well the chemists I came upon was rather shabby and not a patch on the one run by Mr Levy … but needs must. Anyway while I was trying to decide which plaster looked the most suitable, I heard an interesting conversation. A young woman was asking the chemist about a certain Trevor Squires.' Solomon placed his knife and fork at the side of his plate, and nodded meaningfully at his family, as if they all should know to whom he was referring.

Bathsheba's eyes moved from her mother-in–law to her husband and back, but everyone looked nonplussed. So she continued enjoying her food.

'Who are you talking about Dad?' Obadiah could feel his skin smarting beneath his shirt and took a small sip from his small glass of red wine. This was the only time of the week he permitted himself an alcoholic drink.

'Do you remember many years ago, I had the most terrible tenant. I made a bad judgement of character and this evil man swindled me out of lots of money.' Solomon shook his head slowly, for since then he had only rented his flats out to those within the faith.

Obadiah's attention was piqued at the mention of swindle, and his mind once more was filled with thoughts of the evil Neil.' What happened with him?'

'Well, I was renting out one of my properties down the road, you know where old Mrs Zimmerman lives now? This was a long time ago and you were only a young lad Obadiah. But anyway I had completely forgotten, that this dreadful man used to work at this chemist's down the road – where I was yesterday.'

'What did he do that was so awful?' Bathsheba helped herself to a second plateful of food.

'Well he just disappeared … owing six months' rent which was a considerable amount of money. But if that wasn't bad enough … he stole a standard lamp and a set of cutlery.' Solomon sounded as if he were talking about the Crown Jewels. 'I must have visited that place hundreds of times to find out as to his whereabouts but nobody could … or would provide me with any information. It seemed he had just disappeared in a puff of smoke.' When Solomon clapped his hands together for dramatic effect, Esther and Ruth almost jumped out of their seats

'Now I'm starting to remember. It's the cutlery … yes that set of knives and forks.' Sarah looked fondly at the ones she held in her arthritic hands.

‘Don’t forget the spoons Sarah. There were spoons as well.’ Solomon brandished a spoon at his wife as if it were a weapon.’ Anyway, this tall, orange-coloured woman was asking the chemist about him … Trevor Squires of all people.’

‘Orange? Are you sure?’ Asked Obadiah for even his daughter’s attention had been captured by this strange image.

‘Orange coat, ginger hair. You know the type. Well apparently her friend, a Julia Latimer, as she now is called, was once married to him.’ Solomon’s hands were now shaking and his stick toppled over with his excitement.

At the mention of the name Latimer, Obadiah’s ears pricked up. ‘Latimer you say… if she was married to this Trevor Square why is she called Latimer?’

‘Well apparently. This Trevor’s been missing for many years.’ Solomon replayed in his head the conversation between chemist and the red lady.’ So, I think she has married again but it seems the ginger lady and the chemist want to trace Mr Squires because he’s committed some crime in the chemist’s.’ Obadiah’s mind was racing, if this red lady knew this Julia Latimer. Well Latimer wasn’t that common a name and Obadiah’s heart was beating nineteen to the dozen. He needed urgently to write this information down in his little red notebook.

Charles

Charles was spying on Tracy dealing with some customers from his office. She had no idea that she was being watched and her performance was not of the standard that he had come to expect. When Charles had entered his business premises that morning, the two had barely grunted a greeting to each other. This was not how relations between them used to be. Charles noticed that she had dark circles beneath her eyes which made her look tired and old. Also there were dirty makeup smudges on her usually immaculate clothes .Then he observed with distaste, that when she went to the photocopier machine, her false tan had been so badly applied, that her legs were just a big mess of ugly white and orange blotches, like a giraffe's neck. Normally, Charles wouldn't notice these things but her card was marked and he was making it his business to do so.

Over the past few years Charles had clearly been taking his eye off the ball and matters had certainly been slipping. If he hadn't buried his head in the sand, the awful business with Neil could have been avoided. There was no need for the situation to have become so out of control and he wondered how much a part in the escalation of events the now not so delectable Tracy had played. As she strutted about in her white stilettoes and little short skirts, thoughts of mutton and lamb came into his mind. For goodness sake the woman must be fifty if she was a day. Even if his own wife Pamela was sitting in Tracy's chair doing a jigsaw puzzle, the act would be conducted with a little more dignity. Was this really the corporate image OakElmAsh should be projecting? Especially, now his son Max was playing such an important role in the business. Maybe it was time to prune away some of the old dead wood.

Although he'd nursed some reservations about the suitability of his boy for this line of work, the lad had surprisingly come up trumps. During the past few days, offers on properties had been coming in thick and fast and this was all due to his son's incredible transformation. Max was both walking and talking differently. He was projecting himself with such a swagger and poise that one would think he had been taking lessons from Neil. If only he had both of these salesmen as strings in his … but Charles should be grateful for what he had.

As Max came walking into the showroom, with a smile on his face, Charles saw him deliberately blank Tracy and go to make himself a coffee. That was interesting thought Charles and wondered the reason for this. He opened his office door. 'Max have you got a minute. I just wanted a quick word.'

'Yes sure Dad.' Max looked at his watch. 'Yes, I've got about twenty minutes before my next appointment.'

'Sit down son. You know I'm so proud of you. You're a real chip off the old black. You know I was a little scared that I might have thrown you in at the deep end but I needn't have worried, need I?' Charles beamed affectionately at his son.

‘Well to be honest Dad, I have quite surprised myself.’ Max stretched his legs out and made himself comfy on the chair.

‘Well if you keep this up lad, you should be thinking of a treat for yourself.’ Charles thought his son deserved a reward for his amazing success.

‘Really.’ Thoughts of sand, sea and surfing immediately popped into Max’s mind.

‘Yes I reckon so. Anywhere you fancy?’ Charles imagined the Canary Islands would still warm this time of year.

‘Thailand.’

‘Blimey that was quick. You’ve obviously been thinking about it yourself.’ Charles chuckled and remembered his own days as a carefree young man before he was married.

‘There was just something I’ve been meaning to ask you …’ Charles wasn’t quite sure how to broach this question.

‘Oh please Dad. I thought I’d maybe ask Nigel. It wouldn’t be the same if you and Mam came too.’

‘No of course not. I mean I can’t see your Mam in a bikini on a surfboard. Can you?’ Once again Charles laughed .’No it’s just I noticed that you ignored Tracy just before. Was this for any particular reason.’ Charles gave his son an awkward grimace.

‘She’s a mean cow, that’s why.’ Max wouldn’t have dared say this a few days ago.

‘Really.’ Charles hadn’t expected such a blunt answer but he wasn’t disappointed by his son’s honest appraisal of her. ‘And is this for any particular reason?’

‘Where do I begin?’ Max turned his palms upwards.

‘Go on …’ Charles urged, intrigued as to what his son was going to say next.

‘Well do you know how I used to keep cocking up appointments…’

‘To be fair son, you can hardly blame that on her.’

‘Oh yes I can. She kept giving me the wrong times, postcodes and giving me false details. All the things that were bad about the house … well her notes told me to bring them to people’s attention.’ A note of pure hatred crept into Max’s voice.

‘Is that why there were all those complaints?’ Charles was aghast.

Max nodded. ‘Exactly.’

‘You mean she was setting you up to fail on purpose.’ Were there no bounds to this woman’s treachery?

‘That’s it in a nutshell.’

This conversation had had given Charles more food for thought than even he could have imagined.

Chapter 22

Julia

36 Years Ago

As soon as the maroon Ford Cortina had swung into Lowfield Avenue, Carol's spirits had visibly lifted and she took the mirrored compact from her bag to apply some more powder and lipstick. While running her fingers through and patting down her hair, she smiled at her own reflection. The minute the car pulled up, she was out in a flash. Leaving Michael to bring in the cases, she bolted down the path and rammed the key into the door with such speed, it was as if the house were on fire. While Carol disappeared into the house, Julia helped her father bring in the luggage and as he closed the boot, he shook his head wearily.

There had been an awkward knife-cutting silence during most of the journey back from the Lake District. After Penrith, Carol hadn't even got the usual radio playing and a little banal banter from a prattling DJ would have been a welcome distraction. Julia hated to see her parents behaving like this. She couldn't understand it and wished they could just be nice to each other. Julia was scared to say anything to them herself, for fear of making matters even worse.

Her friend Samantha at school, had parents who were no longer together. Samantha said it was great because she spent weekdays with her mum and weekends with her dad. Best of all though she said, was that they both tried to outdo each other in giving her expensive treats. Last week her dad had bought her a Walkman and the latest Michael Jackson tape and her mum tried to outdo this with a gorgeous pink shell suit. Samantha had all the latest gadgets, toys and clothes. She was always going on holiday to Blackpool or Great Yarmouth. Julia didn't care about such things and didn't want this for her parents. The three of them belonged together as a family. Awful terms like separation and the even more dreadful divorce, spun round in her mind creating a malevolent, word web. Julia's eyes filled with tears. When they stopped for a snack, toilet and petrol refill near Penrith, the atmosphere between Michael and Carol showed no improvement and Julia just wished they were home. *Some* holiday this had been and the only fond memories she had were of those walks with her dad.

Julia watched her father's sad face as he brought the heavy cases into the house and wondered why her parents were being so horrible to each other. It was stupid because they were just making each other unhappy. As she walked through to the dining room, she could see her Mum talking to Ian in the garden. While they had been away, he had obviously been doing some work there and Julia could see a new flower bed brimming with red, yellow and pink blooms. Her mother was smiling and laughing with him. She was twirling a strand of hair round her finger and Ian was leaning against his spade, as if it were the edge of a bar where they were both sipping exotic cocktails. Why was her Mum seem so happy and jolly with him?

Over the past few months, Ian had been around in their house quite a lot. First, he had fitted a new kitchen with tangerine coloured units, lemon floor tiles and walnut panelled walls. Then he had ripped out the old white bathroom suite and replaced with a funny, green coloured one. Her mother had told her it was *avocado* and it was quite the latest thing in bathrooms. Ian had raised his eyebrows in a *get you* kind of way, when she had told Julia this piece of information and he given her mother a strange look, which Julia couldn't quite place.
Julia had preferred the old white one. Her father had agreed about this and said he did too.

There was something about Ian that Julia didn't quite like. Perhaps, it was his strange, handlebar moustache, that put Julia in mind of a walrus or the black hairs that poked out from the top of his shirt, like bits of old rag from an old-fashioned proggy mat. Maybe it was the pungent smell of his after shave, which she believed was called Old Spice. Even the name reminded her of a manky jar of herbs, that had been kept in the cupboard too long. Or most likely, the fact that her mother, seemed prefer keeping company with *him* rather than her dad. While Carol and Ian cavorted in their imaginary wine bar in the garden, Michael made himself a cup of tea and Julia went to the sanctity of her bedroom.

30 Years Ago

Once Trevor had realised, that Nick had seen his scarf hanging over the CCTV camera, he knew he was rumbled. Irrespective of the purpose for him actually being in the cupboard, it was an area that he didn't have legitimate access to. Just because of the fact that he lacked those *golden ticket* paper qualifications of a degree, had always infuriated him. As if that made any difference to his competency in pharmaceutical land because he knew which drugs did what and then some.

It was really unfair, especially as his boss Nick and he were of a similar age and were both the most senior workers at the chemists. Trevor had worked in the shop now for many years. Nick should have allowed him more responsibility and a better wage to reflect this. Moreover, it was absurd that he couldn't be trusted with his own key. But therein lay the problem, if it became known the exact purpose for which he had been procuring the Ketamine, from the cupboard with the key from the throat lozenge tin, then the shit really would hit the fan.

But apart from the fact that he had been caught obscuring the security camera, there was no other evidence stacked against him. Surely, it was quite plausible that he had been using the equipment for something as innocent as a clothes stand. After all, it would have been quite likely for him to have encountered some germ-infested rats and thrown his jacket anywhere in shock. This was a chemist where people came to cure their ailments, not catch diseases from filthy rodents. On a road like this, with all the Kosher bakeries and bagels, there would be ample temptations for vermin of all types.

Trevor could see the silhouette of his boss in the office and he wondered what he was doing. Trevor had been very careful only to take small amounts of the Ketamine at any one time, but as Julia was becoming more accustomed to the drug, increasingly larger amounts were becoming necessary. He had been horrified to discover that she had been prancing about in the garden yesterday, especially as the amount of drugs she must have had in her system should have rendered this impossible. Trevor was baffled as to how this had happened. This was why he had made a point of arriving so early and had not expected any one to have been there. Damn Nick. Once the quantities of the drugs were checked, the missing Ketamine would be detected and the finger of suspicion would be pointing in his direction. Also he still had the tin and key in his pocket.

Now, before anyone else arrived was the only time he could do it. He could see that Nick was still busy, so he tiptoed once more to the kitchen and replaced the key in the throat lozenge tin. Perhaps he should have returned the contents of the bottle too but no, time was pressing forward and he couldn't risk placing himself in anymore uncompromising positions. While still in the kitchen, he made himself a cup of coffee and watched as Nick strode through the shop, turned on the main light and used his own lawful key to unlock the cupboard. Trevor felt sick and knew it was now only a matter of time before his crimes were exposed.

He unbolted the back door, ran along the ginnel through the back lanes and to the safety of his car. This wasn't only a matter of theft, once it became known his purpose for wanting the drug who knows what heinous crimes would land in his direction. Just think all the time and effort he had wasted on that bitch. Well, the bank was to be his first port of call and he would take great delight in the money between certain accounts being more fairly adjusted.

Neil

The Present Day

For the third time that week Neil was running late and he couldn't understand it. Julia had made him a cup of tea before leaving for work and even left the shower running this morning, but he had just gone back to sleep and wasted a lot of water. When he had taken a drink from the tea it was cold, then he saw the time and felt sick. Not again, it was becoming like a repeated nightmare. Each night, he had no recollection of going to bed. He fell unconscious rather than asleep and he hadn't even been to the Golf Club for the last couple of nights. The last two mornings he had vowed never again to drink but when he had arrived home from work, Julia had plied him with wine and whiskies in such delightful ways, it was impossible to refuse. It reminded him so much of when they had first got together but that was over twenty years ago and although he was loathe to admit it, he was no longer a young man.

There must be some reason for her doing this but he couldn't for the life of him think what that might be. Did she want him to lose his job? Well that made no sense. Did she want him to become ill or turn into an alcoholic? Why would she want to do that? Also, she was keeping him company and she had to get up even earlier than him for her teaching job. Was she matching him drink for drink because that what she used to do? Last night was just a foggy blur and really he had no idea.

As Neil set off from Washington Village, he noticed that road works on the new bypass were already in full swing and wondered when his cheque would be coming through the post. No doubt it wouldn't be long, and with his new job, things were definitely on the up. However, he was aware that his performance hadn't been quite up to scratch the last couple of days and he was determined to have a booze free early night. Eventually, when Neil pulled into Armstrong Automobiles at ten past nine, Geoff Armstrong was standing outside his showroom tapping his foot and looking at his wristwatch.

'Morning Neil. And how are you today?' He asked and not in a kindly way.

'Not too bad. A little tired but you know …' Neil gave an apologetic half smile.

'Yes I do know Neil. That's why I was wondering if you were all right.' Geoff managed to make this enquiry about his health more than a little aggressive.

'I'll be fine when I've had a coffee. A little caffeine will sort me out. No problem.' Neil knew he was looking decidedly green about the gills.

'I hope no problems … for your sake at least.' Geoff lit a cigar, the smell of which made Neil feel even more queasy.

'What do you mean Geoff?' Neil was seeing a more unpleasant side to his boss that he hadn't seen before.

'Well I don't know, you've just seemed a little off colour the last couple of days. A tad shall we say … not in tip top form. ' The tees alliterated from his tongue like bullets ricocheting.

'Maybe I'm coming down with a cold or something.' Neil knew exactly to what he was referring and didn't like the direction in which this conversation was heading.

'It's the *something* that bothers me Neil. Really, at your age I'd have thought you a little old to be burning the candle at both ends. Don't you think?' Geoff gave Neil a disparaging look up and down whilst flaring his nostrils.' I mean you know the game and you know what is said … you're only as good as the last car you sold. Which in your case was three days ago.'

Neil felt multiple pairs of eyes from within the salesroom, focused on him as if his mortified image had been projected on a big screen. All ears were tuning in on the awkward conversation like ultra-receptive satellite dishes and he wished desperately that the ground could in some pitiful way swallow him up.

Obadiah

Obadiah slept fitfully, having the most vivid and colourful dreams. Much to the annoyance of his wife, he tossed in his bed like a pancake being flipped over and over again. As he flopped about the bed, Bathsheba, groaned, sighed and turned in irritation, before promptly beginning snoring once more. In his head he played through the intriguing monologue delivered by his father earlier that evening.

The chemist had been told by the red lady, that her friend had been married to a Trevor Squires. *The* very Trevor Squires who had worked in that very pharmacy, been his father's regrettable tenant and stolen the valuable spoons. *This* Trevor wasn't married to her anymore because she was now called Latimer. Neil was called Latimer. There had to be a connection. It was all too much of a coincidence. What had happened to this Trevor? He had disappeared mysteriously no doubt with his father's cutlery. Neil steals money and probably spoons too, given half a chance. Why had he not been arrested? Why hadn't Charles Lavender told the police?

Neil was a criminal. Obadiah felt sweat pour from his forehead as if it were glue and he pulled the sticky ringlets from his cheeks like strips of moist, twisted liquorice. He must have done something to Trevor. Perhaps Neil had murdered Trevor so he could marry this Julia. Obadiah could barely contain the excitement that bubbled through his veins. Criminals don't care and they need to be punished. Obadiah needed to sort this out. It seemed Neil's crimes of embezzlement were the mere tip of the iceberg. Neil must have murdered this Trevor. Where had he hidden the body? Obadiah must become the body finder. Where did Neil and this Julia live? This is where the Trevor body must be hidden.

The ginger lady knew Mrs Latimer. Julia – that was her name. He needed to find the red lady, she would lead him to this Julia. The red lady had ginger hair and orange clothes so she would be easy to find. Obadiah must go to the chemist's and he would lead him to the red lady, Julia, Neil and the missing body.

Obadiah sat bolt upright in bed and started screaming.

'For Jehovah's sake what on earth is wrong with you?' It was an understatement that Bathsheba wasn't happy that her husband was stopping her from sleeping.

'I must find the body.' Although his eyes were wide open, he was quite clearly asleep.

'Hush Obadiah, you'll frighten the girls.' Bathsheba pushed her husband's head back down on the pillow.

Max

When Max arrived at work, he felt for his phone in his pocket and was annoyed to find it not there. Could he have left it in the car? No, the last time he remembered seeing it, was just before he had brushed his teeth. Damn, he must have left it in the bathroom. Everything he needed was in his bloody phone .He would just have to go home and get it.

He knew his first appointment wasn't until after eleven, so he had plenty of time to go home and get it. He could tell Tracy to explain this to his dad where he was, but on second thoughts that probably wasn't the greatest of ideas. The miserable cow was watching him at the moment, no doubt wondering what he was dithering about.

'Max are you all right? Is there anything I can help you with?' Tracy fawned, with what he could only interpret as mock concern.

Strangely enough, he had noticed a change in Tracy these past couple of days. It was most disturbing, as if she was attempting to be more friendly towards him, but he still wouldn't trust her an inch. 'No you are all right.' He replied curtly.

Max knocked before barging into his father's office and explained what had happened with his phone.

'Max, I've been thinking about what you told me about Tracy. She must have cost the company thousands.' Charles' face wore on expression of concern as he drummed a pen on his desk.

'She won't care about that, not her. All she thinks about is herself.' Max raised his eyebrows.

'But I'm just surprised she has been so stupid. I mean she must know that we talk to each other as father and son.' Charles felt he had been the stupid one, being such a poor judge of character.

'Well I reckon she must have thought that I was just so useless, that my being here would be very short-lived. So she was doing everyone a favour by making me look even more incompetent that I actually am. To be honest I had little faith in myself.' A few days ago, Max would not be able to rationalise never mind articulate what had been happening. 'Because the sooner I was out. The quicker Neil would be back. In her own weird way, I suppose she thought she was doing everyone a favour.'

Charles had not considered this and for the umpteenth time in the past couple of days Max had astounded him.

'But Max that was never on the cards. I can't have Neil working here because of what he did.' Charles shook his head sadly.

'What did he do?' Finally, thought Max he was getting to the bottom of this great mystery.

'He stole thousands of pounds from the company.' Max thought he had never seen his father look so elderly and bewildered.

'What? Why would he do that?' This was not the answer Max had been expecting.

'That's what I couldn't understand either. I'd had my suspicions for a while but thought I might have been imagining it. That's why I hired Mr Goldstein to check through the books.' The multiple transactions from the miscellaneous business account flashed through his head

'Is that the weird Jewish bloke that keeps hanging around?' Max hadn't been able to fathom what his skulking presence was all about.

'Yes but don't get me started on him.' Charles rolled his eyes.'He can't understand why Neil isn't in prison. I asked the bloody man to check through the accounts not to play judge and jury.'

'But why did Neil steal and why haven't you told the police.' This was all too baffling thought Max.

'Neil's got problems. I only found out the real reason from Julia the other day.' Charles sighed.

'You mean his wife? What did she tell you then? Why did the bastard steal from us?' Max was becoming increasingly angry with his father's ineptitude.

'He's got a gambling addiction. Julia and Neil they have nothing now. He was my best friend, ever since we were young. If I'd realised earlier maybe I could have done something before it came to this.'

'This isn't your fault Dad.' Max's angry voice was temporarily replaced by pity for his father.' If you're not going to tell the police, which I think you should by the way, then you need to get the money back off him.'

'I know son but it's all such a mess.'

'I wish you'd told me this earlier.'

'Max, if you knew Neil wasn't coming back the job would have freaked you out even more.'

'Perhaps if Tracy knew the truth then she wouldn't have tried to sabotage me.' Once more Max's hackles were rising.

'Oh don't get me started on her.'

Chapter 23

30 Years Ago

Julia

At first, Julia was happy that her husband, Trevor was late home from work, as she no longer enjoyed being in his company and for a little longer she could do as she pleased. For the first time that day, she had actually seen him in his true colours. He was a controlling bully who had never loved her at all. Even at the outset, it had all been an evil plan of his to get his hands on what was of interest to him, which could only be her money. And now, she was forced to live like a pauper, when she knew for a fact that her parents had left her well provided for. Not only did he not love her but also he didn't even like her. He quite clearly despised her. Why had she allowed this to happen?

But the most calculating part of this sorry gaslighting melodrama, was the fact that he'd been repeatedly and systematically poisoning her, from the very day of their wedding. The horrible champagne that tasted more like shampoo and its toxic effects, was the actual evidence of that. The bastard knew exactly what he was doing. That was the reason the tea tasted so bad and why he became angry if she failed to drink every last drop. This was why she felt so awful. Now, she understood why he had forced her to give up her friendships and teaching course. He didn't want anyone to suspect his horrible plan and her interaction with others made this more than likely. Her lack of self-worth would have made it difficult for her to function mentally as a teacher and her exhaustion, physically impossible. Zoe would have noticed something was amiss very quickly.

It all made perfect sense now. He just wanted to own a house in the street that he had grown up in with his mother and his eventual aim was quite clearly to live there by himself. Trevor certainly had no desire for a wife in any shape or form; she was clearly a means to an end. And her very end was her husband's ultimate goal. He was a cold-blooded murderer who thought he could get whatever he wanted. How convenient for him to have a job as a chemist. God only knew what pharmaceutical concoction the bastard had been putting in her drinks. Well, for no longer.

She looked out of the window dreading the hated VW pulingl up on the drive. The car he had bought with her parent's money. Her beloved parents, who had died tragically in a car crash. Perhaps he'd been in a road accident. Well good. That would be an excellent, divine retribution. She would be happy if he was lying in a hospital bed with serious injuries or better still – dead. Who would have thought a few short months ago she would be nursing such vitriolic thoughts towards her husband?Who would have dreamt her husband was composed of pure evil?

Julia put on the television to see if there had been any road accidents reported.

The Present Day

Pamela

In the hallway of the Lavender household, lay two unopened jigsaw puzzle boxes, one with a picture of The Angel of the North at sunset and the other a picturesque riverside view of Durham Cathedral. They were both still enveloped in their cellophane packaging and were untouched. For three days, they had sat neglected on the small pedestal table next to the telephone. This was most unlike Pamela, who usually took great delight in sniffing the cardboard pieces of a virgin new puzzle, in the same manner that others take pleasure from inhaling the odour of an expensive box of chocolates. By now in normal times she would probably have completed one and be well on into the second. However, these times were not normal and Pamela had other things on her mind.

Since her husband and son had left for work over an hour ago, she had sat on her chair in the lounge, nursing a box of paper tissues and weeping. When the boys were in the house, she just about managed to hold things together but once they had gone, she allowed her face to crumble into pieces and the tears fall freely. Images of that horrible, Tracy-woman's ghoulish face flashed through her mind with her platinum hair, unnatural white teeth and cruel, taunting eyes. The nasty words spoken by that gleeful common voice repeatedly reverberated - *meetings, on the phone to her nearly all afternoon, I thought it was very peculiar and round to her house.* Pamela tortured herself and hovered over the still unfinished puzzle of Alnwick Castle, tears spilling all over the pieces like a dripping tap. How long had this affair been going on? Why was Julia being so spiteful when she had a perfectly good, well perhaps not good but nevertheless, a husband of her own? Why was Charles not happy with his wife? Admittedly, she knew at times she could be irritating because he repeatedly told her, but this was just so awful.

So wrapped up was Pamela in her own tragic world, that she failed to hear the key in the door and when Max heard the awful wailing noise he ran to find its source. Max was mortified by the pitiful sight of his mother, surrounded by a sea of sodden tissues and sobbing hysterically. He assumed that someone must have died but couldn't think who, as all his grandparents were long gone.

'Mum, whatever's wrong?' Seeing how upset his mother was, he went to put an arm round her shoulder.

'Max. I'm sorry. I didn't know you were here.' Pamela tried to stifle her sobs but perturbing noises somewhere between hiccoughs and snorts filled the room.

'What's happened. Has somebody died?' Max had never seen his mother like this before.

'It's your father.' Pamela's face oscillated from old woman to little girl and back.

'He's fine. I was only with him a few moments ago.' Max tried to reassure her by patting her arm.

Pamela gulped. 'He's having an affair with Julia.'

'Julia?' Whatever was his mother going on about? This was crazy. 'You mean Neil's wife. I don't think so.'

'Yes he is. He was round there the other afternoon. I know for a fact.' Pamela was talking very quickly and hardly making sense.' And he's been talking to her … on the telephone.

I don't know how long it's been going on. I don't know what to do. When he was late home, he said… he said he'd been in a meeting but he wouldn't say with whom. That's because he was in a meeting with her. He's always liked Julia and the way that she dresses. He thinks my clothes are horrible. I don't know what to do. Oh, I'm so sorry son.'

'Mum calm down. I think you are wrong.' Where had his mother got this ridiculous notion from? 'I know he was round at Julia's but it was only because he was worried about Neil.'

'Well he would say that wouldn't he? He's hardly going to tell you the truth is he?' Pamela searched her son's face for a clue that he was right.

'He went to find out why Neil took that money. He's been gambling you know?'

Usually Pamela would love to be learning gossip about Neil. 'Yes, but he said he was in a meeting and he wouldn't tell me with who. He always tells me.'

'Look Mum. Have you been talking to someone?' Surely, she hadn't hired a private detective. 'How did you actually know he'd been round at Julia's.'

'That horrible Tracy woman. She told me.' Pamela thought this was proof enough of her husband's duplicity.

'Well that makes sense.' Max wondered if there were any limits to the damage she was capable of causing.' Tracy is poison. Look Mum you don't want to believe anything that bitch says. Dad isn't having an affair with Julia. I'm certain of that.'

Obadiah

As soon as the clock said quarter to nine, Obadiah was marching along Coatsworth Rd with his mission in mind. This was not a good time as there seemed to be school children and their mother's everywhere, blocking the pavement and generally getting in his way. In fact, Bathsheba had left the house only five minutes before him with their two daughters. Striding along the street, Obadiah was oblivious to the several people who wished him good morning, giving more credence to the belief held locally, that he was rather rude and more than a little bit odd.

The door rang loudly as Obadiah entered the shop and made Nick jump. He had only that very moment opened the chemists and was unaccustomed to having such early customers. Most of the Jewish community favoured the pharmacy at the other end of the street, and he wondered what had brought this distinctive and obviously flustered man here at such an early hour.

'Good morning and how can I help you?' Nick Stewart gave Obadiah one of his most pleasant smiles.

'Did a Trevor Squires used to work here?' Obadiah got straight to the point.

'Well yes he did. But this was a long time ago.' This was a coincidence. No one had mentioned this man for years, and now twice in one week.

'Where is he now?' The Jewish man was not smiling and in his undertaker-like outfit, he looked quite threatening.

'I really have no idea. I think he was last heard of as being described as a missing person.' Nick Stewart shook his head, as such cases were just a sign of these troubled times.

'I think he's been murdered by Neil Latimer.'

Did this strange man just say murdered? 'What? What are you talking about and who is this Neil Latimer?'

'A red lady came to see you the other day didn't she?' Obadiah asked the question as if he were a character from Alice Through The Looking Glass.

Nick thought this was all getting a bit surreal and he wished his assistant was here to bear witness. 'A red lady?'

'Yes. My father was in the shop the other afternoon and he was listening to a conversation you were having with a woman with red hair. And she was asking about the whereabouts of Trevor Squires.' Obadiah held his head to one side and widened his eyes behind his little round glasses.

'And where exactly does this fit into your accusations against this Nigel Latimer?' Nick couldn't decide whether he was amused, scared or bamboozled, but settled on the latter.

'Neil Latimer.' Obadiah corrected.' Well, you see my dad used to be Trevor Squire's landlord. He rented a flat just down the road from here and he left rather suddenly without paying his rent. He owed my poor father a great deal of money and stole some valuable items from him.'

'What sort of things?' Nick was intrigued.

'Spoons and lampstands, that sort of thing. Anyway my father couldn't believe after all these years, that his name was being mentioned. Not very likely he would get any money back but nevertheless, he mentioned to me in conversation over dinner. Also he told me that he used to be married to a Julia Latimer. Is that right?'

'Sorry Mr ...?' Nick was feeling uncomfortable and wasn't sure he should be disclosing this information.

'Mr Goldstein. Mr Obadiah Goldstein.' He made the announcement with a certain pride, as if the Right Honourable should be affixed to his title. 'And my father is Mr Solomon Goldstein. I live just along the street on Berwick Rd.'

'Mr Goldstein, your father was eavesdropping on a private conversation between myself and Mrs Evans.'

'My father was doing no such thing. He is an upstanding member of our community.' Obadiah took the little notebook out of his pocket and made a note of this name.

'Julia Latimer is a friend of this Mrs Zoe Jackson,' Obadiah added this further detail to his book. 'And your Red Lady is trying to find her friend's ex-husband's whereabouts.'

'She won't have any success there. Well at least with finding him alive because … I believe he is buried somewhere in the vicinity of Neil Latimer's house You must give me this Zoe Jackson's phone number. My father saw her giving you it to you.'

'I don't think Mrs Jackson would be very pleased about me giving her number to all and sundry.' Nick looked uneasy.

'I am neither *all* nor *sundry*. I need that number.'

Neil was determined that the performance of the last few nights would not be repeated. At three o'clock that afternoon he had been forced to take more paracetamol because he head was still banging. What could Julia be thinking of with all this drinking? After eight in the evening each night, he had no recollection of what happened. As much as he was loathe to admit it, they were both middle-aged. It was no wonder he couldn't do his job properly. That day he had sold no cars whatsoever. A young woman with a yapping white poodle had come close to buying a three- year- old Pergeot, but she decided against it at the very last moment. Neil had seen Geoff shaking his head, as she left through the door. Needless to say, there were no suggestions for drinks at the Golf Club after work.

When Neil arrived back home, he was there before Julia. Mabel seemed pleased to see him. She brushed her coat against his legs and made the familiar chirruping noises, before manoeuvring him towards the direction of her empty food bowl. This was kept in the utility room and as Neil emptied a can of cat food, he noticed Julia's wellington boots were absolutely caked with mud. That was very strange because he hadn't been aware of her doing any gardening recently. For this was when she usually wore her wellies.

Neil made himself a cup of tea, found that night's edition of The Chase on catch up, and settled on the sofa with Mabel to watch it. When Julia arrived home she noticed the tea and her brow furrowed in annoyance.

'I didn't expect you to be home. I thought you would be at the club with your new mates.' Julia had arrived with the nightly supply of clanking bottles.

'To be honest love. I'm keeping out of there for a while. I need to get my head straight. All this drinking is wrecking me. I'm going on the wagon for a few days.' Neil announced.

'Really. Whatever for?' Julia tried to ask casually.

'Every day I'm getting to work hungover. I'm nearly always late and I can't do my job properly.' Neil sipped his tea piously.

'I'm sure that's an exaggeration.' Julia got two glasses from the cupboard.' I'm just opening a lovely bottle of Chateauneuf du Pape. Why don't you join me in a glass?'

'Julia, why don't you save it for the weekend? It's expensive wine.' Neil was actually feeling a little annoyed with her.

'Too late. It's open now and here you are.' She placed the glass on the table next to him.' I knew you wouldn't be able to resist. So how was your day darling?'

'To be honest Julia, it was awful. I didn't sell any cars at all and if this carries on … well Geoff will be giving me my marching orders and I can't say I blame him.'

Julia hadn't seen this one coming and she still had a lot of nocturnal work to complete. 'Oh don't be so hard on yourself. You haven't been there long. There were bound to be a few teething problems and I'm sure Geoff will cut you a little slack.' She noticed with some concern, that so far his drink was untouched.

'I don't think he will. Geoff's a ruthless businessman and there's only one thing drives him – money. Talking of which, you must have been spending a fortune on drink the last few days. You know even with that money from the council, and my job, we're still not out of the woods.'

'At least you have a job now.' Julia anxiously watched the full glass.

'Not for long though, if my sales record doesn't improve. I wonder when that cheque'll be through. I've noticed the building in the road has started. Not be long now before they're at our garden.' Neil stood up to look through the window knowing that although sooner the garden would be much smaller it was no skin off his nose.

'Are you ready for a top up?' Julia shook the bottle as if in a kitsch advert from the 1970's encouraging people to drink. He was put in mind of the "Nothing sparkles like Babysham" commercial and the little prancing deer his dim and distant past.

'No I'm ok thanks.' Something was starting to bother Neil about his wife's behaviour. She was keeping him company every night with the crazy drinking, but was she? He noticed that her glass of the expensive wine was also untouched. Also every morning she got up to go to work with no bother and with little evidence of any hangover. Furthermore, he was almost sure on several occasions during the night, her side of the bed had been empty. And when he had felt her get in she had been freezing for some reason and there was the matter of those filthy wellington boots. If Neil was to find out what was going on, then he needed to pretend to play her game. While Julia was busy in the kitchen he threw the glass of wine into a plant pot.

'Julia. I'm ready for a refill now.'

Julia smiled with relief.

Zoe

Zoe was eating a cheese and pickle sandwich at lunchtime in the classroom, when she felt her phone ringing once more. Although it was a number she didn't recognise, she'd had phone calls from it before. In fact several times and all in the last couple of days. She had been hoping to hear from Nick Stewart but she had immediately added him to her address book, so she knew it wasn't him. This time however was different because a message had been left on her voicemail.

Hello is that Mrs Zoe Jackson? You don't know me but my name is Obadiah Goldstein and I must speak with you. You know Neil Latimer don't you? He is married to your friend Julia but he is a very bad man. You were looking for Mr Trevor Squires weren't you? He's supposed to be a missing person isn't he? But I think he's dead. And I think that Neil Latimer killed him. Neil Latimer is reckless and he steals large amounts of money. I think he kills people too. He wanted to marry Julia, so I think he murdered Trevor and the body must be at their house. Please Mrs Zoe Jackson tell me where they live. *This is very important please get in touch.*

Goodness gracious, Zoe certainly hadn't been expecting that. Obadiah Goldstein had a very strange voice, with an almost robotic quality and she wondered if this was some sort of joke or scam. But surely this was just too weird for that. She played the message again and after a second listen it seemed even more bizarre, if that were possible. Certainly, she was no fan of Neil's but this was all just too far-fetched. Yet Obadiah knew that Neil had been stealing and that he was Julia's second husband. Well this much was all true. Could Neil Latimer possibly be a murderer? Zoe wouldn't have thought so but one never knew.

Perhaps this was what Julia's secret was and that she was trying to protect him. Maybe this accounted for the haunted look Julia so often wore.

How had this Obadiah Goldstein possibly got her number? There was only one person that it could possibly be. While she was annoyed he had been giving her number out willy-nilly to others, this nevertheless gave her the perfect opportunity to get in touch once more with a certain pharmacist, Nick Stewart.

Tracy

Tracy was filing her nails, while pretending to look through some appointments, when a young woman came into OakElmAsh Properties. Although she looked neat, presentable and rather too pretty for Tracy's liking, she didn't seem to be of the young, flashy type, having the luxury to afford to buy a property at her age. Tracy wondered what her business was, as she eyed her blonde wavy hair and spotted navy dress with suspicion.

'Can I help you?' Tracy sat up straight on her seat, to establish her superiority.

'Yes, I have an appointment with Mr Lavender at 2pm.' The girl smiled to reveal her perfect teeth, which were white but not unnaturally so.

'And can you tell me what the appointment is about.' Tracy was starting to feel worried and there was something about this girl she didn't like.

'It's about a job vacancy actually.' The girl feigned an unbecoming innocence in Tracy's eyes.

Tracy didn't know of any job vacancies especially ones for schoolgirls. 'I will ring him and tell him you are here. What is your name?'

'It's Lauren … Lauren Davies.'

'Mr Lavender.' The days of her calling him Charles were long over. 'There's a Lauren Davies here to see you.'

'Good, send her through.' Charles ordered.

Tracy begrudgingly showed Lauren Davies the way through to Charles Lavender's office, while being desperate to trip her up or push her into the photo-copier machine. Once inside, the door was closed and from her own desk Tracy watched their frosted images through the glass. She'd had a sick feeling in the pit of her stomach, as she knew she had been skating on thin ice for some time. Admittedly, she knew she had been beastly towards Max but she hadn't been to know that he would miraculously turn a corner like he had. She imagined that his ineptness would have been so apparent that he would have been replaced by a reinstated Neil by now. How was she to know that her loyalties would be so misplaced and that Neil seemed no longer to want to be friends with her? Not in any way could she have foreseen, that the feckless Max would take to his job as a duck to water. Obviously, father and son must have been speaking.

All of a sudden, the door to Charles's office flew opened and a beaming Lauren Davies skipped out as if off to the playground.
'So my dear, just help yourself to a coffee and I will be with you in a few moments.' Charles spoke to her as if he were a kindly uncle.
Lauren sashayed across to the coffee machine like she was pretending to be all grown up and Tracy was almost sure she was being smirked at by the child.
'Tracy could you come to my office immediately?' Tracy's eyes focused on the ground, as she put one foot in front of another, images of hangmen and nooses flashed through her mind. While standing awkwardly in her boss's office, she noticed that ominously she wasn't invited to sit down.
'Well Tracy. I expect you know what this is all about don't you? I must say I am very disappointed in you and horrified by your disloyalty.' Charles was not mincing his words.
Tracy felt like she was up before a stern head teacher.' I'm sorry Mr Lavender, it won't happen again, I promise you.'
'No it won't Tracy because from this moment on … you are no longer my employee.' Charles said this, he breathed a huge sigh of relief.
Surely this was all just a bad dream thought Tracy. 'But please. I'm sorry. Just give me one more chance. I didn't mean to be horrible to Max. It was just my little joke. '
'A little *joke* that nobody found funny. Not Max, myself or any customers. If you found it remotely amusing … well there is something seriously wrong with your head. You have cost the company thousands of pounds and I personally find you despicable. What

saddens me most Tracy is that I used to consider us as friends. You know, Neil was sacked for stealing from the company, well your crime is even worse because it was motivated by spite.'

'It was never meant that way. I was thinking what was best for the company.' Tracy sulked knowing her words sounded lame.

'But no Tracy. I haven't finished. Not content with ruining the company. You next had to try and sabotage my marriage. 'You told my wife, I was having an affair with Julia. What ridiculous malicious lies.' Charles' voice booming with anger reverberated round the room.

'Well I didn't say that exactly …' Tracy remembered how he had asked her to find Julia's number, the lengthy phone conversation he'd had with her and the mysterious meeting. It was a conclusion that anyone would have reached and to blame her for this wasn't fair. However, she thought better than to mention this.

'Just go Tracy. You know I even had my suspicions you were blackmailing Neil.'

'Well no, that's definitely not the case.' He would be blaming her for global warming next!

'Just clear your desk and go. There will be two months' salary in your bank and I think that's more than generous.'

Chapter 24

Thirty-Six Years Ago

Julia

It was now well after the summer holidays and Julia was back into the swing of the Autumn term at school. She was in the fourth year of secondary school and the teachers were now in full sail, with all their talk being of impending exams and expected grades, which was ridiculous Julia thought as they were almost two years away. However, the workload was increasing noticeably and Julia wondered if the teachers were participating in a sadistic competition, to see who could upon inflict the pupils with the largest stack of gruelling assignments and sticks to jump over. Julia kicked the orange and yellow leaves that were collecting in piles on the footpath. Soon, she would be home, to the delights of only quadratic equations, French past participles and the memorisation of the periodic table, for company.

In many ways it was just as well, as no doubt handyman Ian would be there working on the new garden shed he was so busy building. Quite what was wrong with the old one was a mystery to Julia but her mother insisted that the wood was rotten and it needed sorting before the winter, so all the tools didn't go rusty. This was strange because all the spades, forks and hoes she was familiar with, were already ancient and looking decidedly worse for wear. However, it seemed that job after job was being found for that horrible man and it much be costing her parents a fortune.

Whenever she got home from school, Julia felt uncomfortable, so she just went straight to her bedroom. Wherever Ian was, it seemed her mother was not far away. How many cups of tea was it possible to drink in an hour? She couldn't bear to hear her mother's pathetic giggling and flirting. It made her feel sick to watch her tottering around on high heels, with her little skirts and skimpy tops. Julia was actually starting to become a little embarrassed for her mother, who seemed to behave much more like a teenager than she did. Why did her poor father put up with it?

When she opened the front door, everything seemed quiet in the house and there was no sign of either her mother or Ian. Julia put her school bag on the kitchen table and helped herself to a glass of orange juice. In the sink was such a large collection of half-drunk cups of coffee and tea, if seemed as if every drinking vessel in the house had been used. Well there was nothing unusual there. Julia was just about to disappear into her bedroom,to get started on her homework when she heard a peculiar noise from upstairs. There were such strange grunting and moaning noises coming from her parents' bedroom. Had an animal somehow got into the house? Were these sounds of pain, pleasure or both? It was difficult to tell. Then she noticed some discarded workman's boots, lying close to the front door, while some dirty jeans, a tiny red skirt, a checked shirt and various items of male and female underwear formed a stomach churning procession leading up the stairs.

lady Chatterleys Lover!

Five Years Later

Julia

Julia was sitting in that very same kitchen with its tangerine-coloured units, lemon floor tiles and walnut panelled walls, wondering what had happened to her husband. Although, she had seen the news at both six and ten o'clock, there had been no mention of any accidents locally. She wondered, if she should ring the hospitals to find if there had been any Trevors admitted but no she couldn't quite bring herself to do so. It was so much more pleasant in the house when she was there by herself and she had even managed to find herself a bottle of wine in a cupboard to drink. It had been there for a long time. Julia hadn't partaken of a drop since her wedding night for obvious reasons. She had even forgotten not only how pleasant it tasted, but also that comforting feeling of well-being it produced. More than likely this had been one bought years ago by her Mum and Dad.

Julia remembered that terrible night when the rain had been lashing and the wind blowing a gale. When the police had come to the house inform her of the dreadful tragedy and she had learned of her parents' death. Everyone wondered how on earth her father could have lost control of the car on a winding country lane in Birtley, but Julia had some ideas. She had kept these close to her chest, not wishing to tarnish her parent's reputation. Julia sighed and caught a glimpse of her parents' wedding photo in the next room. She had always loved the picture of their special day and had hoped one day to have something similar herself. But her parody of a marriage to Trevor had just been a cruel joke hadn't it? However, Julia with her newly found clarity of thought was beginning to remember the warts and all reality of her own parents' marriage.

The idyllic holiday recollections of her early childhood didn't quite tally with those of her teenage years. She called to mind the hostile looks between her parents. The bickering and arguments. Looking now at the sadly dated decoration of the orange kitchen and the avocado bathroom upstairs, she thought once more of her mother's lover; Ian, with his alarming moustache, creepy looks and overbearing smell of Old Spice and sweat. She thought back to the promiscuous behaviour of her mother and the way that the two of them had carried on together so blatantly under her father's very nose. That awful afternoon, when she had caught them in flagrante in her parents' bed had utterly shocked her. But at last, she could see matters for what they were, All those unnecessary jobs, that had been concocted for the house and the garden, but most particularly *that* shed.

Once more the bell jangled loudly on the chemist's door and Nick Stewart was startled. In breezed Zoe, with a look of amused anger on her face. Nick thought she appeared with her bush of long flaming tresses, like a magnificent Boudicca poised for battle.

Despite being a chemist, Nick had always had a keen interest in early history. He was frequently to be found on his days of leisure, marching up and down the Military Road. Upon such occasions, he reflected upon by-gone days and retraced the steps of long-dead Roman soldiers. Recently, Nick had joined an historical enactment society that specialised in all matters Roman. Only last weekend, as he was one of the older members of the group, he had been thrilled to be given the title of Lucias Maximus and the honour of being dressed in a centurion's costume. Then, with some difficulty, he had organised his admittedly small legion of six men into a tortoise formation. So, the idea of combat with a Celtic warrior queen aroused him enormously.

'I expect you know why I am here Nick.' Zoe folded her arms across her chest, meaning business.

'Yes, I have a good idea.' Nick seemed a little embarrassed by his sharing of her phone number, but could not contain in his delight in seeing her again. 'Is it by any chance in connection with a certain Mr Obadiah Goldstein and his mad accusations? I had been meaning to ring you …'

'Whatever. But what do you think you are doing giving my number out to … well he could be anyone. He sounded odd to me, like he might in fact be some sort of pervert.' She viewed him coquettishly from under her eyelids.

'He's an Orthodox Jew.' Nick replied quickly.

'Well, no matter.' Zoe was enjoying the sparring. 'Anyway what's all this nonsense about Neil Latimer being a murderer?'

'Yes. Do you know this Neil?' This was the most excitement Nick had encountered in years.' Do you think there is any truth in his allegations?'

'Well yes, I know him and I'm not his greatest fan but even I wouldn't have thought him capable of *killing* anyone.'

'But he's Julia's current husband?'

'Current? He's her second husband. My friend has hardly been racking up a string of husbands, like a twenty-first century Henry VIII.'

'Obadiah's not accusing *her*, its Neil he's accusing of using the old chopping block.' Nick began cutting with an imaginary axe.

'Nick this isn't funny.' Zoe realised they were making fun of very serious matters. 'My friend Julia is beside herself, what with one thing and another. First, she had Neil being sacked from his job as a property salesman for embezzling money to contend with. Then, she discovered to her distress, he's got a massive gambling problem and has accumulated massive debts.'

'So you could say he's got form.' Nick gave a knowing shake of the head.

'Yes but murder.' Nick seemed to be finding the matter one big joke and Zoe thought he was being wicked involving her in his fun.

'Well … Obadiah seems to think so, but why it should be any of his concern, I really don't know. He said that Trevor Squires used to be a tenant of his dad's. And his dad was furious when he did a moonlight flit years ago, stealing some spoons and owing him money.' At the very mention of the cutlery, Nick was losing miserably in his fight to keep a straight face.

'How has this man made the connection between Trevor, Neil and Julia?' Zoe tried to bring back a serious note to the conversation.

'Ah that's the thing. You know when you were here the other day.'

'Yes, that would be when I gave you my phone number, for you to share with any random folk you came across? What about it?'

'Well Obadiah's father was also in the shop listening to our conversation.'

Zoe looked suspiciously around the shop, expecting several elderly Jewish men to surface from behind the shampoos and hair dyes.

Nick continued. 'So do you think we should give him the Latimer's address?'

Zoe whispered. 'No. For starters neither Neil nor Julia would be pleased to see him looking around outside their house.' She pictured a curious image of a Hasidic Jew hiding in one of her friend's garden bushes. 'And, if Julia finds out I'm the source, well … that's not going to look very good for me is it? He has their names. Surely he can look them up on the internet. That's unless he's as stupid as he sounds.'

'Yes fair point … but Zoe? Would you care to come out for dinner with me this evening?" Nick looked at the floor and became suddenly tongue tied. He was not in the habit of asking women out to dinner. His wife had died of cancer a few years ago and since then he had never really had the inclination, but there was something about this Zoe Jackson he really liked. 'We could discuss the matter some more over food and a few drinks.'

'Well I'll have to check that my mum can keep an eye on my daughter. But I can't see that being a problem. 'A night out with Nick promised to be very good fun she thought.

Neil

Despite not having had a drink for a few days, Neil was struggling not to fall asleep. After a couple of early nights and smooth morning starts, his performance at work had improved dramatically and he was back on friendly terms with Geoff. Yesterday, he had sold an impressive seven cars, including a three year old Corsa that had been previously written off and sitting at the back of the forecourt for months. It had been prettified in an obviously botched up job but its new owner was blissfully ignorant of this fact and was delighted with his bargain buy.

Neil with fine expertise had drawn attention to its fine upholstery and the attractive shade of its paintwork, happily on familiar territory, as if he were selling a house. The boss had been delighted to be shot of the white elephant. In fact, Geoff had even asked him to join him in the Golf Club last night but he had declined the offer, professing to have a dental appointment. So now that matters on work were back on track and the battle of the booze had been won, the mystery with Julia just needed to be solved.

Julia was lying stone still in the bed next to him, but he knew she wasn't asleep. He glanced at the alarm clock which showed 2.30 am and turned over. Making his breath deliberately deep, he shut his eyes tight and affected a few gentle snoring noises. Still, Julia didn't move, so he made his grunts a little louder, for a greater authenticity and waited. Sure enough, a few moments later Julia slid her legs out of bed and crept downstairs like a ninja. Neil listened, as she moved about in the utility room, shushing Mabel to be quiet. Quickly, Neil pulled on jeans and a hoody over his pyjamas, then hovered like a drone on the landing at the top of the stairs. As Julia moved towards the front door bedecked in her wellies and a parka, Neil watched. Once the door closed, he followed her downstairs and saw her through the window, leaving the front garden carrying a spade. Neil was puzzled and wondered where on earth his wife was going and what she could possibly be doing.

Keeping a good distance behind, he followed her as she moved towards the woods nearby the old Bowes Railway line. Once or twice, he saw her glance behind, to check she wasn't being followed and Neil was glad of the handy-to-hide- behind trees. In a particularly dense part of the wood, she stopped and began moving some big boulders. When she rolled them to one side, as if well practised in this, he was surprised at her strength. Then, she began using the spade to remove soil from the ground. It seemed as if she were digging a hole which already was considerably large. She must have been busy with this project for some time. In fact, the sizable cavity she had already made looked as if it were big enough to hold a body.

Charles

Charles was glad that the deed was done and the awkward conversation that he had been dreading with spiteful Tracy was over. In fact, he had been surprised that she hadn't kicked up more of a fuss, professing an unfair dismissal. However, when she had realised that he was fully aware of the enormity of her crimes, she must have known that the game was up. As if all the money she must have cost the company and how her contriving to ruin Max wasn't bad enough. But her trying to sidestep the issue and to profess that it was just her little joke beggared belief.

To be fair, to some small extent he could see that she might have argued that the reinstalment of Neil could have been for the company's good, if she hadn't known about his embezzling. She seemed to have been genuinely unaware of Neil's thieving, so her blackmailing him was unlikely. But deliberately seeking out poor Pamela and misleading her into thinking he was having an affair with Julia was the final nail in her coffin. Definitely, OakElmAsh Residential's was well shot of Tracy and her plague of malice, which had hung about the showroom for way too long.

Charles watched his new receptionist Lauren, with her smart spotty dress and bright smile and knew that he had made the right choice. It was as if the tawdry, white aura of ill will that Tracy had projected about the room, had been replaced by an inviting breath of fresh air. In fact, there was something about Lauren and her shining hair that reminded him of his wife when they had first met. As Charles thought affectionately about his dear Pamela, he thought that he would maybe buy her a small bunch of flowers from garage that evening, as she too had suffered at the evil Tracy's hands.

At that very moment, in walked Max and did a double take when he saw the new occupant of what he had always known as Tracy's seat. Charles watched as the two of them made their introductions and he thought what a handsome couple they made. He imagined Lauren being invited round for dinner and her helping Pamela with a jigsaw puzzle while father and son went out for a pint.

Max came into his father's office beaming. 'So you did it dad. Good on you. Already, the world seems a much better place. Now we don't have to suffer that nasty cow's presence out there.' Max joined his father in watching the new receptionist through the glass of the door.

'So what do you think of Lauren then?' Charles gave his son a knowing look.

'She seems very nice.' Max's cheeks started to flush a slight pink colour.

'Why don't you ask her out for a drink or take her out to the cinema son?' Charles gave Max a gentle nudge with his elbow.

'Oh I don't know. I'm not very good at that sort of thing. 'The pink of his cheeks began turning an unbecoming shade of puce.

'Well there's only one way to get better at it.' Charles winked at his son lasciviously and Max felt a little sick.

After leaving several messages on Zoe Jackson's phone, Obadiah was annoyed not to have received any reply. He felt sure that if he knew Neil and Julia's address, he would be able to find some incriminating evidence. It was all too much of a coincidence. Trevor was married to Julia, Trevor disappeared and Neil was now married to Julia. It was just much too convenient for Trevor to be a missing person. If Neil had managed to siphon off massive amounts of money before being detected, this was no doubt due to the man's wicked cunning. And if he was so innately evil, he was surely capable of even worse. Julia was married to Trevor and Neil wanted to be her husband. What Neil wanted, Neil got. To Obadiah's mind it seemed much more than likely, that Neil was responsible for the missing Trevor and it was down to Obadiah to find what could now only be Trevor's remains.

Obadiah imagined if he wanted to get rid of Bathsheba, not that he did of course, what would he do? Would he poison, strangle, or stab her with a knife? He conjured up disturbing images of his wife laying either in convulsions on the kitchen floor, after he had spiked her coffee with cyanide or with a look of horror as she choked to death with his fingers around her neck. Next he saw her squirting with fountains of blood, as the room turned into an abattoir, after he had lunged at her multiple times with the bread knife. Although all of these examples of uxoricide seemed equally unpleasant, whichever the chosen murder method, the problem of the corpse remained a constant. What would he do with his wife's dead body? Well concealing within the house would seem the most expedient but the giveaway of course would be the smell. He had recently watched a programme on the television about Dennis Nilsen and stench from the bodies under the floorboards had led to his discovery. So in this case, the garden would be a much better bet. However, Obadiah had a small backyard. Yes, but *he* wasn't the one burying bodies and the Latimer's house more than likely had one. Obadiah made a few notes in his little red notebook.

'Would you like a cup of coffee Obadiah?' His wife's voice came from downstairs.

'Yes please Bathsheba.' And a few moments later she brought the drink to him.

‘You look deep in thought my dear. What job are you busy with today?’ She gave him one of her kindly smiles.

To Obadiah the concept of lying to his wife was alien. But he didn’t think it would be wise to share the exact details of his thoughts with her at this moment. ‘It’s a job for an undertaker.’ This he conceded wasn’t stretching the truth too far.

Bathsheba nodded before disappearing downstairs and Obadiah returned once more to the task in hand. He googled on his phone how to trace the whereabouts of names and a site called Tracegenie popped up on his screen. All you needed were their names and the Electoral Roll would supply you with matching addresses. Perfect. He typed in the names Neil and Julia Latimer and blinked. Then, in a digital puff of smoke, the information that a 54 year old Neil and a 48 year old Julia lived in a house at Lowfield Avenue in Washington Village appeared on the screen . This wasn’t too far away. Bingo, thought Obadiah as he pulled on his overcoat, shouted goodbye to his wife and jumped excitedly into his Volvo.

In a matter of minutes, he was outside the house. More than likely, at this time Mr and Mrs Latimer would both be at work. So he stepped out of his car and noticed a garden both at the front and the back. Interesting, thought Obadiah as he wandered up and down conspicuously on the pavement on Lowfield Avenue. Fortunately, he couldn’t see any neighbours about but you never knew what hid behind curtains. Down the road, some builders were making a new front wall on a house, the postman was delivering some letters and from the front window of Neil and Julia’s house, he was being watched by an enormous beast. A massive grey furry cat, more the size of a leopard than a domestic animal was weighing up Obadiah and taking note of his every move.

Julia

Julia breathed a deep sigh of relief, as she arrived back at the house and returned the wheelbarrow to the shed. For the last time her wellies were placed next to Neil’s and her clothes in the machine. The deed at last was done. It was over, at least for the time being and she at last was free. For the first time in years, she was not chained and bound to this horrible house. There was now no reason whatsoever why they couldn't move elsewhere and in fact in might be for the best. Really, they should live as far away from Washington Village as they possibly could and then they could finally put all this behind them. They should put the house on the market and with the money it raised, they could travel wherever they liked. The world would be their oyster. Far flung thoughts of adventures in Asia and South America filled her mind. It was inevitable that at some point the body would be discovered and when this happened, they needed to be elsewhere on the other side of the globe.

Julia knew Neil would find this change of heart strange because since they had first met, she had refused to consider any possibility of moving home. Wanting a fresh start would seem totally out of character for her but she had pulled so much wool over his eyes recently, it was a wonder he hadn't turned into a sheep. As she washed her hands for the last time, she felt exhausted and she couldn't wait to drift into sleep. Thank goodness it was Saturday tomorrow and for the first time in weeks she could enjoy a lie in. For so many nights she had been playing this ridiculous charade. Nightly, after a hard days teaching, she had been forced to keep her husband company pretending to drink and steering him towards oblivion. To be honest, this hadn't been fair on him but then again he had needed little encouragement. Then, waiting until she was certain he was out for the count, she had ventured out into the woods.

During each journey, she had become increasingly paranoid and fearful she was being followed and watched but she just prayed that she hadn't been. On the last couple of times she heard distinct rustling sounds and she had been almost sure she had heard footsteps behind her. But when she had turned round there had been no trace of anyone. On this last time, she had no doubt made more noise herself due to the exertion of moving the body but she just hoped no one had been there. As she slid her freezing body next to that of her husband, his snoring suddenly stopped. Oh my God, thought Julia - he's awake, but then he turned over and resumed the noise.

Before going for a meal, Zoe insisted that they went for a drink in her favourite local pub The Free Trade in the Ouseburn area of Newcastle. Nick didn't mind, as it was only seven and their meal wasn't booked until half past eight, at the nearby Hotel du Vin. As they settled themselves down in a seat next to the window, Nick looked around at the sparse furniture, relaxed atmosphere and stunning views of the bridges over the Tyne. He decided instantly, that he liked this place very much and his company even more.

'Well, what do you think?' Zoe smiled and waved at a couple sitting over the other side of the bar.

'Yes, a great choice. I like it here.' Nick took a the first sip from his beer which tasted good

'I've been coming here for years. In fact I was here with Julia a short while ago.' Zoe thought back to the interesting conversation between the two of them.

'Julia, the murderer's wife according to Obadiah Steinberg.' Nick's eyes brightened.

'Oh yes. I wonder if he's managed to track them down yet.' Zoe laughed remembering the strange messages Obadiah had left on her phone.

'Well if he has, I don't think he will have found any Trevor graves dug in their garden.' Nick took a piece ripped from a newspaper, out of his pocket.

'I never thought he would. I mean Neil maybe many things but a murderer no – way.' Zoe wondered what the paper was that Nick was uncrumpling on the table.

'This Trevor was Trevor Squires wasn't it? Take a look at this.'

There was a newspaper article about some murderer with an unattractive photograph of the criminal attached. Zoe read with interest about:

"Terence Smith (66), from Oakum in Leicestershire, was today sentenced in Leicester Crown Court to life imprisonment. He was found guilty of the murders of Mrs Kathleen Bell (89), Mrs Margaret Reid (79) and Mrs Mary Hutchinson (90). All these unfortunate ladies were residents of the Sunnyday Care Home where Mr Smith worked as a carer The three ladies were all suffering from Alzheimer's Disease and Mr Smith had persuaded them to alter their wills in his favour before administering poison to them in their nightly bedtime drinks. Terence Smith, a former pharmacist's assistant displayed no emotion and appeared unrepentant. All the families of these ladies were horrified by the vile actions of this man but said they were all pleased to see justice done."

'Oh my God, That's him. I'd recognise those eyes anywhere. Terence Smith. It's the same initials and a different name but its him. Definitely'

'Yes that's what I thought. He looks older and his hair's grey, but its him.' Nick pictured Trevor Squires crawling around on the floor supposedly looking for a rat. He remembered the coat over the CCTV camera and the missing drugs.

'How has he remained on the missing person list for so long?' It must be twenty five years since she last had clapped eyes on this miserable man.

'Obviously, he's either kept out of mischief or remained undetected. You know I should have reported him before he fled. I mean I could have saved these ladies lives. And what if there are other crimes he's committed. There might be other deaths …'

'Well he's been caught now.' Zoe put her hand over Nick's, seeing he was upset. This wasn't how she had imagined the night panning out and Trevor was spoiling it. 'I wonder what he did with those drugs he stole from your chemists?' Said Zoe. 'I mean could he have killed someone with those? What drug was it he stole?'

'It's a drug called Ketamine and yes he quite easily could have killed someone.'

Chapter 25

36 Years Ago

Julia

Julia had come home from school to find no trace of anyone in the house. She was becoming used to her mother's absence from home and her being otherwise occupied so that she didn't have time to spend with her daughter. Julia missed the happy times they used to spend together. With nothing else to do she thought she would have a look at the new, garden shed.

Once inside, to be honest, she didn't think the shed was anything special. It was dark and seemed much too big for the collection of rusty, old tools that had been given to Carol by her parents. From out of the small window, she could see the new rose bed that had been dug in the middle of the lawn by Ian and she wondered what unnecessary jobs would be found for him to do next. At the top left-hand corner of the window was a spider's web and she watched fascinated as the giant house spider finished its construction.

A figure walked past the window, crunching the newly laid gravel. She didn't quite see who it was and made to leave the shed to find out. She got halfway across the wooden floor when the door suddenly flew open. The door was quickly closed again and there stood a smiling Ian.

'Hello,' he said casually. 'And what's a not-so-little Julia doing here then.'

There was a menace to his voice and the usual smell of sweat and Old Spice.

'I was just having a look at the new shed.' Julia edged towards the door, already feeling uneasy.

'And does Julia like what she sees then?' Ian pulled his lips back again and showed his teeth rather than smiled. He didn't move from the doorway.

'Well, it's just a shed isn't it?' She tried not to sound nervous but there was a tremor to her voice which annoyed her. She didn't like the way he was blocking the door. Her whole skin began to contract and tighten.

'Just a shed is it?' He moved across pushed up closer towards her and she smelt the revolting halitosis stench from his breath.

'I need to be going. I have my homework to do.' Her heart started to hammer.

Ian placed his hands on her shoulders. She pulled back but he held her tight and she felt his lips clamp on her mouth like putrid wet fish. She wondered how her mother could possibly find this pleasant.

'Please. Please let me go.' She managed to blurt out as she tried to push him away.

'Don't pretend you don't like it. You're your mother's daughter aren't you … little Julia.' His big hands pinched her skin and started to feverishly explore her body.

Julia struggled to push his hands away but it was no use, he was too strong. She turned her face to escape his smell and concentrated on the house spider finishing off its beautifully constructed web; its spinnerets working rapidly, playing out more silk. She was terrified and began to shake. 'Get off, get off. Let me go,' she screamed.

'Keep your voice down girl.' He covered her mouth with his own and bit her lips to stop her making a noise.

Julia could feel his fingers hovering round the top of her thighs. She pulled her right leg back and sent her knee into his groin with as much force as she could. She heard a satisfying yelp of pain from him.

'You little bitch! That hurt.' He pinned her against the wall of the shed and put his hand over her mouth to stop her shouting.

But it was too late. Her screams had been heard.

The shed door flew open again and her mother stood there with a face like fury.

Neil - The Present

t was Saturday morning, Neil wasn't starting work until midday and Julia was having a are lie in bed. Neil couldn't remember when she had last done this. For ages, even when he hadn't been at school, she was up nearly every morning with the lark. It was as if she ad something truly terrible on her conscience which was stopping her from sleeping and ow Neil had some clues as to the reasons of what this might be. As he had lain in bed, uring the early hours of the morning, he had only waited for a short while for Julia to come and join him. Soon, he felt her ice cold body slide in next to him like a corpse in a chapel of rest. He was pretending to be asleep; as if he could sleep after what he had just witnessed. It had been on the tip of his tongue to confront her about what he had just seen there and then, but at the last minute he bit his tongue. He would let her sleep and they could talk about it properly later.

Last night, he had watched in confusion through the window, her digging up the flower bed, throwing rose bushes onto the lawn and putting a collection of black, plastic bags into a wheel barrow. Whatever could she be doing he had wondered? Once again, Neil had followed his wife into the woods. This time, she had been so immersed with the task in hand, that he was able to get quite close and see what she was actually doing. He knew he was making the twigs snap on the ground and the bushes crackle, but it was as if she were in a trance and oblivious to everything around her. Julia's only concern seemed to be completing the bizarre task in hand.

Once more, he was amazed as she moved the heavy boulders to one side with ease. Then, she began transferring the packages into the hole. Some slid into the hole quite easily while others were quite difficult to shift, as if the objects inside were sharp and were catching on the barrow. Julia gave one a heavy kick to dislodge it and when the plastic became ripped, it confirmed his very worst suspicions. Quite clearly the contents in the bags were bones. From their size they were not the bones of a pet, but those of a human and the hole that Julia had made was without any doubt that of a grave. Also, it was clear that body had been removed from the rose bed in the middle of their garden lawn. But how long had it been buried there? Neil's mind was whirring like a clockwork toy, as the peculiar behaviour of his wife over the last few weeks was at last beginning to make some sense.

Mabel was by the French windows purring loudly, as if trying to attract his attention. Neil moved towards her to give her a stroke. Very clearly, he could see where the soil had been tossed across the lawn and the bushes uprooted. Julia obviously hadn't though about this one and neighbours would definitely be speculating; it wasn't normal to be gardening during the middle of the night in November. Events were at last beginning to slip into place in Neil's mind. This was why Julia had not been pleased at the thought of the new road being built. Certainly, it would necessitate the body being dug up. It must be the reason, that Julia had felt it necessary to move this person's remains into the wood as soon as possible.

Now, he understood why Julia had been encouraging him to drink so much every night. It was so she could go hole digging. Matters at last were beginning to make some sense. But whose body was it? As far as Neil could think, there was only one candidate it could possibly be and if Julia had killed him, there must have been a very good reason. This must be the cause of the haunted look Julia had carried round with her for all these years. Poor Julia. Trevor must have been a bloody bastard to her. If he had made her do this, God only knew what had happened between the pair of them .And if she had killed her first husband, it had more than likely on her part been either accidental or self- defence. Despite Julia's attempts to turn him into an alcoholic, this was a means to an end and he thought it unlikely that she was trying to kill husband number two.

But that body in the woods wouldn't remain undiscovered forever. Maybe, Julia and he needed to go to the police with all this. They would talk about this properly this evening. As Neil looked out of the window, at the sorry mess in the garden, he sighed wishing he knew exactly the right thing to do. He had a couple of hours free before he needed to go to work and he supposed he ought to attempt to make last night's exhumation less obvious. When he went out to shed to get some tools, he noticed a figure clad in dark colours skulking in the bushes. The man was tall and thin. Surely that was Obadiah Goldstein but what the hell was he doing in their back garden?

Obadiah

Obadiah could hardly contain his excitement at what he had just witnessed. Not only had he seen the plain evidence in Neil Latimer's back garden, but he just witnessed the murderer attempting to cover his tracks. Obadiah had now been stalking the property for the last couple of days, searching for evidence of a likely place where Neil could have dug Trevor's grave. Then on that morning, he had parked his Volvo around the corner, to appear less conspicuous to the neighbours, and went to watch from his favourite bush. The Latimer's had a large holly bush which although a little prickly, provided excellent coverage.

There

~~Then~~ in the middle of the lawn, where once had been a rose bed was a great massive hole. Rose bushes were strewn across the lawn, soil was all over the grass but most interestingly, there was a great chasm more than large enough to conceal a body right in front of his eyes. Obadiah took out his phone and took several incriminating shots of the recently emptied grave. He had heard somewhere, of the council's plans to make a road nearby. It was a new by-pass he believed to connect Newcastle and Sunderland. More than likely, the route must be running through the Latimer's land, so that must be why the killer had moved the corpse. Although surprised, he was more than delighted that Neil had done such a slipshod job to conceal his tracks. It was most unlike him, considering how long it had taken for his fraud to be detected, to leave this glaring piece of evidence right in the middle of his garden, under anyone's nose to see. How careless of Neil, but how fortunate for Obadiah. Obadiah wondered where Trevor's body was now but that was irrelevant as he had the necessary proof to get the penal ball rolling.

But next, when Neil walked out of the house and came into the garden, Obadiah nearly fell out of the bush in his giddiness. Despite several holly leaves attaching themselves to his bottom, he couldn't have cared less. Before it was obvious that Neil had spotted him, he managed to get a further two shots of Neil holding a spade and hoe with a very shifty look upon his face. He ran back to his car to consider his next plan of action. It would be useful before contacting the police to have some sort of ally. His father would be perfect but he feared the thrill of it all would prove too much for the old man. There was Charles Lavender or Nick Stewart in the chemists, but the latter was probably the better bet, as he was aware he had tried Mr Lavender's patience to full capacity and the Estate Agent would probably not even be at work on a Saturday.

A few moments later, Obadiah was in the chemist's where Nick was providing an old lady with her prescription.

'You will never guess what I have just seen.' Obadiah interrupted.

'Just wait a moment will you? I'm just serving this lady.' The old lady gave him a cross look, as she tutted and put a white package into her bag.

Obadiah jumped from one foot to the other, unable to contain his excitement. Before the old lady was out of the shop he continued. 'You have to believe me now. I've seen the grave. It's right there in the garden. They must have had to move the body because of the new road.' Obadiah's eyes blinked disconcertingly, like a solemn owl, behind his little round glasses.

'Excuse me,' Nick was flustered by this agitated apparition before him. 'What are you talking about?'

'That Trevor who used to work here. He was killed by Neil. Neil Latimer, who that red friend of yours knows. I've seen a grave in his garden. It has to be Trevor's grave. Don't you agree?' Obadiah's head wobbled, as if the weight of this information was too much for his neck to bear and he tried to focus on the main points he needed to get across.

Slow down man. Are you telling you have actually seen Trevor's skeleton in their back garden.' Nick knew this not only unlikely but impossible.

Not exactly… but as good as.' The smile on his face was demonic.

What did you actually see?' Nick was starting to enjoy himself a little now, as he knew the man was talking rubbish.

Well in the middle of their lawn yesterday they had a flower bed. Today, it was all dug up with a big hole in the middle. And the hole was, you know, *body size*.' He stretched his long arms wide, to illustrate his point.

Look you can't go making allegations like this. Have you actually seen a body?'

No, but he must have moved it. It was the right size. It must have been Trevor's grave and now they have moved him because of the *new road*.' Obadiah relayed the information about the new highway, as if he were privy to some top secret information while this building work was already in progress and common knowledge.

That is impossible.' Nick went to his coat pocket hanging up on the wall and retrieved his newspaper article. 'Look,' he placed the paper on the table. 'Here is Trevor Squires. He is now using the name of Terence Smith but its him all right. He's alive, kicking

around in Oakham of all places and just been found guilty of poisoning three old ladies.'
At first, Obadiah was lost for words and then giving matter careful thought asked. "Oakham, I haven't heard of this place. Is it nearby?"
'It's near to Leicester, where they found the body of Richard III in a car park.' Replied Nick but Obadiah just looked nonplussed.

Pamela

Pamela had just finished her latest jigsaw puzzle of the Angel of the North. The picture had the bronzed aeroplane-winged angel, set against the blue of a beautiful summer's day. It contrasted sharply with the dull, grey sky outside but Pamela didn't care, she was feeling the happiest that she had been in years. She had only started what was she had to admit was a very tricky puzzle the day before, but in a matter of a few short hours, it was complete. She ran her fingers in satisfaction across the neatly slotted together orange and blue pieces. Then, as she looked at the small bunch of pink carnations on the mantelpiece, that her wonderful husband had presented her with the night before, her eyes filled up.

But these were tears of joy not sadness. Pamela had not felt such euphoria since her days as a newlywed or when Max was a very young baby. Last night, the three of them had enjoyed a lovely meal of steak and kidney pudding, followed by apple crumble and Midsommer Murders. Of course she had been busy with the jigsaw but nonetheless, they had all sat together for once. Not only had Charles complimented her on the meal but he even said he liked the new turquoise shirt dress with jaunty epaulettes on the shoulders she was wearing.

To be honest the outfit was a little simpler than that she usually wore, but it was still very *her* and not something drab Julia would have ever considered wearing. How she could ever seriously have thought those two were having an affair was beyond her. In hindsight she could see now, that the very idea was ludicrous. She now knew her devoted husband would never dream of looking elsewhere, especially not with the likes of Julia. When he explained that he had felt sorry for her because of the financial predicament feckless Neil had placed her in, it all made perfect sense. Charles was just being the kind man that he was.

There was only one person to blame for all her suspicions and misery. She was pleased to see that person had got her just desserts and had been promptly sacked from OakElmAsh Estate Agents. When Pamela had heard, that not only had the spiteful woman deliberately lead her to believe that Charles was being unfaithful but she had also been making a fool of poor Max, she had felt her blood boil. The twisted receptionist had been deliberately giving him the wrong information about properties, post codes and the timings for viewings. Not only had it undermined Max's confidence, by making him look inept and stupid but it had cost the family company thousands of pounds. Well, good riddance to bad rubbish, thought Pamela. She felt a spring return to her step as she refilled the occasional bowls with a fine-scented potpourri, containing shells, sawdust and the aroma of the sea.

Pamela had just returned from a walk to Low Fell High Street to buy some of the butcher's best mince to make a shepherd's pie for that night's meal. She was especially pleased, that she had decided against taking the car when she noticed a sadistic, female traffic warden, slapping bright, yellow tickets on cars. Pamela observed that the officer's platinum, white hair was pulled into a stringy, ponytail beneath what could only be described as an extremely unbecoming, peaked hat. The woman wore an ugly, high viz jacket, sensible black, mannish shoes and a familiar sulky set to the lips. Good grief, it was Tracy. This must be the only job she could find. A little different to the glamorous, cushy position she had previously held. How apt and what a welcome turn up for the books. Pamela just couldn't resist going over to speak to her.
'Hello there. It's Tracy isn't it?' Pamela couldn't suppress the glee from her voice.
'Yes and what of it?' The surly, traffic warden growled back.
'You *used* to work for my husband didn't you?' Pamela enjoyed stressing the word. 'I can see you have a new job which if you don't mind me saying … seems much more suited to your talents.'

'Whatever. 'Tracy refused to make eye contact with Pamela. 'Where's your car parked by the way?' As Pamela's eyes, like two finely engineered yoyos, scanned Tracy's unflattering uniform up and down, a smile puckered about her lips.
'Fortunately, I haven't brought it with me, As my *big* house isn't that far away." Pamela made an inconsequential gesture with a swish of her wrist. 'Incidentally, the new receptionist is doing an excellent job. Such a sweet, young girl and … so pretty. In fact, guess what? She is coming round to dinner tonight because she's stepping out with Max.

Julia

Julia suddenly awoke from a deep sleep because her mobile was ringing. She ignored it but the caller persisted several times. Whoever this was, the person seemed desperate to speak with her. This couldn't be good news she decided as the terrible events of the previous night flashed through her head and she knew she desperately needed a shower. She looked at the clock, which said half past eleven and groaned. Neil would be on his way to work which in a way was good.

She thought about the mess she must have left in the garden last night and opened the curtains. To her amazement everything was in order. The roses were back in place in the flower bed and the lawn was all neat. How could that be? After removing the body packages from the ground, she had done no tidying up and she knew she had left the garden in turmoil. Had she dreamed last night? Julia looked had her hands and could still see traces of soil beneath her fingernails. No, it had been no dream. Last night, the awful remains had been dug up, she had moved them with the help of the wheelbarrow to the woods, successfully buried them and returned to their home. Mission had been successfully accomplished and hopefully she hadn't been seen. But how could the garden have been sorted?

It must have been Neil. Maybe he imagined that naughty Mabel had created the chaos in the garden but this was totally out of character. She had never done such a thing before.

Did he know what she had done? No, that was impossible because Neil had been flat out when she had got into bed. She remembered that she had thought for one dreadful moment that he was going to wake up … but no he hadn't. Had he any indication of what she had been doing? Surely not.

Night after night, she had made completely sure he had been suitably imbibed before leaving the house. He must have just thought that Mabel had destroyed the rose bed. That was the only possible explanation. Still, it was extremely fortunate for her, as the mess would have set a few tongues wagging in the street. Julia was beginning to feel much more fondly of her husband now he seemed to have got his gambling under control, had secured himself a new job and it seemed that finally, they were getting their life back on track.

Once more the phone rang and she saw that the number was Zoe's. Whatever could she be wanting on a Saturday morning?

'Julia. I have been trying to ring you all morning. Why haven't you been answering your phone?' Zoe was gabbling like she always did when she was excited.

'It's Saturday Zoe and I was having a lie in.' Julia yawned as understandably, she still felt tired.

'You'll never guess what I have found out. Well it was Nick really but…'

'Who's Nick? What are you talking about?' Julia was confused. This Nick was obviously Zoe's latest fling and why she was so excited. A love-struck Zoe was the last thing she needed today and in a couple of weeks it would no doubt end in tears.

'Nick works in a chemist. In fact he used to work with Trevor.'

Zoe could certainly pick her moments and Julia felt more than a little annoyed by her friend's bad timing. 'Trevor? My ex-husband? Zoe I'm not interested in anything about that man.'

'Believe me Julia you'll want to know this. Meet me for a coffee. There's something that I need to show you.' Zoe was insistent.

'Zoe. That man is dead to me. He's been missing for so many years…'

'No arguments Zoe. Meet me at half past 12 in the coffee bar in Sainsbury's on the Team Valley. This is something you will want to know.' Julia had been involved in more than enough drama for twenty-four hours but Zoe wasn't taking no for an answer. Still, she had nothing else to do that day and she was a little intrigued as to what her friend had found out.

After having a long hot shower and blow drying her hair into its usual sleek bob, Julia pulled on her favourite jeans and grey cashmere jumper. As she pulled out of the drive, a forlorn Mabel sat watching from the lounge window. Julia had imagined that she, herself, would have been spending the day gardening and felt very grateful to Neil and his exertions. All things considered, a meeting with her friend for coffee wasn't such a bad idea. For years, she had been pleased to hear nothing about Trevor but after the events of last night any distraction could only be welcome.

Zoe, in a cheery red jumper, with orange zigzags and a matching woolly hat was already there and waiting. She had a flat white coffee ready for her friend and was occupied drinking a cappuccino herself, leaving bits of the creamy foam around her mouth.
'Julia, at last.' She shrieked loudly before giving her friend a hug and planting a coffee kiss on her cheek.
Julia sat down. 'So what have you got to tell me? What's so urgent it can't wait till Monday?'
Zoe pulled some crumpled photocopied papers out of her bag. 'Look, do you recognise this man?'
Julia looked at a picture of an unattractive man in late middle-age with white hair, glasses and a paunch. Although, older and scowling, the man without doubt, was her hated ex-husband Trevor. 'Oh my God, it him. That's Trevor.' Julia didn't think it was possible to feel even more sick than she had upon awakening.
'Calling himself Terence mind these days. It was Nick that recognised him.' Zoe gave a coy look, which Julia correctly interpreted as meaning they were sleeping together.' He works in the same chemist that Trevor did and he knew him. But look, he's killed three elderly ladies. He's poisoned them after getting them to leave their money to him.' Zoe pointed to the three photographs of Kathleen Bell, Margaret Reid and Mary Hutchinson.
'Oh my God, I could have prevented this.' Julia's coffee tasted horrible.
'Don't be silly, none of this was your fault.' Zoe gave a concerned look and held her friend's hand.

'But he tried to poison me. If only I had gone to the police. But I was just so happy that he'd gone away and left me alone.' Julia's eyes welled with tears. 'I'd hoped he'd died. I really did.'

'He poisoned you?' Zoe was incredulous. She suspected the marriage had been a disaster but not that he's tried to kill her. She remembered Nick telling her about his suspicions of him stealing the Ketamin drug. This was obviously what he had been using it for.

'Oh Zoe I was so ill. He made me ill.' Julia had never shared this with anyone, not even Neil. 'The man's a monster you can't imagine what he did to me. There's a word for it now … gaslighting. He made me feel I was worthless and unfit for anything … that's why I gave up my teaching course. That's why I stopped seeing you Zoe. He wouldn't let me.'

'It's all right Julia. I suspected that something like that must have happened. Not the poisoning of course. Although, at the time I wasn't very happy.' Zoe remembered how miffed her younger self had been to lose her chum but she had soon found new friends to hang out with. 'Bloody hell Julia, he could have killed you … like one of these woman.'

'It's my fault these women died. If I had gone to the police years ago these women would be still alive. And who's to say he's not killed more. I mean, it was thirty years ago when he did it to me. What's he been doing all this time.'

'You still can go to the police Julia. In fact you definitely should. I mean there may be others that haven't been discovered yet. In fact we should go now.'

Julia looked at her friend. Awful as all of this was, she was in no mood for visiting a police station on today of all days.

Chapter 26

36 Years Ago

Julia

When Carol saw what Ian was doing to Julia, she saw red.

'You bastard. What are you doing to my daughter?' The mother lion roared.

'Mum.' Julia cried. Never had she been so pleased to see her mother.

Ian immediately released Julia and pulled back.

'It's not what it looks like,' he said. 'The little bitch was coming on to me. I couldn't get her off. It wasn't my fault love. It was her …'

He turned to send an accusatory nod to Julia.

Carol saw her chance to hurt him before he could defend himself. She snatched an old, rusty spade leaning against the side of the shed, whirled it around and smashed it on to the back of his head.

Ian's hands flew up to stem the already gushing blood. He looked at Carol in amazement.

'You fucking maniac …' He bleated, before suddenly collapsing like a rag doll on the wooden floor. The blood, streaming from his head, soon made a red pool on the ground, rapidly getting wider and wider as if ten bottles of watery ketchup had been spilt. Ian lay perfectly still, his eyes glazing over like those of a dead mackerel.

Julia and Carol stared at the prostrate body of Ian.

Julia broke the silence. 'Mum, what have you done?' she gasped. Her mother started to scream. Julia shook her. 'Mum you need to be quiet, somebody will hear!'

But Carol was hysterical, as Ian quite clearly was dead … and what were they going to do next?

The Present

Julia

Julia thought back to that awful day and wondered how she and her mother had pulled it off. Once Ian was dead, their relationship reverted back to how it was when Julia was a small child and the two of them once more became inseparable. Except, it seemed as if the roles were reversed; Julia behaved like an adult and her mother seemed more like the child. Relations between her parents still were not good. Although, Michael was pleased about Ian's disappearance, it was never mentioned and he couldn't forgive his wife for what she had done. He was constantly finding fault and looking for arguments but it just seemed that Carol couldn't be bothered to fight.

After a few days, the stench in the shed had become unbearable and they both knew that something had to be done. Carol was incapable of making any decisions so it was down to the teenage Julia to be proactive and when Michael was away on an auditing course for a couple of days, it was time for action. Julia made her mother help dig a hole in the flower bed. This they did over two nights and prayed that no one was watching. Julia urged her apathetic mother to keep digging but it was down to her to do most.

Then came the really dreadful part. Ian's foul body was black and the blood congealed. As the body was too heavy to move in its entirety somehow they managed to hack it into several parts. Julia had once fancied herself as a butcher but after this turn of events, it quickly lost its appeal. The limbs, head and torso once severed, were rapped into separate heavy duty, black bags and tied with green gardening tape. Then they were buried in the flowery grave, the man himself had made only a few months earlier.

Once the rose bushes were replanted, only they along with the mother and daughter knew the ghoulish secret that lay beneath the roots. Her father had no idea but he couldn't understand the reason why, his pretty, feisty wife had become so docile and no longer seemed to care about her appearance. The once meticulously dressed woman, who always followed the latest fashion trends, now haunted their home in dull, oversized shirts and comfy trousers with elasticated waistbands, as her weight ballooned. Michael who had once been so proud of his wife no longer wanted to be seen with her. And that night, in the terrible storm when they had been out to collect an Indian takeaway, was the first time that they had been out in each other's company for a long time.

.

Obadiah

Obadiah was furious, as he took angry little sips from his strong, black coffee. Bathsheba was always warning him that too much caffeine was bad for him and that it made him behave erratically, but these were exceptional times. He had been so convinced that the body Neil had buried in his garden had belonged to Julia's first husband, Trevor Squires. It had ticked all the boxes so neatly. Neil himself, the other morning, had provided further verification of this, appearing suddenly from his house, looking so shifty and the wielding a spade as if it were a weapon of destruction. Aware that he had been spotted, when he had fallen from the holly tree and yelped from the prickly pain, Obadiah had been forced to retreat to a viewpoint further away.

Yet, from behind the nearby bus stop, assisted by his trusty pair of binoculars, he watched as the man filled in what could only be an empty grave. After having watched avidly, repeats of Inspector Morse on the television, Obadiah knew all the signs: big hole, piles of soil, discarded greenery scattered all over the lawn. Then, Neil hurriedly replanted all the bushes to disguise his evil act. Obadiah was no gardener and there were no flowers on them so he didn't recognise the plants but doubted very much they were weeds. These flowers would be a futile attempt by the murderer, to disguise the evil which had lain beneath.

But if the missing body didn't belong to Trevor who else could it be? Well that, to Obadiah's mind was immaterial. The very fact that Neil had sometime very recently removed what could be a corpse from his garden was surely enough proof. Despite keeping an close watch on the News and the internet, there was no report of any arrests, prosecutions or imprisoning's of a certain Neil Latimer and that needed to be rectified. Before contacting the police there was only one other person he could think of to be a possible ally. And, although he recognised he was grasping at straws, the avenue needed to revisited at least one more time.

Charles

The conversation he'd had with Max a few days ago, had turned Charles's thoughts towards the possibility of he and Pamela having a holiday. As he surfed the net, some very good last minute deals seemed to be coming up for Los Gigantes in Tenerife. He and Pamela had been there a few years back and it had proved an excellent choice. It wasn't too busy but had bars, restaurants and a golf course close by. After all the events recently, he and his wife deserved a little break and the Canary Isles were always a good bet for some decent weather at this time of year.

As he was imagining him swinging his golf clubs in the sunshine and Pamela completing a jigsaw of a banana plantation in a new yellow swim suit, he was disturbed by a phone call.

'Is that Charles Lavender I'm speaking to?' asked a familiar voice down the line.

Immediately, Charles recognised that whiney voice and rolled his eyes. 'Obadiah. And to what matter do I owe the pleasure of this phone call?'

'It's about Neil.' He quickly replied.

'Well there's a surprise.' Here we go again, thought Charles.

'I notice he hasn't been arrested yet. Well not that I have seen any evidence in the news.'

Charles thought they had had this conversation before.

'Look Mr Goldstein.' Charles' patience was running thin.' This is no longer any of your business. I'm the one he stole money from and what I choose to do with this information, is my decision and mine alone.'

'But Mr Lavender this isn't *all* is it?' Obadiah persisted.

'Anything else is of no concern of mine and with all respect Mr Goldstein, will you just back off and leave me alone.' Charles was close to cutting him off..

'Yes but what if I told you that he *murdered* somebody.' Obadiah lit the touch paper and waited …

‘Ridiculous. I’ve known Neil for donkey’s years and in no way is he capable of killing.’ Honestly, this man should be sued for slander.
‘Well you wouldn’t have thought him guilty of *embezzlement* would you?’ He needled.
This man was like an annoying record with the needle stuck thought Charles. ‘That is an entirely different matter. And who do you profess that he has done away with?’
‘Well that was where I was hoping that you might help me. You see at first I thought it might be his wife’s first husband, Trevor Squires but that proved to be a red herring, as he’s alive somewhere in the midlands and busy poisoning people.’
‘Well of course he would be … in your fantasy land. Please Mr Goldstein, I haven’t got time for this nonsense.’
‘I wondered if perhaps you know any of the casino bosses or dodgy, loan sharks he had fallen foul …’
Charles Lavender slammed down the phone and shook his head in exasperation.

Neil

When Neil arrived home from work he was surprised to see a relaxed Julia curled up on the sofa with a contented Mabel, reading a book. He hadn’t been expecting this.
‘Have you had a nice day my dear?’ Neil was worried as to the outcome of this conversation.
‘Yes I met Zoe for a coffee on the Team Valley.’ She smiled at him but seemed nervous. ‘Oh and Mabel and myself, we both want to say thank you.’
‘Really? And what are you both thanking me for?’
‘The mess that Mabel made in the garden in the flowerbed. Thank you for tidying it up.’ Julia didn’t meet his eyes and continued stroking Mabel.
Neil thought Mabel looked very happy, enjoying the attention of Julia and with no sign of any remorse whatsoever. ‘Oh and Mabel did that did she? Come on Julia, I think is high time you were straight with me.’ There was a steely edge creeping into his voice.
‘What do you mean?’ Julia feigned innocence badly.
‘I was watching you last night. You dug up pieces of what looked to be a body from the

back garden didn't you. And then you put the bags into the wheelbarrow and buried them in a grave you have been digging for weeks in the woods, What have you got to say about that?'

Julia wished she could just stick her fingers in her ears and it would all go away.' I don't know what to say.' she replied mournfully.

'And that's why you been plying me with drink each night isn't it?' He looked disappointed with her.

Julia had never seen her husband as serious as this before, not even when the boot had been on the other shoe and he had been the one in trouble. She felt ashamed. 'I didn't want you to know. I thought you were asleep.'

'I watched you the other night as well. Just tell me what is going on?' There were tears in his eyes.

'I can't.' Mabel perceived the seriousness of the conversation and slipped off her mistress's lap.

'The body … who was it? Was it Trevor?' It had to be that bastard thought Neil, as there was no one else's it could be.

'No it wasn't him.' Julia's hands went to the empty space, wishing Mabel was still there to pet.

Who's body was it then. He was so sure it would be Trevor's. After all missing persons usually show up eventually. 'Well. There has definitely been a body buried in the garden for … well, God knows how long. And now for some reason you have moved it to the woods.' A light flicked on in his head.' Hey, wait a minute this is all because of the new road isn't it?'

'I knew they would find it. That's why I hoped the road wouldn't happen.' Julia's face was wet with crying.

'If it's not Trevor. Well, who does the bloody body belong to and why is it buried in our back garden?' Neil was pacing the room.' This explains why you have always been so protective of the damn flower bed. That's why we couldn't move isn't it? Whose body is it? You need to tell me this Julia. Enough is enough.'

'It's Ian.'

This was a new name. Who the hell was Ian? 'Ian … and he is? Was he your boyfriend

before Trevor?'
'No, it's nothing like that. This is from much further back than then.'

Michael – 35 Years Ago

It was a dreadful night. The rain was lashing and the wind howling, as Michael and his wife came back from the Indian Take-Away in Birtley. Carol had said she was hungry and couldn't be bothered to cook. This had become par for the course recently, as she never left the house to get in any shopping. All she did each day was sit glued to the sofa, with eyes fixed on the screen. Yet, she had a vacuous look, as if no thoughts were registering in her brain. Her day seemed only punctuated by the switch from daytime to evening telly and the incessant munching on biscuits. Julia replenished the biscuit barrel regularly, with the misguided notion she was doing her mother a favour.

On that fateful evening, Michael had suggested that she came for the ride along with him, as she hadn't been out of the home for at least three weeks. He looked at the double chin and bloated profile of his once beautiful wife and his eyes became blurry with tears. The Carol he fallen in love with had been so lovely and so full of life but this puffed up creature was the mere husk of his wife. He turned the windscreen wipers on to full speed but visibility still remained poor. They had been so happy together, well it had seemed so once, but that was a very long time ago . Thoughts of the tawdry Ian with his vile moustache flashed through his mind. This was all his fault. How could she have? The car tyres skidded on the wet country lane as he took a corner too fast. He just wanted to be home. As he begged her to tell him why this had happened, he took his eyes off the road for just one brief second and thud. The car hit a stone wall at great speed and whirled across the road like a spinning top.

Death must have been instantaneous but it was difficult to tell because petrol had leaked from the car and their bodies had been barely recognisable, after the inferno that followed.

The Present

Julia

After Julia had explained to Neil what had happened with Ian in brief detail, he fell silent and she wondered what would happen next.

'But you didn't kill him Julia. This isn't your fault.' He was smiling and gave her a hug.

'I'm not sure the police would see it that way. After all, I helped my mother and I was the one who mostly dealt with the body.' She still wasn't convinced.

'Yes but your mother, she was the one who hit him with the spade. Good God Julia, the man was trying to rape you. And how old were you?'

'I was nearly sixteen.'

'You were underage. Still a child. Oh Julia, how awful.' No wonder that she had been engulfed by that tragic cloak of sadness he thought.

'My mother was never the same. You know, after what happened.' She remembered the pitiable specimen her mother had been reduced to in her later days.

'I was sure it was Trevor. I know you had an awful time with him. I for one wouldn't have blamed you if you had killed him. Even though I don't know all the details. But don't you see? This is better for us if you know what I mean. I thought you must have killed him.'

He's not dead Neil. That's what Zoe met me to tell me about. He's no longer a missing person and he's in prison.'

What?' This was some afternoon of revelations thought Neil.

Well, I never did tell you of how he tried to poison me'

Julia, I can't take in anymore. My brain's full.'

Trevor has been convicted of poisoning three old ladies. After they had changed their wills, in his favour of course. Look here at this newspaper clipping.' Julia took a photocopied newspaper report from her pocket.

Julia. Do we have any of that whisky left?'

Epilogue

After all the unpleasant associations the house now held. Julia and Neil decided that they would sell up and move far away. They supposed that at some point, the grisly remains in the forest would be discovered and it was best that they were as far as possible. As it was on the market for much less than it was worth, the property quickly sold and Neil was able to pay back Charles at least some of what he owed. Still this left them with a considerable amount of money and they bought tickets to Mexico.

Mabel had been sent on ahead of them so she would be out of quarantine when they arrived. She had made no secret of her displeasure when she was parcelled up inside a travel cage. Julia was sad to say goodbye to Zoe. But Zoe and Nick promised they would come and visit them during the next summer holidays. Neither Julia or Neil were sorry to leave their jobs.

While they were waiting for their flights to Heathrow and then on to Cancun, Julia spotted a familiar figure at the airport. Max and his friend, both wearing baseball caps and carrying surf boards as hand had just checked onto a flight to Phuket. Before noticing Neil and Julia, a weeping Pamela and encouraging Charles were waving their son goodbye.

'Neil, Julia. So you are really off to Mexico. 'Pamela quickly brushed away her tears, for although she no longer suspected that anything untoward had happened between Julia and her husband, she still didn't entirely trust the woman. So she was pleased they were leaving.

'Neil, thanks for the money you gave me back.'

'The rest will be on its way shortly.'

'Don't worry. There are after all some things more important than money.'

'Look Neil, when you come back. I mean if you want your old job back … I'm sure we can come to some sort of arrangement.'

'We aren't coming back but I'm glad we've cleared the air. We're having a three month touring break, then I've got a new job lined up at Cancun's Sea,Surf,Sun Timeshare Lets. So if you are interested Charles, I'm sure I can organise some 'mates rates'.

Printed in Great Britain
by Amazon

57187629R00154